W9-CMD-336

This Side of Heaven

This Side of Heaven

Karen Robards

A Dell Book

Published by
Dell Publishing
a division of
Bantam Doubleday Dell Publishing Group, Inc.
666 Fifth Avenue
New York, New York 10103

Printed in the United States of America

To Doug, Peter, and Christopher—my three loves

*T*he prow of the *Dove*'s longboat accidentally bumped the first of the landing pilings. The barrels of sugar and molasses that crammed bow and stern teetered, scraping together noisily.

"Careful, there!" Captain Rowse snapped to the oarsmen as the unexpected shifting of its load caused the boat to heel. Seated directly in front of him—he was in the stern, she nearly in the center of the boat—Caroline had to grab the edge of the plank seat to keep her balance. Her slippered feet slid off the leather-bound lid of one of her own sizable trunks, where, for want of another place to put them, they had settled. The large, lidded basket that rested in her lap tilted precariously. She grabbed for it, restoring it to an upright position seconds before its precious contents were tipped into the bay. Her feet returned to their perch. One hand settled on the basket's lid; the other curled around the thick handle, tightening until her knuckles showed white. That was the only outward sign she gave of the nervousness that was making her stomach churn so she could hardly keep her breakfast down. Had she been aware of how much her grip revealed, she would have deliberately relaxed it.

It would be too humiliating to let the silent men around her know just how apprehensive of her reception she was. Carefully she avoided their gazes, her posture both lonely and proud as she looked past the straining sailors toward the unfamiliar land that was to be her new home.

Her eyes remained unreadable. She had learned it was best to keep them so. They showed none of the dismay she felt as she took in the forbidding gray shoreline that sloped upward to end in earthen fortifications, and the ugly raw wood of the dock. Beyond the dock perhaps a hundred acres of grassland had been hacked from the towering blue-green forest. The grassland was studded with rows of tiny, boxlike sheds. What could they be? Fishermen's shacks? Surely they were too small, too mean, too few, to comprise the town that she had supposed lay directly beyond the bay.

The brisk morning air blowing in from the sea smelled strongly of salt and fish. A fine spray splashed from the crest of a playful wave to splatter her cheek and cloak with icy water. Lifting a pale, long-fingered hand, Caroline wiped the beads of moisture from her face. It was early spring of 1684, and at home in England the weather would be misty and cool. But here the March air was plain cold, although the sun shone with almost vulgar intensity. Caroline reminded herself grimly that this was not England. It was unlikely that she would ever see England again.

This was not how she had pictured Saybrook. Her half sister Elizabeth's letters had contained glowing descriptions of her home in Connecticut Colony. During the difficult years that had preceded this moment when every downstroke of the oars brought her nearer to what she very much feared would be a humiliating comeuppance, Caroline had taken her sister's words and elaborated on them to create a picture of a verdant paradise that she could visit anytime she closed her eyes.

But as was ever the case, the reality was already proving far inferior to the fantasy. Doubtless the hope she'd cherished of her sister's warm welcome was misplaced, too. Although in all fairness, given the circumstances, Elizabeth couldn't be blamed if she were to be less than elated to see the baby sister she must scarcely remember.

"Ahoy there! Daniel Mathieson!"

The shout, coming almost in her ear from Captain Rowse, made Caroline jump. Both hands clamped around the basket's handle, and her lips pressed together in an effort to forestall the tart words that rose to her tongue. But the impassive shell she had learned to hide behind remained in place, and she did no more than glance witheringly over her shoulder at the captain, who was waving at someone on the dock. From the last name, she knew the man he hailed had to be her sister's kin. Her heart pounded, but her expression did not change. A facade of haughty dignity was far more effective than cringing apologies, she had learned.

The boat brushed the pilings again, farther along the dock than its first inadvertent contact, and this time a sailor leaped ashore to catch the hawser and make the craft fast. Caroline clenched her teeth. Her time of reckoning was at hand.

"Up with you, missy." Captain Rowse placed a hand under Caroline's elbow and all but lifted her to her feet. "You there, Homer, lend Miss Wetherby a hand. *Cooee,* Daniel Mathieson!"

Wincing from the booming shout, Caroline scorned the sailor's proffered hand and clambered onto the dock without assistance. The wooden boards suddenly seemed to tilt beneath her, and she staggered. A male hand grasped her arm, steadying her.

"Careful there, you ain't got your land legs back yet," a gruff voice cautioned. Caroline jerked free. Shrugging, the sailor turned away to other duties while a man in a wide-brimmed black hat emerged from the chattering crowd gathered to watch the unloading of the tall ship. Captain Rowse, bounding onto the dock beside Caroline, greeted the newcomer with a hearty thump on the shoulder, while at other points along the dock more longboats from the *Dove* arrived and began to unload cargo along with the other passengers.

"What can I do for you, Tobias?" Daniel Mathieson, for that was clearly who he was, greeted the *Dove*'s captain genially. Tall, with auburn hair and weathered skin, Daniel was attractive despite the sober garb and short-cropped hair that marked him as a Roundhead. His blue eyes roamed curiously over Caroline. She met his interested look with frosty composure. Not for anything would she permit him to see her anxiety, which was now so acute that she had to clench her teeth to avoid becoming actively ill.

"Is Matt about?"

"Nay, he's to home. He's expecting naught, and he's too much work to do to waste time on such a useless pursuit as viewing the docking of a ship, he said."

Captain Rowse chuckled. "That sounds like Matt." He sobered, glancing at Caroline. "Fact is, I've something for him. This young—lady, to be precise."

"What?" Daniel turned incredulous eyes back to Caroline. She met his gaze without flinching.

" 'S truth. Claims to be his sister-in-law. Come to make her home with him, she says."

" 'Tis the first I've heard of such!"

Before Daniel could give further voice to the surprise that had widened his eyes and pursed his mouth, Caroline spoke up with chilly dignity. She was not a child, or an idiot, to be discussed as if she were not even present! "I am Caroline Wetherby. Ephraim Mathieson is husband to my sister Elizabeth. From your surname, I presume she is also some connection of yours. Perhaps you would be so good as to take me to her."

"May the good Lord preserve us!" Daniel's tone expressed the same surprise as his expression. Without making any direct reply to her request, he took a quick and thorough inventory of her person. Caroline's eyes narrowed as she was clearly weighed and seemed to be found wanting, although there was little enough of her available for him to see. Except for her face, with its delicate, even features and large, almond-shaped eyes of a brown so golden as to be almost amber, and an inch or so of sleekly pulled back black hair, none of which any gentleman had ever before found displeasing, the vast hooded cloak she wore concealed the rest. But the cloak itself, of deep scarlet velvet purchased when her father had been flush and held on to through the subsequent lean years, was probably quite enough to provoke his dismay. Judging from the drab brown, gray, and black homespun that was the predominant attire of the citizenry around her, the vivid hue alone was likely to be looked upon with disfavor. Indeed, several among the milling crowd were already casting her censorious looks. Those that were most disparaging came from the *Dove*'s other passengers, who had somehow learned, in the mysterious way news travels throughout small communities, of her plight. The story would soon be spread all over Saybrook, Caroline realized as she watched the new arrivals greeting friends and acquaintances among the colonists. Already a few of them had their heads together with those who had come to greet them, and were shooting furtive glances her way. Caroline's spine stiffened at the unwelcome scrutiny, but in no other way did she acknowledge she was aware she was the subject of their gossip.

"You haven't yet heard the worst of it." Captain Rowse, no doubt relieved at the prospect of soon being rid of his unwanted burden, was grimly amused. "Miss Wetherby owes me for her passage. She has spent the better part of the voyage assuring me that her brother-in-law will pay her shot."

"How can that be?" Daniel sounded appalled.

"The young—lady—boarded late and beguiled my first mate into accepting a piece of jewelry instead of hard cash for her fare. The gems turned out to be paste. 'Twas her misfortune that we had a jeweler aboard, or we'd never have known of the deception till we tried to get our money out of them. Which was her plan all along, I've little doubt."

"I've told you and told you: I'd no notion of that! The brooch was my mother's. I thought it real." The outburst escaped before Caroline could stop it. Her eyes blazed with indignation at Captain Rowse; then she caught herself, forcing the passion from her face and her manner and sheathing herself once again in a facade of ice. She held her head high as she faced Daniel Mathieson's baffled uncertainty and Captain Rowse's patent disbelief.

"How much?" There was a hollow ring to Daniel's question. At Captain Rowse's answer his eyes widened, and he gave a low whistle. "Matt won't like that."

"So I guessed. But what's to do? I suppose I could take her before the magistrates. . . ."

"No. No." Daniel shook his head. "If she is in truth some relation to Matt . . ."

"Would you kindly stop talking about me as if I weren't here, and take me to my sister? I'm certain that she, at least, will be glad to see me." Caroline wasn't nearly as confident as she sounded, but no one save herself could know about the queasiness of her stomach or the nervous dampness of her palms.

A helpless expression crossed Daniel's face. He and Captain Rowse exchanged glances, and the captain shrugged.

"Were I you, I'd let Matt sort it out."

"Aye." Clearly coming to a decision, he nodded and reached for Caroline's basket. "You'd best come along with me, miss. I'm brother to Matt —Ephraim, that is. Though he doesn't care overmuch for the name."

"I'll carry my own basket, thank you," she said coolly. "If you would be so good, you may see to my trunks."

"Her trunks?" Daniel asked as Caroline moved away from them, head high.

"Three of 'em," Captain Rowse answered with a crooked grin, indicating the baggage that his men had piled nearby. "Hoity-toity thing, ain't she? Wonder what Matt will make of her?"

Daniel shook his head, and reached down to shoulder a trunk. "He won't be any too pleased, I can tell you that."

2

*T*he dirt road on which Caroline trod behind Daniel and Captain Rowse led through the center of the cluster of buildings that she had seen from the boat. On closer inspection she saw that they were indeed small dwellings made of clapboards that had not yet had time to weather. Yellowed squares of paper, or perhaps hide, covered the windows. Smoke rose from nearly every chimney. Young children under the care of a harassed-looking older sister scampered from one house to another, giggling as they took in the passing trio and the strangeness of Caroline's garb. A homespun-clad woman with a baby on her hip, her hair modestly concealed beneath a white linen cap, waved to them from her stoop, her expression openly curious.

"Morning, Mary!" Daniel called, lifting a hand to the woman.

"Goodwife Mathieson!" Captain Rowse echoed, touching his hat. The surname led Caroline to assume that the young woman was also some connection of her sister's. A sister-in-law, perhaps? She was thankful when Daniel did not stop but continued to set a brisk pace toward the outskirts of the village.

As she walked, she found that the houses surrounded, in somewhat haphazard fashion, a grassy field that she took for the town common. A large, rectangular building with real glass in the windows had been erected in its center. From the four-sided steeple on the top and the little cemetery that lay to its left, Caroline decided that it must be the church. A black-robed, white-wigged dominie emerged to stand at the head of the steps, confirming her guess.

He watched them, unsmiling, although his hand lifted in response to Daniel's greeting.

"Reverend Master Miller looks like he's had a taste of something sour today," Captain Rowse remarked when they were well out of earshot.

Daniel grunted. "He and Matt had a falling-out, and he's not overly fond of any of us as a result. Considers Matt ungodly."

Captain Rowse grinned. "I doubt he says that to Matt's face."

Daniel shook his head. "His folly doesn't stretch to complete lunacy. Though doubtless he'll come nosying around in a day or two to find out about *her.*"

A jerk of his head indicated Caroline. Her shoulders stiffened at what she sensed was the slighting nature of the reference, but she said nothing. In truth, as they drew steadily closer to their destination she was growing more apprehensive by the minute. Certainly she was too nervous to relish quarreling with her escorts. Would Elizabeth welcome her? If she did not, then what was to become of her? Lifting her chin high, Caroline refused to allow herself to speculate.

Once they left the common behind, there was little to see but wide, stumpy fields hacked out of the virgin forest that rose, dark and cool-looking, perhaps a mile away on either side of the road. In civilized England the countryside had been neat and tidy, the norm being grassy meadows and well-cultivated farms bordered by low stone walls or tidy hedgerows. But this—this was rampant wilderness. The surprise of discovering that the wooden shacks were houses was nothing to the astonishment she felt upon realizing that the square with its tiny community of church and boxlike dwellings was Saybrook. *All* of Saybrook. Except for outlying farms, there was no more to the town.

They met a man in a leather jerkin leading a limping horse toward the village. Daniel and Captain Rowse exchanged greetings with him but didn't stop to talk, although from the stranger's interested glance at Caroline he was obviously curious as to her identity. Again Caroline was grateful for her escorts' reticence. In her bright scarlet plumage, which would not have been thought worthy of so much as a second glance at home, she felt as conspicuous as a cardinal amid a flock of sparrows. She barely managed to control the impulse to pull her hood closer about her face. But her pride would not allow her to hide.

"This way." Daniel, who was slightly in the lead with a trunk balanced on each shoulder, turned off the road to stride down a footpath that led toward the woods. Captain Rowse, carrying the third trunk on his shoulder, followed. Caroline, after one appalled glance told her where the path led, also realized that she had no choice. She trailed after them, clutching the basket closer as she picked her way along the narrow trail.

Gloomy shadows enveloped her as she took her first tentative steps into the forest; the trees were huge, their foliage entwined like laced fingers overhead to block out the sun. Cool vines reached out to brush her skin; the very air seemed alive with twittering birds and calling animals. But the men were striding briskly ahead. Already they were nearly out of sight. Plucking up her courage—she had not come so far and dared so much to be put off by a mere woods, no matter how daunting she might find it—she hurried after them. Neither man bothered to hold branches out of her way, so Caroline, with one and sometimes both hands holding the basket, ducked and dodged the overhanging limbs as best she could. A supple sapling sprang back in Captain Rowse's wake to strike her face; with a little cry she clapped a hand to her stinging cheek and glared after the offender, who marched on, oblivious. Then he disappeared around a bend in the path, and she was alone. The hairs on the back of her neck rose as she contemplated the various types of beasts that might at that very moment be watching her hungrily from the undergrowth. Did they have bears in Connecticut Colony, or wolves? Looking around her, she shivered. Catching her skirts up over one arm to free her feet, she almost ran after the men.

During her lifetime she had, with her father, traveled from town to town over the length and breadth of England, and not often in the lap of luxury, either. But her father had earned his living by the turn of a card or the fall of a pair of dice, and such a profession by its very nature was largely carried out within the environs of civilization. She had much experience of town life, and little practical knowledge of farms or the countryside. This wild, primitive place was totally beyond her ken. Caroline felt her skin crawl as she glanced at the shadowy woodland around her. The conviction that she had been a fool to come had been festering inside her for weeks. Never had it been stronger than it was at this moment. But what other choice had she had? She'd been destitute, with no one to turn to and nowhere to go. The only alternative had been to turn whore, and that she would not do.

Daniel had paused at the edge of a clearing. Captain Rowse was just catching up to him as Caroline, remembering her modesty, dropped her skirts and emerged from the trees behind them.

"Here we are. We'll just leave these here"—Daniel lowered the trunks to the ground with obvious relief—"until Matt decides what's best to do."

"That's sensible." Captain Rowse spoke approvingly and set the trunk he'd been carrying down beside the other two. From their unwillingness to tote the heavy load any farther, it was clear to Caroline that they feared they might soon be lugging it back the way they had come. Her stomach churned again; they didn't think she was welcome, and they might well be right. But surely Elizabeth, her own sister, would want her. Although they hadn't set eyes on each other since Caroline had been a child of seven—could it really be fifteen years?

Caroline stopped a pace or so behind the men, surreptitiously straightening her hood and brushing her skirt free of the leaves and twigs that clung to it. Her first view of her destination was at an angle to encompass house, outbuildings, and the surrounding land, and was at least partly reassuring. The town dwellings had been little more than shacks. This establishment looked both comfortable and prosperous.

The house was two stories tall, with long, narrow windows of leaded glass and a massive front door. The upper story overhung the lower in a design most likely intended to provide shelter from bad weather for the rooms below. It also seemed meant to serve as a lookout and would undoubtedly be a strategic place from which to shoot should the need arise, which, in such an unsettled land, it probably did all too often. The whole house was built of rough-hewn logs, with huge chimneys of native stone rising on both sides. Behind the house was a barn with fencing to contain a number of cows and horses. A small, shirt-sleeved boy fed chickens in the barnyard, and beyond him two men could be seen laboring in the nearest of the vast fields that had been carved out of the forest. On one side of the house a youth stirred a steaming kettle that had been suspended over a fire. A large black-and-white mongrel lay at his feet; it sprang up, barking madly, as it caught sight of Daniel, Captain Rowse, and Caroline.

"That's Matt in yonder field." Lifting a hand in greeting to the boy stirring the kettle, Daniel started off again with Caroline and Captain Rowse following. The boy waved back while the dog bounded toward them.

"Mind your manners, Raleigh," Daniel scolded the dog in an indulgent tone as it darted, growling ferociously, toward Captain Rowse's legs. The captain pushed it away with his booted foot, his expression completely unperturbed, as if he were well used to being attacked by a dog the size of a small pony. The beast, thwarted, galloped around the three of them, barking all the while. Then, to Caroline's horror, it turned its attention to her.

She had never had any dealings with dogs, and this particular specimen, besides being enormous, seemed possessed of an extraordinary number of sharp and glistening teeth. All of which it bared at her in a taunting doggy grin before it charged.

"Oh!" Despite her best efforts at aplomb, she could not hold back a squeal.

"'Twould be a pity if you were afraid of dogs," Daniel observed, sounding mildly amused as she clutched her basket closer and whirled, presenting her back to the dreadful beast.

"Wouldn't it?" In the normal way of things, her voice was soft, well modulated, quite melodious, in fact. More than once she had been complimented on its beauty. But in her effort to remain nonchalant as the animal caught and worried the edge of her cloak, her tone might best have been described as shrill.

Neither man made the slightest move to rescue her. Indeed, both grinned widely as they observed the unequal struggle. When the monster next sank its teeth into her flesh, would they still watch so merrily, she wondered, and came to the conclusion that they probably would. Gritting her teeth, trying to keep the lid on both her growing temper and her escalating panic, Caroline yanked cautiously at her cloak. The dog held on. The hem ripped, the dog tugged harder—and then the unthinkable happened. The flimsy catch that fastened her basket gave way as it had threatened to do all morning, the lid lifted, and out popped a furry black head. Caroline saw, knew what was about to happen, and sought to cram the cat safely back inside, but she was too late. Millicent took only an instant to assess the situation. With a yowl she bounded over the side and away.

"What on earth . . . ?" If there was any more to Daniel's exclamation, Caroline didn't hear it. After no more than a heartbeat's worth of frozen surprise, Raleigh let go of the cloak to tear after the streaking cat. Frenzied barking mixed with Caroline's shriek as her pet just managed to elude the dog's teeth. Abandoning all thoughts of dignity and personal safety, Caroline dropped the basket, picked up her skirts, and sped to the rescue. But Millicent clearly had no intention of waiting for succor. She fled under the barnyard fence while Raleigh, no more than a few paces behind, leaped over it.

"Millicent! Stop!"

The cat paid no heed to her scream. Squawking chickens scattered as the animals zigzagged wildly through their midst. The boy who'd been feeding them dropped his pan of meal as Millicent darted between his legs; Raleigh swerved just in time to avoid knocking the windmilling child down. Undeterred by the near collision, the dog continued to pursue his prey with earsplitting intensity. With a shout the boy joined the chase.

"Millicent! Oh, will somebody call off that blasted dog?"

Caroline caught the top of the fence and propelled herself up and over to land in the middle of the bedlam created by chickens, child, dog, and cat. Behind her Daniel yelled for Raleigh to come back between what sounded like fits of laughter. Out in the field the laboring men stopped what they were doing and squinted toward the scene of the commotion. One called out something that was unintelligible to Caroline.

Millicent bolted under the fence on the opposite side of the barnyard while Raleigh and the boy raced after her. Caroline, her caught-up skirts revealing flashes of white petticoats and slim, thrashing calves, followed suit. The child stopped, apparently content to do no more than hang on the gate and watch as dog and cat dashed across the meadow. He yelled something to Caroline as she swarmed up and over the fence. So intent was she on the chase that the words didn't register until she was almost halfway across the field. Then the sense of what he had said sank in. The boy had cried, " 'Ware the bull!"

Bull?

Caroline's step faltered. Her gaze left the dog and cat and swung around in a wide arc. What she saw made her stop dead and drop her skirts. Her mouth opened and her eyes rounded with horror.

There was, indeed, a bull.

It was as black as Satan and as big as a colossus, and it was looking directly at her from no more than a dozen yards away!

For a moment that seemed suspended forever in time, Caroline and the beast stared at each other. Then, with a nod to the adage that discretion was the better part of valor, Caroline snatched up her skirts, whirled about, and fled back toward the safety of the barnyard, her scarlet cloak streaming out behind her like a banner.

Behind her, with a fearsome bellow, the behemoth charged.

"Run!"

The boy on the fence screamed encouragement, but Caroline scarcely heard him. She was deafened, blinded by fear. Her eyes focused on the fence, and her ears were filled with the heaving, snorting creature that pounded after her.

"Come on! Come on!"

The child cheered her on, but it was scarcely necessary. The finest runner in all of London town could not have matched the speed Caroline attained that morning. She sprinted toward the fence like a greyhound. Behind her she could hear the monster's enraged bawls, the pounding of its hooves.

Caroline screamed. The boy on the gate yelled. Men and children converged on the barnyard from seemingly every direction.

She fancied she could feel the creature's hot breath on her back.

"Your cloak! Drop your cloak!"

Still some paces short of the fence, Daniel yelled the advice even as he raced to her assistance.

Caroline clenched one fist around her skirt—tripping at such a juncture might very well prove fatal—and raised the other hand to jerk at the strings of her cloak. An instant later the garment billowed free.

"Good girl!"

Terror gave wings to her feet as she leaped toward the safety of the fence from nearly a yard away. Daniel, vaulting up the other side, grabbed her arm and jerked her up and over. There was a tug as her skirt caught, the sound of ripping cloth, and then she was hurtling through the air to land with an *oomph!* facedown in the filth of the barnyard.

As she lay sprawled, aching in every bone and fighting for breath, Millicent appeared from nowhere and rubbed her head against her mistress's. From the woods beyond the bull's pasture, Raleigh continued to bark frantically as he sought the cat, which had, in the mysterious manner of its kind, managed to elude him. Caroline didn't even have the strength to groan as her pet began, very noisily, to purr.

3

*F*or what seemed like an eternity Caroline lay unmoving, Millicent's consoling rumbles echoing in her ears. The fall had knocked the breath from her; the hardscrabble ground had scraped her face and hands, making them sting. Her entire body felt bruised by the force of her landing, and her heart had yet to slow its panicked beat. To make matters worse, she was sure that when she opened her eyes a huge mouth full of giant doggy teeth would be poised to make a meal of her under the eyes of its grinning masters, none of whom had seemed inclined to lift so much as a finger in her defense.

But finally she could postpone the inevitable no longer. Reaching out an arm, she scooped up Millicent, cradling the cat against her bruised ribcage. With great reluctance, she opened her eyes and rolled cautiously onto an elbow as she looked around. The dog was nowhere in sight. Caroline heaved a sigh of relief. Except for the scowling scrutiny of the small boy who had been feeding the chickens, she was alone. Moving gingerly, she sat up.

"She's alive, Pa."

The child spoke over his shoulder, then turned wide blue eyes back on Caroline. His black hair, fine as silk, formed a ragged fringe above his eyes; it needed trimming, she saw, and there was a rip in the knee of his breeches that cried out for mending. He had an untended look about him, and his manners certainly left a great deal to be desired. But he was not her concern, and for that she must be thankful.

Squinting against the sun, Caroline looked past the urchin to find five grown men and the youth who'd been stirring the kettle leaning against the fence she'd just scaled. Beyond them the bull snorted and stomped as it tossed what was left of her cloak into the air with its horns. All five males regarded the malevolent beast with an anxiety that would have been heartwarming had it been directed at her. But focused on the bull, such concern was maddening.

At the child's pronouncement they all turned their heads. Six pairs of eyes fixed on Caroline with varying degrees of rebuke. Her attention focused on the oldest of the three men she had not yet met. If she was not mistaken, he was the one whom Daniel had earlier referred to as Matt. Her eyes were more than a little hostile as she watched the approach of Ephraim Mathieson.

He was a tall man, taller even than Daniel who had stood beside him at the fence, with broad shoulders and a wide chest that tapered down to narrow hips and long, powerful legs. Like the two boys, he wore no coat or waistcoat. His shirt was long-sleeved, white, and collarless, his breeches black and full, ending just below the knee. His stockings were of gray wool, his shoes simple square-toed leather. He was hatless, and his hair was so black that it glinted blue in the bright sunlight, as rare and fine a shade of black as her own. Like Daniel's, it was cut short in the Roundhead style, but the curls and deep waves it fell into seemed determined to defy that modest fashion.

Even before she got a good look at his face, Caroline decided that her sister's husband was a most attractive man.

It was only as he drew closer that she realized that he limped. His left leg, apparently unable to bend at the knee, swung awkwardly as he moved. A small amount of hostility faded from her gaze. It must be galling for such an obviously vigorous man to be hampered by such an affliction.

When he was but a few paces from her, he stopped, fists on hips, as he studied her, frowning. Self-consciously her gaze followed the same path as his. As she inventoried her own shortcomings, it was all she could do to suppress a wince. She was naturally tall and slender, but once she had been round in all the places where women were meant to be round. The rigors of the voyage and the soul-destroying months that had preceded it had leached the feminine roundness from her, leaving her almost painfully thin. Unfortunately, her gown—it was her best, a once-lovely creation of ruched emerald silk—had been made when her contours were more womanly. Now it hung on her, the neckline far lower than it should be, the elbow-length sleeves and waist drooping, the skirt inches too long. In fact, the garment looked as if it had been made for a much larger person. It was also torn and filthy from her fall. With her hair tumbling from its once-tidy knot at her nape so that thick black strands straggled indecorously around her neck and down her back, and her petticoat hiked to expose her legs almost to the knee, she was, she realized with chagrin, quite a sight to behold.

He was eyeing her bare legs disapprovingly. All her earlier hostility returned in full force.

"Ephraim Mathieson?"

Her tone was frosty. He nodded once in confirmation as, despite her protesting muscles, she scrambled to her feet, trying without much success to brush the grime from her skirt while at the same time keeping a tight grip on Millicent. The cat glared at the man; Caroline barely controlled an urge to do likewise as she strove to set her appearance to rights.

The square neckline of her bodice had slipped off one shoulder, exposing the top of her chemise and far more of her creamy skin than she would have liked. With angry jerks she tugged at her offending corsage until it was at least minimally decent. There was nothing she could do about the rip in her skirt that revealed glimpses of ruffled white petticoat to the waist. As for her hair, with Millicent in her arms she was forced to let it hang where it would. Lifting her chin—she tried not to dwell on the thought that her face was very likely as dirty as her dress—she met his eyes. Never in her life had she felt at such a disadvantage, but she'd be hanged before she'd let it show!

"You may count yourself lucky," he said in a deep, brusque tone, "that you've not caused harm to my bull."

After all she had endured, that statement was too much. Caroline drew in a long, ragged breath, trying without much success to catch the tail end of her runaway self-control.

"*I* harm your bull!" she sputtered, her eyes snapping with indignation. "Yon beast was almost the death of me! To hell with your bloody bull, is what I say!"

"Shut your foul mouth, woman!" The roar from behind her made Caroline jump and almost lose her grip on Millicent. Catching the squirming cat just as it would have leaped for freedom, Caroline swung around to discover the dominie not a dozen paces away, stopped in his tracks by her hasty words. Outrage was writ plain upon his sharp features. Beneath the tight, white curls of his wig, his face was very red.

"Oh, my land," Caroline muttered, put out of countenance by the pastor's unexpected presence. What had emerged from her mouth mortified her nearly as much as it horrified the dominie. She had thought the hardships she had learned to endure had permanently snuffed her inclination toward quick-temperedness and outspokenness. Why did both the blasted dominie and her proposed new family have to be present to witness her newly reawakened delinquency?

"So you're a blasphemer as well as a thief, a strumpet as well as a liar!"

The dominie's voice swelled with affront as his gaze raked over Caroline before fixing on the man behind her. "Ephraim Mathieson, if you have not yet repudiated this shameless woman, I urge you to do so at once, and publicly! When one of my flock told me of her iniquities aboard ship, I shuddered and hurried to warn you! But it seems no warning is necessary: out of her own mouth she is condemned!"

The dominie's denunciation quivered in the air. Caroline's eyes flashed, and she opened her mouth to defend herself with words that were admittedly stronger than was politic. But before she could utter so much as a syllable she was stopped by a strong, warm hand that closed over her arm, squeezing a warning.

"And a very good day to you, too, Mr. Miller."

Matt's greeting was coldly sardonic, but Caroline was too concerned with the crawling sensation engendered by his touch to do more than barely register his tone. Would the feel of a man's hand on her person ever cease to repulse her, she wondered even as she pulled free. With the cessation of the hated contact, her mind cleared, and she was once again able to focus on the exchange between the two men.

Her gaze moving from the bristling dominie to Matt, Caroline saw that her brother-in-law's expression was even more unpleasant than his voice. She saw something else, too, in this, her first closeup view of him, that made her eyes widen involuntarily. He was regarding the pastor with icy distaste, but his expression in no way marred the dark splendor of his face. His features could have graced a classical statue; his jaw and cheekbones had been chiseled by a master hand. His nose was straight, his mouth long and well shaped, with a lower lip that was just slightly fuller than the upper. His eyes were deep set beneath straight, thick black brows. The irises were a brilliant celestial blue, their lightness almost shocking against the sun-weathered swarthiness of his skin. The only note of disharmony was the scar, white and jagged, that sliced across his left cheek from the corner of his eye to just above his mouth. Had it not been for that, Caroline would have easily judged him to be the handsomest man she had ever beheld in her life.

Fortunately, he did not observe her reaction to his appearance. His attention was all for the dominie.

"I charge you to put your household in order, Ephraim Mathieson, and denounce this sinful woman!" the pastor brayed.

Matt's lips tightened, and his eyes narrowed. "It is not for you to tell me how to conduct matters relating to my household, Joachim Miller. Nor to condemn a stranger without proof."

"Proof?" The man tittered angrily. "Proof of her blasphemy I have just heard with my own ears. For proof of her thievery and lying, I have the word of her fellow passengers from the *Dove*! Question Tobias for yourself, if you will; I have no doubt that he will verify the tale! For proof of strumpetry, you have only to look at the way she is displaying herself in that shocking gown! 'Tis an affront to decency, it is! She should be set in the stocks, then sent back across the sea to the Gomorrah from which she came!"

"I believe I am capable of handling my own affairs without your interference."

"You dare to set yourself up in opposition to the word of God?"

"To God's word I'll willingly listen, but to more of your blather, no! Take yourself from my sight, Mr. Miller, whilst you still can!"

"So now you go so far as to threaten a man of the cloth! You will be held accountable for your actions, Ephraim Mathieson!" The dominie, chin quivering with anger, turned away. "You'll rue this day, I promise you!" Robe flapping, he marched across the barnyard, heading with jerky haste for the path through the trees.

"It might be less than wise to make more of an enemy of the dominie, Matt." Daniel's uneasy pronouncement brought his brother's and Caroline's gaze around to him. She had not noticed their approach during the exchange between Matt and the pastor, but now Daniel, a younger man who must, from his resemblance to Daniel, be another brother, a third man with sandy hair and a lurking grin, and the two boys formed a semicircle behind Matt. Tobias Rowse stood a little to one side, shaking his head with a frown.

"Daniel's in the right of it, you know," the sandy-haired man said.

Matt shrugged, clearly indifferent to the warning. His attention shifted to Caroline. Blue eyes met amber ones and held.

"Are you always this much trouble?" he asked after a moment. Caroline's chin came up. Ephraim Mathieson was clearly as uncivilized as the land in which he lived!

"I am rarely any trouble at all, when I am not plagued by monstrous dogs and charging bulls and rude men," she replied tartly. Having once lost her grip on the remote facade she had thought was well on its way to becoming her true nature, she could not seem to recover it again.

Matt grunted. Behind him, Daniel started to speak, his expression worried. With a wave of his hand Matt silenced him. "From what my brother and Tobias have managed to impart to me, I gather that you have arrived from England just this morn, and are claiming to be a near relation to our family. Perhaps, now that you've dragged us all from our work and caused such a commotion as we are not likely to see again, you would care to explain how this can be?"

Caroline's eyes glinted, and she ached to give him the rough side of her tongue. But instead she took a deep breath, suddenly realizing that to alienate the very man whose support she most needed would be foolhardy. What would she do if he, in his capacity as her sister's husband, sent her packing? The notion did not bear thinking of.

"I am Elizabeth's sister," she said evenly. "I am Caroline Wetherby."

There was a shocked sound from the young man who looked like Daniel, and wide-eyed stares from the two boys. Matt's eyes flickered, then ran slowly over her before returning to her face. "I see little resemblance."

"Believe me, I am who I say. I have papers to prove my identity. Although Elizabeth will surely know me."

"Ah, you saw her recently, then?"

"You must know that I have not seen her for some fifteen years." There was anger in her voice. "Since shortly before she ran away with you, to be precise."

His mouth twitched once, then was stilled. His expression was unreadable. "She spoke of you."

His acknowledgment that she was indeed who she claimed to be, meager as it was in the face of all that she required of him, sent a wave of relief through Caroline. Until she registered precisely what it was that he had said.

"She *spoke* of me?" she asked carefully, feeling an icy finger of premonition run along her spine. "Does she no longer do so?"

"You cannot have had my letter."

"N-no. I have received no letter from you."

"I wrote last year. To you and your father. He is not with you?"

"He died a little more than two months ago."

"Ah. You have my condolences, then."

"Thank you."

There was a watchfulness in his blue eyes, and he seemed to hesitate as if weighing his next words. Coupled with the ponderous silence of the others, his reticence confirmed Caroline's worst suspicion.

"Elizabeth is dead, isn't she?" Although it felt as though a giant hand was squeezing her insides, her words were steady.

His lips tightened, and then he nodded once. "Yes."

"Oh, no." Caroline closed her eyes tightly, taking deep breaths to combat the nausea that suddenly resurrected itself with swirling insistence.

"Oh, no!" There was heavy silence on the part of the watching males. After a moment, her eyes opened again. This time they were cloudy with shock. "How—how did she die?"

"She drowned," Matt said tersely. " 'Twill be two years ago in May."

"Oh, no!" It seemed to be all she could say. The children, the men—their faces grew suddenly blurry. The thought of how far she had come, of how much she had risked to make this journey, made her feel light-headed. All in vain, all in vain—the words ran through her head in ringing chorus. Her stomach churned; she clenched her teeth, determined not to give way. But this time incipient illness was not to be denied. With a gasp, she thrust Millicent blindly into Ephraim Mathieson's surprised arms. Pressing a hand to her mouth, she turned quickly away, stumbling in her haste to reach the nearest concealment.

The barn was nearby; she barely managed to get around the corner of it before collapsing onto her knees and becoming violently sick. When she was finished, she crawled away to sit huddled in the structure's cool shadow with her head resting back against the rough wood. She had never felt so miserable, both physically and spiritually.

Elizabeth was dead. Caroline had no strength left even to mourn for her sister. At that moment her concern was all for herself: she was destitute, cast adrift in a strange land with no one left to turn to. In England she had burned her bridges with a vengeance, but even if she hadn't she had not the funds to return. What could she do, except cast herself on the mercy of her unwelcoming brother-in-law?

Caroline cringed in humiliation at the very idea.

The object of her thoughts came around the corner of the barn toward her. Caroline watched him approach, vaguely registering the limping gait that he must despise. He kept coming until he stood over her. She said nothing for a moment, merely looked up at him with eyes that were slightly unfocused. It was an effort to return to the present.

"What have you done with my cat?" Millicent was all she had left to love in the world, and the animal's well-being was the first thing that popped into Caroline's mind.

"Daniel has the creature. It's safe enough."

He studied her briefly. Then he reached inside his sleeve and withdrew a square of linen, which he held out to her.

"Wipe your face."

After a moment's hesitation Caroline took the cloth and did as he bade her. When she was finished, she automatically handed the crumpled ball back to him. Only the slightest of grimaces betrayed the distaste he must have felt as he accepted it and tucked it into his waistband.

"That's better." His gaze ran over her, his eyes narrowed. "I remember your mincing Cavalier of a father well. You resemble him physically. I hold scant hope that the resemblance is only surface deep, but I am willing to be proved wrong. Tobias informs me that you have come to make your home with us. He also tells me that I owe him for your passage, spinning me a tale I can hardly credit. I have no patience with thieves, but I cannot in all fairness condemn you without giving you a chance to speak. So, Miss Caroline Wetherby, here is your chance: tell me what you will, and I will listen. More than that I cannot promise."

4

"**Y**ou will not speak slightingly of my father!"

Caroline's eyes flashed as she defended the honor of the parent who had been, admittedly, somewhat lacking in stability and possessed of myriad other faults, but dearly beloved even so.

"Will I not? It is no more than the truth, although Marcellus Wetherby's failings are certainly not the central issue here."

Caroline scrambled to her feet, clenching her fists as she returned his somber gaze with a glare. "I'll not listen to you befoul his memory. He was a fine man, a kind and good one!"

"He was an irresponsible profligate with a misguided love for a debauched king, among other less-than-pleasant traits." Matt's voice was dry.

"Fine talk from the scion of a family of regicides! I don't doubt you'd sing another tune if King Charles had not seen fit to confiscate the property of all traitors!"

According to what her father had told her of her sister's husband, his family had lost land and fortune with the restoration of the rightful monarch in the aftermath of Cromwell's death. For the next several years, the once-powerful Mathiesons had scratched out a living from the soil of what had been one of their tenant farms. Then Mathieson *père*, still a staunch Puritan, had died, and Ephraim, or Matt as he apparently was called, as the new head of the family, had decided to emigrate. An unknown number of family members had sailed from England with him—as had Elizabeth Wetherby, who had then been twenty years old. It was not precisely tactful to fling such a recollection in the face of a man whose help she needed, Caroline realized even as she said it, but anger governed her tongue and the words were out before she could stop them.

Fortunately, his temper did not heat to match hers.

"The regicides were in the right of it. 'Twas the first King Charles who was gravely in error, and the son is cast from the same mold as the father.

But I'll not discuss politics with a chit who was not even born when the mess began. You may tell me, instead, what prompted you to come to Connecticut Colony. Was there no one in England you could turn to after the death of your father?"

Caroline eyed him resentfully, but prudence prompted her to forbear continuing the argument. "No."

"An attractive young woman like yourself must have had at least one suitor. Could you not have wed?"

"I had no wish to wed."

"You preferred instead to leave hearth and country and undertake a perilous journey to a wilderness to make your home with strangers?" His eyebrows lifted skeptically.

"Elizabeth is—was—the only family remaining to me. I wished to see her, to be with her. So I came. Had I known that—had I known of her death, I would have made other arrangements."

"I see. So now we come to the heart of the matter. Having made up your mind to come, you chose to pay for your passage with worthless jewelry. What I would know is whether you knew the gems were paste."

Caroline's eyes flickered. "No."

"The truth, mind. I have no love for liars."

"I am not a liar!"

Matt looked at her reflectively. "Tobias showed me the brooch. 'Tis a lovely thing, most distinctive. So distinctive, in fact, that it called to mind a memory: years ago Elizabeth told me of a fine-looking brooch made in the same shape of a peacock as yours that your father used to wager in his games of chance when he was low on funds. 'Twas a good thing he usually won, she said, because the gems were fake, and he'd have been hanged had he been found out. That both brooches should be fashioned alike is quite a coincidence, wouldn't you say?"

His eyes seemed to be burning a hole through her. Caroline had to fight the urge to close her lids against that searing look. Instead she gritted her teeth and lifted her chin at him.

"Very well, then. I knew," she said abruptly.

"Ah."

"What exactly does that mean?" Her question was fierce.

"It means that you had better tell me the whole story whilst you still may. My inclination is to wash my hands of all responsibility for you. I told you I have no love for liars, and I have even less for thieves."

Bitterness twisted her mouth. "You want the whole story? All right, I'll tell you. For the last two years of his life my father was ill, and unable to provide for us. I took in sewing for what little income we had, but it was scarce enough to pay for a roof over our heads, much less feed us. We had to sell everything we possessed of value, but still there wasn't enough. The landlord—the man who owned the rooms we stayed in—took a fancy to me, and stopped asking for the rent the last few months. When my father died, he demanded to be paid. With—with my person.''

Caroline stopped, unable to go on as the dreadful memories washed over her. Simon Denker's hands running over her body, his mouth, fetid and wet, forcing kisses on her. Fists clenching, she fought back the tears that burned at the back of her eyes. She had demeaned herself enough; she would not cry.

Matt's lips were pursed, his eyes thoughtful as they surveyed her.

"You need not look at me like that!" she burst out. "What would you have done in my shoes? Using Papa's lucky brooch would not seem so dreadful had the choice faced *you.*"

He seemed to weigh her words. Then he nodded. "Presented with two evils, you chose the lesser. Although it would have been better had you not lied about it when asked."

Caroline drew a deep, shaken breath. As always happened when the recollections of that day assaulted her mind, she felt curiously weak and sick. She swayed once, then caught herself, resting a hand against the side of the barn for support. Resentment blazed in her eyes as she looked at her brother-in-law where he stood passing judgment on her. It was easy to take the moral high ground when one was not in desperate need!

"Does being sanctimonious come naturally to you, Mr. Mathieson, or do you have to work at it?"

"I would control that vixen's tongue, were I you." Faint amusement suddenly lightened his expression. "And don't bother fainting, if that's the next trick you mean to employ to win my sympathy. I have already decided to reimburse Tobias for your passage."

"How very kind of you." Sarcasm turned the polite words cold. Abandoning the support of the wall, she stood rigidly erect. She would not collapse now if it killed her to stay on her feet. "But unnecessary, after all. I find that I no longer require your assistance."

The icy hauteur she assumed was balm for her shamed spirit. Pride and temper might have combined to crowd out sound good judgment, but at the moment Caroline meant what she said.

"If I do not reimburse Tobias for your passage, he will have you taken before the magistrate and sold as a bound servant to recoup the cost."

Caroline was proud, but she was not stupid, and his calm pronouncement shocked her.

"Surely such a thing cannot be legal?"

"I assure you that it is."

"Of course it would be, in this barbarous country! Do you Roundheads
practice any other abominations besides slavery?" Bitterness edged her
words.

His eyes narrowed. "A word of advice, my girl. Do not be spewing your
Royalist twaddle on this side of the ocean. Our punishments for such loose
talk are severe."

"Must I live in fear, then, of such as your sour-faced dominie?"

"Enough! I'll tolerate no more of your insolence, I warn you. If you are
to be a member of my household, then you will comport yourself in a
seemly fashion. That means, at the very least, no thievery, no lying, no
blasphemous language, and no Royalist harangues." If she had been in any
fit state to notice, she would have perceived the faintest of humorous glints
at the back of his eyes. Unfortunately, she wasn't.

"It may surprise you to learn that I no longer have the slightest desire to
become a member of your household!" Caroline, speaking through her
teeth, threw good sense to the winds and was surprised by how wonderful
it felt.

"You prefer to be sold as a bound servant?" He arched his eyebrows at
her.

"I prefer to find some kind of employment. I am no stranger to hard
work. I can cook, keep house, and sew. If you will pay Captain Rowse his
money, I will repay you out of my earnings as soon as I can. You would be
making me a loan only."

Matt snorted. "Who around here would employ a rudespoken, outlandishly dressed female of the Royalist persuasion, do you suppose? You
would starve before you'd earned so much as a crust."

Thwarted, Caroline scowled at him. "You're uncommonly lacking in
courtesy, sir!"

"Then I'd say we're a well-matched pair. As you are the sister of my
dead wife and the aunt of my boys, I am willing to provide you with a
home. You will work to earn your keep, and to repay the monies given to
Tobias for your passage. We have some need of a cook-housekeeper ourselves, and that's the function you will fill. All I ask is that you try not to
be more of a bother than you can help. I would not care to suffer through
daily repeats of this morning's idiocy."

"Idiocy!" Before Caroline could say more—and there was certainly a great deal more she wished to say—a loud noise arose from the barnyard. Caroline stiffened, but ere she could move Millicent careered around the corner of the barn with the hound from hell in baying pursuit. Spying her mistress, Millicent made a beeline toward her, tearing painfully up Caroline's gown to perch on her shoulder, fur on end, hissing at the slavering beast that galloped after her.

"Go away! Shoo!" Caroline cried, one hand steadying her cat as the other extended in a frantic attempt to ward off the oncoming dog.

"Raleigh, no!" Matt boomed, but it was too late. Raleigh launched himself forward, paws outstretched. The dog crashed into Caroline with the velocity of a runaway wagon, knocking her sprawling to the ground. She cried out; Millicent tumbled, hissed, and lashed out with a razor-tipped paw; Raleigh yelped; Matt yelled. Some few yards away, the thundering herd of remaining Mathiesons burst into view.

Then, as Caroline once again lay stunned in the dirt, Millicent clawed straight up the side of the barn while Raleigh barked hysterically and the onlookers variously shouted, laughed, and grabbed at the leaping dog.

For the second time that day, pandemonium reigned.

5

"**D**own, Raleigh! I'll stand no more of your nonsense, sir!" Matt roared, thoroughly exasperated as he seized the frenzied animal by the scruff of his neck. Recognizing the voice of authority, the dog ceased his deafening howls in midcry and dropped to grovel on the ground at Matt's feet. From the roof of the barn, Millicent looked down with malevolent satisfaction at her tormentor's comeuppance. Then, assured that he was thoroughly cowed, she proceeded to sit and calmly wash her face. Caroline struggled to a sitting position and surreptitiously rubbed her abused posterior. Suddenly realizing that she was a source of extreme amusement to her audience, she stopped, embarrassed.

"Damned cat! I should have had one of the seamen toss it overboard. Thing's been nothing but a passel of trouble from the start." Captain Rowse—who, besides Matt, was the only one of the many males present not choking back laughter—came over to offer Caroline a hand as he spoke. Scowling at the captain—he'd been almost as unpleasant over the smuggled-aboard Millicent as over the worthless brooch—she coldly declined his offer of assistance and got to her feet on her own.

"Millicent caused no trouble aboard ship," she protested hotly.

"Oh, no? Is it not a fact that we were becalmed for four days, and had to break out the oars? Did the flour not become moldy, and have to be thrown out? Did Goody Shoemaker's specially bespoke chair not split its back when a barrel tipped over on it? Did my quartermaster not cut his leg to the bone while doing something as simple as slicing a rope? Eh, missy?"

"None of that can be blamed on Millicent!"

"Cat on board ship's bad luck, as everyone knows. Black cat's worse. I've never had such a string of calamities befall a craft of mine in a single voyage. Had to be the cat."

"What utter nonsense!" Caroline exclaimed scornfully.

"The mistress, more like," Matt said under his breath. Caroline was not sure whether anyone besides herself could hear his words. "She's caused enough havoc here."

He had tied a rope around Raleigh's neck. Even as Caroline turned fuming eyes on him he was beckoning to the older of the two boys. Like his little brother, this child had a shock of stick-straight black hair and blue eyes. But he was far taller than the younger boy and thin as a reed. As close as Caroline could judge, he looked to be about ten years old.

"Take him and tie him out back of the house." Matt handed the rope to his son.

"But, Pa . . . !"

"Just till things get straightened away. He'll take no harm. Do as you're told now."

"Yes, sir." The boy was sullen but obedient, and a visibly reluctant Raleigh was partly coaxed, partly dragged away. Caroline gave an audible sigh of relief as the animal disappeared from sight.

"You can't lay the blame for this morning's upheaval at my door!" Caroline said indignantly to Matt. " 'Tis all the fault of yon ill-trained monster, and you know it!"

"You should really strive to get over your fear of dogs," Daniel observed, grinning, before Matt could reply.

"Any but a fool would be afraid of a great ferocious beast such as that!" Caroline snapped, her eyes swinging around to him. Daniel was flanked by both his nearly identical brother and the sandy-haired man. On all three faces were lunatic grins. She raked the three of them with dagger looks.

"Ferocious! Raleigh is not! You're just a coward, is what it is!" The younger boy scowled at her. Caroline had to resist an impulse to scowl right back. The child couldn't be more than five years old, and to take umbrage at a barely breeched babe was certainly beneath her, but she'd had about enough of each and every one of these arrogant males!

"Hold your tongue, David Mathieson." Matt silenced him with a stern look. "You'll be polite to your aunt, or you'll feel the flat of my hand where you sit."

"She's not my aunt! Is she?" The child sounded fascinated and appalled at the same time.

"Indeed she is. This is your Aunt Caroline, who it seems will be making her home with us for the forseeable future." Matt glanced at Caroline. She was nearly as taken aback at the idea of their kinship as the wide-eyed boy, but of course it was true. If these were Elizabeth's children, then she was their aunt. Or half aunt, as she and her sister had had different mothers.

"How do you do, David," she said to him, managing to sound reasonably pleasant, upon which feat she congratulated herself, considering the circumstances.

"I don't want no aunt living with us!" David burst out, glaring at Caroline. "We're fine on our own, just us men!"

"Silence!" Matt's roar had worked on Raleigh, and it worked again on David. Abashed, the child shut his mouth, but his expression was belligerent as he glowered at Caroline.

"She says she can cook and clean and sew, and that's something we can use around here. Besides that, she's family. She'll be staying, and that's all I have to say on the subject!" As if he expected to be challenged, his gaze swept around the semicircle formed by the three men and his son. The adults looked dubious, the child mutinous. Caroline scowled at the lot of them. Off to the right, Captain Rowse made a choking sound that he hastily turned into a cough, but no one even glanced his way.

"You know Daniel, and that's our brother Thomas to his left"—Matt indicated the sandy-haired man—"and Robert to his right. They live here, work the farm with me and my boys. John's my older son. This one's David." His eyes slid over to Captain Rowse. "Tobias, if you'll come with me into the house, I'll settle our business and offer you a drink at the same time."

"Sounds fair enough to me." Captain Rowse grinned at Daniel and the other men behind Matt's back.

"Caroline, you may come with me, too. I'll show you where things are kept, how we like things done. The rest of you, get back to work. You, too, Davey. Get some more corn and finish feeding the chickens." His tone gentled as he spoke to his son.

"What about her trunks?" Daniel asked.

"Trunks?" Matt looked at Caroline with raised brows.

"Three of 'em," Daniel replied. "Heavy, too. And a basket."

Matt grunted. "Bring them in." He shook his head. "Three trunks!"

He started for the house, disappearing around the corner of the barn with Captain Rowse as the others moved off to do his bidding. But instead of following him, as Matt had clearly intended her to do, Caroline turned to look up at the cat perched on the peaked roof high above her head.

"Come on, Millicent," she coaxed.

Millicent stared back at her, her golden eyes unblinking.

"Millicent, come down!"

Millicent blinked once, slowly, then got to her feet and stretched. Her sleek black body rippled, and her tail stood up.

"Woman, where are you? Are you coming?" Matt's annoyed shout from somewhere outside her field of vision caused Caroline to jump.

"In just a minute!" she called back. To the animal, who was sauntering along the roofline as if she had not a care in the world, Caroline added in an urgent tone: "Millicent! Come!"

"Bother the cat! The creature'll come down when it's good and ready, and not before." Matt had reappeared. When he saw what she was about he stalked over to her, caught her by the arm, and propelled her in the direction he wanted her to go. "I've lost enough time for one day. I don't propose to lose more waiting on the whims of a confounded cat."

Caroline pulled free. "But the dog will get her!"

Matt stopped walking, planted his fists on his hips, and glowered at her. "He's tied, and anyway he'd not hurt her. We've cats aplenty around the barn, and they've all survived him quite handily. He just likes to give chase to anything that will run." He reached for her arm again. Caroline quickly stepped back to avoid his touch.

"She'll get lost! I've had her since she was a kitten, and . . ." Her voice was unconsciously pleading.

Matt's lips tightened. He hesitated, looking distinctly displeased. Then he sighed. "If I fetch your infernal nuisance of a cat down for you, will you then go into the house and do your utmost to stay out of trouble for the rest of the day?"

His offer—ungraciously phrased as it was—surprised her. In gratitude Caroline almost smiled at him before she caught herself. "I promise."

"Very well, then." He turned to call over his shoulder. "One minute, Tobias."

He walked into the barn. Emerging moments later with a ladder, he placed it against the side of the building and proceeded, rather awkwardly because of his stiff leg, to climb. Millicent eyed him with wary attention as he stepped onto the roof and moved toward her. Just as he leaned down to scoop her up, the cat hissed, spat, and bolted, flying down the slope of the roof and leaping agilely to the ground.

"Millicent!"

The cat darted toward Caroline, who bent and gathered her pet up in her arms. Captain Rowse, who'd walked over to join her as they waited for Matt, was convulsed with silent laughter. Caroline ignored him as his shoulders heaved.

Aggravation visible in every lean line of his body, Matt turned to survey man, woman, and cat from his vantage point on the barn roof before retracing his steps. Some short time later, having restored the ladder to the barn, he came toward them, fixing Caroline and Millicent with a jaundiced eye.

"Did I not tell you about the accursed beast?" Matt demanded. Without waiting for her reply, he stalked past her, heading for the house. Captain Rowse, miraculously sobered now that Matt was within sight and sound, fell in beside him.

Meekly, Caroline followed, Millicent clutched to her breast. However it had turned out, he had tried to be kind. Her spirits lifted infinitesimally. Perhaps, just perhaps, life with the Mathiesons would not be so terrible after all.

6

Matt might have been kind about her cat, but his manners were no better than Daniel's or Captain Rowse's. Caroline discovered that as he shouldered his way through the unbolted door without so much as glancing at her some few paces behind the pair of men. Had she really expected him to stand back to let her precede them? Given her experiences of the morning, no, she decided, she had not. Every colonial she had met so far, from the pickle-faced dominie to the youngest Mathieson boy, had been as rude as he could be. Apparently the outward conventions of gentlemanly behavior were not highly prized in the New World.

"Come in, Tobias, and have some ale. 'Twill make your head spin, I promise you. How much is it the chit owes you?"

" 'Tis a fair amount."

"I gathered that." Matt sounded as if he were mentally bracing himself. "How much?"

The amount Captain Rowse named made Matt groan. He shot Caroline, who had just stepped over the threshold, a darkling look. Then, shaking his head, he disappeared through a doorway on the opposite side of the room with Captain Rowse at his heels.

Feeling slightly chastened, Caroline stayed where she was, blinking as she looked around the dim interior of the house.

It took only seconds for her eyes to adjust to the change of light. When they did, they swept the large front room before her, widening with disbelief.

Clutter was everywhere—saddles and hats, boots and farm implements, a half-carved tree trunk that was apparently in the process of being fashioned into a stool, an open sea chest piled haphazardly with bedding. The furniture was strewn with clothing, whether clean or dirty Caroline couldn't tell. The wide plank floor sported a circular path of caked mud that ran the circumference of the room, clearly marking the path where the house's inhabitants habitually walked. To the left of the door, a narrow staircase climbed steeply upward, the wall side of each tread providing space for a collection of piled objects. The air in the house bore a decided chill, and over everything there was a layer of dust. A musty smell, combined with an odor of onions that must have been part of the previous night's dinner, assaulted her nostrils. Wrinkling her nose against the smell, Caroline took a cautious step forward. If she had ever possessed such a house, it would have been spotless. She could not imagine anyone, not even such barbarians as the Mathiesons clearly were, letting a dwelling get into such a state.

In the next room she could hear Matt talking in a low voice to Captain Rowse. Certain that she was the subject of their discourse, she was of no mind to let them discuss her without her presence. Picking her way through the miscellany of items littering the floor, she at last reached her destination. Pausing in the doorway, she glanced around the room. As she had feared, the kitchen was a disaster.

A ridiculously tiny fire flickered in the huge fireplace that filled half of one side of the room. Made of creekstone that was blackened to the ceiling from lack of regular cleaning, it clearly, from the smoke that stung her eyes, needed its chimney swept. A collection of dingy-looking pots hung forlornly over the hearth, which was heaped with ashes from previous fires. In here the odor of smoke overlaid the memory of onions. The plain board table in front of the fire had been cleared, but the floor had not been swept, and the crude wooden plates, though scraped (as far as she could see), were piled in a pail near the door along with pewter mugs and spoons. Apparently someone had meant to take them outside for washing but had forgotten or found some other task more worth his attention.

Matt stood with both arms crossed over the back of a chair, leaning forward as he talked to Captain Rowse. The captain, looking well satisfied, was in the act of rising from the bench beside the table as Caroline appeared. Both men, glancing at her, abruptly broke off their conversation. After a barely perceptible hesitation, Captain Rowse took a swallow from his mug. It must have contained a particularly tasty kind of ale if his lip-smacking appreciation of it was any indication.

"'Tis glad I am that this matter has been settled so beneficially." Captain Rowse put the mug down and nodded at Caroline in a way that was now entirely friendly. "Matt's taken care of the cost of your passage, Mistress Wetherby. I hope there'll be no ill feeling between us."

"Not at all," Caroline said coolly. Her hands tightened on Millicent as she squashed the urge to let him know just what she thought of his treatment of her aboard the *Dove*. At the least, Captain Rowse had made it clear that he held her in contempt. His attitude had caused the sailors and her fellow passengers to treat her almost as a pariah. Would he really have turned her over to the magistrate to be sold as a servant had he not received the money he was owed? Looking at him, bluff and beefy and good-humored as he now appeared, she knew that had Matt repudiated her, he would have. Caroline felt a sudden welling of gratitude toward her frowning brother-in-law. Immediately she forced the emotion back. Such feelings made one dangerously vulnerable, and that was one thing she meant never to be again.

"Good, good!" Captain Rowse's tone was just a shade too hearty. Caroline regarded him, unsmiling. In place of the banished gratitude sprang a nearly overwhelming sense of relief. She was free of him and his ship, free of the uncertainty of not knowing what awaited her at her journey's end. The anxiety that had been her constant companion for the six weeks of the voyage was a thing of the past.

"Oh, by the by, this is yours, then, if you want it." Fumbling in the pouch that hung at his side, Captain Rowse extracted the peacock brooch. Lips tightening, head high, Caroline held out her hand for it. With a quick look at Matt, who curtly nodded permission, the captain dropped it onto her palm. Her fingers closed tightly over the jewel. Worthless or not, it was her last link to her father. A pang smote her heart as his well-loved face rose before her mind's eye, but she refused to allow herself to acknowledge the aching. Even her grief for her father she meant to put behind her. In this new land, she would start her life afresh. She would simply refuse to allow herself to remember England and all that had happened there.

But for those few seconds her fingers tightened convulsively around the brooch. Millicent squirmed, and Caroline set her down. Then she tucked the brooch into her waistband. When she had the chance she would store the ornament in her trunks, and not look at it again.

"I've no love for animals in the house," Matt said. He straightened and regarded Millicent, who was sniffing cautiously at an overturned milk pail, with suspicion.

Caroline laughed, the sound brittle as she still fought to suppress the sorrow that she would not allow herself to feel.

"What harm do you imagine my poor cat will do, pray? She's far cleaner by nature than others who live here."

Matt's frown darkened as Caroline's glance swept around the room with obvious disdain.

Captain Rowse cleared his throat, looking from one to the other uneasily.

"Well, now that all's settled happily, I'd best be getting back to my ship," he said.

Matt nodded. Giving Caroline a quelling look, he escorted the captain from the room. There was the murmur of their voices, and then Caroline heard the door open and shut. She wandered around the kitchen, increasingly appalled as she encountered spiderwebs and dust balls and clear evidence of mice, which Millicent sniffed with interest. For a woman who loved to cook, as she did, such an ill-kept kitchen was an abomination. What manner of people were these, who possessed so much and clearly valued it so little?

When Matt returned, Caroline was standing near the fireplace, peering disbelievingly into a pot that was half-filled with some food that had been charred to no more than a burnt offering. Without seeming to notice her disgusted expression, he crossed to a covered wooden bin in the corner. Millicent, who sat on top of it, tail twitching, put her ears back at him. With an impatient mutter he shooed her away.

"This in here is corn meal," Matt said, lifting the lid briefly to give her a glimpse of the contents before shutting it again. "There's meat and suet in the smokehouse around back, butter and cheese in the spring. 'Tis out behind the smokehouse. You'll have no trouble finding it. Flour is in here" —he lifted the lid of another bin—"and we've apples and potatoes in the larder. Anything else you need, ask. It's probably around somewhere."

He paused, shoving a piece of harness out of his way with his foot without ever seeming to consider that it had no business being jumbled in a heap on the kitchen floor in the first place. "We'll work through nuncheon, as we've lost so much time, but by sunset we'll be ready to eat. There are six of us, and except for Davey we've big appetites. I hope you were telling the truth when you claimed you could cook."

Then, before Caroline could say aye, nay, or maybe, he turned on his heel and started for the door, apparently meaning simply to leave her to it.

7

"*H*old just a minute, if you please!" Caroline's voice quivered with ire. "You surely do not expect me to prepare a meal in this—this pigsty!"

His back stiffened at her words, and he turned around to eye her measuringly.

"If the accommodations do not suit your ladyship," he said with an edge to his voice, "you have my permission to clean them up."

Caroline laughed. "It would take six women working all day every day for a fortnight to clean this mess up! I will not cook in filthy pots, nor serve a meal in a kitchen so dirty that I cannot even see out the windows! Even to make this one room minimally decent will take the rest of the day! If I am to prepare an edible meal by sunset as well, I must help!"

"Lazy, are you? I should have expected it."

"I am not," Caroline said through her teeth, "lazy!"

Matt lifted an eyebrow, but before he could reply there was the sound of the outside door opening, and the solid thump of something heavy hitting the floor. Matt turned and headed into the front room, where Daniel was carrying inside the last of Caroline's trunks.

"You told me before you left this morn that you'd quite finished building the calving shed," Matt said abruptly.

"Aye." Daniel straightened, eyeing his brother. "What of it?"

"Good. As there is nothing else urgent requiring your attention, you may spend the remainder of the day helping the duchess here around the house. She requires assistance cleaning, she says, because the place is such a pigsty."

Daniel looked aghast. "Clean house? But, Matt . . . !"

"Look to it."

With that Matt walked past his brother and out the door. Daniel swiveled to stare after him, then turned slowly back to look at Caroline with an expression of such dismay that, had she been in a better frame of mind, she would have been hard put not to laugh.

"I know naught of women's work." There was a hollow note to Daniel's voice.

" 'Tis obvious that all of you know naught of women's work," Caroline ground out.

" 'Tis planting season." There was an apologetic note to Daniel's voice. "Usually the place is not so bad."

"Oh?" Caroline raised her eyebrows. "If the floor has seen a broom anytime this past six months, I'll count myself surprised. But there's no point in bewailing what's done. If you will carry my trunks in to where I am to sleep, we will get started. The kitchen first, I think, as it's the most urgent—and the dirtiest."

"Well, now, there's another problem," Daniel said. "I've no notion where you're to sleep. There's four bedchambers abovestairs, but Davey and John share one, Thomas and Robert another. I've the third, and Matt the fourth."

"Then you and Matt will just have to share, won't you?" Caroline smiled with false sweetness. "For I've no intention of sleeping in the stair-well!"

"But there's only one bed in each." Caroline could already see that Daniel was a man to whom improvisation did not come easily. "I doubt Matt would take kindly to sharing bed with me. We've shared one before, and he said he'd sooner sleep with a grizzly. I would, too."

"Bother Matt!" Caroline snapped, then sighed, knowing herself defeated. "Very well, just carry my trunks abovestairs so that they're out of the way. We'll sort it out when *Matt* returns."

Her mockery of the way he spoke of Matt as some kind of supreme being either sailed completely over Daniel's head or didn't bother him. In any case, he looked relieved as he hefted the first of the trunks and started up the stairs with it.

By the time he had finished, Caroline was already busy. She had discovered a small keeping room off the kitchen that held a variety of supplies as well as a washstand. The mirror above the washstand was tiny, allowing her to see only a portion of her face at a time, but it was enough to permit her to repair the worst of the ravages wrought by her encounters with the farm's livestock. She washed her face and hands, pinned up her hair, and —with a mental sigh of regret for the ruination of her best gown—set to mucking out the kitchen. At least she wouldn't have to worry about further damaging her dress. With a section of hem tucked into her waistband to hide the rip, the dress was acceptable for the work she intended doing, but the jagged tear rendered the garment unsalvageable. It would undoubtedly soon find its way to the ragbag.

"What do you want me to do now?" Daniel asked dismally from the doorway. Caroline set him to building up the fire, then had him carry the cooking utensils to the stream, where they had to be scraped until their bottoms were reached and then scrubbed with sand. Toiling side by side with him, arms plunged deep in icy water, Caroline struggled to dismiss the sense of unreality that assailed her whenever her mind wandered from the task at hand. Was this really she, Caroline Wetherby, the toast of a hundred smoky gaming hells, who worked with cold-benumbed fingers at such a homely chore? How all the men who had clamored in vain to bed if not wed her would laugh if they could see her brought so low! Yet, strangely, she was content to have it so. Honest labor seemed suddenly far preferable to the deceit which, were she honest, she would admit had long been her stock in trade. For years she had been little more than her father's shill, the glittering enticement he had used to lure fools for his fleecing. Marcellus Wetherby's victims had ogled his beautiful daughter covetously while he palmed a card or produced an overlooked ace, never realizing until their purses were considerably lightened that they were not to be consoled for their losses in the way they had imagined. Though until her father's final illness she had been subjected almost nightly to lecherous eyes and bawdy suggestions, physically he had kept her safe. He had been a rogue, but not so much a rogue as to permit the forced dishonor of his own flesh and blood. But as she had grown up and become more aware of exactly what those leering men thought of her, she had felt soiled. In this new land, she need never endure such again, and the knowledge heartened her. She would turn her hand to the most backbreaking of tasks, so long as she could hold her head high in the doing.

"Is this good enough?" Daniel asked, exhibiting a well-scoured pot. Brought abruptly back to the present, Caroline nodded approval, glad enough to focus once again on the work at hand.

Despite his initial reluctance, Daniel proved to be an able worker. When that chore was completed, Caroline set him to lugging the farm implements scattered about the house back to the barn where they belonged while she sorted clothing into piles according to its need for washing, mending, or pressing. Nearly every item required some sort of attention, and as she surveyed the size of the piles she wanted to groan. Keeping six males in decent wearing apparel was clearly going to be a never-ending task. But it was one she could do, and do well.

Like cooking and housekeeping, stitchery was a skill she had learned in the long-ago days of her childhood. With her mother, who had wearied of Marcellus's constant traveling once the first bloom of wedded bliss had passed into the reality of raising a child, she had occupied a small cottage in the tiny village of Bishop's Lynn. There she had lived happily until her mother died under the wheels of a runaway wagon, and her father, who had visited only rarely, came to fetch her away with him. She was nearly twelve at the time, and Marcellus, with his handsome face, fine clothes, and elegant ways, seemed a magnificent being. Willingly she had gone adventuring with him, and let him mold her into the kind of woman he wished her to be. But in the last few years she had begun to find their peripatetic existence both tiring and tawdry, and longed to settle someplace. As she grew to love her father dearly, she never expressed what she felt for fear of hurting him. Now the thought of having a home again, with meals to prepare and a house to clean and people to care for, was so appealing that she was almost afraid to allow herself to believe that it lay within her grasp. Over painful years she had learned the value of hearth and home and domesticity, and she suddenly found herself craving them as a starving man might food. Though she was tired and worn down from all that had brought her to this place, she tackled the waiting work with an energy that made Daniel groan.

Some hours later, swept, scrubbed, and dusted, the front two rooms were marginally presentable. There was still much polishing and waxing to do, and Caroline had decided that the windows as well as the wash would have to wait for another day, but the change was remarkable. Even Daniel, who was wearily chopping vegetables on the sideboard in the kitchen, was impressed with the change they had wrought.

"I suppose we've let things slide," he said ruefully. "None of us is a dab hand at housework, so we've just done what was needed to get by. With planting season upon us, that's hardly more than cooking an occasional meal. But I must admit, 'tis nice to be able to walk across the room without forever tripping over something."

Caroline stood over a steaming pot of water, dropping in chunks of meat as she cut them into cubes. The fare for the evening meal would be rabbit stew with girdlecakes; she'd mixed dough for bread and set it to rise, but it would not be ready for baking until the next morn. It was simple food, but tasty and filling, and she had not had time to concoct anything more elaborate. Fortunately, the preparing of savory meals from whatever one could catch or cadge was a skill she had already learned well.

" 'Tis understandable that the housekeeping should suffer since Elizabeth's passing," Caroline replied. She and Daniel, after a somewhat rocky start, were now on fairly good terms. He was an amiable man, if not forced to make decisions that might put him in conflict with his older brother, and a likable one. He even seemed willing to tolerate Millicent, who was purring contentedly from the top of the settle, which put her in the vicinity of Daniel's left elbow. From time to time he absentmindedly scratched her head.

"Elizabeth was no housekeeper. She . . ." Daniel cast Caroline a swift glance and shut up.

"She what?" Caroline asked curiously, turning away from the steaming pot to look at him.

"Nothing. She just did not much like cleaning house, is all," Daniel mumbled, chopping a carrot as if his life depended on it.

Caroline eyed him thoughtfully.

"Daniel," she began, "if I am to be a member of this household, it would help me a great deal to know as much as I can about it. Was there some reason why Elizabeth did not clean house? Please tell me."

Daniel frowned at the carrot he was reducing to shreds. Caroline was too anxious to hear what he might tell her to rescue the vegetable from him while it was still in a state fit for the pot.

"She was ill—really ill from the time Davey was born," Daniel said to the carrot. "She rarely left her bed. Matt had to bunk with me, so as not to disturb her. She could never sleep when he was with her, she said."

"So she was ill for a long time—but your brother said that she died of drowning. If she rarely left her bed, how did that come about?"

"She left it that day. She left it and went to the spring. And she drowned." Daniel's words were stark. "More I can't tell you. I was away. By the time I got home, she was already buried."

Something in his voice made Caroline frown.

"Did you not like her, Daniel?"

He glanced at her then, his eyes opaque.

"She was Matt's wife. 'Twas not my place to like or dislike her."

His tone told her that she would get no more from him on the subject of Elizabeth. Tossing the last of the meat into the boiling water, she went to retrieve the vegetables. The sight of the inexpertly chopped chunks made her grimace as she added them to the pot.

"Who on earth has been doing the cooking for the lot of you? Not you, 'tis obvious."

Clearly relieved to be off the subject of Elizabeth, Daniel turned around on his stool and shrugged.

"Rob's a fair enough cook, when he wishes to be. And sometimes Mary

—that's James's wife, he's our brother who lives in the town—will invite the lot of us to their house to eat. The Widow Forrester has set her cap for Matt, and she's forever sending out bread and pies and such, much good may it do her. Patience Smith has her eye on Rob, and she makes a tasty pot of soup. Thom has a whole gaggle of girls after him, and they vie to tempt him—and of necessity, the rest of us—with their culinary talents. For the rest, we forage fairly well for ourselves. None of us has starved."

Caroline was mixing the buttermilk and flour for the girdlecakes. "I'm surprised that none of the ladies you mentioned thought to volunteer to take on the housekeeping. 'Tis not as sure a way to a man's heart as through his belly, but it is certainly a way."

"Matt's no use for women forever hanging about the place. He's told them to keep away."

Caroline looked at him in some surprise. "Quite the gentleman, your brother," she muttered, setting the batter aside to thicken. Then, turning away from the hearth, she motioned to Daniel. " 'Tis an hour or more yet till supper. Let's start on the upstairs."

Daniel groaned, but followed her as she left the room.

8

"*I* won't eat what she cooks!"

Caroline could hear Davey's piping voice from the larder where she had gone to fetch a crock of fruit preserve. From what Daniel had told her, she assumed it was an offering from one of the brothers' female admirers, but when she tasted it with a cautious finger earlier she realized that it had been made with some sort of berry she could not identify. But whatever it was, it was both tart and sweet, and it would serve to go with the girdle-cakes. In the summer, when the fruits and berries were once again ripe, she would make her own jams. Caroline frowned as she realized how much pleasure the thought gave her; perhaps, she reminded herself fiercely, she would be gone by then. It would not do to allow herself to imagine that she had found a permanent home. Davey did not like her, and none of the other Mathiesons seemed much happier about her presence. Besides, she herself might choose to go elsewhere. Certainly she did not mean to spend longer than she had to tending these impossible males. She could leave whenever the whim took her—or they could toss her out.

"Hush up, Davey! She'll hear you!" said John. Like Davey's, his voice was still youthfully high.

Putting a hand to the small of her back, Caroline stretched the aching muscles there. Lord, she was tired! Too tired to take umbrage with an ill-behaved child, or anyone else. Too tired almost to think. Sweat had curled the tendrils of hair at her temples and nape, and there were damp circles staining the green gown under her armpits. Her head ached, her legs hurt, and she longed for a bed.

Then she remembered she didn't have a bed. And she was reminded, again, that this was not her home. She was here on sufferance only.

"You'll eat what's put before you, and keep your mouth shut in the meanwhile." Matt's reproof came as Caroline entered the kitchen. He and Davey met her gaze with identical scowls. Behind them stood John, hands shoved awkwardly into his waistband, and Thomas. All of them looked as wary as Caroline felt. From the sound of it, Robert was talking to Daniel in the front room. Likely they wanted nothing to do with her either.

"You may all wash up and sit down," Caroline said curtly. "The meal's ready."

"Wash up!" The aghast words came from Davey, but from the expressions on the faces of the males she could see, every one of them was thinking the same thing.

She paused in the act of sliding another girdlecake onto the heap already piled on a pewter plate and glared from one appalled face to another.

"If you want to eat in this kitchen, each and every one of you will wash your hands and face before you sit down. I'll not serve pigs."

Running the back of her hand over her damp forehead, she turned away to spoon more batter onto the sizzling hot girdle. Behind her she sensed the issue of cleanliness hung in the balance. But she meant what she had said: if they tried to eat without washing, she'd throw the food in the fire! And if her behavior didn't suit them, they could just cast her out for it! She would not let the knowledge that she had nowhere to go bind her into groveling servitude. She had managed under impossible odds before, and if necessary she could again!

"Davey, John, your aunt is in the right of it. Out back to the pump, both of you. All of you. Thomas, go fetch Robert and Daniel." Matt's was the voice of authority, but even so the boys protested.

"But, Pa . . . !"

"You'll do as you're told," he responded, shepherding his sons out the door. Caroline's spine sagged a little with relief. She'd won that round, without any of the dire consequences she'd been braced for. It would have been fatally easy to say nothing, to let them do as they pleased. Just for tonight, when she was so tired, it would not have hurt for them to sit down in all their dirt to a meal she had prepared. But it was best to start as she meant to continue, she reminded herself, and she was not yet so spineless as to let them treat her with disrespect.

A moment or so later Thomas, Robert, and Daniel passed through the kitchen and out the door, shooting Caroline sidelong looks as they went. She continued her cooking, ignoring them. When they returned, they were silent as they took their places around the table. Hands and faces were conspicuously clean.

Caroline turned toward the table with plates heaped with the flat, fragrant girdlecakes. If she felt a tad triumphant, she was careful not to show it.

"We say grace in this house." Matt sat at the head of the table, and his words were a clear challenge.

"Very well," Caroline answered, setting the plates on the table and folding her hands in front of her. "Please proceed."

The menfolk cast furtive glances at one another, then all rose and bowed their heads. Matt made a brief invocation, and then they all sat down again, maintaining the same uneasy silence as before.

Caroline's lips tightened as she ladled stew into wooden trenchers and carried them, two at a time, to the table to the accompaniment of deafening silence. When food was set before each of them, along with mugs of water, she served herself and carried her own trencher and mug to the table to join them. Men and boys ate hungrily, but no one spoke or looked up as she drew near. All eyes were on their plates as they shoveled down the food.

There were benches along both sides of the table, and a large wooden chair at each end. Matt and Daniel occupied the chairs, while David and Thomas filled one bench and John and Robert the other. There was no place for Caroline to sit.

She stood there, holding her plate and mug, waiting for someone to notice her predicament. But no one did.

"If you *gentlemen* don't mind, I would like to sit down."

They looked up at that. Matt frowned, looking around the table.

"Scoot over, Davey," he directed.

"I don't want her sitting by me!" It was a wail.

"Do as you're told, and be quick about it!"

" 'Tisn't fair," Davey muttered, his expression sullen. But as he caught his father's eye he obediently moved closer to Thomas, his plate and cup making a scraping noise as he shoved them along the table.

"So sit." Matt returned his attention to his food. Lips tightening, Caroline sat, trying not to notice that Davey crowded as close to Thomas as he could, presumably so that no part of him would suffer her contaminating touch.

"Is there more?" Thomas sopped his girdlecake in the last of the gravy on his plate, popped it into his mouth, and looked around as though expecting food to appear magically in front of him.

"In the kettle," Caroline said, her spoon suspended halfway to her mouth. She had not yet had a chance to take a single bite.

" 'Tis good." Daniel stopped eating long enough to compliment her as Thomas passed her his plate. Like his brothers and nephews, Thomas was blue-eyed and attractive. His fair hair and skin served to disguise his resemblance to the others, but it became apparent when he talked, or moved. Caroline judged him to be the youngest of the foursome, still lanky in the manner of a young man not quite grown into his height. Robert too was more bone than muscle, while Daniel was more solid. Matt, who was the tallest, was also the most muscular. His physique looked both tough and powerful. There was a time when such a physique would have made Caroline's pulse quicken, but no longer. The girl who would have once responded instinctively to Matt's sheer masculine appeal was now buried deep within the frozen shell she had erected to keep hurt out.

"I'll have some, then—please." Thomas's reluctant courtesy earned him the response he sought. Returning her spoon to her plate, its steaming contents untasted, Caroline took his trencher and rose to fill it. When she handed it back to him, he accepted it with a nod and fell to. Sitting again, Caroline began to eat. This time she actually was able to swallow a spoonful before Matt wanted seconds. After that, Caroline managed a few mouthfuls in between trips from table to pot and back again, but not many. It was with a feeling of relief that she realized that at last the pot was empty. Finally she could finish her own meal!

"I want more." This was Davey. A slower eater than the rest, he was just polishing off his first plateful.

"I'm sorry, but it's all gone." Caroline took another bite as she spoke. She was still on her original serving, and only halfway through with that. These Mathieson men must have hollow legs to put away such a quantity of food so quickly!

"No more!" Davey's face puckered as if he would cry. From all around the table, the five remaining males looked up at her with identical disbelieving expressions.

"No more?" Uttered in Matt's deep voice, the words were a careful question.

"No. No more," Caroline said firmly, as if she were dealing with a sextet of idiots. Really, didn't they understand plain English?

"But I told you that there are six of us, and that we have big appetites."

"Except for David, you've had three helpings each!" Putting her spoon down again, she stared at Matt indignantly.

"Aye, and we've worked all day, too. Hard, outdoor work, with no nuncheon. We're men, and we're hungry. In future you will please remember that."

As rebukes go, that one was fairly mild, but still it made Caroline see red.

"In future I'll prepare enough for a barnyard full of hogs, as that's what

I seem to be feeding!" She tried to jump to her feet, only to be thwarted as the solidly weighted down bench refused to budge. Fuming, she slid off the end of the bench and stood, fists clenched, glaring at the bunch of them.

"There's no need to get angry. We're all willing to make allowances, considering this is your first day with us. We'll fill up on the girdlecakes. There are more girdlecakes?" Matt's tone was that of a reasonable man dealing with the unreasonable.

"No. There are not. I made two dozen girdlecakes, and you've wolfed down every one!" If there was a hysterical edge to her voice, it was nothing compared to the way she was feeling. She wanted to scream, wanted to curse and stomp her feet. She wanted to grind these unappreciative males to dust! To have worked so hard, for such a reward as this, was infuriating.

"No more cakes!" This was Davey again, and this time he burst into noisy tears. Staring at him, Caroline felt like crying herself. She was tired, and hungry too, because she hadn't even had a chance to finish her own meal, and she didn't have a bed, and the table still had to be cleared and the dishes washed and . . .

It was too much. She clamped her lips together, turned on her heel, and walked with careful dignity from the kitchen through the keeping room and out the rear door.

It was twilight, near to total dark. Stars were beginning to appear overhead. A quarter moon floated on the edge of the sky, its light obscured by blowing clouds. The sounds of chirping insects and croaking frogs filled the air. From somewhere in the distance came a mournful howl.

The howl was what did it. Nothing ever howled like that in England. Shivering as the cold night air blew through her thin dress, Caroline walked as far as the fence that edged the barnyard. Placing her hand on top of the gate, she laid her forehead on her hand.

Then she cried.

9

Despite the lightness of his tread, Caroline was aware of Matt's approach even with her back turned. There was something, a sixth sense, that told her he was there.

Straightening, she angrily dashed the tears from her cheeks, glad for the covering darkness that, she hoped, hid her weakness. The very last thing in the world she wanted was pity, from him or anyone else.

"Thank the Lord you've stopped sniveling. I can't abide women who weep."

At that unfeeling statement her spine stiffened into ramrod erectness. Fists clenching at her sides, she pivoted to face him.

"I am not weeping! I never weep!"

The night enveloped him as it did her, making it difficult to read his expression. She was aware of the height and breadth of him as he stood perhaps half a dozen paces from her, of the whiteness of his shirt, of his musky male scent, but the details of his appearance were hidden from her. As, she hoped, the details of hers were from him.

"All women weep like watering pots, hoping for sympathy. I'll not tolerate it in my household."

Caroline took a deep breath. "You," she said with forced calm, "have obviously had very limited experience with women."

"I was wed for thirteen years."

"Are you saying that Elizabeth was a watering pot? I don't wonder at it, having met you and your sons and brothers."

"You know nothing about me or my family."

"Believe me, I know as much about you and your family as I care to know. I'm leaving in the morning. There must be something, some work I can do, in the town."

"You're not leaving." The quite surety of that statement took Caroline aback.

"I most certainly am! You can't stop me! You're every one of you filthy, rude, and unappreciative, and that's being kind! I'd rather work as a—as a —as anything I can find rather than slave away for the lot of you!"

"Strong words, but I'm afraid the choice isn't yours to make."

"Of course the choice is mine! What do you mean, the choice isn't mine?"

"You forget that I paid for your passage. You are legally indebted to me. You can work the amount off informally, as a member of the family, or we can go to the magistrate and make it official. I've no objection to taking you on as a bound girl."

"A bound girl!"

"I'm sure Tobias would be willing to testify as to your indebtedness."

"You wouldn't do such a thing!"

"I would—if you force me to it." He was silent as disbelief and outrage combined to stun her into silence as well. When he spoke again, some of the grimness had left his voice. "But I'd rather you didn't make it necessary. 'Twould be best for all concerned if we could try to come to some mutually agreeable accommodation. I admit, when I was first presented with you and your—ah—difficulties, I was not best pleased. But now I see that the situation might well offer real benefits for all of us. You need a home. We need a woman's touch around here. In particular, my boys need mothering. You are their aunt. Who better than you to take on the task?"

"If you want a mother for your sons, why don't you simply remarry?" Resentment sharpened her voice.

"I've no wish to wed again. Ever." There was a cold finality to his tone that told her that he meant what he said.

"I'm a thief and a liar of the Royalist persuasion, remember? Surely you don't want the likes of me corrupting your innocent children?"

"I've no fear that you'll teach them to steal or to lie," he said. Then, just as Caroline was recovering from her surprise at the apparent compliment, he added, "Their morals are too firmly ingrained for that. Besides, they've a healthy fear of my wrath. As for your Royalist leanings, 'tis apparent that they were learned at your father's knee, and thus are not entirely your fault. We shall simply have to relearn you."

"You may try!"

"We just might succeed."

"Not very likely!"

"Not much that happens in life is very likely, I've found. Take your arrival, for example. I spent the better part of the afternoon pondering it, and finally decided that you just might be a gift from Providence. According to the Scripture, the Lord works in mysterious ways." There was a glint of humor in his voice. "In your case, I would say, very mysterious."

"Thank you." Her response was icy.

"Come, I was but teasing you." He paused a moment to study what he could see of her expression through the darkness. When he spoke again, his voice had altered so that it sounded almost coaxing. "Tonight is the first time in a long while that we've come in to a clean house and a cooked supper. It felt good to have a woman in the kitchen, even at your insistence that we wash up. It struck me then that you can offer something my boys need, something I can't give them: a woman's kind of caring."

"Well." Though she was loath to admit it even to herself, the picture he painted of six males hungering for a woman's gentling touch softened her. They needed her, that was what he was telling her. As she realized that, she also realized that what he was offering her was balm for her sore and weary heart: the home and family she had recognized only that afternoon that she craved. "I'm not averse to doing what I can for my nephews, but I'll not be treated with disrespect, mind, nor ordered about like a maidservant."

"We'll treat you with all honor, I promise you, though in return I trust you'll not enact us a tragedy over every misspoken word or unthinking deed. We've been on our own for a long time, and it may be that our manners are a trifle rougher than they should be. As a case in point, what was said tonight was not meant to hurt your feelings. The food was good; in fact, 'twas as tasty a meal as I've eaten since I don't remember when."

"I enjoy cooking." Caroline cautiously lowered her guard a degree more. His cajolery was having the effect he intended. She realized that he was using soft words to get what he wanted from her, but she responded nonetheless. Almost greedily she contemplated taking them all in hand.

"Well, then, as we enjoy eating, you are clearly heaven-sent."

He smiled at her then, a slow, crooked grin that was illuminated as the moon slid out from behind a cloud. It eased something inside her that had been wound up tight since her father died. Until that moment she had not thought that he could smile. It made him look younger, far younger than she had imagined he could be, and almost dazzlingly handsome. Once, oh, once, how he would have appealed to her!

"How old are you?" The question popped into her head, and from there to her mouth, without volition. As soon as she uttered it, Caroline blushed to her hairline. Once again she was thankful for the darkness. His age was none of her business, and her question implied an interest in him that she certainly did not feel!

The smile died. His eyes narrowed, and a measure of distance entered his voice as he replied. "Thirty-two."

"But Elizabeth is—would have been . . ." His answer surprised her so much that she couldn't let the topic go.

"She was three years older than I."

"You must have been only seventeen when you wed her and left England!"

"Did she not tell you that, in the letters she was forever writing you and your father?"

There was an undertone to his voice that she did not understand. Was it bitterness, or hurt, or anger, or some combination of all three? Or was it simply annoyance at her questions?

"To tell you the truth, she rarely mentioned you." As soon as she said it, Caroline realized how tactless the remark was.

"Or, I'll wager, the boys." There was no mistaking the bitterness this time.

"No." It surprised Caroline to realize that this was so. Such an omission had never struck her as strange before, but then before today she had never met her sister's family and had had no notion of them as living, breathing human beings. How any woman could have failed to brag about two sturdy sons and a swooningly handsome husband was puzzling. But Elizabeth's letters, which had come frequently at first and then grown increasingly rare with the passing years, had been mostly concerned with the scenic beauty of the New World and how different it was from the old. Caroline frowned as she realized how truly devoid of personal information her sister's correspondence had been. She had never mentioned Matt's—or Mr. Mathieson's, as Elizabeth had always very properly referred to him—age, or his remarkable handsomeness, or his limp. She had written nothing of his brothers who had made their home with them, and little of the circumstances in which she lived. Occasionally Elizabeth had made vague reference to her children, but she had never written anything that would convey the vigorous reality of those two vital little boys. How could she have made so little of those things that were surely essential to her life? If there was an answer to that, Caroline couldn't at the moment find it.

In the distance an animal howled again. From behind the house where he was still tied, Raleigh joined in in mournful reply. Caroline shivered, suddenly cold. Or had the shiver been prompted by something else entirely?

Matt made a sound under his breath. "I must loose the dog." His gaze slid to her face. "Come with me. If you are to make your home with us, you and Raleigh must needs be friends."

"No, I thank you." Caroline was suddenly eager to be safely back inside the four walls of the house. When she rushed outside, she had scarcely noticed the encroaching gloom of the forest in her upset. Now it loomed close and forbidding, more sinister in the dark than it had been even by day. The howling continued in eerie chorus as more and more of the baying creatures joined in. Caroline wrapped her arms about herself and looked nervously around.

"What *is* that?" Despite her best efforts, she could not quite conceal her apprehension. Matt reached for her, the gesture one of automatic reassurance as his hand curled around her arm just above her elbow. Starting toward the house, he pulled her along with him. Caroline felt the heat of his palm, the hard strength of his fingers, even through the silk of her sleeve, and tried to fight what she knew was coming. But for all her determination to overcome it the distaste arose like bile, clouding her thoughts, making her want to thrust his hand away. His touch was more unnerving than the pagan chorus reverberating around her. Unable to stop herself, she jerked her arm free. To her relief, he seemed scarcely to notice.

"That?" His voice was casual. "Wolves. Not close."

"Wolves!" That got her attention. Her eyes darted fearfully along the shadowy perimeter of the woods. More afraid of the wolves now than she was leery of him, she moved closer to the solid warmth of his body. Still she did not touch him, merely walked at his side, but it was comforting to have him near. Though if wolves attacked, she wouldn't wager her life that he wouldn't abandon her to them. He seemed to have almost as little use for women as she had for men.

"Aye. But don't worry. They stay away from the settled areas, for the most part. Even when hunger drives them in, they don't usually devour young women. Jacob is more to their liking, which is why he's locked in the barn at night.

"Jacob?"

"The bull. Surely you remember Jacob from the Holy Writ? He was a most prolific sire, and that's what we hope for from his namesake." Amusement crept into his words as he cast her a sidelong look. Caroline knew that he was remembering her mortifying introduction to the animal. If she hadn't been so afraid of whatever might lurk within the woods, she would have stalked away from him in righteous indignation. As it was, she contented herself with giving him a darkling look.

"I hope the wolves get your blasted Jacob. And I am going in."

They had rounded the corner of the house, and were now near enough to the door that she felt safe in doing so. Sighting them, Raleigh left off his howling to bark excitedly, leaping about on the end of his rope. Instinctively Caroline stepped behind Matt, who shook his head.

"Afraid of dogs, bulls, and wolves. At least we may count ourselves fortunate that you're not afraid of men."

His words followed her as she left him before he could loose the dog and hurried toward the safety of the house. Then he said something that for a brace of seconds stopped her in her tracks.

"Or are you?" she thought he muttered, but when she turned back to stare at him, he had his back to her and was untying that moose of a dog.

Knowing the creature would be free at any second, she picked up her skirts and ran for the house. But the half-heard words haunted her. Had he really uttered them—or had it been only the wind?

"Down, Raleigh!" As Matt untied the rope, the ecstatic dog almost knocked him over. Straightening, he suffered a couple of doggy licks to the cheek despite his attempts to fend off the animal. As Raleigh jumped around and on him, he caught the dog's paws and pushed him away. Which was fine with Raleigh, who seemed to think everything that occurred was a wonderful new game. Barking madly, the dog tore off around the yard to race in scrabbling, concentric circles, loudly expressing his joy in being free again.

A half-smile played about Matt's mouth as he watched the animal's antics. As a watchdog, the purpose for which he had been intended, Raleigh was a dubious success. Although his sheer size was intimidating, the dog had never been known to harm so much as the cheekiest squirrel. But the boys loved him, his brothers treated the dog as the veriest pet, and he was passing fond of the huge pest himself. It needed only for the newest member of their household to discover that what she considered to be the monster in their midst was, in actuality, almost all bark and no bite, and Raleigh would find himself a universal favorite.

At the thought, Matt shifted his eyes to the rear door, through which he had watched Caroline vanish just moments before. Reminded of the events of the day, he grimaced. It was very possible that he'd made another colossal mistake. Caroline Wetherby was no demure Puritan miss but a gambler's daughter, a Royalist, a thief, a liar, and God alone knew what else. Yet he had agreed to let her stay, had moreover asked her to provide female nurturing to his boys. Why? Demmed if he knew.

Which wasn't entirely true, of course. He knew very well. He'd always been easy prey for a beautiful woman down on her luck. That was how he had acquired his late, unlamented wife, whom he would classify as the worst mistake of his life had it not been for the sons she had given him.

Like Elizabeth, her half sister was a looker, although in a very different style. Caroline was tall for a woman, and much too thin, which he supposed was the result of the recent hard times it was clear she had experienced. Elizabeth had been shorter, and well rounded, voluptuous almost, although the word carried with it a connotation that he preferred not to think about. Some memories were so unpleasant that they were best forgotten.

Where Caroline's hair was as black as a crow's wing, as black as his own, in fact, Elizabeth's had been auburn, and curly where Caroline's was straight. Elizabeth had been as round of face as she was of body, with a peaches-and-cream complexion that had, in later years, turned ruddy. Caroline's face was fine-boned, with small, delicate features and skin so white and smooth that his fingers itched to touch it, just once, to see if it felt as velvety as it looked. Although of course he would do no such thing. He was no longer a foolish boy, but a man, well tempered by the fires of life. Never again would he succumb to lust unleavened by love. The destruction such folly wrought was well-nigh unmendable.

Although he, and his boys, were mending.

Now it lacked only to teach them that not all women were as their mother had been. And that, he supposed, was what had, ultimately, persuaded him to let Caroline stay. The scars left from his marriage were more physical than mental; his boys, he feared, would be scarred in their minds unless steps were taken. Their mother had been no mother to them, but instead a source of embarrassment and dread. They needed to learn that all women were not like Elizabeth. He had been remiss not to consider that before. But then, he had had his own hurtful memories to contend with. Caroline, as he had told her, might well be considered a godsend.

So his decision to permit Elizabeth's sister to become a member of their household had been prompted by paternal concern. It had not been influenced one whit by black-lashed, provocatively slanted, tawny gold eyes that spoke to him of things better left unrecognized, nor a wide, full-lipped mouth that promised more of sensuality than had the curves of Elizabeth's entire body.

At least, not much. It occurred to him to wonder if she were promiscuous. He remembered how she had shrunk from his touch, and his brow cleared. Whatever Caroline Wetherby's faults, and he was sure they were many and varied, they did not include that.

The realization carried with it a sense of profound relief. He did not think he could face dealing with such again.

A flicker of light caught his attention in the woods off to his right. Not one, but two or three flickers deep in the woods. Near the spring.

Raleigh's joyous barks changed in character as he, too, spied the lights. For a decidedly nonferocious dog, he was sounding almost menacing. Apparently the possessors of the lights thought so, because the flickering gleams abruptly vanished.

Lanterns, he thought, blown out.

They were at it again, the shadowy disciples of Satan who haunted the woods, damn them to bloody hell. They practiced their evil witches' rites in the forest at night with none but themselves the wiser as to their identities, although Matt knew, or had known, the name of at least one: Elizabeth Mathieson.

Wicca was their religion, she had told him once as she told him everything, hurling the information at him furiously at the height of a bitter argument. They used the power of the earth to summon spirits and cast spells. Over their sulphurous campfires—they chose a different site each time to escape detection, marking the spot with an incantation scribbled in their own ancient language so that the coven would know where to gather when the moon was right—she had seen the Devil himself, writhing in the smoke.

Elizabeth's descent into madness had begun when she had started fancying herself a witch. When he discovered her nocturnal ramblings and their purpose, he was horrified, revolted, and yes, if he was honest with himself, even a little frightened. He had forbidden her excursions, of course, and when she refused to heed him he took the extreme course of locking her in her bedchamber at night. When she discovered that he would not be swayed from his determination to keep her from the woods, she cursed him, a true witch's curse, in full hearing of his brothers and a neighboring farmer who happened to be visiting. Ranting in sometimes unintelligible syllables, her unbrushed hair hanging over her shoulders and down her back, clad in no more than a nightgown, she had hung out her bedroom window and shrieked to Satan to exact vengeance on him. It was after that that the rumors that she was a witch began. When confronted, as only one or two of the villagers were bold enough to do, he responded with laughter and scorn. But until the very day of her death he had lived in fear that one day she would be arrested, tried, and convicted of witchcraft. The penalty for that was death, by hanging or burning at the stake as they had done in neighboring colonies. As much as he had grown to despise his wife, he could not wish such an end on her. While for his boys, such a denouement would be a horror that would haunt them for the rest of their lives. Which was why, though it might say much about the lack of God's grace in his heart, when she drowned he had not inquired too closely into the circumstances, nor felt anything but profound relief. If, as he suspected, a group of townspeople had taken it upon themselves to test the truthfulness of the witch rumor by subjecting Elizabeth to a water trial, and the dunking had ended in her death, nothing he could do would restore her to life. He had seen to it that she was given a Christian burial, but other than that he had let the matter rest.

But the followers of the serpent still haunted the forest, and their very existence was an abomination to all God-fearing folk. It was just that he had more reason than most to hate and fear them.

A coven of witches would likely not be dispatched by a volley of shot, but Matt snatched up the musket always kept by the back door and fired in the direction in which the lights had vanished anyway. The yellow flash and sharp report made him feel better, as did the jarring of the musket into his shoulder and the acrid smell of gunpowder. No matter how futile his effort, at least he'd done something.

He stood for a moment, staring into the darkness, but saw nothing more. After a moment Raleigh bounded up to him, tongue lolling as he begged in doggy fashion for a game. For Raleigh the incident was apparently over.

And for himself too. With Elizabeth gone, there was no reason for him to become involved with the dark doings in the forest. As long as no member of his household was involved, it was none of his concern.

Cradling the musket in his arm, Matt turned and went into the house.

10

*T*he crowing of a raucous pair of roosters announced the coming of dawn. Caroline would have slept through it, heedless, had it not been for the tremendous booming sound that arose to fill the house at the same time. After an astounded moment, during which her eyes opened blearily to peer through the graying darkness with disbelief, she realized that the hideous noise was actually a man singing at the top of his lungs. Another moment passed. Still groggy with sleep, Caroline imagined that she was abed in one of the hedge taverns in which she and her father had passed so many nights. Then her head cleared. She remembered where she was, and ascertained that the singer was Matt. His voice was tuneless in the extreme, and he was punctuating his songs with crashes of some metal implement against the walls and doors of the house so that the din was earsplitting. Millicent, who'd been curled on Caroline's pillow, jumped up, fur bristling as she listened to the noise. Then she leaped for the floor and disappeared beneath the bed. Caroline only wished that she could disappear so readily.

"All people that on Earth do dwell!" Bang!

"Sing to the Lord with cheerful voice!" Bang!

"Him serve with mirth, His praise forth tell!" Bang!

"Come ye before Him and rejoice!" Bang!

A chorus of groans and shouts for the singer to be silent arose, but the bellowed hymn showed no signs of abating. Caroline moaned, covering her ears with a pillow as she sought to drown out the noise. By the time all her work had been done the night before, she'd been dead on her feet with fatigue. Now the tiniest fingers of light were just beginning to streak the sky, and already she was being forced awake! It wasn't fair!

"For the Lord's sake, Matt, do you have to be so blamed loud?" The first intelligible grumble belonged to either Thomas or Robert, Caroline couldn't be sure which.

" 'Tis time to rise, slacker. I'll tolerate no idleness in this house. *All people that on Earth do dwell!*" Bang!

"Oh, Pa, do we have to get up right now?" That was John, groaning.

"You know you do. Davey, out of that bed. 'Twill not do to be late to school. *Sing to the Lord with cheerful voice!*" Bang!

"Can't we stay home today, Pa? Most of the boys are helping out with the planting. You said we were a big help yesterday."

"You had a holiday yesterday because the schoolmaster was wed. He'll be back today, and so will you. School's important, John, as you well know. Your uncles and I can manage the planting well enough without you, big help or not. I'd rather you learn to read and write and cipher whilst you have the chance. *Him serve with mirth, His praise forth tell!*" Bang!

"All right, we're up, we're up! Your caterwauling's enough to rouse the dead!" That was Daniel, she thought.

"Good. *Come ye before Him and rejoice!*" Bang!

This time whatever it was that was causing the bang slammed into the outside of Caroline's door. She jumped, her head emerging from beneath the pillow as she glowered at the still-closed door. Maybe, if she ignored him, the sadistic beast would give up and go away.

"Up, Madam Slugabed!" The shout reverbated through the door. "The Royalist fashion of lying abed till all hours will not do around here! 'Tis breakfast time!"

Caroline considered yelling back the suggestion that he journey to a far warmer region than could be found on this earth, then thought better of it. After all, Matt had been kind enough to give up his bed to her the night before (although he'd stipulated that he would sleep with Daniel only until other arrangements for Caroline's accommodations could be made), and generous enough to offer her a home in the first place (self-interested though the offer might have been). But those considerations were only a small part of what prompted her to hold her tongue. The real silencer was her conviction that if she shouted back at him, he would be through that door in a trice to personally tip her out of bed.

The object crashed into her door again.

"I'm up, I'm up!" she cried.

"And about time too!"

His footsteps retreated to the accompaniment of more out-of-tune verses and earsplitting bangs. Caroline sighed and rolled out of bed.

A quarter of an hour later she was semidressed and in the kitchen preparing porridge. Her hair she had twisted up any which way, and wayward strands had already worked free to straggle around her ears and down her back. In her haste in doing up the back of her gown she had misfastened a pair of hooks, so that the bodice was twisted in an awkward fashion beneath her breasts. Her too-long skirts kept tripping her, and she longed for a moment to pin them up. But a moment was what she didn't have. The household was abustle, and Matt had informed her that she had somewhere in the neighborhood of half an hour to get breakfast prepared and the boys off to school.

Inside the house it was still as dark as night. A pair of sputtering candles provided most of the illumination for her cooking. Daniel had been dispatched to the spring for butter and milk, and the children were outside at the pump. Matt, Thomas, and Robert vied with one another for glimpses into the one small mirror as they tried, all at the same time, to shave. Steaming water now rose from the battered wash tin that Matt had used to effect the unvocal portion of his morning concert, and it was this water that the men used for shaving. The kettle, Caroline discovered when it turned up missing, had been emptied and abandoned by the wash tin. As she fetched it, trying not to look at or touch the half-clad men—which was quite a feat, because the keeping room was both tiny and crowded—she felt a pair of eyes lingering on her averted cheek. Glancing up instinctively, she was surprised to meet Matt's intent gaze. For a single unwary moment before he lowered his lids, deliberately breaking contact, she could read purely masculine appreciation for a desirable female in the cobalt depths. The spell that held her motionless shattered, and she turned away. She felt shaky, and her heart pounded as she refilled the kettle and restored it to its crane over the fire. It took some few minutes before she was able to calm down. Not even to herself would she admit how that brief exchange of glances had affected her. Spine ramrod stiff with silent rejection, Caroline resolutely kept her back to the adjoining room. However, it was impossible to remain totally oblivious to so much naked male flesh. All three of them were bare to the waist and seemed completely unconcerned about the close proximity of a strange female. But then excessive modesty, as she had already learned, was not a male affliction.

"You might bring us a meal out in the field at noon. We'll be too busy to take the time to come back to the house." Matt, clean-shaven now and seemingly oblivious to the undercurrents that only a brief time ago had quivered between them, walked into the kitchen, wiping soap from his face with a linen towel. Caroline tried not to see the black whorls of hair that covered his chest, nor the bronzed rippling muscles of his shoulders and arms as he reached for his shirt, which hung over the back of a chair, and shrugged into it. Despite the man's many shortcomings, she had to admit that physically he was glorious-looking. At an earlier time and under different circumstances, the sight of him without his shirt might have dazzled her. As it was, she afforded him no more than a single leery glance as she began to dish up the porridge, and tried, by ignoring it, to quell the discomfort that his half-dressed presence caused her.

"Whatever it is, it smells good." This admission, made in an almost grudging tone, came from Thomas. She had already learned that he was a dedicated trencherman, and as he donned his shirt she glanced at him. His torso was lean and muscular, nearly hairless as might be expected with his fair coloring, but it had not the same effect on her as had Matt's more massive build. Nor, as he too emerged from the keeping room, did Robert, whose chest was sprinkled with auburn hair. They were attractive, these Mathieson males, she had to admit, but only Matt had the looks to stop a woman's breath.

If she were the kind of woman, that is, to have her breath stopped by such things. Which, Caroline assured herself as she stirred the porridge with more force than was necessary, she emphatically was not!

"I'm hungry." This announcement came from David, who entered along with John. Both boys stopped just inside the door to watch Caroline uncertainly. From the way they, and Thomas and Robert as well, behaved in her presence, Caroline felt herself to be some kind of alien creature. Had they had so little experience of women that they actually considered females dangerous? Matt and Daniel, who were older, were far less wary of her, although neither of them could be termed effusive in their welcome.

"The meal's ready as soon as your uncle gets back with the milk." She tried a tentative smile on the boys. Really, it was a shame for their father and uncles to raise them in an atmosphere so distrustful of women. Although surely they must retain some soft memories of their mother.

"I want to eat *now!*"

"Be patient, Davey. And polite," Matt said, frowning his son into silence.

"Will she leave today?" It was a whine.

"I told you that your Aunt Caroline will be staying here."

"I don't want her to! I want her to go!"

"Silence!" His patience at an end, Matt roared the order. David was quelled, although his lower lip jutted ominously.

Heaping porridge into bowls, Caroline sighed inwardly. It would take some time to win David's friendship, it was clear.

"Have you learned your lesson for the day?" Matt, his tone gentled, asked his younger son. Davey, still mutinous, nodded.

"Let's hear it." Matt sat down at the table, his eyes on his son.

"In Adam's fall, we sinned all." There was more, but Caroline was too preoccupied to hear it. Watching the little boy reciting to the father of whom he was a near miniature, she felt a pang somewhere in the region of her heart. Whether they wanted her or not, these children were her nephews, the last blood kin she had left in the world. She would do her best by them.

Today each wore a badly wrinkled shirt of blue-and-white speckled homespun with what appeared, from rips and stains that seemed identical, to be the same breeches they'd worn the previous day. David's stockings had been torn and most inexpertly mended; John's had not been mended at all, so that a glimpse of skinny shin was evident whenever he moved. Both boys had wet hair that had been slicked with a comb, and both had clean faces. Other than that, they looked sorely in need of care. Since the task was now hers, she meant to do her utmost to remedy the lack. The first item on her day's agenda would be the washing and mending of their clothes.

Daniel entered with the milk and butter, Caroline set bowls of steaming porridge on the table, and the menfolk fell to with a will. Five minutes later they were done and the boys were on their way out the door.

"What's this?" Caroline had started to clear the table when she found on it a small wooden slab with a piece of precious paper attached. The surface of the contraption was covered with a sheet of transparent horn. The alphabet was inscribed on the top of the slab, with the Lord's Prayer on the bottom.

"Davey, you forgot your hornbook!" shouted Robert. He snatched the thing from Caroline and then was out the door after his nephews, waving the wooden slab by its stout handle. The door stood open behind him; the rising sun touched the keeping room and the kitchen beyond it with a warm light.

"We'll be in the south field," Matt said to Caroline, as he, Daniel, and Thomas prepared to depart. " 'Tis not so far that you need fear to come alone. Walk along the stream and you can't miss us. If you encounter a problem, shout and we'll hear you. Cold meat, bread, a few apples, and some ale will do us till dinner."

"Yes, master," Caroline responded tartly, her hands loaded down with emptied bowls that she was removing from the table. Her head full of the improvements she would make to the boys' wardrobes, she had completely forgotten the other seemingly endless tasks that awaited her. Matt's bland assumption that she had nothing better to do than interrupt her work in the middle of the day to carry a meal to him and his brothers was maddening. Besides the time she needed to put order into the boys' garments, there were windows to wash, bedrooms to be turned out, furniture and floors to scrub and polish, other clothes to wash, press, and mend, and countless additional jobs to be done. Today she would be on her own, and there was so much work waiting that she was tired already from just thinking about it. But Matt acted as if his request was perfectly reasonable. Which, Caroline supposed, to one who had nothing to do with the meal's preparation, delivery, and cleanup, it was.

"If you have some objection, pray state it baldly. I've no time or patience to waste on female megrims."

"Megrims!" Caroline dropped the bowls into the bucket with a clatter and turned to face him, fists on hips. "I'll have you know that I suffer from no megrims, sir! 'Tis your lack of consideration that pricks my temper!"

"Oh, I see. It's too much to expect you to carry a cold meal out to us in the middle of the day, is it? In that case, we'll return to the house for something hot."

They locked eyes. Annoyed, Caroline had to admit that he had her there. Carrying a meal out to them would be a deal of trouble, but the alternative would involve even more work. She had longed for a home and family with an intensity that had been almost physical for at least the last four years. Now that she had what she had wished for, she should be thankful, not cross. But Matt's attitude made her want to heave something at his head.

"No, I'll bring the meal out," she said through her teeth.

Matt shrugged. "As you will."

Then without so much as a victorious glimmer he followed Robert and Thomas out the door, leaving Caroline alone to sizzle. For a moment after they left she was tempted to kick the table leg to vent her spleen, but the realization that the only likely outcome of that would be to hurt her toes dissuaded her. Really, the Mathieson males were aggravating, and Matt was the most aggravating one of all!

With no one to be affected by her anger, nursing it was useless. So Caroline gave it up, scraped the pot clean to find enough porridge for herself, poured Millicent a saucer of milk, and sat down at the cleared table to make her own meal. Taking care of a houseful of men and boys was going to be a daunting task. It was clear that it would require working her fingers to the bone from dawn to midnight, day after day, with scant reward. But still—'twas good to have a home. Not since her mother died had she known such stability, and the lack made it all the sweeter now that she had found it again. To know with certainty that there would be food on the table for each meal, that she would lay her head in the same spot for countless nights to come, that there was no one or nothing to menace her, brought with it a relief so profound that she could only savor it. Accustoming herself to the vagaries of so many males might require some effort, but it could be done. She would just have to give both herself and her graceless new relatives time to adjust to the situation. The trick would be to hang on to her temper in the meantime.

Several hours later she was wrapping fresh-baked bread in a cloth and placing it in the bucket atop the sliced remains of an end of cured ham she had found in the smokehouse. Four grown men would eat a considerable amount, and she had already had an unhappy experience with this group's appetite. Frowning thoughtfully, she wrapped another loaf of bread and put it into the bucket, then added several apples and a good supply of green onions. To feed them adequately, it was plain that she would be forever cooking. Caroline rolled her eyes as she looked at the two loaves of bread that remained on the table. Four loaves baked that morning, and already, with one meal, half were gone. Well, she would just have to set more dough to rise when she returned.

Hefting the bucket in one hand and the jug of ale in the other, Caroline started out the door. The air was cold, the sunlight bright as it had been the previous day. Ordinarily she would have put on a bonnet to protect her skin from the sun, but she did not feel like going back upstairs to unearth one from her trunks. She had finally found time to brush her hair, and she wore it as she usually did, in a simple knot at her nape. Her dress already bore a number of spots from the scrubbing she had done, but at least it was now fastened correctly. It was the plainest gown she possessed, but it was still far too fine for such menial labor as she had been doing. The fitted bodice of heavy pink cotton was edged with swaths of white muslin around its wide oval neckline, and the white muslin sleeves of her chemise were visible to the elbow. The overskirt, which was fashionably looped up in back, was of the same pink cotton as the bodice, while the linen underskirt was maroon and white-striped. It had once been an elegant dress, commissioned at the same time as the rest of her wardrobe. All her gowns had been designed to attract attention as well as play up her unusual beauty. Her father had taken a great deal of pleasure in escorting her about whatever town they had happened to find themselves in, making sure that she was well seen by day in order to lure opponents to his table at night. But her weight loss had rendered it too large, and it showed signs of wear about the hem. The high-heeled shoes that went with it she had left off in favor of more practical flat ones of light brown leather. As a result, the hem trailed even more than it might have; fortunately she had at last had a chance to get at her pins and had fastened up the underskirt just enough to free her feet. Certainly no one could take exception to the small amount of ankle that her makeshift remedy displayed. Besides, who would there be to see?

The brisk wind raised chill bumps along her arms, and Caroline spent a useless moment regretting the loss of her cloak. She had no other; before the coming of winter she must procure some cloth and make one. Or perhaps some of Elizabeth's garments remained that she could make use of. Caroline felt a momentary pang for the loss of the sister she had barely known. Then she dismissed the emotion; never again, she reminded herself, would she look to the past.

As she walked along, she cast sideways glances at the forest that seemed far more menacing now that she was alone. Follow the stream, Matt had said. Well, she would, so long as that stream cut through cleared ground. Not for anything did she mean to venture alone into the woods. The Mathiesons could starve first!

Fortunately, the stream stayed in the open. Caroline hurried, trying not to start nervously at every unfamiliar sound. Her shoulders ached as the bucket and jug grew heavier with each step. The countryside was vast, the trees tall as mountains. Everything in this new world seemed bigger than its English counterpart! As she thought about that, Caroline pictured the well-muscled height of the Mathiesons and added silently, even the men.

Something moved in the forest. Something large, which seemed to be traveling parallel to her path. She caught the merest glimpse of it from the corner of her eye. Her head pivoted to her left, her eyes searching the leafy undergrowth. But now that she was looking at it directly, not a twig stirred.

Still, the movement had not come from her imagination. She was sure of that.

The weight of the bucket and jug ceased to bother her as she quickened her step. Constant quick glances at the forest yielded the same results: nothing. Yet she could not rid herself of the notion that someone, or something, was watching her.

The stream led over a grassy knob. Caroline vowed that if she did not see the men from its top, she was heading back to the house. But the hideous thought occurred, would she be any safer then? Whatever was following her—if indeed something was—would in all likelihood turn around when she did.

Fear built inside her as she hurried up the knob. Her palms grew slippery with it even as her throat went dry. Gaining the top of the knob, she looked back over her shoulder—and found to her horror that something had, indeed, been watching her. Or, rather, someone.

A savage, naked except for a cloth swathing his loins and a few stripes of bright paint, stood beneath the overhanging trees. His skin was a deep clay color, his hair hung black and lank to his shoulders, and his face was as harsh as a hunting hawk's. He was watching her intently, and even as Caroline registered his presence he began to move toward her, his swift stride graceful.

Caroline gaped, willing the apparition to be no more than a figment of her imagination. When he didn't vanish, but instead kept coming toward her, she started to back away. The bucket slipped unnoticed from her hand and rolled clanking down the way she had come, spilling its contents as it went. The jug dropped too, with a heavy thud. It landed on its side in the tall grass, but, being stoppered, held on to its contents.

"Unnhh!" The man glared at her, gesturing fiercely—and that was enough for Caroline. She raised both hands in fists to her mouth and screamed.

Behind her she heard a volley of shouts, and realized with devout thankfulness that the Mathiesons were somewhere close at hand. The savage heard too, and stopped as if undecided. Caroline screamed again, and turned to run. Even as she did so Raleigh hurtled past her, barking ferociously and flying toward the savage. The man took one look at the huge dog, turned on his heel, and fled.

"What the devil?" Despite his limp, it was Matt who reached her first. Whether he had been the closest or whether her obvious terror had spurred him to superhuman effort she had no idea. All she knew as she threw herself against his chest was that he was solid and safe and known and *there*, and that in her fright she needed him. She clung, gasping, unable to force out words, her face pressed into the hard warmth of his chest, her fingers wrapped in the soft linen of his shirt. Against her breasts she could feel the unyielding strength of him; her thighs pressed against the iron muscles of his legs. Her nostrils were filled with the scent of man —and then his arms, which had wrapped around her, instinctively, she thought, dropped. His hands came up to close over her elbows and thrust her back from him. The gesture was unnecessary. As soon as Caroline realized where her fright had put her, she was pulling away. A blush suffused her cheeks. Even as she colored up, her gaze met his.

For just a moment, as they looked at each other, the memory of the morning hung between them. Caroline's eyes widened at what she again thought she read in his. They were bright blue, blazing blue in the hard darkness of his face, restless eyes, wanting—and then, before she could be sure, or even respond with a shudder of distaste, they changed. Even as Robert and Thomas and Daniel thundered up beside them, the heat went out of the blue depths. They grew shuttered, cold, and distant, leaving Caroline to wonder if she had mistaken the brief flare of masculine awareness. Had she only imagined, out of her own oversensitivity to such matters, the hunger she thought she saw in his eyes?

"What happened?" Daniel demanded, panting. Matt's hands released their grip on her elbows. Still shaken and unsure, Caroline pulled her eyes away from Matt's to look at his brother.

"It was a savage," she answered in an unsteady voice, pointing back toward where the man had stood. "He came out of the woods over there."

"All that fuss over an Indian?" Robert said in a scathing tone. Caroline's gaze slewed around to him, but before she could speak Thomas forestalled her with a shout.

"Our food!" he yelped, pointing back down the knob toward where only the apples and onions remained of her carefully prepared luncheon. Raleigh, an expression of what looked like utter delight on his face, was wolfing down a loaf of bread. Even as the men bellowed in unison, the dog gulped down that loaf and grabbed the second, shaking it free of its cloth.

"Drop it! Drop it, you mangy beast!"

All four men started running down the knob in instinctive response. Raleigh, sensing that his prize was about to be stolen, raced into the woods with the loaf in his mouth and Robert and Thomas in shouting pursuit. Matt and Daniel, already perceiving their mission's uselessness, had left off the chase a quarter of the way and halfway down the knob, respectively. Feeling somehow guilty—although how anything that had happened could be laid at her door she didn't know—Caroline watched as Matt, without so much as a glance at her, began to gather up the scattered apples and onions. The meat had apparently gone the way of the bread.

"It was truly a savage," Caroline said, succumbing to the absurd urge to justify herself as Matt, arms full of reclaimed apples and onions, climbed up the knob again and stopped beside her, looking down into her upturned face.

"The Indians hereabouts are friendly, as a general rule. We even trade with them from time to time. Likely he wanted something, and your screams scared him off." Matt's expression was completely unreadable, but Caroline felt guiltier than ever. She also felt foolish, both for her panic over the savage (though it hadn't seemed at all foolish at the time) and her feeling that Matt had experienced a bout of intense masculine interest in her person. He was as cool and remote as ever now, and she was sure that what she thought she had seen and recognized in him had been as much in her head as in his eyes.

"At least the ale didn't suffer." Daniel, ever cheerful, had picked up the jug and was hefting it aloft as he joined them.

"Wonderful. We'll dine on apples and onions and ale," Robert said sourly as he, too, reclaimed the top of the knob with Thomas, who bore the now-empty bucket in his hand.

"Because she was afeared of an Indian." Thomas's voice dripped scorn.

"Because your ill-behaved dog ate the food intended for you, rather!" Caroline rounded on Thomas, arms akimbo.

"You can't put the blame on Raleigh when 'twas you who dropped the bucket in the first place!"

"Oh, can't I just? That beast may think himself fortunate if he does not end up in my stewpot!"

"Harm him, and . . ."

"Enough!" Matt roared, and Caroline winced at the sheer volume of the sound. But it silenced Thomas and the rest of them. "Apples and ale will do us until supper. We've passed many a day with less. Though 'twould be nice if you would keep in mind that we've had little in our stomachs today when you prepare the evening meal."

This last, directed to Caroline, was a not too subtle reminder of the previous night's shortcomings.

"Oh, I'll prepare enough for the King's entire army this time, you may be sure!"

"Cromwell's, rather." At that Matt smiled at her. It was a mere curve of his lips sparked by amusement, but her eyes widened at the sheer dazzling handsomeness it gave to his face. Roundhead or not, maddening or not, man or not, he was a gorgeous specimen. Had her heart not been permanently armored against men, it might be in grave danger from such as him.

"I'll leave you to your meal, then," she muttered, dragging her gaze away from him with an effort.

"Such as it is," Thomas sniffed, even as Caroline started back down the hill.

"Caroline!" Daniel stopped her. She looked over her shoulder at him inquiringly. "If you're afraid to walk home alone, I'll be glad to accompany you."

From the expressions on his brothers' faces as they turned as one to stare at him, such an offer was going to earn Daniel a good deal of ridicule. The memory of the savage surfaced to scare Caroline a little, but Matt had said that he was harmless and she trusted Matt. Besides, she would be boiled in oil before she would admit to fear again before the unfeeling lot of them!

"Thank you for your kind offer, but I'm not afraid," she said rather more shortly than the occasion warranted, and started off again.

"Caroline!" She had not gone half a dozen paces when she was stopped once more, this time by Matt.

"What now?" Turning, she frowned at him, surprised to see that he was coming down the knob toward her. Surely he was not going to be so chivalrous as to walk her home? Strange how her pulse quickened at the thought.

Her brows lifted at him as he stopped in front of her.

"Now that you have treated us all to a rare display of your bare ankles . . ." His voice was low, meant for her ears alone, and there was an undertone of anger to it that raised her hackles even before his words penetrated. "You might consider spending the afternoon in fashioning yourself some more seemly gowns. The one you wore when you arrived was almost equally as revealing of your bosom."

As the sense of what he was saying sank in, Caroline's spine stiffened and her eyes flashed with indignation. "The other gown was too large, and I merely pinned the hem up on this one so that I could walk unencumbered!"

"Be that as it may"—he was unsmiling still—"here in Connecticut Colony we are accustomed to seeing our womenfolk more modestly dressed."

Then, before Caroline could give voice to any of the many outraged replies that popped into her head, he turned on his heel and strode away to rejoin his brothers, who were already disappearing over the knob.

11

*T*hat evening, after supper, their little group was, on the surface at least, pleasantly domestic in appearance. While Caroline scoured trenchers and cleaned the kitchen, fully aware of how ridiculous it was to take such satisfaction in so homely a task but enjoying it nonetheless, the boys sat at the table doing their homework by candlelight. John worked on what seemed to be a vast number of sums, while Davey labored mightily to write the alphabet. Daniel mended harnesses and Thomas sharpened blades. Robert had retrieved the treetrunk-size chunk of wood that had graced the front room on Caroline's arrival, which she had promptly ordered Daniel to carry off to the barn. Now Robert was carving what he said would be a chair out of it, although it presently bore little resemblance to one, to Caroline's thinking. Matt was outside, doing chores. He had taken himself off immediately after the meal was finished, and Caroline had not seen him since. She had spoken not a word to him since that last exchange on the hill, nor had he spoken to her. And she still wore the dress that provoked his ire. The whole time she dished up the meal, she silently flaunted it like a badge of independence. But if Matt even noticed, he said nary a word. Having geared herself for battle, Caroline felt almost disappointed.

Now, as she sprinkled fresh sand on the floor, Caroline watched Davey. He had his lower lip caught firmly between his teeth as he strove to scratch out the letters in a fair hand. Beside him an overturned mug contained his newest possession, a small pond frog. Every few seconds he swept back the ragged edges of his bangs, as they hung down over his eyes and threatened to obscure his vision. She had already spent the afternoon in washing, mending, and ironing his and John's clothes and was looking forward to viewing their much-improved appearance when they left for school on the morrow. The only thing lacking, she decided, was a haircut. She was bound and determined to remedy the lack.

"Whew!" Davey said at last, shoving the bench back in an exuberant gesture of release.

"You made me make a blot!" John glowered at his brother from across the table.

"All done?" Caroline asked brightly, having already assembled scissors, chair, and comb. Not unexpectedly, Davey didn't favor her with a reply, but the way he skipped away from the table to join Daniel by the fire gave Caroline her answer.

"Good," she continued, just as if the child had spoken. "Now we have time to trim your hair before you go to bed. And John's too, of course."

Both boys' heads swiveled toward her as if pulled by invisible strings.

"What?" John asked, mouth agape, while Davey, spying the waiting scissors and chair, reacted more vehemently.

"Don't want no haircut!" He scowled at her and sidled strategically behind Daniel even as she beckoned to him.

"You'll look so handsome with your hair cut so as to show off your face. And you'll be able to see a whole lot better," Caroline coaxed, edging toward him with the stealthy movements a hunter might have used toward a rabbit.

"No!"

"Now, Davey . . . ." said Daniel quietly.

"What's the matter?" asked Robert, poking his head in the door from the front room, where he'd been working.

"'Twould be best if you just left the boy alone." Thomas, openly hostile, had come to join Robert in the doorway. Davey, sensing which uncle would prove his best ally, moved away from Daniel to edge around the perimeter of the room toward Thomas.

"Thom, you're not helping matters," Daniel chided.

"I don't suppose the boy has to get his hair cut if he doesn't want to," Thomas returned.

Caroline, gritting her teeth, willed her expression to remain pleasant.

"Davey, surely you're not afraid of a little thing like getting your hair cut! Why, it won't hurt a bit!" she said.

Davey gained Thomas's side and clung to his leg like a limpet.

"Don't let her touch me, Uncle Thom! I hate her!"

"David Mathieson!" Matt appeared in the keeping room door, shrugging out of his coat and bringing a whiff of cold night air with him. His eyes fastened warningly on his younger son. "You will be polite to your Aunt Caroline, do you hear me?"

"But, Pa, she wants to cut my hair!" Davey wailed, and abandoned Thomas to hurtle toward his father. He wrapped his arms around Matt's leg just as he had Thomas's. Matt put his hand on the child's head, smoothing Davey's hair off his forehead as the boy looked pleadingly up at him.

"Mine too!" John put in hurriedly.

"It looks to me like you both could use haircuts," Matt said.

"Pa!" The boys responded in identical tones of betrayal.

"In fact, I fancy we all could." Matt looked across the room at Caroline. "Including me. Think you're up to taking on so many?"

"Why—certainly." If she was faintly taken aback at the idea of performing so intimate a task for Matt—and, of course, his brothers—she had enough presence of mind not to let it show.

"Good, then. Who'll be first?"

"Let's draw straws!" said John, sounding suddenly enthusiastic.

"Good thinking." Matt went into the keeping room, where he pulled straws from the broom kept there and emerged with six of them sticking out of his fist. "Short one's first. John?"

John drew a straw.

"Davey?"

"But I don't want my hair cut, Pa!"

"Davey!"

Davey drew a straw.

"Rob?"

Robert drew a straw.

"Dan?"

Daniel drew a straw.

"Thom?"

"Wait a minute! I don't think I want my hair cut, either!"

Matt fixed him with a look. Thomas drew a straw.

"So where's the short one?" John demanded, frowning. Everyone held up his straw.

"Pa has it!" Davey exclaimed with delight, and it was true. Matt had been left with the short straw. He looked at it for a moment, appeared slightly nonplussed, then glanced over to where Caroline stood watching him. If she felt a trifle nervous, she was determined not to let it show.

"Sit down, then," she said as casually as possible, indicating the chair she had set out. "And we'll get it done. And it won't hurt a bit, either."

"You relieve my mind." If there was an edge of dryness to that, Caroline took it in good part. Indeed, the prospect of having Matt at her mercy, even for so small a matter as the cutting of his hair, made her spirits rise enormously. Just let him say one unpleasant thing to her while she had the scissors in her hand, and he would leave the chair as bald as an egg.

Matt must have read her mind. Even as he seated himself, and suffered her to secure a cloth around his neck to catch the cut hairs, he pinned glinting blue eyes on her.

"One lock falls amiss, and I'll see your hair shorn before morning," he threatened under his breath.

"Don't you trust me?" Caroline asked just as softly and snapped the scissors together in a way that might have passed as teasing.

Then all five remaining Mathiesons gathered round, open fascination in their eyes as they prepared to watch the shearing of the first, and most fearsome, sheep. Of necessity, all covert exchanges between Caroline and Matt ceased.

Picking up the comb, she walked around behind him. For a moment she hesitated, studying the wealth of thick black hair. His shoulders and back dwarfed the narrow-back chair, his long legs were stretched out in front of him, and his arms were crossed almost menacingly over his chest. His jaw was set, his eyes stared straight ahead. Above the pinned cloth, his neck was bronzed and strong-looking. Staring at the vulnerable nape, where a myriad of blue-black curls nestled in almost feminine beauty, Caroline felt a queer little stirring deep inside her. For no more than an instant, the impulse came to her to run her finger along that bared, vulnerable neck. The image this conjured up made her stiffen. She almost dropped the comb and turned away. Then, supremely conscious of her interested audience, she took a firm grip on her emotions, along with a deep breath, and ran the comb through Matt's hair.

Each curl and wave sprang immediately back into place, leaving no mark of the comb's passing. Over his forehead and around his ears and neck were the spots that needed trimming. Abandoning the comb, which was doing no good at all, Caroline cautiously ran her fingers through the curly mass. His scalp felt warm beneath her touch. The strands of his hair were cool and crisp as she drew them away from his head.

Snip. She trimmed the ends so that they were just longer than his right ear. *Snip.* She did the same for his left. Then she stood behind him again, trying to pretend that he was no older, no more threatening to her peace of mind, than Davey. She threaded her fingers through the curls at his nape. Still she could not quite control the unsteadiness of her hands as she stretched the hair away from his scalp.

Strangely she felt no repulsion. Whether it was because she knew he was no threat to her, with or without their interested audience, or because she so thoroughly controlled the situation, she didn't know. But he seemed to sense that something in her attitude toward him had changed as she cut his hair. When she came around to stand in front of him and trim the locks that fell over his forehead, he looked up to meet her eyes with a speculative look in his own.

"You next, Davey," he said, breaking the spell along with their eye contact as his gaze found his son, who was watching wide-eyed along with the rest. Even before she had finished, Matt was rising from the chair, pulling the cloth from his shoulders and installing Davey where he had sat. Although Matt still had a few locks that needed trimming, Caroline made no protest. What had occurred—and had not occurred—inside her body when she had touched Matt needed some thinking on. What she did not need was to go on touching him.

With her mind on Matt, she smoothed her hands over Davey's silky hair without thought, only to be rewarded by having him jerk his head away from her touch. The look he gave her over his shoulder was black with loathing and quickly recalled Caroline to herself. In a very businesslike fashion she cut his hair, trying not to feel hurt as he held himself stiffly erect beneath her ministrations. The instant she finished he jumped up with a sigh of relief and retreated to the opposite end of the room. Clearly winning the child over was not going to be easy. If anything, he seemed to dislike her more now than he had when she first arrived.

Robert was next, and she made short work of him and the others. In half an hour all were done, and Matt was ordering the boys off to bed. Sleepy-eyed but still resentful, Davey at first defied his father, refusing to budge from the corner where he was comfortably curled up. Fists on hips, Matt eyed his recalcitrant son, and Caroline winced as she considered the form his wrath might take. For a moment the two stared at each other while the issue trembled in the balance. Then Matt's face abruptly softened. He swooped down on the boy, catching him up with his hands beneath the child's armpits and tossing him high in the air before catching him again. Giggling as he wrapped his arms around his father's neck and his legs around his waist, Davey made no further protest as he was borne off toward the stairs. John, trailing them, was smiling, and Caroline smiled too. The sheer coziness of the scene touched her heart. Watching them go, she admired her own handiwork on the three eye-catchingly similar heads of black hair, and to her surprise she felt a totally unexpected tingle of pride in the sheer handsomeness of the man and his sons. Hastily she attributed the feeling to nothing more than satisfaction in a job well done and then shied away from examining her emotions altogether.

Caroline tidied the kitchen one last time, put more dough out to rise, and went upstairs herself. As no one had told her otherwise, she supposed she would once again be sleeping in Matt's bed.

But not alone. Caroline made that discovery as she climbed between the sheets in the dark. Her toes touched something—and it moved! Something alive was under there! Something cold and faintly damp and . . . surely it wasn't a snake!

Caroline was out of that bed before the thought was half-formed. Instinct alone held back a scream—along with, perhaps, the memory of how scornfully her screams had been received earlier in the day. Shuddering, she struck flint to steel and lighted the bedside candle. Turning back to the bed, prepared to jump out of the way as fast as could be if whatever was under there warranted it, she flung back the bedcoverings.

From the very end of the bed, where her feet had been, a frog jumped to the center of the mattress.

For a moment Caroline stared at it. Frogs held no particular horrors for her—but how on earth had such a thing gotten into her bed? She remembered Davey and his newly captured pet.

Rivet! The frog croaked and jumped again, this time landing at the very edge of the mattress. One more leap and it would be on the floor.

Catching up the pitcher that stood on the bedside table, Caroline used it to scoop up the frog. The pitcher would keep it safely imprisoned for the night—and in the morning she knew just what she would do with it.

Return it to its rightful owner, of course. Because, if her suspicions were correct, and they almost certainly were, the frog was a gift from Davey, designed to send her shrieking from the house, never to return. He must be listening hard at that very moment, waiting for her earsplitting scream.

A smile sneaked around her lips. The child would have a long, tiring wait, with a surprise at the end of it.

Feeling better than she would have imagined she could twenty-four hours before, Caroline climbed back into bed. This time her head barely touched the pillow before she was asleep.

12

*C*aroline waited for her opportunity, then dropped the frog in Davey's lap the next morning with no one the wiser. The men were seated around the table, wolfing down their breakfast as was their wont. Only Davey had seemed somewhat off his feed. He had been eyeing her a trifle nervously ever since he came downstairs and discovered her, deliberately serene, stirring the porridge as though she had not a care in the world. She greeted him with no sign of anything wrong, and it was then that he started looking perturbed. Now, as the men rose from the table and John shoveled in the last bite of porridge before doing likewise, Davey looked very worried indeed. It was at that moment that Caroline chose to return the frog.

Rivet! The creature jumped and croaked, but Davey's hand was already cupping it, pinning it to his knee, and in the general hubbub the sound went unnoticed.

Davey cast her a guilty look. Caroline bent over him and whispered in his ear.

"If you want to keep him, you'd best not let him come in the house again. Millicent has quite an appetite for frogs, I'm sorry to say."

At that Davey looked appalled and glanced swiftly down at his cupped hand. Caroline, keeping her expression carefully bland, straightened—and found Matt looking at her, a frown darkening his brow and his eyes keen on her face.

"Is aught amiss?" he asked, as his glance traveled between Caroline and his younger son. Davey looked guiltier than ever, but his hand stayed firm over the frog.

"Not a thing in the world," Caroline answered cheerfully. She could have sworn that the glance Davey shot her was almost grateful as he slid off the bench.

"Come on, John, we don't want to be late for school," he reminded his brother hurriedly. The hand holding the frog slid into his pocket and he snatched up his hornbook. Then he was out the door with his brother, complaining of his haste, at his heels.

"Nothing, eh?" Matt's gaze returned from following his sons to fix on her again, sharply. Caroline shook her head. Matt, though still frowning suspiciously, let the matter pass.

"We'll be in the south field again" was the only other thing he said as he and the others were leaving. Caroline straightened from where she was scrubbing the table to frown at him, not immediately comprehending.

"When time comes for lunch," he clarified, then added, as he took himself off, "and this time, try to keep it away from the dog."

She was expected to bring them lunch again! Remembering yesterday's misadventure, and considering how tired she was already and how much work awaited her besides preparing and delivering the meal, Caroline groaned. But the men were gone, and there was no one save Millicent to hear her. So she poured the cat a saucer of milk, fixed herself the leavings of the porridge, and looked on the bright side: at least she had given Davey something to think about. He might respect her after this, even if the rest of them did not.

The meal she prepared was much the same as yesterday's, except that she substituted venison for the ham. When the time came to deliver it, she started out again along the stream just as she had the day before. But this time her step was quicker, and she walked on the side of the stream away from the forest, though that meant that she had to ford the creek in its shallowest spot. The water was cold, the day windy, and she was soon thoroughly chilled. Thus as she hurried along, bucket and jug weighing her down, her feet were wet and she was not in a very good humor. She was also scared. For the life of her, she could not help casting wary glances at the forest. What would she do if the Indian reappeared? The very thought gave her the shivers, and she knew, with the best will in the world, that she would not be able to repress a scream.

And then the blasted Mathiesons would laugh at her again!

She was so busy keeping an eye on the forest that she did not realize how far she had come until she heard the rhythmic whack of an ax. An off-key hymn being roared as accompaniment clinched the matter. Her destination was at hand.

Caroline took a deep breath, almost surprised to discover that she was still unaccosted. The Indian had not appeared, and nothing had jumped out of the woods to devour her—yet. But of course she wasn't safely over the knoll yet either.

It was with a feeling of relief that she finally topped the small knob and saw them. Daniel and Robert were at work in the middle of the field. Daniel was gouging furrows out of the dark soil with a hand plow while Robert, walking behind him, dropped in seed and shoved the earth back into place. At one end of the field Matt, singing, wielded an ax while Thomas pushed against the trunk of a gigantic oak they were chopping down. The tree towered over its neighbors. Its shadow was far-reaching enough to block the bright sunlight from much of the field. Which, Caroline supposed, was the reason Matt and Thomas labored so mightily to bring it down.

Despite the chilliness of the day, Matt's shirt was off as he worked, and his torso gleamed with sweat. Even at that modest distance, the well-defined vee of his physique was evident. The muscles in his back and arms bulged as he swung the ax. Caroline, watching, felt a stirring of purely female appreciation. Vexatious or not, he was certainly a beautiful man.

Raleigh, who had apparently been exploring the woods near where Matt and Thomas labored, was the first to catch sight of her. He exploded across the field with an earsplitting volley of barks that made Caroline jump a foot in the air. All four men looked around to see what had caused the dog's excitement, while Caroline, unable to help herself, started backing away from the animal's onslaught. It took a tremendous effort of will for her to stop and stand her ground. She would conquer her fear of the dog if it was the last thing she ever did! And really, he had not even eaten the Indian; it was quite unlikely that he would devour her.

"Ahoy, there! Food!" Daniel, spotting Caroline, let out a shout. Putting down their tools, Robert and Daniel came to meet her. Matt, after one brief glance, continued to chop at the tree, although he stopped singing. Thomas stayed with him. Raleigh beat the lot of them. He jumped excitedly around Caroline, yapping until her ears rang from the noise. She expected him to leap at her at any moment and knock her to the ground. Tightening her grip on the bucket, she prepared to swing it in her own defense if need be. It was stout wood bound with iron, and heavily loaded, but would it be enough to hold off that monster of a dog? Not that she expected to have to use it, of course.

Just then the wind caught her skirt and sent it billowing. With her hands full, there was nothing she could do to prevent the approaching men from getting an eyeful of her stockinged legs halfway to the knee. To their credit, neither Daniel nor Robert so much as blinked. She could only be thankful that Matt's attention continued to focus on the tree. She was in no mood for another scolding, and had he offered her one she would probably have clouted him with the jug.

"Stop it, Raleigh!" Despite his words, Daniel did not sound particularly convincing as he and Robert converged on her at the edge of the field. It came as no surprise to Caroline when the dog ignored him. Daniel shushed the animal again as he reached to take the bucket from her, while Robert, unspeaking, relieved her of the jug. The wind had died again, as she should have expected it would now that her hands were free to control her skirt. Keeping a wary eye on Raleigh, who finally quit barking in favor of sniffing interestedly at the air as the men rooted through the bucket, Caroline flexed her shoulders. From the aches that bedeviled her already, it was clear that her body was unused to physical labor; if she was to uphold her part of the arrangement, she would have to toughen up.

"Fresh-baked bread!" Daniel sounded like a child with a new toy as he held aloft a loaf. "And venison! 'Tis a veritable feast! See, Rob?" He sounded triumphant.

"At least this time the dog didn't get it," Rob responded, but despite his words he accepted a chunk of bread from Daniel and popped it into his mouth. Swallowing, he turned to shout to his other brothers, who glanced around, waved, and then abandoned their labors in favor of joining the three of them. A great gash, looking for all the world like a huge whitish smile, had been hacked from the oak's trunk, but still the behemoth stood. Caroline supposed that Matt and Thomas would tackle the job with renewed energy after they had eaten.

"Hey, save us some!" Thomas bellowed good-naturedly to his brothers. He was several yards ahead of Matt, his hand cupped around his mouth to call to them as he hurried across the field. Behind him, Matt came toward them at a more deliberate pace, the ax slung over his shoulder.

"You'd best hurry!" Robert yelled back, grinning as he pulled off more bread to stuff into his mouth. The elaborate gesture was clearly meant to tease his brother, and it worked as Thomas, with a loud protest, broke into a run.

Another strong gust of wind caught Caroline's skirt and ruffled the men's hair. This time she clapped both hands to the front of her dress as the hem swirled upward, thus managing to preserve her modesty. As she did so, a great tearing noise rent the air.

For a moment Caroline was puzzled. Then her attention was caught by the great oak as it slowly began to tilt toward the field. The wind in its branches had apparently finished what the men with their axes had begun. She watched with wide-eyed interest as, first with majestic dignity and then with hurtling force, the mighty tree fell.

Beside her, Daniel gave a sudden hoarse cry. Following his horrified gaze, Caroline saw the reason for his fear. Trapped in the shadow of the falling tree Matt, who like Thomas had run for safety at the first loud crack, stumbled and fell. Though he scrambled almost at once to his feet, his bad leg slowed him down so that he wasn't going to get clear. Then with an earth-shaking crash the tree hit the ground, bounced once, and, with its branches quivering, lay still.

As Caroline screamed, Daniel and Robert were already off and running toward the spot where Matt had disappeared.

13

"Matt! Matt! Damn it, where is he?"

"Here he is! Quick, help me get these branches out of the way!"

"Oh, God, is he . . . ?"

Sprinting toward the site of the accident, Caroline was still not nearly as quick as Daniel or Robert. They reached the tree just an instant after Thomas, who had been much nearer, and the three of them spent an agonizing few seconds looking through the still-trembling foliage. She came panting up as they found him. Daniel went down on his hands and knees, worming his way between branches stuck into the earth like the tines of upended forks as he fought to reach his brother.

"He's alive!" At Daniel's muffled cry Caroline released the breath she had not even realized she was holding. "Quick! We've got to get this tree off him! He's trapped, and he's hurt!"

Robert and Thomas had worked their way through the tangle of branches to where Daniel, kneeling, was almost hidden from view. Caroline scrambled after them, her heart pounding with dread. The tree was huge, its weight immense. Matt must surely be crushed beneath it. Please God that he was unconscious, so that he wasn't suffering, she thought. But then she heard him groan. If he had been unconscious, he was no longer. The low sounds he made were those of pain.

Caroline felt her heart twist even as she reached the men and was able to see, through the heavy curtain of greenery, Matt's black head flung back against the rich earth of the new-turned field. From what she could discern, he was prone, with his hands outflung. His eyes were closed, his skin white as paper, his lips drawn apart as those awful groans emerged from between his clenched teeth.

Around him his brothers worked furiously, their faces nearly as pale as his as they fought to shift the tree.

"Rob, get over on the other side. Thom, you pull him out when we lift. Rob, when I say three."

Daniel's voice was urgent but determinedly calm. He counted three, and he and Robert strained with all their might. The tree moved just the tiniest bit, then thudded down again.

Matt screamed. Caroline shuddered, her hands rising to clench her breast. If the pain was so bad that it forced such a cry from a man as strong and stoical as Matt, it must be unbearable. Was he dying, even as they struggled to get him out? Please God, she thought, please don't let him die! The very thought pierced her like a knife to the heart.

"It wasn't enough! I didn't have time to pull him out! Oh, sweet Jesus, we've hurt him more!" Thomas cried. There was no further sound from Matt. The agony that had caused him to scream must have been excruciating enough to render him unconscious. At least, so Caroline hoped. The alternative was unthinkable.

"Dear God, give us strength in this our hour of need!" Daniel prayed aloud. Then he and Robert braced themselves and, bending, wrapped their arms around the massive trunk, oblivious of the many branches that scraped and poked at their skin.

"Wait!" Caroline clambered over the last of the branches separating her from Thomas. "I'll help you pull," she told him. Neither he nor his brothers argued. Caroline bent down and caught hold of one of Matt's arms, while Thomas grabbed the other.

"At three!" Daniel said. Then he counted to three and, with mighty groans, he and Robert lifted the tree. Just a few inches; their faces turned as red as though their hearts would burst as they held the huge oak off the ground. Caroline pulled with all her strength; Thomas did the same. Matt was a big man, and heavy. Injured as he was, he was also a dead weight. It seemed impossible that they could move him, but they did. Matt slid forward—and then the tree crashed to earth again.

But this time Matt did not scream. Did it miss him, or was he beyond pain?

"He's free! We've got him free!" Robert scrabbled to take Caroline's place, pushing her aside with scant ceremony.

"Let's get him out of here!" Daniel took hold of Matt too, and the three of them dragged him clear. When he was out in the open, lying supine in the rich soil, his brothers let him go and knelt over him. Raleigh joined them, sniffing anxiously at Matt's hair until Daniel, with an impatient exclamation, shoved him away. Pushing out of the entangling foliage, Caroline blanched as she came up to them and took in the extent of Matt's injuries.

His eyes were closed, his lashes dark stubby crescents against cheeks that were as white as death except for the places where seeping blood painted his skin scarlet. Scratches covered his face and neck and criss-crossed the right side of his chest. More blood spread across his breeches in a widening stain. As Caroline looked more closely, she had to bite back a gasp. His right leg was broken below the knee; the white, shattered end of a bone, surrounded by welling blood, protruded through flesh and stockings. The sight of the jagged shards made Caroline feel sick.

"Is he . . . ?" She couldn't finish the question.

"He's fainted," Daniel answered curtly, his large hands surprisingly gentle as they ran along his brother's skull and neck, then probed his shoulders and ribcage. "The only serious damage I can find is the leg, but that's bad enough. There's no telling about his insides. In any case, he'll be hurting bad when he wakens. We'd best get him to the house quick. Thomas, you go for Mr. Williams."

"Is he the doctor?" Caroline asked, her voice hoarse. To see Matt's hard-muscled body lying broken and bloody in the dirt bothered her more than she would have thought possible. If he were to die . . . Caroline was surprised at the distress the thought caused her. How, in the short time she had known him, had he come to represent security to her?

"The apothecary. We've no doctor in Saybrook at present. Go, Thomas!"

Thomas got up off his knees and ran off in the direction of the village. Matt's eyelids fluttered, and he groaned.

"Stay out, Matt," Daniel muttered, and to Caroline's relief Matt obliged, subsiding into waxen stillness once more. "We need a branch to brace that leg before we move him. Rob . . ."

But Robert was already stripping the limbs from a sturdy branch that had broken off from the oak when it fell.

"Here." He handed it to Daniel, who hesitated a moment, looking from it to his injured brother. Then Daniel glanced up at Caroline.

"We must needs slit his breeches," he said, sounding ridiculously prim, considering the circumstances. " 'Twould be best were you to go back to the house and ready a bed for him."

"Yes. Yes, of course." It occurred to Caroline to argue that under the circumstances she was certainly not squeamish about seeing Matt's bare leg. But then she realized that Daniel's suggestion had merit. Even as she turned away to hurry back to the house she heard the sound of ripping cloth, and, seconds later, another groan. Poor man, poor man, she thought, and broke into a run.

By the time they carried him into the house, she had the kettle boiling, her own best petticoat ('twas the cleanest linen in the house, as she had not yet time to do that portion of the wash) torn into strips for bandages, and Matt's bed readied. In one of her trunks were the remnants of the medicines she had used in nursing her father. The most likely of these she set by the bed. She heard them enter, and hurried to the top of the stairs just as they began to ascend.

They barely acknowledged her presence as they bore him straight up to the second floor. Robert had his hands under Matt's armpits, bearing the weight of his shoulders and chest, while Daniel had carefully positioned himself so that he supported his brother's hips. The broken leg, bound to the branch with strips of what must once have been Matt's shirt, jutted over Daniel's shoulder. Despite their care, they were unable to avoid banging Matt's foot into the wall as they maneuvered him through the narrow doorway.

"Oh, do be careful!" Caroline cried as she retreated before them, wincing for Matt's pain. But if he felt anything, he made no sound. His head lolled back against Robert's chest. His eyes were closed, and she thought that he must be unconscious again. Blood dripped onto the floor with a rhythmic plopping sound from the gaping wound in his broken leg. His skin was ashen. His lips had taken on a bluish tinge.

"We *are* being careful," Robert snarled, shooting her an unfriendly look. His hostility put her firmly in her place. Caroline was reminded that Matt was their brother, while she was no blood kin at all, but little more than a stranger who'd been taken in on sufferance. They expected her to have scant feeling for Matt's pain, and indeed she wondered at herself that her empathy for his suffering was so strong. But at the moment she had no time to dwell on the ramifications of that. She was needed, and she would do what must be done.

As they carefully lowered him onto the mattress, she dipped a strip of linen into the bowl of steaming water that she had set beside the medicines on the bedside table.

"What are you about?" Daniel asked, frowning warily as Caroline wrung out the cloth and turned to Matt. He was bare to the waist, his face, neck, shoulders, and chest streaked with blood. The waist-to-kneeband slit in his breeches revealed a narrow portion of muscle-ridged abdomen and hairy, strong-looking thigh before the rest of the right leg was obscured by the bindings of the splint. Besides what was left of his breeches, he still wore his left stocking and shoe. The latter, caked with earth, had already smeared mud liberally over the lower section of the sheet.

"Now what do you imagine I'm about? I would wipe away the blood so that we may determine the true extent of the injuries."

Without waiting for a response, she ran the cloth over Matt's sweat-beaded forehead, then brought it down over his temples and cheeks, gently cleaning away the gore. Some of the scratches were fairly deep, others were not; she hoped he would not bear further facial scars from them. The one he had already, though not disfiguring, was enough of an insult to a face that, without it, would have been flawless in its handsomeness.

When she eased the cloth along his scarred cheek, Matt turned his head to escape her ministrations. Persistent, she continued her efforts. He mumbled something, and to her surprise his hand shot up to close around her wrist. Despite his injury, there was still considerable strength in the long fingers. Caroline found herself quite unable to tug free; not wanting to hurt him more, she held still. 'Twas the first time that he had held her against her will, and she waited to see if repulsion would surface at so direct a reminder. Funnily enough, it did not. Because he was injured and helpless, or because he was Matt? But she had no time at the moment to speculate.

"Who . . . ?" he muttered, his eyes opening to seek the owner of the wrist he had captured. Caroline guessed that in his half-aware state, its feminine softness mystified him, and the expression on his face as his gaze met hers seemed to bear that out. For a moment longer he seemed not to recognize her; his eyes narrowed, and the hand holding hers tensed. Then his grip relaxed.

"Caroline," he said, and as he identified her his lids fluttered closed again. His hand dropped back to rest at his side.

"If you hurt him . . ." Robert's voice was suddenly fierce. In the act of wringing the cloth out for the third time over the now-bloodied water in the bowl, Caroline glanced at him in surprise.

"Why on earth would I hurt him? And how, pray, could I do so?" She was nettled by his continued enmity. Daniel, too, now watched her every move as if he suspected her of wishing to slip a knife between Matt's ribs. Really, what was wrong with the pair of them? They must be addled when it came to women, and so she meant to tell them when the moment was more propitious!

"Of course she won't hurt him," Daniel said, his expression easing as her words reached him. The look he sent Robert contained a message she couldn't decipher. "Don't be an ass, Rob."

Their behavior was mystifying, but Caroline had not the leisure to ponder it. Turning her attention to Matt again, she very gently wiped the blood from his chest. There were no gaping wounds there, she was happy to see, but the scratches were numerous and bloody. The worst of them were on his right side, where the skin covering the lower section of his ribs was already beginning to turn black and blue; fearful of causing him unnecessary pain, Caroline left that area alone. A deep scratch below his right nipple caught her attention. It was bleeding profusely. The hair covering his chest brushed her knuckles as she worked to staunch the flow. With vague surprise she registered just how fine and silky that hair felt. Not at all coarse, as she had imagined it would be.

"Where is that fool Williams?" Daniel spoke through his teeth, startling her. As she glanced at him she saw that his hands were clenched around the spool footboard. While Daniel stood tensely watching her, Robert paced.

The question was not meant to be answered, and it was not. Caroline continued to sponge the blood and sweat gently from Matt's body. He stirred and muttered under her ministrations but did not rouse.

Except for internal damage, the possibility of which could not be excluded, Matt's right leg was the most severe of his injuries. It was swollen to thrice its normal size, so that its circumference surpassed that of Caroline's waist. Caroline winced at the hideous bruising she could already see spreading over his thigh above the top of the makeshift splint. Blood had soaked the ripped-up shirt that bound his leg to the branch and was seeping in an ever-widening stain across the bedding beneath the shattered leg. Caroline was thankful that she had thought to put padding on that side of the bed to protect the mattress. If the apothecary did not arrive soon, something would have to be done to staunch the flow of blood from that leg. But unless she had to, Caroline was loath to disturb the splint and thereby cause Matt more pain. And 'twould be near impossible to stop the blood until the bone was returned to its proper position.

"Sweet Jesus, it's as if he *were* accursed! Do you suppose all that blather about witches they've been nattering about in town could be true?" Robert stopped his pacing long enough to bang his fist into the palm of his other hand.

"Hold your tongue!" Daniel growled back with real menace, and for a moment the two glared at each other. Then, with a conscious look at Caroline, Robert clamped his lips together and resumed his pacing, while Caroline scowled at the pair of them. Witches! she thought with contempt. What idiocy!

"You two arguing is not helping anything! If you wish to do something constructive, you could start by removing his shoe! It's caked with mud!"

Despite her snappish tone, their concern for their injured brother in part made up for their overt hostility toward her. However misogynistic the Mathieson men might be, they plainly loved one another.

At her words Robert stopped his pacing, and both he and Daniel scowled at Caroline.

"She's right. It does no good to bleat at each other," Daniel said after a moment and moved toward the bed. As he grasped the heel of Matt's left shoe, Caroline picked up the bowl and headed for the door. There would be a need for more hot water when the apothecary arrived, she knew.

14

*W*hen Caroline returned some few minutes later, a stained quilt was tucked beneath Matt's armpits. His splinted leg had been left carefully uncovered, and she could see that they had removed what was left of his breeches as well as his stocking and shoe. Against the white sheet his shoulders looked dark and very wide. His hair was black as coal in contrast to the grayed paleness of his face.

As she approached the bed he began to fidget restlessly, moaning and thrashing until he had kicked quite clear of the quilt. With an opaque look at Caroline, Daniel pulled the covering back into place. Caroline kept her eyes carefully averted; Matt's nakedness was something that she preferred not to see. Though the revulsion that most men engendered in her did not seem any longer to apply to Matt, she had no wish to hurry its return. The very thought of seeing a male organ, even under such innocent, accidental circumstances, made her shudder inwardly with dread.

Matt's unconscious thrashing continued. Robert and Daniel ranged themselves on either side of the bed, trying their best to soothe their brother and hold him still so that he would not do himself further injury.

"If the apothecary does not come soon, I fear that we will have to do what we can without him. Though we know little more than the rudiments of doctoring." Daniel's eyes were anxious.

"I have some experience of it." Caroline said it almost reluctantly. She had learned much of what she knew from her mother; Judith Wetherby had been a renowned healer, with much knowledge of herbs and potions. But all Caroline's efforts had not helped her father as he had wasted away despite everything that she tried. It hurt now to remember. Had Matt not been so obviously in need of her help, she would have banished the recollections from her mind.

As Caroline replied to Daniel, she moved around him and placed a hand on Matt's forehead. Gaining confidence as her secret revulsion remained at bay, she flattened her palm against the contours of his skull. The skin beneath her palm was fine-textured and damp and warm—too warm? Was he already developing a fever? Strands of silky black hair curled about her questing fingers; unthinking, Caroline smoothed them back out of her way.

Her gaze moved down over Matt's face to his body. His eyes were closed, the white lines around his mouth pronounced. Both legs were now free of the quilt, which just barely preserved his modesty. His left leg was straight and strong-looking, covered with dark hair except in the area around his knee; the knee was hideously scarred, and Caroline was reminded forcibly of his lameness. Then the dreadful thought occurred: 'twas his good leg that was so badly broken. How would he walk, should it not heal properly? Instinctively she knew that he would rather die than spend the rest of his life confined to a bed, or a chair.

"I will do what I can," she said, and turned away to the medicines on the bedside table.

Matt groaned, and as she glanced at him his lids fluttered open. There was a glaze of pain in his blue eyes, and his teeth were clenched so tightly that the area around his lips was white, but there was no doubt that he was, however tenuously, aware.

"How—bad?" he asked groggily, the question directed at Daniel, who bent toward him.

"You've busted up your leg right proper," Daniel answered. "Thomas has gone for Mr. Williams."

"Williams is—an old woman," Matt said, his face so pale now that Caroline feared he might faint again at any moment. "You watch out for me, Dan."

"I will. You needn't worry."

The effort of talking obviously left Matt exhausted. His eyes closed just as, at long last, a sudden commotion belowstairs announced the arrival of Thomas with Mr. Williams. Daniel's and Robert's relief was almost palpable. As Mr. Williams, followed by Thomas, bustled importantly into the room, Caroline understood Matt's concern. He was a short, plumpish old man, with straggly white hair to his shoulders surrounding a bald pink dome. His features were delicate in a round florid face. His clothing, of coarsely woven charcoal homespun, was none too clean. Caroline looked at his hands, and winced. Like his clothing, they would have been much improved by a good scrubbing. In healing, her mother had always told her, cleanliness was all-important.

"Knife." That was the only word Mr. Williams spoke as, after favoring Caroline and Daniel with a condescending glance and a twitch of his lips, he moved to the bedside. Tight-lipped, Daniel passed him the knife he requested. Caroline and the rest of the brothers watched anxiously as he proceeded to cut through the bindings wrapping Matt's injured leg.

"Nasty," Mr. Williams observed, shaking his head as the wound was laid bare. Caroline tried to keep her eyes on Matt's face rather than look at his gruesomely mutilated limb. His skin was putty-colored now, and rivulets of sweat ran down his temples. Even as she watched him, his eyes opened again. For a moment they met hers; shaken at the pain she saw there, she managed a small smile for him. He didn't acknowledge the gesture by so much as the flicker of an eyelid; instead he seemed to gather all his resources. His eyes left hers, moved to Mr. Williams, who had commenced poking at the bruises over his ribcage.

But as the hand nearest her curled convulsively, grasping at the sheet, Caroline gave in to some unnamed impulse and laid her fingers over his. He didn't say anything, didn't even look at her, but his fingers closed tightly around her hand.

"The ribs are badly bruised, but they'll heal right enough." Matt's face grayed as the apothecary shifted his attention, prodding the immensely swollen flesh around the protruding bone. "But the leg—now that's a different matter. It might be best to just go ahead and take it off. If putrefaction should set in . . ."

"Just set it," Matt interrupted, speaking through his teeth. His grip on Caroline's hand was suddenly so tight that it was all she could do not to wince. But if he even knew he was holding her hand he didn't appear to. His attention was all for the apothecary.

"Should infection set in . . ."

"Just set it!"

"Very well." Mr. Williams was clearly miffed by the curtness of the order. "But I tell you now I'll not be held responsible for the consequences." His eyes moved to Daniel. "If you would hold him, Mr. Mathieson, you and your brother, and your other brother were to help me pull . . ." His gaze touched Caroline, chilled. " 'Twould be best if you were to leave us now, miss." From his tone it was clear that he had heard of her, and equally clear that what he had heard was nothing to her credit.

Caroline was too concerned for Matt even to take affront. She glanced down at his scratched, gray, and sweating face, at the broad bare shoulders, at the hideously swollen and bloody leg. Her fingers tightened over the hand that was clutching hers with unconscious need. She realized that despite her hard-won wisdom, what she had determined to avoid was occurring: she was once again starting to care what happened to a person besides herself.

Over the previous decade she had lost everyone she had ever loved: her mother, father, and sister. Even the few young men she had fancied in her teens before she learned to guard her too-open heart had moved on when she made it clear that she would not consent to grace their beds without the benefit of matrimony. Though she had been as virginal as a nun, she had been forced to recognize that her mere presence in the establishments in which her father gambled caused men to regard her as a light-skirts. The knowledge had wounded her deeply, but she had hidden the hurt behind an aloofly haughty facade. The lesson she had learned during those years had been simple: caring for someone brought pain as its inevitable corollary. Her father's death and all that had come after it had frozen the last of her ability to feel tender emotions, she'd thought. But Matt—there was something about him that threatened to melt the ice that sheathed her heart. The notion frightened her. She would not open herself to pain again.

"Yes, of course," she said woodenly, acting on her newly strengthened resolve by easing her fingers from his as carefully as she could. Matt glanced up at her then, his eyes cloudy with pain and, she thought, fear. Her instincts told her that he wished her to stay. Tightening her lips, she tried to ignore the small pang that smote her heart.

Still he looked at her, not seeming to understand that she was deserting him. Her eyes met his; it took an effort of will to pull them away. He had been kind to her, in his fashion; 'twould after all be no more than a fitting recompense were she to do what she could to lessen his pain, and no admission of caring need enter into it at all.

She raised her eyes to the apothecary. "I've something that might make the setting of his leg easier for him to bear. Some medicine to ease him through the worst of it."

Turning to the small store of medicines she had set out on the bedside table, she reached for a brown glass vial.

"What have you there?" Mr. Williams sounded unnaturally shrill. Caroline wondered precisely what it was that he feared. Did he imagine she meant to poison Matt? she wondered. Had gossip labeled her a would-be murderess as well as a thief?

"I told you. Medicine. 'Twill make him sleep." She poured out a dose as she spoke. Daniel, Robert, and Thomas watched her as warily as Mr. Williams.

"Hold a minute, there!" This was Robert. He looked alarmed as Caroline turned toward Matt, glass in hand. "We'll not permit . . ."

"If 'twill make the pain easier, give it to me," Matt interrupted, reaching out for the glass. Caroline put it into his hand, and when he was unable to hold it, she helped him guide the glass to his mouth. He swallowed its contents quickly, then lay back on the pillows with his eyes closed.

For a moment no one said anything while all eyes fastened on Matt.

"If he takes ill of this, the blame will rest on you," Mr. Williams said. Caroline was not surprised to hear near hatred in his voice. She had given up expecting anything approaching reason from men.

" 'Tis something to make him sleep, no more." Caroline's words were even as she set the glass back on the bedside table and turned to leave the room. As she exited with regal dignity, she felt four pairs of male eyes boring into her back.

The sensation made her skin prickle with unease.

15

*M*att's scream of pain when the bone was set into place made Caroline grit her teeth. Even the haze induced by her medicine could not shield him entirely from what must be done, though she prayed he would drop back into sleep as soon as the moments of acutest agony were over. She continued with what she was doing, refusing to give into the impulse to go back up the stairs to Matt's side. He had the apothecary with him, and his brothers. He could have no need of her.

Still, despite her resolution, her ears were attuned to the departure of Mr. Williams as she kneaded the bread dough, covered it with a cloth, and set it aside to rise. 'Twas strange how quickly she had fallen into the routine of caring for this rowdy crew. Already she could do what required doing without the need for even thinking about it. The afternoon was well advanced by now, and she should be planning supper. For Matt, if he could eat at all, a thin broth would be best. But the rest of them would want a full meal. Their luncheon, unless consumed by Raleigh or some other animal, lay forgotten in the field.

Peeling a veritable mountain of potatoes, she set them to boil with a few handfuls of greens, then retrieved a joint of venison from the smokehouse and put it on the spit over the fire. A small chunk of the venison she dropped into a separate pot, where it would boil until it was so soft it fell apart. Strained, the liquid would be Matt's supper.

It was taking Mr. Williams an unconscionable time to leave, she decided finally. He had already been abovestairs near an hour. Curiosity at last got the better of Caroline, and she left the meal to cook while she ascended the stairs. Pausing on the threshold of Matt's chamber, she drew in a shocked breath at the sight that met her eyes.

Mr. Williams clutched Matt's arm, holding his wrist over a cup held by Thomas, who was kneeling at bedside. Thomas's eyes were averted from the bright scarlet blood that ran from Matt's vein into the receiving vessel. Daniel and Robert leaned against the wall on either side of the bed, watching intently. All three brothers were nearly as pale as Matt, who was as white as a corpse and still insensible, either from pain or the drug she had given him, or some combination of the two.

"Stop!" she cried with more urgency than tact. "He doesn't need to be bled! He's lost a bucketful of blood already!"

Thomas, Robert, and Daniel looked at her with identical expressions of surprise. Mr. Williams straightened, regarding her with lofty disdain.

"Bleeding is necessary to remove the poisons from the system," Mr. Williams said as he continued with what he was about. To Caroline's horror, she spied a basin that had been set on the floor beside Thomas. It held blood perhaps a quarter of an inch deep. Apparently Mr. Williams had seen fit to bleed Matt more than once.

"If you keep that up, you'll kill him!" Her voice was fierce as she hurried to the foot of Matt's bed.

"If he dies, 'twill be from the potion you administered to him, and not from anything I have done!" Mr. Williams's lip curled angrily at her, and he turned his back in deliberate insult. Matt's blood still gushed into the cup.

"Daniel . . . !" Caroline's gaze shifted in desperate appeal to the brother she knew best. "Two ounces of blood is the prescribed amount in cases like this, and he has lost far more than that at Mr. Williams's hands alone. To lose too much invariably proves fatal!"

"And how would a chit like that know anything about it?" Mr. Williams demanded of Daniel in wrathful rebuttal.

Daniel's brow knit with worry. For a moment he looked undecided. Then, with a glance at Robert, who was scowling fiercely at Caroline, and at Matt's limp form, he stepped forward to place a forestalling hand on the apothecary's arm.

"There's no need to take more, is there? If there was poison in his system, surely 'tis let now."

"So you would take the advice of this—this female, over mine? It shall be as you wish, then, and the consequences shall be yours! Do not think to summon me back when he worsens!" Mr. Williams straightened, glaring at Daniel, whose hand dropped from the other's arm. But at least Mr. Williams was binding the wound he had opened in Matt's wrist, and the bleeding was at an end. Caroline did not even mind the venomous look the apothecary gave her as he jerkily restored the implements of his trade to his bag.

" 'Tis not that we take her word over yours, but merely that enough is enough. Bleeding him was surely beneficial, but he needs have some left to recover on." Daniel's attempt at soothing the irate apothecary with gentle humor fell flat. Mr. Williams, bag closed and in hand, responded to this with a glowering look.

"I'll have my fee, if you please," he said stiffly.

"Aye, of course." With a defeated nod Daniel ushered Mr. Williams from the room.

Caroline moved around the bed, her fingers seeking and finding the pulse in Matt's untapped wrist. Robert came to stand beside her, as if to put himself between his injured brother and harm.

"Williams may be nine parts a fool, but he made a good point: what can you possibly know of doctoring?" Robert's question was hostile. His eyes as she glanced up to meet them were cold.

"My mother was skilled in the healing arts. I learned what I know from her." Caroline silently counted the beats. Matt's pulse was weak and slow, and she feared that the blood loss had weakened him severely.

" 'Tis passing strange that your sister had no such skills." It was almost a sneer.

Putting Matt's wrist down, Caroline straightened to regard Robert steadily. Although he was some inches shorter than Matt, he still topped her by half a head. His stance was belligerent, his eyes narrowed with distrust. Caroline felt her temper begin to heat, and deliberately reined it in.

"Elizabeth and I were half sisters only. Our father was the same, but while her mother was of noble lineage, mine was a gypsy whom my father met in his travels. She knew much of herbs and medicines and healing and taught what she knew to me. Now, will you permit me to use that knowledge on your brother, or will you stand here and watch him die?"

Despite her efforts to remain cool in the face of Robert's attack, fierceness crept into her words. Her gaze did not flinch as Robert glowered at her. Behind her, she was aware of Thomas approaching. He went to Robert and put his hand on his brother's shoulder. They exchanged glances, then both of them looked at her. Thomas was perhaps an inch the shorter, and his sandy hair and fair skin made him seem like little more than a boy. Still, by the determined jut of his chin, Caroline knew that he was as opposed to her interference as his brother.

"We have little choice but to allow you to do what you can for him, as Daniel permitted you to run off the apothecary." Thomas's voice grated. "But be warned: we'll be watching you, and if anything amiss occurs, we'll know it."

Daniel reentered the room then and took in his brothers' posture with a glance.

"Take shame to yourselves, the both of you," he said sharply. "She has given you no reason to think ill of her."

"The sins of the fathers are visited upon the sons," Robert retorted.

"It says nothing of sisters, and in any case Caroline is not Elizabeth." Daniel's words were nearly as mystifying as Robert's. What was becoming abundantly clear was that for some unknown reason Matt's brothers had distrusted and disliked Elizabeth, and their feelings were being carried over to her. Caroline would have liked to ask questions, to discover what had occurred to earn her sister so much enmity, but that would have to wait for another time.

Matt stirred, and all eyes shifted expectantly to him. But he did not rouse, and after a moment it became clear that he would not.

"If one of you will sit with him, and summon me should he awaken or seem to grow worse, I will finish preparing the meal."

The three of them looked at each other.

"I'll stay," Daniel said at once. "Rob, you and Thomas had best go back to work. With Matt bedridden, we've no time to waste if we mean to get the planting done."

Still the two of them hesitated, and from the glances they cast at her Caroline had no difficulty laying their hesitation at her door.

"Oh, for goodness' sake," she snapped, exasperated. "If you're that suspicious of me, then I doubt you'll care to eat the supper I'm cooking. For all you know, I might have poisoned it, or put a spell on it to turn you all into jackasses. Though," she added with a mocking smile, "that's hardly necessary, is it?"

And with that masterly shot she left the room. Moments later, the clatter of feet on the stairs told her that Thomas and Robert had done the same.

16

"**W**ill Pa die?"

Caroline, in the act of sponging Matt's burning forehead with cool water, looked up to find John standing in the doorway watching her. It was midnight or thereabouts of the day following the accident, and the boys had, at their uncles' insistence, retired long since. John wore his nightshirt, and his feet were bare. By the light of the single candle that sputtered on the bedside table, he looked very young and defenseless as he stared with fear in his eyes at his father lying unconscious in the big bed. Caroline's heart ached for him: she knew what it was to despair for the life of a beloved parent.

"No, he won't die."

At least, she prayed he would not. The bloodletting had left Matt very weak, and he had developed a raging fever over the course of the day. She had been able to rouse him only enough to take a few spoonfuls of broth and swallow a draught of medicine. Other than that, he'd been insensible.

His leg was hugely swollen and inflamed above and below the new, sturdier splint. When she had adjusted the dressings so that she could check the wound where the bone had thrust through his flesh, she had found that it was still bleeding sluggishly. The loss of blood was a danger; she'd seen nothing for it but to sprinkle basilicum powder on the gash and pad it as solidly as she could with lint and clean rags. When after a few hours no new blood appeared on the surface of the bandage, she judged— hoped—that the bleeding had stopped at last.

Fever was the primary threat now, along with gangrene. If such should set in, she would not like to wager on Matt's chances of survival, with or without his leg intact. But there was no need to tell his son that.

Because John looked so pathetic, she smiled at him. The gesture felt strange, rusty; she had not smiled often in the last few months. But if she'd hoped to touch a chord of fellowship in him, there was no sign that she had succeeded. He did not smile back but looked uncertainly at his father.

"If I said good night to him, do you think he could hear me?"

"Oh, I think so."

Caroline sounded far more confident than she felt. Her smile died, but her compassion for the boy did not. If it was a comfort to him to imagine that his father could hear, what harm would it do? She beckoned John nearer. He came to stand beside her, his tousled black head just topping her shoulder. He was so thin that she could see, through the neck opening in his nightshirt, his shoulder bones pushing against his skin.

"Good night, Pa," John murmured almost inaudibly and reached with a tentative finger to touch Matt's outflung hand where it lay against the quilt.

There was not the slightest flicker of response. Caroline started to say something, anything, to try to make the child feel better. But before she could frame the words, a gush of tears filled his eyes that were already red-rimmed with crying.

Despite what Caroline could tell was a supreme effort to maintain his composure, John sobbed once, a great gulping sound, before catching himself and biting down hard on his lower lip. His pain was so raw that it made her hurt too. Instinctively her arm encircled his shoulders, and she hugged him. But instead of responding positively to her effort to console him, he gave a muffled cry, shoved her roughly aside, and, turning, ran from the room.

She understood that reaction too. Regaining her balance, Caroline frowned as she listened to John's feet thudding down the steps. Instead of returning to bed, he had rushed belowstairs, probably to cry his heart out without awakening David. In his distress he needed someone with him, but that person was clearly not herself.

Drawing her wrapper more closely about her—she wore her nightdress beneath it, and slippers on her feet—she padded down the narrow, dark hall to stand hesitating for a moment outside Daniel's door. Under the circumstances, she should have known better than to dress for bed, she supposed. But the gown she had worn all day had been bloodstained and filthy, and she had felt dirty too. When the men had retired she had treated herself to a quick sponge bath in the keeping room, which she had, of necessity, converted into a chamber for her own use. After her bath she had longed for something clean and loose and had donned her night attire. She would snatch what sleep she could on a pallet on Matt's floor.

But as she stood there, shifting from foot to foot outside Daniel's door, it occurred to her that he, like his brothers, was no blood kin of hers at all but a stranger. She did not really imagine that the sight of her in dishabille would move him to lustful thoughts or worse, but still . . .

The dilemma was resolved when without warning Daniel snatched open his door. For an instant they gaped at each other, mutually taken aback. In the deep shadows of the hall, which was lighted only by the faint glow from Matt's room, Caroline saw that he slept naked. Blessedly, he had wrapped a quilt around himself before coming to the door.

As if he couldn't quite remember who she was, Daniel blinked owlishly at her. His gaze ran down her body, then jerked back to her face. This time his expression was alert.

"Matt?" It was a terse question. Caroline shook her head.

" 'Tis John," she whispered, mindful of the others who still slept. She had no wish to rouse anyone else. "He's belowstairs, crying. He came to see his father, then ran from the room. He won't take comfort from me, but I think someone should go to him."

Daniel glanced toward the stairs. "Aye," he said, then turned away, closing the door in her face. Caroline, already grown too accustomed to the Mathieson men's casual rudeness to take affront, presumed he meant to dress, and slipped back into Matt's room. Her presumption was proved correct when, scant moments later, she heard Daniel's door open again and the sound of his feet, first moving along the hall and then descending the stairs.

Knowing that John was being dealt with made her easier in her mind. Tucking a long strand back into the loose plait in which she wore her hair for sleeping, Caroline returned her attention to Matt.

He lay flat on his back with his arms flung out beside him so that his hands rested, palms uppermost and fingers curled, on top of the quilt, which had been carefully tented around his splinted leg. His hands, large, strong-looking hands, their skin toughened by hard work, touched her by their look of vulnerability. Such hands were not meant to be helpless. A blazing fire, built at Caroline's insistence in the hearth that had clearly not been used in a long while, kept the room toasty warm. As a result she had no qualms about his bare arms and shoulders being left outside the coverings, nor his nakedness beneath—at least, not as far as his health was concerned. But she had to admit that she found caring for such a very masculine man, even if that man was Matt, disquieting. The muscles that bulged in his arms, the width of his shoulders, the thick pelt of hair that formed a wedge down the center of his chest, and the companion hairiness of his forearms and legs made her more than a trifle uneasy if she permitted herself to dwell on it. The thought of what else lay hidden beneath the quilt brought waves of discomfort with it. So she simply refused to think about it. Matt was helpless, and under her care, and she would not allow the fact that he was a virile man to influence her. He had been kind to her, in his fashion, and without him her position in the household would be in serious jeopardy. For that reason if for no other—and she was not admitting to any other—he deserved her best, and he would get it. Besides, she could not let a man as obviously beloved by his sons as Matt was die for want of care. Her heart broke at the thought of those boys without him.

But keeping him alive, to say nothing of saving his injured leg, could prove to be a formidable task. Despite her best effort to remain optimistic, he did not look good. A blue-black stubble now shaded his cheeks and jaw, which she thought must serve to emphasize the pallor of his skin. Surely no man who was so naturally dark-complected could be that pale and live. Ominously, he was no longer sweating; his skin was hot and dry.

Placing gentle fingers against his forehead to assess the degree of heat, she frowned and drew them back again as her fingers felt burned. If the fever did not break soon, drastic measures, with their not inconsiderable risk, would need to be employed.

Matt had not opened his eyes since the apothecary set his leg. Whether he was unconscious or deeply asleep from the draught she regularly administered to keep him from thrashing about, she could not be sure. His breathing was fast and shallow, more pants than breaths. His lips were parted, moving as he fought for air. Already they were starting to crack with dryness.

Pouring a little water into a cup, Caroline dipped her cloth in it and dribbled the cool moisture between Matt's parted lips. At first he seemed oblivious; his breathing continued unchanged. But then as the water slid along his tongue he swallowed, and she continued, encouraged. At this point simply keeping him quiet and as comfortable as possible was paramount. All she could do was wait to see if his fever rose, or broke.

"How is he?" Daniel spoke from the doorway, making Caroline start. Her hand inadvertently squeezed the cloth too hard, sending a trickle of water running down Matt's cheek. Disregarding Daniel for the moment, she wiped the errant stream away, her hands gentle as they ran the cool cloth over the hard contours of Matt's hot face. Then she looked up again at Daniel, even as, with a tiny section of her consciousness, she noted the sandpaper roughness of Matt's cheek.

"Much the same." Her reply was husky.

Daniel had pulled on breeches and a shirt, but left the latter unbuttoned so that a wide section of hair-sprinkled chest was on view. His calves and feet were bare too. In the sputtering light of the candle he held, his hair gleamed like old copper. His eyes gleamed, too, if only briefly, as they rested on her. In an instinctive reaction to that unmistakable masculine glint, Caroline glanced down at herself to find that her wrapper had fallen open to the waist, revealing the delicate lawn of her nightdress in a narrow vee. Hastily she clutched the edges closed again, feeling her stomach churn even as she did so. It required an effort to force down the repugnance brought on by his appreciative glance, and even more of an effort to look at him again.

"John's gone back to bed. He was through crying when I got down to him. He's a tough lad, is John." Daniel's words were abrupt, his eyes hooded as they fixed unwaveringly on her face. If they had fallen below her neck once, instinctively, it was clear from his dogged expression that he did not mean to permit such a lapse again. Caroline felt some of the tension leave her. Daniel was a decent man, she reminded herself. He had meant nothing by that look and certainly posed no threat to her.

"John can't be more than ten years old. He shouldn't have to be tough."

"Everyone in this world needs to be tough to survive—and John's nine."

"He's very tall for his age. But thin."

"Aye. But then, so was Matt as a boy. So were we all. I must have been about ten or eleven when I first met Elizabeth—I'm six years Matt's junior —and I remember that she laughed at me for being, as she said, nothing more than a collection of long bones."

It was the first time Caroline had heard anyone mention Elizabeth in an unguarded way. By the tone of Daniel's voice, the memory was not a fond one.

"You didn't like Elizabeth, did you? Won't you tell me why? You must know that I can remember scarcely anything about her."

Daniel's expression was suddenly inscrutable. Clearly he regretted saying as much as he had.

"If you want to know about Elizabeth, you must ask Matt. When he recovers, that is."

"I would not like to revive his grief by speaking of her to him."

Daniel laughed, the sound harsh. "I think you need have no fear of that."

"Are you implying that he feels no grief?"

"I am implying nothing. As I said, you must ask Matt." Daniel turned away abruptly. "If you need me for anything, you have only to call. I'm a light sleeper." His eyes glimmered back over his shoulder at her. "Another Mathieson trait."

Then he was gone, back along the hall to his own chamber. Caroline frowned, listening to the opening and closing of his bedroom door. There was something very wrong here, about Elizabeth. The matter would not be allowed to rest until she discovered what.

Caroline sensed rather than saw Matt's awakening. When she glanced down she found his head half-lifted from the pillow. His body was rigid, his eyes open and vividly blue. There was a wild kind of fear in the cerulean depths as they stared, not at her but at a point just beyond her.

"Matt . . ." she began, instinctively glancing around to discover for herself the cause of that terror-stricken look.

Before she could say more he began to scream.

17

*H*is cries were hoarse and panicked, his fight to escape whatever he imagined threatened him desperate. He beat at the mattress, kicked with his unbroken leg, and floundered about until he nearly succeeded in throwing himself off the bed.

"Matt, stop it! You'll hurt yourself!" she cried, and flung herself atop him in an effort to prevent him from doing himself an injury. "Daniel! Daniel, help!"

Instead of heaving himself toward the floor Matt was now struggling with her, shoving at her shoulders and back and hips as he fought to be free of her, landing blows that hurt despite their glancing nature. Afraid of his strength, Caroline nevertheless hung on, wrapping her arms around his neck and her legs around his good leg and clinging like a limpet. Her head was buried in the hollow of his neck as she sought to hide her face from the punches she feared must surely fall at any moment. He could easily do her an injury—and yet she could not let go and thus let him do harm to himself.

"Fire! Fire!" It was a hoarse scream. He beat at the mattress again, the pounding of his fists frantic. It was clear that in his delirium he imagined the bed was aflame.

"Matt, it's all right! There's no fire! Please don't!" Her voice was muffled by the skin of his throat as he bucked to throw her off. She smelled the acrid scent of his feverish body, felt the burning heat of his skin, the softness of his chest hairs against the underside of her chin, the enormous strength in his work-tempered muscles as he thrashed against the terror that threatened him. Her weight alone would not have been nearly enough to hold him down. But coupled with the immobility of his splinted leg and the excruciating pain he must be causing himself with his frenzied movements, it was sufficient to keep him on the bed for those few minutes before Daniel came.

"What in the name of all that's holy . . . ? Matt, for God's sake! Matt!"

As Caroline rolled out of the way, Daniel grappled with his brother. But even Daniel alone was no match for Matt's maddened strength. Fortunately Thomas, followed by Robert, ran into the room, and the three of them managed to subdue their brother.

Matt was still thrashing as Caroline poured a large portion of the sleeping draught down his throat. She stood by, trembling, for what seemed like an eon waiting for the medicine to take effect. It took all three of his brothers to hold him on the bed. Finally his struggles grew feeble and then quieted altogether. Still his brothers let him go only with a great deal of caution and stood by the bed frowning down at him. It was clear from their expressions that they feared for their brother's life.

"What did you do to him?" Thomas turned on her, his eyes flashing. Only then did Caroline register that he was naked. She recoiled, her gaze hastily shifting elsewhere. It took a moment for her to concentrate on the accusation he was making.

"Do to him!" she gasped when his charge sank in, and barely kept her gaze from snapping back to him. She fixed her gaze firmly on the small table to his left and opened her mouth to blister his ears. But before she could let fly, Daniel intervened. Having apparently been given just enough time to remove his shirt, Daniel was clad in breeches only. Robert had had the forethought to grab a quilt, which he held wrapped around his waist. Surrounded by a bevy of naked and nearly naked men, Caroline still managed to seethe.

"Of course Caroline did nothing to him." Daniel seemed to see Thomas's nakedness for the first time. His eyes widened as they swept over his brother. "For heaven's sake, Thom, there's a lady present! Cover yourself!"

Thomas looked down at himself, his cheeks reddening as he was made aware of his state. He grabbed a corner of Robert's quilt to wrap around his own waist, throwing his brother off-balance as he did so. Robert staggered and nearly lost his grip on his own modesty. Only a quick snatch saved his portion of the quilt, and his cheeks turned as red as Thomas's as he gave Caroline a furtive glance to see if she had noticed.

Though Robert glared at his brother, he didn't try to recover full use of the quilt. Much of Caroline's anger was dissipated as she watched the pair of them knocking shoulders and exchanging scowls as they came together in the middle of the coverlet. That bit of byplay, along with Daniel's defense of her, cooled her ire enough to permit her to bite back the words with which she would have annihilated Thomas. Matt's sickroom was no place for a bitter quarrel, though if either of them said such to her again she might speedily whistle that notion down the wind.

Once his brother was decent, Daniel turned his attention back to Caroline. "Suppose you tell us just what did happen."

"I hardly know." Ignoring the other two, who were still struggling over who would have the largest portion of quilt, Caroline spoke to Daniel. "When you left, he woke up. He was staring at something behind me, and he looked—frightened. I checked, but there wasn't anything there, at least nothing that I could see. Then he started to yell, and fight, and I thought he would do himself harm. So I tried to hold him still until you could arrive to help. Oh, and he seemed to think the mattress was burning. He kept beating at it, and twice he yelled 'Fire!' "

There was a sudden heavy silence among her listeners. Thomas and Robert left off their shoving, and the three brothers glanced at one another, their eyes pregnant with knowledge that Caroline was not privy to.

"What is it?" she asked sharply.

Still, though they looked at her instead of each other, they said nothing.

"You must tell me. If I don't know the cause of his upset, how can I prevent it happening again?"

This provoked another exchange of glances. Then Daniel, his eyes clearly conveying a silent warning to his brothers, spoke.

"Matt was burned, severely burned, years ago. 'Tis how he was lamed, and how he came by the scar on his face. Since then he has had an understandable aversion to flames. He has always eschewed having a fire in his chamber, and likes those in the rest of the house kept as small as possible. You'll notice that he never builds them himself, nor tends them, nor draws too near. He must have opened his eyes and seen the fire in the hearth. He was groggy, and the sight brought the memory of when he was burned back to him. 'Tis perfectly understandable that he panicked. Fire is anathema to him."

"Why did no one warn me?" Caroline looked over at the hearth where flames danced merrily among a veritable mountain of logs. Her gaze returned to Matt, rendered unconscious by, she hoped, her draught. His chest was heaving and his fingers were twitching as if, even in sleep, he fought to escape his particular terror.

Daniel's eyes shifted momentarily to his brothers, then returned to her. "None of us thought to, I suppose. Besides, he needs to be kept warm. Under the circumstances, a fire in his chamber is a necessity."

"It can be hidden from his sight." There was a certain tartness to her voice as she moved to pull from a corner the dressing screen that, from the accumulation of dust that afflicted it, had obviously been long unused. It was lightweight, and she dragged it to stand between the bed and the fire. Daniel moved to help her position it, and in moments the deed was done.

"Is there anything else I should know? Anything else that might upset him?"

"The only thing that Matt fears besides fire is God, and He's hardly likely to trouble you." Daniel gave her a faint smile. "Why don't you go on to bed, and let us take turns sitting with him? You're no match for his strength, should he wake again."

Caroline glanced at Matt, who lay motionless now except for the occasional twitching of his fingers. The bed he slept in was a large one, but he filled it, his shoulders covering over half the width of the mattress and his toes stretching clear down to the foot of the bed. His skin looked very dark against the white sheet, and his hair as it waved and curled back from his broad brow was the color of a starling's wing. Even the blue-black bristle that covered his jaw and the scar on his cheek contributed to his handsomeness and to the impression he gave of overwhelming masculinity. By rights Caroline knew that she should have been frightened to death of him. But she was not. He was not a soft man, nor one given to gentle words or gestures, but instinctively she knew that he was, at heart, a man on whom one could rely. Already she had started to feel safe in his household, to take root here and make it her home.

Had he been another sort of man, the kind from whom she had fled in England, what would she have done? The thought made her shiver.

She would take the skills learned from her mother and use them to repay him for that which he had given her. She would save his life, and his leg, if it possibly could be done.

Looking up, Caroline met Daniel's eyes. " 'Tis best that I stay with him, at least until the fever breaks. If a crisis is to occur, I would recognize it right away, whereas you or your brothers might not."

"Crisis?" asked Robert, frowning at her.

Caroline fixed him with an unblinking gaze. "The fever must break soon, or it must be broken."

"And if it does not?" Thomas stood very quiet now, still wound close to his brother but no longer competing with him for space.

"If it does not, he'll die," Caroline said and was repaid for her bluntness by the graying of all their faces.

"Should we get Williams back out here?" Robert addressed Daniel.

"I doubt he'd consent to come." Thomas's interjection was dry, his eyes moving pointedly to Caroline, leaving little doubt as to the reason for his skepticism.

"He'll only bleed him again, because that's the accepted treatment for fever. Much more blood loss will kill your brother as surely as the heat in his body." Caroline spoke to Daniel now, her tone urgent. It was Daniel who would make the decision, and for Matt's sake it had to be the right one.

"Do you know anything better to do?" Thomas said scathingly to Caroline.

"Yes. I do."

"Pray enlighten us, then."

The sarcasm in Thomas's voice made Caroline's eyes snap, but there was too much at stake to afford her the luxury of losing her temper. Ignoring Thomas, she looked again at Daniel. "If he does not start to sweat on his own, and thereby lower his temperature, then we must lower it for him. The best method is to wrap him in cold wet sheets."

"And thereby kill him with the ague rather than the fever!" Thomas gave an angry snort.

"That's ridiculous!" She glared at him.

"Hold, now." Daniel sounded impatient as he mediated. He looked at Thomas, then at Robert. "We all know that Williams is no doctor. The question is, can Caroline do better by Matt?" He looked at Caroline, and held her gaze. "Can you? Our brother is very important to us, remember."

"If he dies because of what you do to him, we'll string you up!"

"Thomas!" Daniel's reproof was sharp. His gaze swung back to Caroline. "Well?"

"I cannot guarantee that he will live, whatever cure is employed on him," she said slowly, wanting to be as honest as she could in the face of Daniel's trust. "But I am sure that what I will do for him will have a better chance of success than getting that awful man out here to bleed him again."

"Mr. Williams is a godly member of our church," Robert interjected. "Whereas you—we know nothing about you. Except that you are Elizabeth's sister."

From his tone, this was far from a compliment. All three brothers stared at her as if the statement was well worth considering.

"Your brother is the father of my nephews, and has given me a home. You may be sure I'll do my best for him."

If ever there was an understatement, this was it. Her cool response gave no inkling of the complex state of her feelings for Matt. He aggravated her, it was true, but the solid strength of his character and the capacity for tenderness that she sensed lay at its core drew her bruised spirit as a flame might a moth. Her father had been charming and amusing and had loved her as much as he was capable of loving anyone, but she had been the strong one of the pair. It was she who had pretended, the last few years, to be well content with the life he had chosen for her when her very soul hankered after respectability, so as not to hurt his pride. It was she who had managed their money when they were flush, prudently tucking aside enough to get them through the hard patch that inevitably came. When winnings were sparse, it was she who had dickered with coachmen and innkeepers for better prices on transportation, food, and lodging. At the end, when her father lay so terribly ill, it was she who had borne the burden of caring for him. But Matt was a different breed from her gay, feckless father. For all his sometimes less than polished manners, he had carved out a stable home for himself and his family from the raw material of this harsh new land. It was he who held the boisterous group together, and he whom everyone turned to instinctively as the family's head. He was clearly deeply loved by his sons and brothers alike, and deservedly so. She felt a greedy longing to envelop herself in the security he represented, and she admired and respected him too. But none of that would she tell his brothers. It was all she could do to admit it to herself.

They looked at her, Robert and Thomas wary, Daniel thoughtful. Caroline held her ground, jaw set, head high. Should they object to her ministrations to their brother, there was little she could do. She would not grovel for the right to try to save his life. And besides, even if Williams were to be summoned and bled Matt again, it was always possible that Matt had the kind of constitution that would simply refuse to die.

Please God that he did!

Daniel was frowning, his arms crossed over his chest. She was almost sure that he was going to tell one of his brothers to fetch Mr. Williams. She held her breath while silently she prayed. Which was noteworthy in and of itself. Prayer was not something she turned to easily or often. Then Daniel nodded curtly at her, and she breathed again.

"We will leave Matt's care in your hands. For the nonce, at any rate." His eyes shifted to his brothers. "If need be, we can always summon Williams later."

And on that note of confidence, the three of them left her.

18

*B*y midmorning it was clear the crisis was at hand. Matt was unconscious, muttering restlessly, his head tossing against the pillow, his skin burning up. He constantly kicked the quilt off, and Caroline had finally stopped replacing it. To preserve his modesty, she had draped a linen towel over his hips. But as his feverish movements grew more frenzied, the towel was off as much as it was on. After an initial period of clenching her teeth and averting her eyes whenever his male parts popped into view, Caroline could now treat his nudity with equanimity. To her surprise and relief, the sick revulsion that such a sight should have engendered in her did not materialize. Apparently even her instincts realized that Matt, desperately ill and unaware even of her presence, was not a threat.

Daniel had sent John and David on to school, despite both boys' protests. Caroline was glad they were out of the way as Matt started to gasp for air. Daniel and Thomas—he, she supposed, to keep an eye on her—were already in the room. Robert, who had gone outside to chop some wood for the fire, was recalled with a shout. Caroline was thankful that they had elected to remain near at hand despite her assurances that she would summon them if and when needed. The crisis had come on far more swiftly than she had anticipated.

"I need buckets of water, the coldest water you can obtain. Quickly!" she said to the three of them as she sought to quiet Matt. Robert and Thomas rushed to do her bidding, while Daniel stayed at her side. When Robert and Thomas returned with four buckets of icy spring water, Caroline was ready. With Daniel's help, she plunged sheets into the buckets, soaking them. Robert and Thomas lifted and turned Matt—a difficult procedure because of his splinted leg—while she and Daniel wrapped him in the dripping sheets. As soon as the raging heat of Matt's body took the chill from the cloth, the sheet was replaced with a freshly soaked one. During it all, Matt muttered and thrashed about.

At the end of a quarter hour, Matt's temperature still soared. He was moaning, trying to thrust Caroline and his brothers away with gestures that were frighteningly feeble, his skin so searingly hot that Caroline nearly despaired.

"It's not working!" Thomas spoke through his teeth, his blue eyes flashing with animosity as they turned on Caroline. She shook her head at him. "He's getting worse!"

Caroline said nothing as she wrapped the newest sheet around Matt's body. What could she say? Despite her best efforts, there was merit to what Thomas said. After he helped Robert lower Matt back to the mattress, Thomas straightened up.

"I'm going to fetch Mr. Williams. This farce has gone on long enough." His eyes challenged his brothers to disagree with him.

Instead, Daniel looked up worriedly. "Aye, maybe you should. If 'tis bleeding he recommends, then 'tis bleeding we'll try. This is not helping."

Although neither his voice nor his eyes accused her as did Thomas's, Caroline felt to blame. She also felt frustrated and afraid. Matt's body was so hot that the sheets grew warm before they could stay on him long enough to bring his temperature down. What was needed was some way to keep cold water on him for a longer period of time.

"The water trough!" Thomas was already on his way out the door as the solution occurred to her. "We'll dunk him in the water trough!"

She stood upright for the first time in what seemed like hours, hand on spine as she eased her aching back. Thomas, stopped by her words, had turned to stare at her. Daniel and Robert looked at her too, but their eyes contained more questioning and less dislike.

"We'll fill the water trough with spring water and rest him in it! 'Tis the answer, I know it!"

Matt moaned, stirring. All eyes shifted to him. His skin was scarlet with heat, his lips parched and cracked. His case was desperate; even the least perceptive of them could not mistake that.

" 'Tis naught but more foolishness!" Thomas said in disgust and turned to leave.

"Wait!" Daniel stopped him. "We'll try it. It makes more sense to me than bleeding him again." His eyes locked with Thomas's, clashed.

"What makes sense to me is that you've developed an eye for her." Thomas jerked his head in Caroline's direction. His face was taut with anger.

"That's a lie!" Red patches popped out high on his cheekbones as Daniel came upright.

"Is it?" Thomas's words were almost a taunt.

"A damned lie, and an irresponsible one too! As if I would endanger Matt's life over any female, even if I did have an eye for her, which in Caroline's case I do not!"

"You're very quick to take her orders!"

"Enough!" To Caroline's amazement, Robert roared the word in fair imitation of Matt's stentorian tones. Except for Matt himself, who remained insensible, the rest of them started and looked at Robert in surprise.

"Would you quarrel over Matt's deathbed?" he demanded fiercely. "Which is what you'll be doing if you don't cease at once. Come on, Thom, and help me fill the trough. If that does not work, then you can go for Mr. Williams. You know as well as I that he's not much use as a doctor."

Robert headed around the side of the bed as he spoke. Thomas eyed his brother with some belligerence even as he was pushed into the hall.

"But she's . . ." The last of Thomas's statement was inaudible, which, Caroline reflected, was probably just as well. Because there was no doubt the "she" referred to herself, and the comment was sure to be uncomplimentary, if not downright inflammatory.

When Robert and Thomas—the latter looking sullen—returned some quarter of an hour later to report the deed done, Matt was no longer making any sounds at all, or even moving. His breathing was alarmingly fast and shallow, and Caroline was sore afraid that they might be losing him. Daniel leaned over him, encouraging him with words made gruff by emotion.

"Hold on, Matt. Think of Davey, and John, and the rest of us, and just hold on."

Caroline and Daniel had already rigged a makeshift stretcher of blankets for the journey to the barnyard, and with the three men to heft it getting Matt to the trough was no great problem. But when they arrived, Daniel as well as Thomas seemed reluctant to just plunge Matt into the water, as Caroline directed.

"What about his leg? The bindings will get wet." Daniel's objection seemed to be designed to cover second thoughts.

"Bindings can be changed. Lower him in, please!"

Although the three men looked doubtful, Thomas even going so far as to wince, Matt's inert body was lowered, blankets and all, into the trough with special care taken not to jar his broken leg. He was too big for it, of course. His splinted leg thrust stiffly out over one end while the other hung limply from the edge of the trough, his foot trailing on the ground. His head and shoulders stuck out at the other end. Thomas stood behind him, supporting his lolling head, as Caroline scooped up water in her hands to pour over his neck and shoulders. His trunk, hips, and thighs were almost completely submerged. Caroline prayed that this was enough.

Except for his splint, Matt was completely naked. The clear water hid nothing of his person from the view of anyone who cared to look, which Caroline did not. But despite her scruples about invading his modesty, his bareness no longer bothered her, nor did it seem to occur to the rest of them. All knew that at this point they were fighting for his life.

At first his skin remained ragingly hot, and Caroline nearly despaired. But gradually, by degrees so infinitesimal that at first she thought she was imagining it, his skin began to cool. Finally she laid a hand on his forehead and found it no more than moderately warm to her fingers. Her shoulder muscles eased; it was only then that she realized just how tense she had been.

"I think the worst is over," she said slowly, her gaze going first to Daniel then to Robert and Thomas. They looked at her for a moment, Thomas narrow-eyed, Robert thoughtful. Then Daniel broke into a broad smile.

"By the rood, we've done it! You've done it, Caroline!"

Before she had any inkling what he would do, he caught her up in a bear hug, swinging her off her feet and around in an exuberant circle. Caroline, taken by surprise, shoved at his shoulders to be free. Being held so close to a hard male body brought the familiar repulsion surging into her throat; her stomach heaved.

"Let me go!" Her voice was far sharper than the occasion warranted.

Daniel immediately stopped what he was doing and set her down. Almost shuddering with distaste, Caroline pushed him away.

"I'm sorry. I meant no offense," he said quietly. Caroline knew her reaction was far more severe than the offense warranted, and she knew too that she was bringing down on her own head the speculation that was rife in all three men's eyes, but she simply could not help it. With the best will in the world she could not mitigate her distaste.

" 'Tis all right," she managed, still battling inward queasiness. Her eyes shifted to Matt. "Let's get him back inside."

She was careful not to look at any of the three of them as they did as she directed.

By the time they got him into the house, all three men were thoroughly wet from the soaked blankets, while Caroline, who had walked beside the procession, was merely splotched. After Matt, still apparently senseless but no longer sizzlingly hot to the touch, had been settled in his bed, Daniel, Robert, and Thomas retired to change into dry clothes. Caroline perched on the edge of the bed to swap the soaked bindings securing the splint for dry ones. A quilt folded beneath the leg protected the mattress from getting wet; another quilt covering Matt to the shoulders restored his modesty. She was bone tired, having gotten no rest at all the night before. After his leg was rebound, she promised herself a nap. The idea of sleep was almost irresistibly alluring.

Her head was nodding even as she tossed the wet bandages aside and began to rewrap the lower half of the splint in dry ones. She would do the exchange in sections; that would limit the possibility of jarring the bone out of position. The leg was still grotesquely swollen, and the gash where the bone had come through was open and ugly. Barely able to drag herself up, she fetched basilicum powder from her store of medicines and sprinkled it over the wound, then set herself to finishing the rebinding of the splint. Even as she knotted the ends of the bandage below his knee, she heard a sound behind her and turned.

To her dismay, she beheld Mr. Williams standing in the doorway glaring at her. Behind him stood a tall man with hair as black as Matt's dressed in the sober Puritan garb of the community, and a diminutive white-capped woman in a gray dress of coarse homespun. Their eyes were fixed on Matt instead of herself, and they were frowning with concern.

Behind them was the dominie.

19

"**S**abotaging my good work, are you?" Mr. Williams demanded wrathfully, his plump chin quivering with annoyance as he stalked across the room to hover at her side.

"Daughter of Belial, what evil are you about now?" The dominie squeezed around the couple to follow Mr. Williams into the room. "But we may take heart from the certain knowledge that your sins are about to catch up with you. As you see, James, it is as I have told you."

"I am the daughter of Marcellus Wetherby, and not Belial at all, whoever he may be. Good afternoon, Mr. Miller. Mr. Williams." Caroline rose to her feet to sketch the new arrivals a brief curtsy. Prudence tempered her wish to skewer the pair of them with her tongue, but she could not quite control the satirical edge to her reply. Both men already harbored a considerable amount of enmity toward her; Mr. Williams's opinion mattered little to her, but Daniel had warned Matt about making an enemy of the pastor. Caroline would not like to bring trouble down upon the household for no more reason than an inability to hold her tongue.

"Belial is the Devil," the dominie spat, plainly scandalized at her ignorance. Before he could say more, Robert appeared in the hall buttoning his shirt. His frown cleared as he clapped a hearty hand down upon the shoulder of the man in the doorway.

"Well met, James. Good afternoon, Mary."

"I've just returned from Wethersfield, to be greeted with the news that Matt lies at death's door. Why was I not sent for?" James demanded hotly.

Now that she was permitted a good look at him, Caroline would have known him for another Mathieson brother even if his name had not previously been mentioned to her. He very much resembled Matt, though he was perhaps a few inches shorter and a great deal leaner. But the features were similar, as was the coloring. James's eyes, while light, were more gray than blue, and his black hair had reddish highlights and a degree less curl. He lacked both scar and limp, which should have made him handsomer than his brother, but oddly enough, in Caroline's eye at least, it did not. Though James was without doubt a very attractive man, he lacked the indefinable something that made Matt breathtaking.

"Why, I suppose because we never thought to do so. We've been somewhat busy, you see." Daniel emerged from his bedroom in time to answer that question. "Hello, Mary." He nodded at the woman, who smiled at him. Caroline recognized her then: she was the woman whom Daniel and Captain Rowse had greeted as they escorted her through the village. Clearly, she was James's wife.

"But be assured we would have summoned you at once if he had died," Robert quipped, grinning at his brother. Mary looked shocked. James frowned.

"I take it from your manner that Matt is not going to die?" James, sounding surprised, cast a sidelong look at Mr. Williams, who bristled.

"Perhaps it may still be prevented, if we take his leg," Mr. Williams took it upon himself to answer, manipulating the swollen, purpled flesh of Matt's thigh above the splint. He sounded almost disappointed at the prediction that Matt would live. It was all Caroline could do not to push him aside; Matt stirred under his ministrations, and she guessed that they must be causing him considerable pain even in his unconscious state.

"He will not die or lose his leg," Caroline said firmly to James, controlling her nearly overwhelming impulse with herculean effort. She had stepped a little away from the bed when she had curtsied, which had given Mr. Williams room to maneuver around her to stand at Matt's side. A mistake, but at least the apothecary had left off squeezing Matt's leg to take his pulse, which would at the very least not cause him pain.

"That is for God, not you, to say." Contempt shone from Mr. Miller's eyes as they moved over her. He gave a disdainful sniff. Caroline was reminded that she was a mess. Her hair, which she had barely had time to brush, much less dress, was in the same type of plait she wore for sleeping. It hung to her waist, the braid thick as a man's wrist and black and gleaming, but still woefully unsuitable for daytime wear or viewing by strangers. To make matters worse, she had that morning pulled on the first dress that came to hand. Following the reverend's eyes, she really looked at it for the first time in months. The white dimity with the once-cunning cherry ribbons trimming skirt and sleeves was no longer white: it had yellowed with age, and was splotched with water and medicines and dirt and God alone knew what else. In addition, it was sadly crushed. But what prompted the minister's condemning frown was the bodice, she was certain. It was cut too low to suit the man's stiff-rumped Puritan sensibilities.

The oval neckline revealed just the tops of her breasts and a hint of cleavage, but Mr. Miller was looking at her décolletage with as much horror as if she had been naked. Nasty man, Caroline thought.

"Have you met Caroline, by the by?" Daniel said to James and Mary. "She's the newest addition to our family."

"How do you do?" Mary smiled at her. Caroline thought that with her round placid-looking face and gentle brown eyes, she would be kind. James, on the other hand, regarded her with suspicion and merely inclined his head to acknowledge the introduction. Was it inbred in the Mathieson men to distrust women, Caroline wondered with some exasperation as she nodded at them in turn.

"So she has already wormed her way into your full acceptance, has she?" Mr. Miller said. "I should not be surprised at it, I suppose. Evil is ever cunning."

"I am not evil!" Caroline's gaze snapped around to the dominie. Their eyes met and clashed. But before either of them could say more, they were interrupted by a voice from a most unexpected source.

"I do not recall inviting you into my home, Mr. Miller."

Amazement silenced Caroline and the rest of them for the space of a heartbeat. Then Caroline pivoted. The voice, raspy and weak as it was, belonged to Matt. Not more than two hours earlier they had battled to bring him back from the verge of death. Now he was not only very much alive, but clearly aware. His eyes were open and focused on the dominie, dislike turning them a darker shade of blue than she had yet seen them.

"Matt!" It was a collective gasp, coming from at least two and possibly all four of his brothers, as Thomas entered the bedchamber.

"I came in my calling as God's representative to ease your passing into eternal life," Mr. Miller replied, moving toward the bedside, the piousness of his words not matched by his expression as he looked down at Matt.

"You are premature," Matt said, his eyes never leaving the minister. Caroline could tell that talking even so briefly was tiring him.

" 'Tis as well I am, for your soul's sake. You have much repenting to do before you can enter the Garden of Heaven, Ephraim Mathieson! Your harboring of this daughter of the serpent cannot enhance your standing in the eyes of the Lord."

"You slander a member of my family at your peril, Mr. Miller. We have laws against such, you know." Anger strengthened Matt's voice. "And I would have it known, by you and everyone else in the community, that Caroline *is* a member of my family. I will tolerate no slights to her."

The firm statement warmed Caroline's heart. Her eyes moved to Matt in silent gratitude, but his attention was all for the dominie.

"So yet another angel of the bottomless pit has seduced you, has she? You are weak, Ephraim Mathieson, an easy target for Lucifer's minions. Your only hope of salvation is to cast her, and your weakness, out!"

"I would cast out you and your twaddle instead. Understand me, and understand me well. If you fling unfounded aspersions against Caroline again, I will have you before the authorities for the spreading of malicious lies. The punishment for that is a public lashing, and so I would remind you, Mr. Miller."

The dominie looked as if he might suffer an attack of apoplexy. His face reddened, and his eyes bulged. "You dare for a second time to threaten a servant of the Lord!" He drew in a deep breath and turned to look at James and Mary, his hands outflung as if in appeal. "I fear your brother is lost to us, James. But you and your dear wife need not be, nor your other brothers, nor your poor defenseless nephews. I call upon you all to turn your backs on him and the temptress who is leading him astray, and leave him to suffer the righteous afflictions that beset the wicked with no one but the cause of his pain to succor him. I . . . ."

James stiffened, but Mary, by a quick shake of her head at him, intervened. With a gentle smile she reached out to grasp the sleeve of the incensed pastor and draw him toward the hall.

"Do you come belowstairs, and let me fix you a cup of tea. Then James and I would be most grateful if you would pray for the salvation of all within this house, Reverend Master Miller. I am sure that neither Caroline nor Matt is beyond the reach of prayer by such an august disciple of the Church as you. Just think: perhaps you were intended by God to be the instrument of their salvation! And you know Matt: he can be very tetchy, but he means little of what he says. Pray do not take offense."

To Caroline's amazement, Mary succeeded in coaxing Mr. Miller from the room. Her soothing words faded as they traversed the hall together and began to descend the stairs.

"Your wife is truly a saint, James," Thomas said to his brother under his breath, sounding awestricken as he stared after them.

"Is she not?" James turned away to stride to Matt's bedside, where he frowned at Mr. Williams.

"Do you see aught that's amiss?" he asked.

"I fear the massive swelling and bruising heralds blood poisoning. I tell you again, the leg needs to come off."

"I'll kill the man who tries it!" Matt spoke bitingly, his expression ferocious as he glared at Mr. Williams.

" 'Tis the only alternative I see to your death!"

"Mr. Williams, if you would go belowstairs to join my wife and the Reverend Miller in a cup of tea, I will endeavor to reason with my unreasonable brother." James put his hand on the apothecary's arm and turned him away from the bedside. "There's naught to be served by setting up his back, you know." This last was said in a lowered tone as Mr. Williams, with James's assistance, gained the doorway, but Caroline—and she suspected Matt as well—heard it. But if he did, he said nothing as Mr. Williams sulkily quitted the chamber, and James returned to frown down at him.

"Now, Matt, I know that losing your leg is hard to face, but if 'tis needful to save your life . . ." James began in a persuasive tone.

"I'll not lose the leg," Matt replied doggedly. From the raggedness of his voice, it was clear that he was exhausted. Caroline moved to stand at the opposite side of the bed, frowning across Matt's supine form at James. But before she could say anything, Daniel spoke.

"After today, I have great faith in Caroline's powers as a healer, and she says amputating the leg is not needful. I trust her, James." Daniel's words were quiet.

"She brought him out of a fever that should by rights have killed him," Robert chimed in. "Is that not right, Thom?"

"Aye," Thomas said after the barest hesitation. Though the single word had a grudging note to it, it was agreement. Caroline shot him a surprised and faintly grateful look. Earlier today he had thoroughly distrusted her; now it seemed as if he was at least prepared to give her a chance.

"She is Elizabeth's sister, is she not?" James said, as if reminding them.

"Half sister, and there is no harm in her that I have seen," Daniel answered firmly.

"Your tongues must be hinged in the middle, to flap at both ends like they do!" This was from Matt, who scowled at his brothers as they spoke above him.

"If you will forgive me, gentlemen, I believe your brother would be best served if you were to continue your discussion elsewhere. He needs to rest." The black scowl as much as the sweat popping out on Matt's brow and upper lip prompted Caroline's intervention. It could do Matt no good to be further upset.

James looked at her in somewhat haughty surprise, while the others, more used to both her presence and her tendency to be outspoken, nodded.

"You're right, of course," Daniel said, and with shooing gestures ushered his brothers from the room. Not even James protested, though he seemed not overpleased at being asked to leave by such an upstart as he plainly considered Caroline to be. But fortunately his care for his brother was such that he could put Matt's welfare before his own indignation.

"I'll not lose the leg," Matt told her, when she came back to his bedside with a draught of the sleeping medicine in her hand.

"No." Caroline sat down on the edge of the bed beside him and slid a hand behind his head to lift it so that he could swallow.

"I'm not a babe," he said irritably, and moved his hand as though he would hold the glass himself. But he was too weak, and his hand fell back. "What is it that you would pour down my throat, anyway?" he asked, glaring at her as if his weakness were somehow her fault.

" 'Twill help you rest." She guided the glass to his mouth, and touched it to his lips, which remained obstinately closed. "Drink."

"I won't lose the leg!" he said again, fiercely, as he resisted her efforts by turning his head. Caroline, understanding that he feared that, were he asleep, he could not defend his person against whatever might be done to him, spoke gently in reply.

"I tell you, there is no need for it, and your brothers are too fond of you to maim you without reason. You need have no fear of having your leg missing when you awaken."

"Need I not?"

"No. Now please drink this. If you do not rest, I fear a return of the fever, and that might kill you where the condition of your leg will not. Please."

She held the glass to his mouth once more. Over its rim, his eyes met hers. They burned fiercely, a bright searing blue. Again Caroline feared a return of the fever, but his skin, when she lifted her other hand to touch his temple gently, did not seem overhot.

"Promise me you won't let them take my leg." Despite his weakness, his hand managed to grasp the wrist of the hand holding the glass. The strength that remained in his long fingers surprised her.

"I promise." She gently pried his fingers loose. Despite his illness, she was not strong enough to force him to release her had he not wished to. But he did, slowly.

"I promise," she repeated, and pressed the glass to his lips. With another long look at her, he opened his mouth and allowed her to pour the contents down his throat.

"That's a good boy." Caroline murmured the words automatically, intending only encouragement. Swallowing, he shuddered at the bitter taste. As she stood up to rinse the glass with the water remaining in the pitcher and wipe it dry, his eyes followed her. There was a thoughtful quality to his frown.

"I am not," he said quietly, "a boy. Injured or not."

Startled, Caroline looked around at him. Then she remembered her words. "No," she agreed, setting the glass on the bedside table.

"Just so you know."

"I know."

"Yet you're not afraid of me any longer."

That made her almost drop the bowl she'd been emptying into the slop jar. Looking at him, her eyes widened. He was watching her intently as if she were a puzzle he was determined to solve.

"I was never afraid of you." The half-lie made her hands clumsy, and she had to snatch at the bowl as it nearly slipped again. Lips tightening, she returned it to its perch on the lower level of the washstand before she could reveal how close his perception was to the mark.

"Oh, yes, you were. Or at least, of my touch."

There was nothing Caroline could find to say to that. Suddenly she was very busy rearranging the vials of medicines on the bedside table. He said nothing for a while, but she could feel him watching her. Finally she could bear his silent scrutiny no longer. Turning to face him, her arms folding over her chest, she eyed him defensively. But he no longer seemed interested in the topic under discussion. His lids were drooping over eyes that had lost their keenness. Suddenly he yawned. Disarmed, Caroline relaxed her belligerent stance. Her arms dropped, and she crossed to his bedside to straighten the quilt that had, in the course of his examination by Mr. Williams, gone sadly awry.

"Don't leave me," he said suddenly, his lids opening so that, leaning over him, she received the full force of that dazzling blue gaze. For a moment Caroline, caught by surprise, could say nothing. She realized that he was actually expressing a need of her. Her guarded heart leaped and quivered, and not all her fine resolutions could prevent the crumbling of the barriers she had so carefully erected for its protection. Looking down at Matt, she felt a blossoming, a kind of greening such as occurs when spring comes after a hard, cold winter.

"I won't. You need have no fear," she answered, the huskiness of her voice surprising her. Then, completely without volition, she smiled at him. This time the smile was genuine, and not tentative at all. But Matt's lids had closed, and he did not see it.

For a moment she watched him sleeping, not liking what she felt at all. As if keeping him safe were her responsibility, which it most emphatically was not. Then she remembered the others and bethought herself of the debate that was doubtless raging at that very moment in the kitchen.

Dragging a chair close to the bed, Caroline settled herself in it. Her brows twitched together in a fierce frown. Her lips stretched into a hard, straight line. Her arms folded over her bosom. Her eyes fixed on the open doorway, their expression so forbidding that Millicent, who had approached her chair with the evident intention of jumping into her lap, desisted and instead slunk beneath the bed where she crouched, her eyes glowing as yellow as her mistress's.

Thus girded for battle, Caroline set herself to wait. They would do Matt unnecessary hurt over her dead body!

20

"*C*aroline!"

Caroline made it all the way to the foot of the stairs before Matt recalled her with a bellow. It was a week after the battle over his leg, which had resulted in James being persuaded to side with his brothers and Caroline against the Reverend Mr. Miller and Mr. Williams, who consequently went away furious. Caroline found herself thoroughly accepted by her new family, at least where domestic chores were concerned, but that was sometimes a mixed blessing. Matt was a fractious, demanding patient, and Caroline was worn out from looking after him. Being bedridden did not suit him at all, and he expected Caroline to be at his beck and call morning, noon, and night. Exasperation thinning her lips, she turned to retrace her steps to his bedchamber. Her hands tightened on the untouched breakfast tray she held as he yelled for her a second time.

"Caroline! From the smell, I'm thinking the bread's burning!" Daniel's shout froze her on the first tread. She looked in the direction of the kitchen, and opened her mouth to reply.

"Aunt Caroline! Is there any more porridge?" yelled Davey, who had become somewhat reconciled to her presence in the household over the past few days. Whether that was because of her care of his father, her kindness toward himself and John, or her cooking Caroline couldn't begin to guess. But at the moment he was clearly most concerned with her cooking.

"Would you mind mending these before Meeting on Sunday?"

With her head turned toward the kitchen, Caroline didn't see Robert until he was standing two steps above her, holding out a pair of gray woolen hose with a large hole in one toe.

Caroline juggled the tray, accepted the hose, and automatically stepped down and aside so that he could pass.

" 'Tis a blessing that you can sew. Those are my best hose, and I'd hate to have my toes sticking out during Meeting. The Lord could see them, if no one else could."

Robert headed for the kitchen, where the rest of them were eating. Caroline had just carried Matt's breakfast up to him, and he had just refused to take so much as a bite of it because she had brought him tea instead of ale to drink. Consequently her humor was not the sunniest. She wrinkled her nose in silent protest at the unwashed state of the hose.

"Caroline! Where in the name of all that's holy are you? Bring that tray back up here!" bellowed Matt again.

"The bread's burning! *Ouch!* Confound it, that's hot!" Daniel yelled.

"I'm still hungry!" moaned Davey.

Ruff! Ruff! came Raleigh's contribution to the general chaos. Raleigh? In the house? Juggling tray and hose, Caroline mentally consigned Matt to the devil and hastened in the direction of the kitchen, from whence the barks had surely come. What was the blasted dog doing in the house?

Stepping over the threshold, she cast one quick, harried glance around.

"*Ouch!* Thank the Lord! Caroline, the bread's burning, and I burned my hand trying to get it out!" Daniel stood by the hearth, sucking the side of his hand like an injured child.

"Aunt Caroline, Uncle Thom ate all the porridge and I'm still hungry!" Davey, seated with John and Thomas at the table, looked woebegone.

"You can have some of mine if you'll just hush up." John shoved his bowl in Davey's direction.

"I want my own!"

"I did not eat all the porridge!" said Thomas, who sounded almost as childish as Davey.

"Did too! Look at this, empty as can be! And with me not getting so much as a bite!" Robert, peering into the pot, tipped it toward the room to confirm his statement.

"The bread . . ." Daniel gestured frantically toward the brick domed oven at the side of the hearth with the hand that was not attached to his mouth.

"Caroline!" From abovestairs, Matt was still shouting for her.

Ruff!

"Where the dickens is that dog?" The question burst from her mouth. Setting the tray down with a clatter on the nearest chair and dropping the hose on the floor, Caroline stormed to the oven, grabbing a cloth on the way, and opened the iron door just in time to rescue a pair of slightly overdone loaves.

"They're burned!" cried Davey.

"Aunt Caroline will make some more." Daniel consoled him.

"I wish she'd make some more porridge," muttered Robert.

"You should get down on time, if you want some," said Thomas.

Ruff! Ruff!

Looking ferociously around as Raleigh, sounding delighted, barked again, Caroline lost the tenuous hold she'd managed to maintain on her composure. *"Where is that dog?"*

Without waiting for an answer she rushed toward the keeping room, which by default had become her bedchamber. Not that she'd had much time to sleep in it, of course, what with sitting up with Matt and attending to the unending needs of the rest of the household as well. Against all logic, the barks had seemed to come from there. Surely the creature could not be in her room. . . .

She threw open the door. Her eyes widened as she stared aghast at the sight that greeted her. The outside door was open; dawn's graying light provided just enough illumination to reveal Raleigh's huge form in the middle of the truckle bed she'd set up for herself in one corner. He was in a semicrouch, front paws flat against the mattress, rear end and madly waving tail in the air as he worried one of her best boots!

"Out! Out! Out!" she screamed, snatching a broom from a corner of the kitchen and rushing into the room. Her boot, of fine black leather with a delicate high heel, already bore signs of being badly chewed. "Out, you benighted beast! Who left the door open so this animal could get in?"

Raleigh, pleased at this new game, leaped from the bed as she flailed at him and ran, madly barking, around the room. Millicent, who'd been curled up before the fire in the kitchen, took one look at her nemesis and streaked for the stairs. Spying her, Raleigh gave chase with a bound and a volley of earsplitting woofs.

"Get that animal out of this house!" Broom held threateningly aloft, Caroline ran after the enormous animal as he bounded up the stairs in vocal pursuit of the fleeing Millicent. "Blasted dog! Get out, get out, *get out!*"

Millicent gained the top of the stairs and darted for Matt's room, as his was the only open door. Behind her, nails scrabbling on the plank floor, came Raleigh in full cry. Like Millicent, he tore through the open door.

"What in the name of . . . !" Matt's muffled protest ended in a yell.

"Out! Out! Out!" Waving the broom, Caroline burst through the door just as Raleigh, all hundred and some odd pounds of him, jumped onto Matt's bed. A hissing black streak leaped from the mattress and disappeared under the bed; Caroline, incensed, swung the broom at the bouncing dog. He bounded from the bed in pursuit of the cat just before the broom would have connected with his furry backside. Caroline ended up whacking the mattress instead. Fortunately, she just missed Matt, who cowered in the face of so much avenging fury, his arms lifted to protect his head.

"Stop it, now! Caroline, that's enough! Raleigh, sit! Blasted troublesome cat!"

"Don't you dare blame this—this debacle on Millicent!" Caroline screeched, using the broom to rout the dog from beneath the bed, where he had wedged himself in pursuit of the cat. Unfortunately, she routed Millicent as well. The cat tore around the room with Raleigh, barking deafeningly after her. Caroline, wielding the broom with grand disregard for what it hit, pounded floor and furniture as she chased the galloping dog. One particularly wild swing hit the washstand, causing bowl and pitcher to teeter; before she could so much as grab at them, they crashed to the floor, shattering. Shrieking with fury, Caroline at last succeeded in making contact with the dog—and got knocked to the bed for her trouble when the huge animal, with a shocked yelp, leaped by her in a lunge for the door.

"I'll kill that bloody dog!" Caroline gasped into Matt's chest. Broom and all, she had fallen across him, and he was holding her by the arms to prevent her from getting up. His chest was heaving. Had she hurt him? She looked up, frowning with concern, to discover that the maddening devil was laughing at her!

"She hit Raleigh!"

"Here, Raleigh! Here, boy! Aunt Caroline didn't mean it!"

"He won't hurt that cat!"

"If you hadn't gone off half-cocked . . . !"

" 'Tis time and past you stopped acting like Raleigh was some kind of wild beast!"

Like a Greek chorus, the five Mathieson males crowded through the doorway, voicing their opinions and giving Caroline condemning looks without restraint. Caroline stiffened even as Matt's grip tightened on her arms.

"I hate you, Aunt Caroline! I hate you!"

That was the final straw. The entire morning had been a disaster, and it wasn't even full daylight yet! She'd worked herself to the bone waiting on the ungrateful crew, cleaning and cooking and mending and nursing, and what did she get for it? A chewed-up shoe, and Davey telling her he hated her! Caroline felt the hot rush of tears. Blinking frantically, she tried to force them back, but she was terribly afraid she was going to make a fool of herself before them all.

"Hold, now," Matt whispered in her ear. "Davey, you may apologize to your aunt later. For now, 'tis time and past that you and your brother left for school. You know your aunt didn't hurt Raleigh. Why, he outweighs her by a good half stone! Daniel, see them off to school, would you? And take yourself, and Rob, and Thom, off as well."

"But, Pa . . . !"

Caroline could feel all their eyes on her, but she refused to look at them. Instead she ducked her head to hide the incipient tears and found her face pressed against the warm, hair-roughened muscles of Matt's chest. It was all she could do to hold back a sniffle. Matt's hands were hard around her upper arms, but his grip didn't hurt her.

"Go on, now. All of you. Daniel. Close the door."

Daniel must have sensed something amiss—indeed, with her sprawled facedown and unmoving across Matt and Matt telling him to leave them alone and close the door, it would be hard to think otherwise. Daniel ushered his nephews and brothers from the room without comment. When she heard the click of the door closing behind them, Caroline's shoulders sagged. Matt's grip on her arms gentled, becoming more comforting than confining.

"Go ahead and cry, if you want to. Your guilty secret's safe with me." His words, soft and only faintly teasing, were addressed to the top of her head, as her face was still buried in his chest.

"I never cry." The protest was muffled and then entirely spoiled by a watery gulp.

"So you've told me."

"I broke the pitcher and bowl."

"They can be replaced."

"And the bread burned."

"We've all eaten burned bread before. If you cut off the worst parts, 'tisn't bad."

"And I didn't make enough porridge."

"Now that," he said, and she could hear the humor lacing the words, "you should be ashamed of."

He was teasing her, she knew he was, but she couldn't help it: despite her best efforts, she burst into noisy tears.

21

"*H*ere, now. I was but teasing you! I thought to make you laugh, not cry!"

Despite Matt's protest and her own mortification, Caroline could not seem to dam the flow of tears. She gulped and gasped and sobbed, weeping until it seemed there must be no more moisture left anywhere in her body. After a few futile attempts, Matt gave up trying to cajole her out of her blubbering. Instead his arms came around her, and he settled her more comfortably against him while she wept away all the pent-up sorrows of the past two years. That he was a man, and naked beneath the bedcoverings, never even occurred to her. In the explosion of her grief, he was simply Matt.

" 'Tis all right then, poppet. Go ahead and cry." Matt's murmur made Caroline burrow closer. Her hands found his shoulders and curled over them, and she held on to him as though for dear life. What she had told him was true: she never cried. There had never seemed much point in it. Her father, dearly beloved as he had been, had had no patience with feminine emotionalism, and even as a child Caroline had learned not to cry in front of him. With her mother dead when Caroline was twelve, there had been nobody left in the world for her to run weeping to. Consequently, she had learned to keep her tears to herself. But something, perhaps the cessation of fear, or the new security she had found, or the Lord alone knew what, had ripped the lid off years of accumulated sorrows. For the life of her, she could not stop crying.

It was probably healthy. But if Caroline had had her wish, she would have wept her woes away anywhere but on Matt's chest.

But if wishes were horses, why, then, beggars would ride. Caroline did not get her wish. She cried in Matt's arms until she was sure no more tears would come. Then she cried some more.

"There, poppet. There, now." Clearly he had had some experience in dealing with tears. He patted her back, his hand warm even through the layers of her blue silk dress and underlying shift. He smoothed the tangles of inky hair from her hot and soggy face, murmured to her soothingly, and let her cry. Hazily Caroline wondered at his expertise, then realized with a gulp and a hiccup that he was probably treating her exactly as he would treat five-year-old Davey in a similar case.

"I'm not Davey!" Her indignant protest was rendered considerably less potent by the strangled sob that punctuated it.

"Believe me, I'm well aware of that."

There was a measure of dryness to his voice that filtered through to her after an incomprehending moment. Hiccuping again, she at last managed to bring her tears under control. For a while longer she lay unmoving, limp and exhausted from the expenditure of so much emotion. Gradually awareness began to return. To her horror, she discovered that she lay almost full length against him, with luck to thank far more than good judgment for keeping her off his splinted leg. One hand clung to his neck while the other splayed across his chest. Her ear rested squarely over his heart. She could hear its steady beat beneath her cheek.

Her breasts, belly, and thighs were pressed tight against the warm strength of his body, which was bare to the waist as his movements during all the commotion had twisted the quilt about his hips and legs. The smell of man was in her nostrils, the salty taste of his skin—flavored perhaps by her tears?—was on her tongue. His arms were around her waist and shoulders, holding her close while his hands wandered freely over her hair and exposed cheek and down her spine. And yet—there was no feeling of revulsion. Her skin did not crawl, her stomach did not heave, her body did not shudder.

In fact, except for a certain mild embarrassment, she was glad to be held so. She felt so wonderfully—safe.

"I suppose now you'll consider me a watering pot too." The chest hairs into which her right cheek nestled tickled her lips as she spoke. Above her head she sensed rather than saw him smile.

"You were provoked," he said.

That handsome admission caused her to lift her head to look at him. As she had thought, he was smiling, an amused smile tinged with kindness that lent a devastating warmth to his eyes.

Caroline blinked, dazzled. Then she stiffened. The realization of what was beginning to happen to her frightened her. Dear Lord, what she was feeling was a jumble of attraction, liking, and—and wanting. For Matt— for a man!

"Wait a minute. There's no need to poker up." His arms tightened around her, one hand coming up to rub along the smooth softness of her cheek. "I'm not going to hurt you, you know. There's no need to look at me like I suddenly turned into Oliver Cromwell."

"I'm not afraid of Oliver Cromwell," Caroline responded, feeling her instinctive resistance start to melt. It had been so long since someone had held her in a comforting, nonthreatening way—how long? Since her mother had died? "Or, for that matter, of you."

"Then perhaps you'll tell me why you suddenly looked at me just so. Did horns pop out on either side of my head?"

"No." Caroline had to smile a little at that.

"Then what?"

"I wish you would let me go."

"I will, presently. In fact, if you tell me you truly wish it, you may get up now."

"I truly wish it."

"Liar."

It was a soft word, and she could hear his smile through it. She didn't see the smile because, out of fear that he would be able to read in her eyes how very accurate his assessment of her was, she ducked her head. 'Twould be for the best that she pull away from him, right that very instant. She knew perfectly well that he would let her go. Matt Mathieson, she knew as surely as she knew her name, was not the man to hold a woman against her will.

But then, if she were very honest with herself, she would admit that she was not being held against her will at all.

"I must go and see the boys off to school."

Although she made no move to do so. Lying against him, she absorbed the smell of him, the taste of him, the feel of him. His chest was bronzed and darkened with hair, his pectoral muscles rising and falling, rising and falling. She lay quiescent against his chest and watched, fascinated, the interplay of work-hardened muscles that rippled with every breath.

"Daniel will see to them. They managed to get to school quite adequately before you came, you know."

"Yes."

Her answer was abstracted, her attention caught by the sheer rugged beauty of the naked masculine torso upon which she rested. Never in her wildest dreams would she have imagined that she would find a man's nudity intoxicating.

"Caroline."

Some few minutes had passed since they had last spoken. Matt was taking deeper, more deliberate breaths.

"Mmm?"

His stomach was flat as a board and ridged with muscle. Like his chest, it was roughened with dark hair, and it undulated when he breathed.

"Perhaps you should get up, after all."

When the sense of that registered, her eyes slid up to his, surprised. The smile was still there for her, but there was something else in the blue depths, something that glittered with bright fire. It hit Caroline then that what she had been feeling, that sudden, intense pull of attraction, had not happened to her alone. He felt it too. It was there in his eyes, this time without mistake. She'd seen a similar hard masculine gleam enough times in her life to know what it portended.

Only this time, because the man looking at her *so* was Matt, she felt no disgust, nor even fear.

Because he was the man he was, he was making no move to do anything save look at her. In fact, his arms had deliberately loosened about her. He wanted her, the expression in his eyes made that abundantly clear. Yet he was prepared to let her go, had even urged her to leave him.

Perversely, this had the effect of keeping her right where she was. If anything, she lay more fully against his chest and adjusted herself so that she could easily look up at him, luxuriating in his masculinity and the wonderful effect it was having on her body. After Simon Denker, she had not thought to feel anything like this ever again. She had supposed that the the part of her that had been designed to enjoy and respond to a man had been killed forever.

"Caroline . . ." For all Matt's flickering smile, he sounded strained.

"I told you, I'm not afraid of you." Her hands moved slowly down his chest to flatten one on top of the other as she rested her chin on them. Her palms tingled from the slight abrasion of his chest hair against them. The sensation was as unexpected as it was enjoyable. "You need not try to make me think you would do me harm, Matt Mathieson. I know you for the fraud you are."

"Elizabeth has been dead for nigh on two years. Before that she was ill, really ill, from the time of Davey's birth."

For a moment Caroline could not fathom what that had to do with anything. Then the sense of what he was trying to tell her hit her. Her eyes widened, and her chin came up off her hands.

"Are you telling me that you've not—that there's been—that you . . ."

Her outspokenness was not quite equal to framing the question she had in mind. But he seemed to know what she meant.

"I'm not the kind of man to play a wife false."

Caroline caught her breath. The notion that he had not loved a woman for over five years was unbelievably seductive. When she exhaled, the sound was a soft sigh.

"Do you understand what I'm saying?" There was a rough edge to his voice.

Caroline nodded, her eyes rapt as she watched his face slowly darken from the hot blood rising beneath his skin. She could feel the new tension in the hard-muscled body beneath her. The heat of him burned through her clothes to sear her skin. Her breasts swelled and hardened against his chest—and the sensation startled her. Eyes very wide, she simply stared for a long, speechless moment into his.

"Caroline, if you have any sense at all, you will get off this bed. Now." The words were forced through his teeth. His hands had moved away from her altogether, to lie flat against the mattress at his sides. As he spoke his fists clenched.

Her gaze locked with his, and her lips parted. Her body began a hot, sweet clamoring the likes of which she had never in her life even imagined she could feel—and then she took fright and rolled off the bed.

Her knees were not quite steady as she got to her feet, her back turned to him so that he could not see the full extent of her discomposure. She could feel his eyes on her, hear the rasp of his breathing.

"I've work to do, if you'll excuse me," she said without looking around. Then, in the hardest move she had ever made in her life, she walked, spine straight and head held high, from his room.

Not until she was safely in the kitchen did she permit herself to acknowledge that her hands, like her knees, had begun to shake uncontrollably. She just barely made it to a chair before she had to sit down.

22

" Caroline!"

Matt was annoyed, and that annoyance was expressed in the deafening volume of his roar. He had called her at least a half dozen times since his stomach had told him that it was time and past for lunch, and had gotten absolutely no answer. Had he not been certain, by the rattling of pots and the thud of a log dropped on the kitchen fire, that she was belowstairs, he would have been out of his head with worry. As it was, he was growing angrier by the minute.

"Caroline!"

The shout was made with enough force to hurt his throat. Coughing, Matt glowered at his open door, sure that this time she would appear. But though he waited, and waited, she did not.

"Caroline!"

The growling of his stomach reminded him that it was past noon, and he had had nothing to eat all day. But there was nothing he could do but shout for her and wait, fuming, for a response. His helplessness heaped fuel on the fire of his fury. Confound the woman, just because he'd had a momentary lapse of judgment was no reason to starve him! So he'd found her attractive, and made the mistake of letting her see it! She'd been attracted to him too—he was no green lad not to recognize the signs—so she need not behave as if he'd insulted her by a bodily response to her person that was beyond his conscious control. If he had had control of it, she could be sure that she was the last female in the world he would have allowed himself to respond to. She was a member of his household, his kinswoman by marriage, and a pert, bad-tempered, troublesome chit besides!

Fiend take her! Where was she?

"Caroline!"

If she had but known it, he was as appalled by what had sprung to life between them as she obviously was. Since Davey's conception in a moment of devil-inspired weakness, he had deliberately turned his back on the desires of the flesh. Recognizing lust as his besetting sin, as well as the author of most of his earthly troubles, he had vowed not to succumb to temptation again.

And so far he had not. Resisting Elizabeth had been no challenge. She had held scant appeal for him for years; only a shamefully strong physical hunger for a willing female body, even *her* willing female body, had brought him into her bed to conceive his sons. Afterward, when he realized the true measure of the depth to which his carnality had caused him to sink, he was sickened at his own degradation.

"Caroline!"

Yet in the eyes of God and man, Elizabeth had been his wife. That had precluded him from taking any other woman to his bed. It shocked him now to realize that he had been six years celibate. Six years without the comfort of a woman's flesh enfolding him! His wife was two years in her grave; he should look about him for another, and then he could indulge his one vice until it no longer bedeviled him.

'Twas an obvious solution, but his mind rebelled at the thought of saddling himself with another wife. His experience of marriage had been such as would put any rational man off it for life.

"Caroline!"

Yet he had never really intended to remain celibate for the remainder of his days. Perhaps, in the winter, when he was healed and there was less work to be done, he would make a trip to Boston. Loose women could be had for the price of a coin in the larger township, and he could appease the hidden baseness of his nature with no one whose opinion he cared for being any the wiser.

After all, he was a single man again. 'Twas not so very great a sin.

And between them, his brothers and Caroline could look after John and Davey very well.

For six years he had denied himself. Caroline was beautiful, and very, very feminine. No wonder her attraction for him was so strong.

But he was older now, far older and far wiser than he had been fifteen years before when he had wed Elizabeth. Then he was a randy youth with far more sexuality than sense. Now he was a man, who knew that all acts, for good or ill, must be paid for. If he allowed his body to rule his head where Caroline was concerned, it would cost him a mouth-watering cook, an indefatigable housekeeper, a skilled nurse, and a mother-figure for his sons who came with no strings of permanency attached. The only other way to acquire such a paragon would be to wed one. And that he would not do.

"Caroline!"

But demon lust, now that time and circumstances had conspired to rouse the sleeping beast, would not, he feared, rest again until it was slaked. He would just have to keep his personal cross under tight rein until he could get away to Boston and rectify the problem.

The devil of it was that in his present invalided state there was no escaping Caroline. She would be in daily close contact with him until he healed. For his sanity's sake, it was necessary to convince her, and himself as well, that the heat that had flared between them had been the natural result of too great a degree of physical proximity, and nothing else.

He desired her simply because she was a woman; certainly he did not desire her because she was Caroline.

If she would only condescend to come upstairs, he would tell her that. And in so doing would completely banish from his mind the knowledge that her skin had felt just as he had imagined it would: like the velvety soft petals of a white rose.

"Caroline!"

Suddenly she was there in the doorway, her face cold and stiff as she carefully did not quite look at him. The fine white skin of her face no longer bore the faintest trace of tears. Her elegantly modeled features were composed, and her soft pink lips were firmly compressed into a no-non-sense line. Her crow-black hair, which her weeping had left in a most appealing disarray, had been freshly brushed and confined in a thick knot at her nape. But if, as appeared to be the case, she had done her best to render herself plain, she had not succeeded. Despite her scraped-back hair and deliberately thinned lips, she was delectable. His body responded to her presence quite independently of his mind.

Thank the Lord for the protection of the quilt, that she could not see! Feeling a guilty heat steal up his face, Matt willed the embarrassment away.

"It took you long enough!" he grumbled, his mind focused more on his problem and its source than on what he was saying.

That earned him a fulminating glare. As she stood there slaying him with her eyes, it occurred to him that she'd changed her gown as well as her hairstyle since that morning. The blue silk that had felt so smooth under his fingertips had been replaced with a gown of dark green serge. Though slightly overlarge, it was becoming, as were all her clothes, no matter how outlandishly they were colored or styled. But he imagined that this particular garment would feel scratchy to the touch. Which, of course, was probably why she had chosen it.

Not that the changed dress, which was clearly intended to rebuff, was necessary. He would not be touching her again. But she could not know that until he told her so.

"I'm not an animal, or a child, to be coerced by a shout!" Her voice was as hostile as her eyes. Her fingers were clenched so tightly on the edges of the tray she carried that her knuckles showed white.

"I was not trying to coerce you. I was trying to get you up here!"

"You've succeeded." The iciness of her reply was matched by the ram-rod stiffness of her spine. Matt's eyes followed her as she marched around the bed to set the tray on the bedside table. Even all pokered up, she was a beautiful, desirable woman. He'd thought so from the first, and he thought so, with an almost painful physicality, now. Until he'd held her, all soft and warm and weeping, in his arms, he had not realized how much the ice-over-fire contradiction of her appealed to his senses. He'd wanted her that morning—dear God in heaven, how he'd wanted her!—and to his dismay he discovered that he wanted her still. The feel of her, the shape and scent of her, the sensation of her breasts pressing into his chest and her legs against his and her hands on his skin, were imprinted on his brain. The memory assailed him and made him grit his teeth.

Watching her as she angrily rattled bowl and mug, Matt exercised iron control and willed the shameful thoughts away. What he had to remind himself, over and over and over until his body was as convinced as his mind, was that any woman would do. It need not be Caroline. . . .

"Lift up."

Still he was not quite prepared when Caroline turned from the table to lean over him, shoving a second and then a third pillow beneath his head as he obediently lifted it. Her scent, a mixture of spice and woman, over-whelmed him, setting his head momentarily awhirl. His loins ached; his fists clenched; in a desperate effort to defend himself, he refused to breathe. Not while she was so near. He would not allow himself to make the same mistake a second time, especially when her intentions toward him were so clearly innocent. With the best will in the world, he could not blame his stumble on the path of righteousness on the lures of a Jezebel. From the first she had been blameless in her dealings with him. 'Twas he who must bear the onus for thinking sin.

From the look of her as she punched his topmost pillow into shape, it was certain that she wished she were pummeling his person instead. It was doubtful—no, sure, rather—that she would not listen to so much as a word he had to say. But if he could not convince himself of the innocence of his feelings toward her, it was imperative to both his comfort and peace of mind that he at least convince her. Life would be much simpler if she would continue to treat him with the same ease she had seemed to feel before this morning's idiocy.

Knowing that it was probably a mistake to touch her, and knowing too that if he didn't seize this chance of insuring her attention, she would in all probability plunk the tray down on his lap and sail out of the room, not to be seen again until dusk, he caught her wrist.

For a moment she jerked angrily against his hold, which he refused to release. Her eyes were as yellow as those of that blasted cat of hers; if she'd had a tail, he imagined she'd be lashing it.

"Let me go."

"Caroline . . ."

"I said, let me go!"

"Will you just listen, please?" Desperation quickened his words. "I did not intend what happened this morning any more than you did. That—feeling—that arose between us was not by design on either of our parts, but rather because nature prompts men and women to desire each other. 'Tis no blame attached to you for it—or to me."

That attempt at smoothing her down, soothing as it was meant to be, clearly missed its objective by a mile. Her eyes flashed at him; her wrist jerked again in his hold.

"Desire—you? I assure you, I do—did—no such thing." Outrage quivered in her voice.

"If you will have it so," he said, not wanting to fan her anger by arguing the point. "Then I will not contradict you."

" 'Twas you who—who . . ." She yanked at her wrist. Matt tightened his grip. Her face was flushed with anger, her eyes bright with it. Her brows, which were black and silky and straight, formed a displeased vee above the bridge of her small nose. As she spoke, he could see her even white teeth, and beyond them her tongue. It was the deep pink of raspberries, and shiny wet. A bolt of heat shot through him at the thought of how it might taste. Shifting uncomfortably, he dragged his eyes away from her mouth.

"Desired you?" In his befuddled state, truth was the only defense he dared trust. "Aye, I'll admit it. Why not? You're beautiful to look at, and made as God intended women to be made. When you threw yourself into my bed—"

"I did not," she interrupted wrathfully, "throw myself into your bed! Your monstrosity of a dog knocked me there!"

"All right," he conceded. "When Raleigh knocked you into my bed, and you started to cry—"

"I never cry!"

"Would you please stop interrupting?" Nettled, Matt forged on. "When, by whatever means it occurred, you lay in my arms, it was natural—"

"If you say that again . . ." Caroline went very still suddenly. "I'll hit you. I swear I will!"

"What?" He was bewildered.

"That what happened between us was 'natural'!" There was a wealth of loathing in her voice.

"But it was!"

"It was not! It was shameful, and disgusting, and—"

"Stop it, Caroline!" The sharpness of his voice silenced her just as he feared she might grow hysterical. She yanked at her wrist, trying futilely to free herself, and his hand tightened in response. To his consternation she winced; he hadn't realized that he was gripping her so hard. At once he loosened his hold, although still not enough so that she could escape. But he would not want to cause her an injury, which he could easily do. Her wrist was so fragile that his fingers were able to span it with inches to spare. It occurred to him that, for a tall woman, she was very delicately made. Even the skin of her wrist was silky soft.

That bolt of heat struck him anew, shocking him so that he nearly released her. But he narrowed his eyes, gritted his teeth, and hung on. If there was to be any peace between them at all, they had to settle this once and for all. If he released her, he knew she would flee.

He tried to ignore the effects of the lightning bolt and appeal to her with the coolness of reason. "What precisely did happen between us this morning? Nothing, except that you discovered that I am a perfectly normal man, and that you're not as averse to men as you'd thought."

"I *am* averse to men! I hate men—and especially you!" She jerked at her wrist again.

"Will you please just be still and listen?" Exasperated beyond bearing by her inability to be rational, he inadvertently tightened his hand around her wrist to such a degree that she cried out. Appalled at himself, he released her. Immediately she whisked herself beyond his reach.

"I'm sorry. I didn't mean to hurt you." If there was anger in his voice, it was for himself rather than her.

"Men are all the same! Nasty, violent beasts . . ."

"It was an accident!!"

"I hope you rot! I hope your leg falls off! I hope you never walk again!" An edge of what sounded like hysteria made the words shrill. Matt realized that instead of mending matters, his attempt to get her to see reason had only made things between them worse. He should have kept his mouth shut and simply allowed her anger to run its course. But of course, like all wisdom, it came too late to do any good.

"Caroline! Caroline, listen! I—"

"I hope you starve!" she finished for him and with a swirl of her scratchy skirt turned and ran from the room.

"Come back here!" he roared, both angered and frightened at something he had seen in her face.

But of course she did not. He was left to worry and fume in solitude for the rest of that day, while the tantalizing aroma of venison stew danced under his nose.

23

"*G*ood afternoon, Mistress Wetherby. I trust we have not come at a bad time?"

Caroline was on her knees, furiously scrubbing the hopelessly blackened stones of the hearth with sand in an effort to make them clean again. The previous day had been the Sabbath, and all but the most essential work was forbidden, she had been informed. Thus she had a great deal to catch up on, and was hard at it. The soft voice startled her so that she knocked against the bucket that rested beside her, sloshing dirty water over her skirt, the floor, and the hearth. Not that a wetting would do any of the three any particular harm. Her skirt was already filthy from her labors, and the floor was next on her list of things to wash after the hearth.

"Oh, I startled you. I'm so sorry!" The speaker, Caroline looked around to discover, was James's wife, Mary. She stood just outside the door that led outside through the keeping room and overlooked the kitchen. A gurgling baby rode her hip, and behind her were two more females, young like Mary but slender where Mary was comfortably plump, both bearing cloth-covered dishes.

"Not at all. Do please come in." Caroline got to her feet, brushing at her dripping skirt as she smiled with some degree of wariness at her entering visitors. She had developed a tentative liking for Mary on the day of the dominie's visit, when Matt's sister-in-law had rid the house of Mr. Miller and Mr. Williams with a great deal of tact and had been all that was pleasant and polite to herself besides. But though Mary's smile was friendly, and the baby was adorable, the smiles of the two women behind her were stiff.

"This is Hannah Forrester, and her sister Patience Smith." Mary introduced them. "And this"—she joggled the infant—"is Hope."

"Hello, Hope." The happy innocence of the wide-eyed child breached the careful barriers she usually erected when faced with strangers, and Caroline smiled at her. Her reaction to the women was more guarded. Like

Mary, they were dressed in the sober style favored by the Puritans. The elder sister, Hannah, was lovely, with smooth pale skin, simply dressed dark blond hair, and hazel eyes given a greenish cast by the deep blue of her gown. Patience looked like her sister, although her features were a trifle less delicate and her eyes were blue. Unlike Hannah, who was busy taking in the details of Caroline's person, Patience seemed shy. Caroline immediately liked her the better of the two.

"How do you do, Mistress Forrester. Mistress Smith."

"*Goodwife* Forrester," Hannah corrected. "I am a widow, unfortunately. How do you do, Mistress Wetherby."

"They've brought an apple pie for Matt," Mary informed her.

"Two, actually." Patience smiled. "With all these hungry men, one wouldn't go very far, would it?"

"And apple is Mr. Matt Mathieson's particular favorite." Hannah said it with the air of a woman who knew whereof she spoke.

"How very kind." For the life of her, Caroline could not keep the coolness from her voice. "Would you like to set them on the table? The men will certainly enjoy them, I know."

The women put the pies down. The aroma the confections gave off was quite delectable, Caroline had to admit.

"I believe I will just pop abovestairs and bid Mr. Mathieson good-day, while I am here." Hannah smiled brightly at the other three women.

"But, sister, should you? Perhaps it might not be quite the thing." Patience frowned as she cautioned Hannah.

"Indeed, I am quite convinced that it is my Christian duty to do so. He must be dying for some company other than his own." Hannah's response to her sister came even as she flitted through the kitchen toward the front room and from there, presumably, to the stairs.

With Hannah already whisking away behind her, Patience looked at Caroline and Mary with resignation. "Perhaps I will just go with her," she murmured, and followed her sister from the room.

"How good of you to come." Left alone with Mary, Caroline felt she must make conversation, although she had little enough notion of what to say. Her life had never included an opportunity to make friends with members of her own sex. Besides, at the moment her attention was focused on what was occurring abovestairs. Daniel had described the Widow Forrester as having set her cap for Matt, and Caroline was belatedly remembering the conversation. An unpleasant prickle of some nameless emotion stirred to life inside her. Caroline resolutely ignored it, shifting her focus to the child Mary was bouncing rhythmically on her hip.

"She's lovely."

"Isn't she?" Mary smiled and tickled the little girl's cheek, causing the round baby face to produce a huge, toothless grin. "I hope you don't object to me bringing Hannah and Patience to call. They are dears, really, and particular friends of the family. Besides, I thought you might be growing lonesome for the sight and sound of other females. You've not gotten into town since you arrived, I believe."

"Things have been a trifle hectic around here," Caroline responded with what she considered vast understatement. Was Matt pleased to see his visitors, she wondered even as she gestured to Mary to sit. And if so, to what degree?

"They certainly have." Mary sat, chuckling, and the baby echoed the sound.

There was no harm in Mary, Caroline was certain. Taking the chair across the table from her guest, she dredged forth a social smile. But even while she offered Mary a cup of tea, she could not get her mind off the scene of tender reunion that might or might not be taking place in Matt's chamber at that very moment. The Widow Forrester was very lovely, and not, from what Caroline had seen of her, the type to be easily dissuaded. If Matt was even interested in dissuading her, of course. Perhaps his professed disinterest in remarrying was naught but a sham to mask his true intentions.

Mary took a sip of tea and smiled comfortably. "I am glad 'tis you and not me who has to deal with Matt bedridden. I have always harbored a healthy fear of James's elder brother, I must confess, and the thought of dealing with him when he is in pain and cannot move about quite alarms me."

"He is not the easiest patient," Caroline admitted. The murmur of voices from the others was just audible, and Caroline realized that Matt's chamber must be directly overhead. It was an effort to stop trying to decipher their words and focus on Mary instead.

"Perhaps Hannah will discover that and will no longer be so determined to land Matt as her second husband. I have assured her that he is not, in my opinion, the best material for such, but she is so taken by his looks that she cannot see beyond them. Of course, I understand that, because he is so like my dear James, who is the handsomest man imaginable, but inside— what his marriage did to him cannot, I fear, be fixed."

"What it did to him?" Caroline suddenly had no difficulty at all concentrating on Mary.

"He has not much use for us women, you know. It was a most disastrous union. Oh, that's right, his wife was your sister, was she not? Forgive me, then. I must not say more."

"Please." Caroline leaned forward in her eagerness to persuade Mary, the goings-on abovestairs temporarily forgotten. "I've gathered already that something was very wrong here. 'Twould make things so much easier for me if I knew what. Will you not tell me? You would be doing me the greatest favor, I assure you."

Mary looked troubled. Hope fussed and kicked to get down, momentarily distracting her attention. Putting her on the floor at her feet, Mary pulled a rag doll from the pocket of her apron and handed it to the child. The baby promptly popped it into her mouth and sat there happily gumming its stuffed linen head.

"You are sure to hear it from someone, and what you hear may be distorted," Mary decided, her face earnest as she looked at Caroline. " 'Tis not that I disliked Elizabeth, you understand—indeed, I scarcely had the opportunity to become acquainted with her, because Matt kept her very close indeed—but she was a—difficult person." Mary hesitated, and her mouth firmed. "If I am to tell you at all, then I must tell you the truth. You will not be offended?"

"On the contrary, I welcome your plainspeaking."

"Very well, then." Mary took a deep breath. "I only knew your sister after she came to these shores, and she was older than I, so my first impressions are those of a young girl for a married lady. She was never popular with the community, and she kept very much to herself, which I thought was the cause of most of the rumors about her. 'Twas not until I wed James that I realized that the rumors had basis in fact."

Mary paused, her eyes troubled as they met Caroline's.

"What were the rumors?" Caroline prompted.

"That she was a disciple of the Black Man."

"The Black Man?" Caroline stared at Mary. "Who or what is the Black Man?"

"You don't know of the Black Man?" Mary sounded faintly scandalized. "He is the Devil, of course. 'Twas said about the town that Goodwife Mathieson had made a pact with him. In later years, after Davey was born, she was seen, disheveled and muttering, roaming the woods at all hours of the day and night. Toward the last, Matt had to keep her locked in her room. He feared she might take her own life, which in the end she did."

"What?" Caroline could scarcely believe what her ears insisted they had heard.

"Oh, dear. You didn't know. Mercy me, had I any idea . . ." Mary's voice petered out unhappily.

"I was told only that she drowned." Caroline's voice was quiet. "Please tell me the truth. I—need to know."

"That she drowned is true enough, but . . ." Mary paused, looking troubled. "Perhaps I should not be telling you this. If she was your sister, you must have loved her. I fear that the knowing will cause you pain."

"We were sisters, half sisters, really, but I had not seen her in fifteen years, and we did not grow up together. I saw her perhaps twice a year until she left England. Though I loved her as I remembered her to be, I know little more of her than if she had been a stranger. Your words will not cause me any pain that I cannot bear. And if I am to make my home here, it will help me to know."

"Yes." Mary seemed to accept that, but still she hesitated. When at last she continued, her words were almost reluctant. "From what James has told me, I gather that she imagined herself a witch. She was not, of course, or she would not have ended so miserably, because of course we all know that witches float. What she was, was mad. She—oh, I cannot tell you this!"

"Please!"

Mary flushed, and looked down at her baby playing happily on the floor. When her gaze returned to Caroline, Caroline saw embarrassment, but also determination, in the soft brown eyes.

"She pursued—men. Any man. All men. She was insatiable, I was told. James—she tried to seduce James, which was what led to his moving out of the house and, eventually, to our being wed. And Daniel too, I think. He was gone when—when she died, and he would not have left Matt except for cause. They are all most devoted to Matt, you know. 'Twould not surprise me if she had tried her wiles on all of them. She certainly attempted many in the town, until Matt took to keeping her locked up. You see, there was once a latch on the outside of the door where Matt now sleeps. 'Twas her room then, and Matt would lock her in it, for her own safety and that of everyone else."

"He locked her up?" It was scarcely more than a whisper. Caroline was so appalled by what she was hearing that it was all she could do to form the words.

"After she first tried to kill herself, so that she would not get the chance again. He saved her that time, you know, though it ended up costing him dear."

"Matt?"

Mary nodded. " 'Twas one night when Davey was but an infant. She escaped from her room, no one knew how, and fled to the barn, where she barricaded the doors from the inside. Then she set the place afire, meaning to incinerate herself along with the animals that were put up for the night. In the end, 'twas the animals that were her salvation. Matt heard them screaming to be free and, with the others, ran to put out what he thought was no more than an accidental conflagration. Discovering the door barricaded, they burst it down, though flames by that time had spread everywhere. Robert told James that Elizabeth was halfway up the ladder to the loft when they won through. She cursed them most foully as she climbed, in words so hideous that Robert would not repeat them to James. Matt went after her while the others fought to rescue the animals. He managed to drag her down from the loft and thrust her out the door just as the roof came down."

"Dear God!"

"Had it not been for his brothers, Matt would have perished that night. A beam fell on him, trapping him. He was afire when they got to him, and they risked their own lives to get him out."

"No wonder he is afraid of fire!"

"So you know that much, do you? 'Tis as well. Quite innocently one time when he came for a meal I asked him to build up the fire in my kitchen, and he gave me such a look and walked out of my house. 'Twas only then that James told me how he had been affected by what he had suffered. I was quite mortified, but James forbade me to speak of it to Matt, not even to apologize, and the matter was never mentioned by anyone again. Perhaps the knowledge will save you from a similar mistake."

"Yes." Caroline felt dazed as she tried to assimilate what Mary had told her. Of course, so many things now made sense—the wariness of the Mathieson men toward her as a woman, the distrust of the children, the tension in all their voices when they spoke of Elizabeth. Why had she not been told? Thinking back, Caroline hit upon what she guessed was the answer: with his particular brand of arbitrary chivalry, Matt had thought to protect her.

"Are you all right?"

"Yes, of course." But Caroline wondered if her answer was true. It was impossible to imagine her sister mad. Caroline thought back to the lively, auburn-haired young woman whom she only vaguely remembered. Her clearest recollection was of Elizabeth patting her much younger self on the head and laughing. The reason for the pat, and the laughter, were shrouded in the mists of time.

Quite suddenly the aroma of the apple pies at her elbow made Caroline feel ill.

"I should not have told you." Mary, who had been watching her changing expressions, sounded remorseful.

Caroline gathered herself. "No. No, I needed to know. I understand much now that I did not before. They—Matt and his brothers—were careful in what they said of Elizabeth before me. But I knew that something was wrong."

Hope, having lost her poppet, began to wail. Mary leaned down and scooped up the child and her toy.

"Perhaps I had best rout out Hannah and Patience, so that we may go."

"Wait!" The sharpness of Caroline's voice surprised even herself. When she continued, she moderated her tone. "Can you tell me—what became of her? The—the body, I mean." She would visit, take flowers, try to understand what had driven her sister to lose her reason. Perhaps, if she, Caroline, had arrived sooner, she might have been able to make a difference in Elizabeth's life. But then came the guilty thought: had Elizabeth lived, she would still have possession of Matt.

"You need not worry. She had a Christian burial." Mary's voice was soft with compassion. "Indeed, Matt had quite a battle with the dominie over it, which is the reason for the bad feeling between them that persists to this day. The Reverend Master Miller refused to allow Elizabeth to be laid to rest in the cemetery beside the church on the grounds that she was a witch. So Matt got out there and dug the grave himself, with his brothers pitching in to help, and dared anyone to stop him. Of course, no one tried. The Mathiesons are very wealthy, you know. Why, this farm is the finest for miles around! Anyway, the family said words over her, and the grave was later blessed by an itinerant minister who did not care if he incurred the dominie's wrath. For a long while I feared that some who took the dominie's side might try to dig her up, but the grave has been undisturbed. Perhaps common sense prevailed in the end: after all, she did drown. Or perhaps they are afraid of Matt. But in any case you may take comfort from the knowledge that she is now at peace."

Caroline said nothing as Mary rose from her chair, restoring the poppet to her pocket and rebalancing the baby on her hip.

"I hope I haven't caused you too much distress. But I agree with you, 'tis best that you know."

"Yes." Caroline rose too. "I do thank you for telling me."

"If there is anything else you wish to know, or if I can help you decipher the sometimes incomprehensible behavior of these Mathieson men, please do not hesitate to come to me. I would like to count myself your friend."

"Why, thank you. I would like that too."

"And now I really must round up Hannah and Patience. I fear James will be wroth with me if I do not get home in time to have supper on the table when he comes in. One trait they all have in common is a fondness for having their stomachs well filled. As you must know. Robert has raved to James about your cooking."

"Has he indeed? How very nice." Caroline's response was mechanical.

Mary headed for the stairs, while Caroline, still in a state of semishock, trailed behind. She had much to mull over as she climbed. Only when she entered Matt's room was she at last wrested from her abstraction.

What did it was the sight of Matt, his bare shoulders broad and muscular against the sheet that *she* had painstakingly laundered, his crisp curls inky black against the pillow slip that *she* had bleached in the sun, smiling and trading quips with Hannah Forrester, who simpered as she sat on the edge of the bed feeding Matt spoonfuls of broth that *she,* Caroline, had prepared and carried up to him only minutes before the visitors arrived!

Confound the duplicitous wretch! 'Twould serve him right if he choked on the bloody broth!

24

"**W**ell, hello there, Mary. Did you bring my niece to visit me, then neglect to carry her upstairs?"

Matt looked up to spy them in the doorway. He seemed completely unembarrassed to be caught sipping broth from a visitor's spoon. Considering the fact that he had insisted to Caroline from the very day after he was injured that he was perfectly capable of feeding himself, she could only suppose that he was quite without shame.

"'Tis good to see you, Matt, although I actually came to further my acquaintance with Mistress Wetherby and cannot stay longer even to allow you to visit with Hope. James will be getting hungry this evening as usual, I fear, so I must hurry home. Ladies, 'tis time we were going. The afternoon grows advanced."

It was probably as well, Caroline decided, that this exchange between Matt and Mary took place without so much as a glance being cast at her. Caroline, biting her lip, barely managed to keep her tongue still as it was. If Matt had spoken to her in terms that had required an answer, she couldn't have been held responsible for what she said. Though why she should feel so outraged by the scene she and Mary had interrupted she couldn't imagine. She certainly had no claim on Matt! Nor, she told herself vehemently, did she wish to have a claim on him!

"Oh!" In response to Mary's words, Hannah looked around with a trilling little laugh. "I had not realized how the time was passing. When I saw that Mr. Mathieson was not eating, I just had to see if I could not coax him to take a bite or two. He must keep up his strength, you know, if he is to heal."

"Mr. Mathieson said the broth tasted much better when Sister wielded the spoon." Patience got to her feet from where she had been sitting in the high-back chair near the bed, decorously playing propriety.

"I am sure it does," Caroline answered sweetly, for the remark had been directed to her. Nobly she refrained from giving into the impulse to cast a dagger look at Matt, who at last turned his eyes toward her. He frowned at something he apparently saw in her face, and opened his mouth as if to speak. Before he could get the words out he was silenced when Hannah, with commendable dexterity, slid a spoonful of broth between his parted lips.

"Hannah? If you are quite ready . . . ?" Mary lifted her eyebrows at her friend while Matt swallowed.

"Oh, yes. I don't believe that even my help can get any more of this down him. It's been allowed to grow quite cold. But he's taken a good bit —and may have some of my apple pie for dessert," Hannah concluded, getting to her feet as she addressed the latter with a smile to Matt. She placed the spoon in the bowl, set the bowl on the bedside table, and turned to survey Matt with a proprietary air that made Caroline, for no reason that she could think of except that the woman plain irked her, want to stomp her feet.

"I will look forward to it." Although Matt didn't return Hannah's smile with other than a faint twitching of his lips, there was to Caroline's ears more gallantry in that one statement than in anything he had said to *her* since he had met her. Deliberately forcing herself not to scowl, Caroline strove to maintain a pleasant expression as the sisters moved toward the door, and she stepped back to let them pass.

"Perhaps I should leave you my recipe for broth? I'm sure what you've prepared is quite nourishing, but mine is extremely tasty as well. I'm convinced that Mr. Mathieson wouldn't find it such a trial to get it down." The condescending tone of this brought a militant sparkle to Caroline's eyes. But before she could reply, Mary most fortunately forestalled her.

"Eating Mistress Wetherby's broth is surely not a trial, Hannah," Mary chided gently as the sisters joined her in the hall.

Hannah gave a trill of guilty laughter. "Oh, you know I didn't mean that! It's just that I am so concerned for Mr. Mathieson's welfare—although of course I'm sure you are doing the best you can."

This was addressed to Caroline in the tone one might use to a superior servant. It caused Caroline to wonder just what the town grapevine made of her position in the Mathieson household. With a silent grinding of her teeth she concluded that, courtesy of Captain Rowse and the Lord alone knew whom else, her status was that of an unofficial kind of bound girl. The thought rankled and brought with it angry blood that rose to stain her cheeks. She could feel Matt's eyes on her back and thought that he might be able to see her profile as well. Thus despite her annoyance she managed a stretching of her lips that she hoped might be mistaken for a smile.

"I would very much appreciate your recipe," she said with absolute falsity. "Although perhaps some other day, since Mistress Mathieson is in a hurry to get home."

"Oh, yes, we really must be going. And please, call me Mary." This was said to Caroline with a smile. James's wife, at least, was prepared to treat her as a member of the family. Although, upon consideration, Caroline decided that that was at best a dubious honor!

"Thank you. And you must call me Caroline." Another forced stretching of her lips made her feel as if her cheeks might crack.

"You need not see us out. I know the way." Mary, Hope riding on her hip, was already heading down the stairs with Hannah and Patience trailing her. Moments later they exited with a wave. Caroline, determined not to say what she felt like saying to Matt, waved back, started down the hallway, remembered the bowl and spoon on the bedside table, and turned back to retrieve it. She would have no more reason to return to Matt's room for the remainder of the day. Daniel could carry up his brother's supper just as he had done the night before, and the night before that! Since their disastrous encounter of two days previous, Caroline had avoided Matt as much as possible. On the Sabbath, which was the day just past, Matt's brothers and sons had attended Meeting. To Caroline's amazement the service was apparently held in two sessions, one in the morning and one in the afternoon. Worship, which the colonial Roundheads seemed to take even more seriously than did their English brethren, therefore took up most of the daylight hours. Everyone who could was expected to attend. Matt was excused only because he was bedridden, and Caroline because someone had to stay with Matt. Since she had had no choice but to carry him his meals and perform other services for him until his brothers returned to relieve her of the burden, the two of them had effected a chilly truce. Which she had adhered to all day, and would continue to adhere to until hell froze over! It might even be longer than that before he got a friendly word from her again!

"If 'tis not too much trouble, I believe I'll have a slice of Mistress Forrester's apple pie. She's a most delectable cook. You should try a piece yourself."

That remark, coming as Caroline stalked across the room to retrieve the bowl and spoon, made her spine stiffen. But not by word or look would she reveal how much his eagerness for the treat irritated her.

"Certainly I'll bring you some. Though personally I have little taste for sweets."

"Do you not? 'Tis just as well. Even with two pies, there'll hardly be enough. Davey and John as well as my brothers are wild about Mistress Forrester's pies."

"I wonder that you don't wed her then, that you may have them every day." Caroline could not resist jibing as she took herself out of the room before she could give in to her impulse to give his thick skull a sound crack with the bowl in her hand.

"A good cook is worth much, but not that much," Matt called after her in great good humor. Of course he would have marked her irritation and been amused by it. He was too canny a man not to see when she was annoyed.

In the kitchen Caroline dropped the bowl and spoon into the bucket of dishes to be washed, then turned to slice the pie. The aroma of cinnamon and apples wafted up to her, tempting her to sample a taste that had somehow found its way onto her finger. It was truly excellent pie, Caroline had to admit. Matt would enjoy it.

The notion rankled. At her feet Millicent meowed, and Caroline cut her a large piece of the precious pie, slid it onto a plate, and set it on the floor. Her cat, from whom she had hoped for better taste, sniffed, took a tentative nibble, and then fell to with a will.

"*Et tu*, Millicent?" Caroline muttered sourly. It was at that moment that she had the idea.

Had she been a Puritan, she would have said that she had become suddenly possessed by the devil. But being a level-headed Royalist sort, she could only plead an irresistible response to an overwhelming urge. Before she could think better of the deed, she slipped the blade of a knife between pastry and filling of the piece she had cut for Matt, lifted the top crust, and anointed the luscious apples beneath with a liberal sprinkling of salt. Then, still possessed of the devil or whatever evil spirit it was that had slipped inside her skin, she gleefully added an extravagant dash of bitters, a few slivers of finely chopped onion, a glob of mutton tallow, and a couple of cherry pits. She consumed the fruit herself, grinning as she licked the pits clean and pushed them deep inside the pie. She replaced the crust, removed the slice to a clean plate, and carried it upstairs along with a nice cup of tea for Matt.

"Here you go." 'Twas the most cheerful remark she had addressed to him for days.

"Thank you."

He was still propped up from lunch. Caroline had only to hand him plate and cup, which she did. Trying to disguise her eagerness for him to get to the pie, she watched as he balanced the plate on his stomach and took a sip from the cup.

" 'Tis good." He appeared to savor the tea, his eyes bright blue and curious as he surveyed her over the rim. Doubtless he was speculating as to why she was remaining in the room, after having taken such pains to avoid him for the last two days. To divert suspicion, she turned partially away from him and began to dust the bedside table with the edge of her apron.

He sipped his tea and watched her work. The pie sat untouched on his lap.

"Shall I help you with the pie?" she cooed at last, unable to stand the suspense any longer. Her words were perhaps more acidic than she had intended them to be—the memory of him meekly sipping broth from a spoon held by Hannah Forrester still rankled—but if anything, that should only serve to allay any suspicions that might occur to him.

"I can manage very well without help, as you well know."

"Well, I own I had thought so, but you seemed to appreciate the Widow Forrester's assistance so much."

His eyes narrowed at that, then to Caroline's annoyance took on what she could only interpret as a distinctly amused gleam. She could have bitten off her tongue; she should not have said so much.

"Ah, but you and Hannah Forrester are very different kettles of fish," he said obscurely.

"And what does that mean?" she demanded, rounding on him, arms akimbo as she thought she recognized an insult. But he merely lifted an eyebrow at her, shook his head, and continued to look amused as he sipped his tea without deigning to answer. After a moment Caroline turned away in a huff.

" 'Tis good of Mary to want to make a friend of you. A kind woman, is James's wife."

Caroline, dusting the screen now as she waited for Matt to take a bite of his pie, stiffened at that.

"And why should we not be friends, pray? Is there something about either of us that would preclude such?" Her eyes had a distinctly militant sparkle as they slewed around to his face. Had he been a prudent man, her expression should have given him pause.

"You have little enough in common with her, I believe. Mary has led a most sheltered life and is a very virtuous woman."

"Are you saying that I am not?" Outrage made her voice quiver.

Matt looked up from the cup he was in the act of draining, his expression innocently surprised.

"I meant no comparison at all. But your backgrounds could not be more different."

"Indeed!" Her bosom swelled inside the faded green cotton gown she wore for cleaning.

"In fact, your background is different from that of every woman in the community. Take Hannah Forrester, for example. Now she has never set a foot amiss that I know of. A fine woman, is Hannah Forrester." The suspicion that he was making sport of her entered Caroline's head. There was the faintest suggestion of a smirk about his mouth, and his eyes were a vivid blue beneath what she suspected were deliberately lowered lids.

"Add to that the fact that she is a fine cook and you have sung her praises well."

Now that she suspected that he was teasing, she was able to refrain from rising to his bait. Instead, she smiled at him. "Eat your pie."

"I will then." Holding out his empty cup—Caroline was so aquiver with anticipation that she nearly dropped it—he picked up his fork and attacked the pie. The bite he cut off and lifted to his mouth was huge. Agog, Caroline watched as he shoveled it in.

For a moment only he continued to look exaggeratedly blissful. Then his eyes widened, his face contorted—and he spat the mouthful onto his plate.

Shocked blue eyes met innocent amber ones. "Is something amiss?" Caroline asked with simulated concern.

"You—little—vixen!" he said. "You deliberately ruined a perfectly good pie!"

"I?" She rounded her eyes at him. Inwardly she was laughing so hard that her throat ached from the effort of holding it in, but she managed to preserve her guiltless front.

"Yes, you! You put salt and God knows what else in it!"

"You're being ridiculous! Mistress Forrester made it, not I."

"Out of sheer spite!"

"Spite?"

"And jealousy!"

"Jealousy!"

Their gazes met and clashed. Caroline stuck her nose in the air and prepared to sail from the room. Matt crossed his arms over his chest and glowered—and then the strangest expression flickered over his face. Even as Caroline looked at him, arrested, his eyes rolled back in his head, and he went limp. His head lolled lifelessly back against the pillows.

"Matt!"

He didn't move. His eyes were closed, and he wasn't breathing. Was he playing her for a fool? Or, dear God, had he perhaps been suffocated by a cherry pit, or poisoned by some mixture of ingredients in the pie?

"Matt!"

Alarmed, she stepped closer. Still he didn't move. And—she was sure of it now—his chest was utterly still.

"Matt!"

She swooped down upon him, catching him by the arms and shaking him even as she cried his name.

Then his eyes opened, his hands clamped over her elbows, and to her shock Caroline found herself tumbling down into his arms. She shrieked and struggled, but before she could free herself he managed to turn at the waist and pin her to the bed. She lay on her back, trapped by his weight and the hands on her arms, her eyes huge with surprise. Then, as he met her gaze with satisfaction plain in his face, she stiffened angrily.

"Let me up this instant!"

"Oh, no. You've had your sport of me. Now 'tis time to pay the piper, Madam Jealousy."

"I am not jealous!"

"Aren't you?" He was taunting her to repay her for her trick with the pie. "If I did not know better, I would think you had a care for me, Caroline."

"You conceited . . ." She struggled but could not get free as he held her wrists piniened on either side of her head. "If you don't let me up this instant, you'll be eating cold gruel at every meal until your leg heals!"

"Aha, she threatens! I'll not be intimidated, and so I warn you. I won't let you up until you admit it: you salted that pie because you were jealous!"

"I was not jealous!" She glared up at him with the tawny ferociousness of a cornered lioness. When he grinned back at her, clearly unconvinced, her temper got the better of her. Turning her head more quickly than he could move to avoid her, she sank her teeth into the wrist nearest her mouth.

"Yoww!" He let go with one hand even as he hung on with the other. Despite her frantic wriggling Caroline discovered that she could not win free—but she could let fly with a stinging slap.

Her hand glanced off his scarred cheek with a resounding crack.

25

*T*hey stared at each other for a long moment as the echo of the slap died away.

"Now what do you deserve for that, I wonder?" he asked with commendable mildness under the circumstances. As shocked by her action as he was, Caroline was determined not to let it show. She put her chin up at him, difficult as that was when one was lying flat on one's back, imprisoned by a man's hard weight.

"You deserved that!"

"Aye, I very likely did." The admission surprised her almost as much as the tone in which it was uttered. He was studying her, his expression grave. Seriousness became him every bit as well as laughter, she discovered. His mouth, unsmiling, was perfectly shaped. His eyes were darker than usual, a deep sea blue, breathtaking in the swarthiness of his face. Since he had not shaved for a fortnight, the stubble on his jaw and chin had grown thick. But instead of obscuring, the blue-black bristles only served to emphasize the hard planes of his face. The classic elegance of his high-carved cheekbones, long, straight nose, and wide brow made a dazzling contrast to the rugged masculinity of his newborn beard. With a plethora of black curls tumbling over his forehead—they needed another trim, she saw, and she felt a strange little ache at the memory of her hands in his hair—he was as handsome as a dark-visaged angel. Gabriel without the horn, Caroline thought, and she shivered.

At her shiver he stiffened, and her gaze rose to meet his. Blue eyes locked with amber, both dark with guilty knowledge: against her hip Caroline felt the unmistakable rising of male passion, even through the quilt that covered him and her clothing. He was, clearly, even more aware of what was happening to his body than was she. As their eyes met a hot tide of color rose to stain his cheekbones. His eyes darkened still more.

So Gabriel had his horn after all. The knowledge seemed to steal the breath from her, and she parted her lips to take in more air.

Thick black brows twitched together over his eyes. His mouth turned down violently at one corner.

"May the devil fly away with you, Caroline!" he muttered as if goaded, and then he bent his head. Caroline knew what was coming, knew that he would kiss her, and instead of turning her head aside or whispering "no!" or doing any one of the half dozen things that she knew would win her release, she merely watched, mesmerized, as his mouth descended toward her own.

She thought that she would die if anything happened to stop that kiss.

His mouth, warmly seductive, just touched her lips. Caroline closed her eyes, quivering at the wonder of it. Her body, of its own accord, turned into his, seeking the heat and hardness of him with instinctive greed. Her hands, freed now, found their way upward to wrap around his neck. Her head slanted to allow him greater access to her mouth.

But still he held back, his lips barely grazing the surface of hers. One arm, braced against the mattress, kept his weight from her. She could tell by the rigidity of his muscles beneath her hands that he kept rein on himself with great effort. Head awhirl at the promise his lips had made her and had yet to keep, Caroline forced open her lids. His eyes were just inches above hers, afire with the brilliance of a thousand diamonds, blue as the sky, and burning as they stared down into hers. Their lips were brushing, no more, in the barest butterfly contact. With the whole length of her she could feel him: his body was as hard as iron. Yet his kiss was as gentle as the fluttering touch of a moth.

"Matt?" It was the merest breath of a question. The muscles of his bare shoulders bunched beneath her hands. He lifted his head so that, when he spoke, his hoarse reply was uttered an inch or so above her mouth.

"I would not force myself on you, Caroline."

It was a battle for her to breathe. Her hands tightened on his shoulders, her nails dug into his smooth flesh. Her heart began a ragged drumbeat that resounded in her ears.

"No," she said.

"No?" He tensed still more. It came to Caroline then that he thought the single word that she had barely managed to get out was a rejection, when it was anything but that.

"I don't feel the least—forced." Her hand slid up the back of his neck to shape his skull beneath the crisp, springy hair. "You—you may kiss me, Matt."

A glimmer of a smile quirked his lips, was gone. "With your permission, then," he said, and lowered his mouth to hers again. The kiss was soft, a brief, sweet salute, but it was enough to send shivers shooting along Caroline's nerve endings. Her eyes closed, her lips parted in a quest for air—and then, instead of withdrawing as she had thought he meant to do, he was kissing her again, his mouth suddenly fierce.

His tongue parted her lips still more, slid inside her mouth, took fierce possession. The arm that had held his weight carefully away from her enfolded her instead. He was wrapped around her, the size and strength of him making her the most delicious kind of prisoner, holding her against him while the raging heat of his skin and unyielding hardness of his muscles screamed of the passion that he could no longer deny.

Even as she tasted him, even as the feel and smell and heat of him combined to make her blood race, a memory was jarred to life. He was not the first man to thrust his tongue inside her mouth; Simon Denker had kissed her so, several times, as payment on account, as he called it, for his self-described generosity in letting her and her father stay on in his house without payment. He had shoved her up against the wall and slammed himself atop her to hold her still and thrust his tongue inside her mouth so that she had wanted to gag, wanted to scream and fight and vomit to rid herself of the offensiveness of his touch. But she had been able to do nothing but endure because, had she totally and completely rejected him as she had longed to do, he would have thrown her and her father out into the street without a second thought. So she had been forced to accept the indignity of unwanted intimacies with him, been forced to let him kiss her and paw her, all the while withholding the ultimate surrender with every iota of guile in her nature while searching, searching for a way of escape.

But in the end there had been no escape.

"No!" she shrieked even as Matt's hand slid over her ribcage, aiming, she knew, for her breast. "No, no, no!"

Like an animal gone berserk she began to fight, beating at him with her fists, kicking and scratching without regard for any damage she might do him. He had ceased to be Matt for her, ceased to be the one man whose touch she had thought might be able to heal her. Instead she experienced again the horror of Simon Denker. . . .

"Whoa, there! Caroline! Caroline, stop it!"

He was no longer kissing her, no longer holding her as a lover might but rather holding her off as she attacked him with sobbing, spitting fury. Her eyes opened even as her nails raked down his unscarred cheek. The sight of blood beading in the scratches she had inflicted shocked her back into some semblance of sense.

"What the deuce is the matter with you?" It was a roar. His hands were tight on her upper arms, pinning her once again to the bed.

"I'm sorry," she said in a small voice. She shut her eyes to block out the mixed bewilderment and fury in the dear face she had just done an injury to.

"Sorry!" For a moment his fingers tightened. Then his grip eased. "Caroline, look at me."

Briefly she resisted. Then, most unwillingly, she opened her eyes.

He was frowning, his brows twitched together over those breathtakingly blue eyes as he searched her face. There were three parallel scratches on his cheek, she saw, blood-spotted and angry-looking against his skin. Scratches he had not deserved.

"I'm so sorry," she said again, helplessly. In response, his eyes narrowed, and his mouth twitched down at one corner.

" 'Tis I who should apologize. I should not have allowed this thing between us to get out of hand."

" 'Twasn't you—" Her voice broke off, strangled by guilt. That he would beg pardon of her after that! The enormity of it made her throat ache.

"Wasn't it?" His voice gentled. "What was it, then, Caroline? Or should I ask, rather, who? The man you told me about, the one who wanted you in payment for your rent?"

26

She flushed a deep, painful scarlet. There was no need to answer after that. Realization was plain in his eyes.

"He forced you, didn't he? Forced you to bed him. That's what this is all about."

Caroline closed her eyes, shuddering. The memories came flooding back, disgusting, horrible memories—and she could no more stem them than she could hold back her tears.

"I'm so—ashamed," she whispered, turning her face away as she felt her eyes brim over. The wet saltiness seeped beneath her lashes to trickle down her cheeks unchecked. Above her—she could not, would not, look—she thought she heard him draw in a harsh breath.

"You've no need to be ashamed." His arms came around her again, tenderly this time. She curled into the hard warmth of them as he eased over onto his back, pulling her with him to cradle her against his chest. "Don't cry, my poppet. 'Tis no blame attached to you."

"You—I—I can't bear to be touched." Her face was burrowed against his chest, her hands clutching him as if he was her lifeline in a raging river. She was not sobbing, but weeping silently, her eyes tightly shut, her face awash in tears. "By men, that is. But you—you can touch me and I don't get sick. . . ."

"Just hysterical," he muttered dryly, and her eyes flew open at that.

" 'Tisn't funny!" she cried, shoving against his chest as she thrust herself into a sitting position. With a grab he caught her hand, barely in time to stop her from scrambling off the bed and fleeing. He held it just tightly enough to keep her beside him.

"Believe me, I am not laughing," he said, and from the grim set to his mouth she knew that he spoke the truth. With one more halfhearted effort she tried to free herself. When he would not let her go, she didn't struggle but continued to sit beside him, legs curled beneath her, her hand in his. In truth, she scarcely knew whether or not she wanted to leave him. She ached for his comfort but feared discovering that her revelation had given him a disgust of her. But even if he did not despise her, she despised herself enough for the both of them. She felt despoiled.

A despairing heaviness settled in her chest as she realized that not even with Matt could she escape the nightmare Simon Denker had thrust upon her.

"I had best go—there's supper to prepare, and . . ."

"Supper can go hang." His hand tightened around hers. "Can you tell me what happened? 'Twould do us both good, I think."

"Oh, no! I—I can't talk about it!" Her stomach churned at the thought.

"Maybe talking about it is what you need to do, to take the hurt away."

Caroline stared at him. He was watching her steadily, his fingers entwined with hers. He was bare to the waist, blatantly male with his bristled jaw and heavy muscles and black hair, but neither the sight of him nor the touch of his hand on hers repelled her. On the contrary, she wanted to curl up in his arms and take shelter there, where she knew as well as she knew that the sun would rise in the morning she would be safe forever.

"I have a stake in this too, you know," he said softly, and as the sense of that sank in, her eyes widened. Her heart began a queer, almost painful hammering in her chest.

"You do?"

He gave her a small, ruefully crooked smile. "You don't think I go around kissing every female who throws herself in my path, do you? Tell me, Caroline."

So she told him, though it nigh tore her apart to do so. Told him about her father lying on the pallet before the tiny fire that was all that they could afford although he shivered constantly with the chill, told him about the meager food with which she had tried to rebuild her father's strength, eating as little as possible herself as she had saved the lion's share for him, told him about watching her father die by degrees right before her eyes while knowing herself helpless to save him—and told him, finally, about Simon Denker. Her voice emptied of all emotion as she spoke of that.

After weeks of putting him off she had thought herself finally free when her father died. Despite her grief at his passing, she had been fiercely relieved to know that she need no longer suffer Simon Denker's maulings, which had been growing more and more intimate. She needed only to retrieve Millicent and her own and her father's belongings from the flat and then she would be on her own. The prospect had frightened her, but not nearly as much as Simon Denker did.

He had been waiting for her in the flat, and when he saw that she meant to leave, he threw her down on the floor and forced himself on her. She fought, but her struggles availed her nothing. Quickly, brutally, he had his way with her. Then, smirking, he got up to go, leaving her lying there, exposed and bleeding. To her horror she heard the key turn in the lock. When she banged on the door, screaming at him to let her out, he said that it would take more than that one lifting of her skirts to repay him for weeks of lost rent. He would keep her till he tired of her, and only then would she be free to go.

The flat was a tiny one on the third floor, the one window too small to allow escape. Had she screamed for help until her lungs ached, no one would have come to her aid. Such screams were all too common in that slum neighborhood.

So she had waited behind the door and knocked him unconscious with a chamber pot when he thought to come to her next. Then she grabbed Millicent and her belongings, locked him in the flat, pocketed the key, and fled. A hansom cab had taken her to dockside, where the *Dove* was ready to sail with the morning tide.

When she finished the telling, she was lying beside him in the position into which he silently had coaxed her, her head on his shoulder, her hand on his chest. As she glanced up at him, sore afraid of what she would read in his face, she saw that his jaw was set, his eyes hard. But that grim look was not, she thought, for her.

"So you see why I had to use the brooch," she ended miserably. "I had no money, and he would have come looking for me."

"You did exactly the right thing. Had I known all this, I would have applauded your courage rather than scolding you as I did upon your arrival."

"Courage?" She peeped up at him, surprised out of her grief.

"Aye, courage. Anyone can be overcome by an enemy's superior strength. Look at me, felled by a deuced tree! But instead of allowing yourself to be beaten, you fought back with the best weapons you could muster, and you prevailed. To knock the dastard over the head with a chamber pot was but a small recompense for what he did to you, my poppet, but I can promise you it made him smart for days."

"I hope so!" She drew in a deep, shuddering breath. Then, conscious suddenly of how cozily she lay against him, she sat up and gave him a wavering smile as she struggled to get herself under control again. Her voice was a shade too bright when she next spoke. "I must put some salve on those scratches. And then I really should get started on supper. There are the pies your lady friends brought, but I must give the boys more than that. . . ."

His hand kept its hold on hers, though she tugged discreetly to be free. "Caroline."

She cast a quick glance at him.

"You must not do this to yourself any longer. By allowing that—lame excuse for a man to affect you so, you give him power over you out of all proportion to his importance to your life. What happened to you was a terrible, brutal assault—but it is over. You have to let go of it, so that you can heal."

"But I feel so—unclean." She whispered the confession, ducking her head in shame that refused to be dismissed, eyes closing even as her hand unconsciously tightened around his.

"So you feel unclean, do you?" There was an undertone of harshness to his words that made her open her eyes and look at him in surprise. "Because of something that was done to you, by force, that you had absolutely no way of preventing, *you* feel unclean."

He made a sound that was midway between a laugh and a snort. "If you want to hear about unclean, my poppet, let me tell you about unclean."

27

She looked lovely, sitting there on the edge of his bed, her delicately boned fingers curled with unconscious trust around his. Her raven hair had escaped its pins yet again, to tumble in artless disarray over her shoulders and down her back. The remnant of tears trembled on her lashes and left damp patches on her pale cheeks. Her mouth was soft, vulnerable, her eyes haunted with memories and the shame they provoked. They glittered a luminous gold through the wash of moisture that still lingered in them, unfallen. Her tongue—the tongue that did not taste of raspberries after all but something infinitely darker and sweeter—was just visible between her lips, which had parted in surprise at his words.

Matt had his fury for the man who had dared to harm her under tight rein. Had the dastard been within his reach, he, God-fearing Puritan though he might be, would have strangled the life from him without a second's pause. But the man was not within his reach and probably never would be. All he could do was try to repair the damage he had done to Caroline.

Caroline. Beautiful, dauntless Caroline. The image of her felling her attacker with a chamber pot made him want to shake with laughter and, at the same time, howl with tears. That was so typically Caroline, courageous, spirited, yet vulnerable beneath the flinty skin she assumed for the benefit of the world. Her eyes were defenseless now as she waited for him to speak. Her head was slightly bent on her slender neck, drooping like a flower weighted down after a heavy rain.

He could not change time and undo what had been done to her. He would give nearly all he possessed were that possible, but it was not. He could help her only by laying himself as open to her as she had laid herself to him. He would reach out to her in the only way he could, by sharing the bitter secrets that he had thought never to speak of to a living soul.

"Just what do you remember of Elizabeth?" he asked, after a moment's careful consideration of how to proceed. He did not want to hurt her further by needless revelations about her sister. Yet he thought that it would help her to know.

She blinked at him. "Very little. Although Mary has told me quite a lot."

That surprised him. His eyes narrowed. "Gossiping, was she? I would not have thought it of Mary."

Caroline shook her head. "It was more in the nature of telling me something that I needed to know."

"She told you that Elizabeth was—not perfectly well in her mind?"

"Yes."

"Did she tell you that one of the symptoms of her illness was a—an appetite for men?" This was more awkward than even he had expected. How did one phrase, for gentle feminine ears, a description of how Elizabeth had been?

"Yes."

Where first he had been nettled to think of James's wife gossiping about his private affairs, Matt now had occasion to be grateful. It would make the telling so much easier.

"All right then. I had no inkling that she was not the innocent young girl she seemed to be when I met her. She lived with an aunt in a cottage on land that was—used to be—ours, and if the Civil War had not thrown our family into poverty, Elizabeth would most likely have never crossed my path. So you may blame all that subsequently happened on your good King Charles."

He tossed in the jibe to tease her and was rewarded by a faint smile. But she did not rise further to the bait, and so he continued: "But of necessity we had taken up farming, and one of our fields lay near her dwelling. Nearly every day that we were there, she would come out to watch us work. It never occurred to me, then, that she did so because she had an—unhealthy interest in men. She was older, but I didn't know it then. Besides, I was old for my years myself. She was a pretty thing, very playful and kittenish, and very interested in me. Like a fool, I let her attentions go to my head and—" He paused, searching for the right phrase, and eventually bypassed a description of what he had done in favor of the results. "Eventually she told me she was with child. Again like a fool, I wed her." He smiled faintly, as an errant fragment of memory momentarily alleviated his self-disgust. "I even went to ask your father for her hand, which was how I became acquainted with Marcellus Wetherby. Where you were, I do not know, but I don't recall ever setting eyes on you."

And, he told himself silently, he would have remembered. He couldn't imagine anyone who had ever seen Caroline forgetting her, especially himself.

"When I was younger, I lived with my mother," she replied. "She and my father were married soon after Elizabeth's mother died, but my mother soon grew tired of living flush one minute and hand to mouth the next, and so she returned with me to her own home. Not until she died did my father come and take me away."

He nodded. "That would explain it, then—and also account for why you are so unlike Elizabeth, for which I heartily give thanks to God. But to go on, I soon discovered that the child Elizabeth expected was not mine. She had used me for a dupe to hide her sin."

Caroline's eyes widened. "Do you mean John . . . ?"

Matt shook his head. "John is mine, I am reasonably sure. As is Davey. The timing—and their looks. Although 'tis God's grace merely that she didn't spawn a bevy of bastards. Despite the fact that I kept as close a watch on her as I could, I know there were others. The—she even tried with my own brothers." The remembrance of that tasted bitter even as he said it.

"So Mary said."

"God in heaven, is there anything Mary didn't tell you? And Mary, I suppose, got her information from James. I had no idea the lad was so loose-tongued." Matt's lips tightened in annoyance at having his private affairs bruited about for strangers to hear. Although he was quite sure—at least he thought he was quite sure—that Mary would have revealed so much to Caroline and none other. And Caroline was not precisely a stranger—although Mary could have no way of knowing that. He made a mental note to have a word with James about his habit of confiding intimate family business to his wife.

"But if John is not—what happened to the child?"

"Elizabeth lost it soon after we were wed. I would have thought it mine still had she not confessed the whole, not in penitence, but to taunt me during a fit of anger because I would not do something she wished. She very soon regretted being so frank, but it was too late: I began to recognize her for what she was."

"And what was that?"

He hesitated, then shook his head. "I'll not give a name to it. She was my wife, after all, and the mother of my sons. I thought, when I moved her and my brothers here, that we could start afresh. But she never got better, only worse."

"And for that you feel unclean? I think you behaved very nobly, given the circumstances."

Matt said nothing for a moment as he grappled with a sudden cravenness that was foreign to his nature. She looked so very young and naïve, sitting there with her head tilted slightly to one side, her tears forgotten now as she listened with interest. For a moment he was tempted to keep the rest to himself. He need not reveal his shame—but he realized then that it was important that she know him for the base sinner that he was. When the truth was told, she could not fail to see him as despicable, while she herself, as victim rather than perpetrator of evil, was totally innocent in a way that he decidedly was not.

"You have not heard the worst yet, my poppet," he said softly, and his hand tightened around hers as instinctively he sought the will to continue. Her rose-petal skin was silky beneath his touch, her bones fragile. Her eyes as she waited for him to continue were wide. He dreaded to see the change that would come over them when she knew—yet he wanted her to know. Telling her the truth about himself was the only palliative he had to offer her sick spirit.

"So tell me."

Matt swallowed to combat the sudden dryness of his throat. "I did beget my sons on her, you see. Though I knew her for a whore and a madwoman, though her spirit repelled me as much as her flesh tempted me, I did enter her bed and take my ease with her—and more often than the two times that would have got me my sons. She would mock me for my weakness, flaunting herself, and I could not steel myself to resist. Only when I awakened to find her drunken and laughing at me on the morning after Davey's conception did I afterward succeed in keeping my vow to stay away. And meager though that credit sounds, I cannot claim even that much grace. I admit I stayed away from her because, physically, her body was repulsive to me after that."

Her eyes widened, darkened, flickered during his stark recital, but Matt could not tell what she was thinking. Now he watched her, almost shrinking inside himself, although he hoped he gave no outward sign. It was only when he felt her hand moving in his that he realized how tight his grip on her fingers was: 'twas a wonder he hadn't broken her bones.

"Well?" His voice was harsh, far harsher than he had intended, but she sat there watching him and saying nothing, and he was sore afraid.

At that her eyes flickered again, and her tongue came out to wet her lips.

"Elizabeth was your wife," she said at last. Her hand turned in his to cling to his fingers when he would have released her. "You had every right to use her as you did."

His eyes darkened. "Aye, I know it. Yet the right was legal, not moral. The memory of it sickens me."

"Just as the memory of Simon Denker sickens me."

"Was that his name, the bloody bastard? From tonight onward I'll add to my prayers the devout request that he roast forever in Hell."

The merest hint of a smile touched her lips. "Good Roundhead that you are, you should not use such language."

"I consider myself strongly provoked. And the term is Puritan, if you please."

At that they smiled at each other, and Matt was conscious of a great easing of the weight he had carried about inside him for so long. Caroline didn't seem to despise him for his weakness, and so perhaps he could stop despising himself.

"So now we have no more secrets between us," he said after a moment that he spent idly turning her hand palm up in his and examining the slender fingers.

"No," she agreed, watching him study her hand. After a moment she clenched her fist and withdrew it from his hold. He looked up at her inquiringly as she got to her feet.

"You need salve on those scratches," she said, with a clear intent to return to business. Briskly she turned to the bedside table and started rooting through her store of medicines.

"And how shall I explain them, I wonder, if someone asks?" He was content to let her go. She had opened up to him, cautiously and not yet willing to stay so, and now like a shy flower had perforce to close again for a spell. He could understand that, and saw no need to push her for more than she could at present give.

"You may blame them on Millicent." She turned to him, smiling, and with gentle fingers anointed his cheek with salve. Matt suffered her ministrations, setting himself to endure without allowing his senses to be overwhelmed by the sight and touch and smell of her as she hovered so near. If she were to heal, she needed time to do so. The boil of her shame had been lanced, the poison spilled. With careful handling she could recover fully. In the meantime he must keep his own baseness in check. As much as his body hungered for her, he would make no further move. Not unless and until she showed him that she was ready to welcome such.

She finished with his cheek, restored the tiny pot to the bedside table, and picked up the ruined and rejected piece of pie.

"I must see to supper," she said, and started for the door. Once there, she hesitated, looked back over her shoulder.

"And Matt," she said softly, her cheeks flushing palest rose, "thank you."

For the longest time after she had gone, he could do nothing but stare at the spot where she had been.

28

*S*pring turned into summer, and summer waxed and waned. Caroline grew accustomed to her new place in the world and even found the time to fashion herself some dresses in the sober Puritan style. Though she turned up her nose at their plainness, the simplicity of the garments served to emphasize her beauty, which grew extraordinary as ample food and happiness rounded her figure and pinkened her cheeks. Despite, or perhaps even because of, her questionable status with the elders of the community, she attracted a great deal of notice and turned more than a few masculine heads on the few times she ventured into town unescorted. When Matt or one of the others was with her, of course, none dared to so much as give her an admiring glance. The combined physical might of the Mathiesons was a force to be reckoned with.

Matt's leg healed, though he spent much of the summer hobbling around, first on crutches carved for him by Robert and later with the aid of a stick. He made no further advances toward her, and Caroline was content to have it so. With their exchange of confidences, their affinity for each other deepened. She liked to think that they enjoyed an intimacy, not of the body but of the soul.

Her relationship with his brothers improved, aided tremendously by their devout appreciation of her cooking. Once Matt no longer required constant attendance, she was able to put herself heart and soul into outdoing the culinary efforts of Hannah Forrester. At this she achieved general success, although Goody Forrester's offerings were still accepted by the brethren with great good will. As were Patience Smith's (who had an eye on Robert), Abigail Fulsom's and Joy Hendrick's (who vied for Thomas), and Lissie Peters's (who was after Daniel). Indeed, as the battle for the allegiance of the Mathieson men's stomachs escalated, Caroline got the feeling that the men themselves were growing amused at the competition. They downed whatever delicacies came their way without prejudice or seeming preference, which was galling to the females concerned. As for

Robert and Thomas, being assiduously courted by comely girls at ages twenty-three and twenty-one, respectively, was a novel and clearly not unpleasant experience. Although not completely cured of their misogyny, they appeared willing to suspend disbelief for the nonce.

Daniel, on the other hand, who had never been as thoroughly distrustful of women as his younger brothers, gave Lissie Peters minimal encouragement. It occurred to Caroline more than once that he might be developing a slight tendre for herself, but she refused to entertain the notion seriously. If she did, it might disturb the peace of mind that she had finally achieved, and she refused to let that happen. It was too wonderful to be at ease in her own skin again.

John and Davey, while still slightly wary of her, seemed to take her presence in their household for granted. Certainly they enjoyed having washed, pressed, and mended clothes to wear to school, meals prepared, and a well-kept house and clean linens for their beds. Caroline realized that it made them feel more like the other children who had loving mothers in their homes, and she was glad that she was able to give them that, even if they were not yet ready to accept more tangible gestures of affection from her. But that, she assured herself, would come in the fullness of time, or so she hoped.

On a particularly warm afternoon in early August, when she was engaged in pegging items of the wash out on the grass to bleach in the sun, she was surprised to discover Davey, who along with his schoolmates was enjoying a holiday from studies, huddled behind a large lilac bush that graced the west corner of the yard. His arms were wrapped tight about Millicent—the cat had grown surprisingly tolerant of Davey's small-boy roughness, and the child exhibited an amazing degree of fondness for the cat when there were, as he thought, no eyes to see—and his face was buried in her fur. For a moment Caroline hesitated, unsure whether or not she should question him. Though he tolerated her, she was not Davey's favorite member of the household, and she knew it. But such a posture from the normally cocksure little boy must mean that something was amiss with him. Leaving the rest of the wash unpegged, Caroline approached and then crouched in front of him.

"Davey?"

His shoulders tensed, but he didn't lift his face. "Go 'way!"

"Are you ill?"

No response.

"Did you hurt yourself?"

No response.

"Shall I fetch your pa?"

At that he lifted his head to glare at her. "No!"

Tears stained his cheeks, and cat hairs clung to the wet tracks, but what really caught her eye was his bottom lip. It was puffy and swollen, with a little trickle of dried blood decorating the left corner.

"What happened?" Caroline asked, thinking that he must have been stung, or fallen, or injured himself in any of the dozens of ways particular to small boys.

"Nothin'." He glanced down at Millicent, and made a ferocious face. "Stupid ol' cat!"

He thrust her away from him more roughly than Caroline might have liked, but Millicent did not seem offended. With a glance at Caroline as if to enjoin her sympathy for the small human, she returned to the boy, butting his arm with her head, purring loudly.

"Go 'way!" He pushed at her, glowering at Caroline all the while so that she understood that his rejection was aimed at her and not the cat at all. This time Millicent walked away, waving her tail proudly in the air as if to make it clear that it was her choice to do so.

"Davey, if you won't tell me what happened I don't have any choice but to fetch your pa." She spoke gently.

"I got in a fight." It was a furiously resentful mutter.

"A fight! Why?"

"They was sayin' bad things about my ma. The boys in town, that is."

"What kind of bad things?"

He hesitated, and the damaged lip quivered tellingly. But the need to confide in someone was too strong to resist.

"They said she was a witch."

"A witch!" Caroline caught her breath. A swift survey of Davey's face told her how much he needed her to deny what had been said, and indeed she had no hesitation in doing so.

"What nonsense!" she continued lightly.

He hesitated, and it was clear that he wanted to believe. But he was unable to take comfort from her so easily. "How would you know?" The question was rude.

"I know," Caroline said with conviction. Despite what Mary had told her, she knew that, whatever the truth of the matter was, it was important to convince Davey that his mother was innocent. "Your mother was my sister, and I knew her when I was just a little girl. She used to sing to me, oh, lovely songs."

"Did she?" It was obvious that Davey was fascinated. "Like what?"

Caroline nodded, and then hummed a lilting melody. Whether or not Elizabeth had ever actually sung that particular song to her she didn't know, but then it didn't matter. What mattered was that Davey have a vision of his mother that he could feel proud of.

"What else did she do?" Davey's eyes were bright as he forgot his resentment of her in his excitement.

"She laughed a lot, and told wonderful stories, and always looked beautiful. I was so proud to be seen with her. You would have been too."

But this was clearly the wrong thing to say. His eyes darkened, and he scowled at her. "I would not have. She was ugly, and mean, and she hated me and I hated her! Just like I hate you!"

Before Caroline could answer, he jumped to his feet and ran away. She stood up more slowly, knowing better than to go after him. Despite his rejection in the end, she could only hope that her words had helped him come to terms with his mother in some small way.

Once Matt's leg had healed enough to permit him to get out and about, he had insisted that she accompany the rest of the family to Meeting, and Caroline reluctantly did. After her talk with Davey she made it a point to stop at Elizabeth's grave. As she stood there, reading the simple inscription—ELIZABETH, WIFE OF EPHRAIM MATHIESON, DIED MAY 1682 AGED 33 YEARS—she felt a sense of release as she finally let go of the image she had cherished of her sister over all the intervening years. The woman in the grave, though bound to her by blood, was a stranger and had always been. The remaining Mathiesons had become more her family than Elizabeth had ever been.

Except for its length—there were two four-hour sessions, one in the morning and one in the afternoon with a short break for the midday meal on every single Sabbath, world without end—Meeting had not been as unbearable an ordeal as Caroline had feared it might be. The Reverend Master Miller had directed a few fulminating looks in her direction and preached more than one pointed sermon on the general subject of daughters of Babylon, thieves, and liars, but he had not denounced her from the pulpit. Quite possibly, she considered, Matt's scowling presence in the hard pew beside her deterred him. As far as the rest of the congregation were concerned, some of the ladies, swayed, no doubt, by the continued disapprobation of the dominie and the apothecary, who were both very important men in the town, kept their distance. But there was no general outcry of "witch," as Caroline had half feared after Davey's unfortunate experience, and nearly as many women were surprisingly cordial, which Caroline had little trouble laying at the door of the handsome Mathieson men. The ladies who would be her friends were, almost to a woman, young and single, and she guessed that they thought her the best avenue to the Mathieson of their choice. In the past Matt had discouraged female callers, and anyway it hadn't been quite right for an unwed female to call on a household of bachelor men, but now that there was a woman in the family calls became unexceptional. If Caroline had wished, she could have entertained visitors every day of the week, but she let it be known that she was busy and thus had to contend only with men-hungry women on an occasional basis. Mary was a different story, and Caroline grew genuinely fond of James's wife. And little Hope was an angel. Caroline greatly enjoyed their company, and at least once a week she would visit their house in town or they would come out to while away an hour or so with her.

During the busy summer there had been a house-raising and a wedding, but Meeting was the main form of social intercourse. Now that it was September, however, and the corn was in, there was to be a husking bee at the Smiths'. To her surprise, Caroline found herself looking forward to the simple entertainment, which the entire family was to attend. After supper she made sure the boys were brushed and scrubbed, then went to don a fresh dress herself. The gown she chose was of black grosgrain with a fitted bodice and a wide collar of white lace. As she was a handy needlewoman, the dress was better made than the average gown worn by the community women, and she had allowed herself the small luxury of trimming her sleeves with double rows of black velvet ribbon edged by flourishes of black silk embroidery. The white muslin sleeves of her chemise were allowed to fall into view below the sleeves of her gown, and she wore a semisheer white muslin apron tied about her waist with a huge, crisp bow at her back. The finer materials were salvaged from the dresses she had worn in England, but she had reworked them so cleverly that no one would suspect they were other than new.

Her hair she dressed in a loose knot at the crown of her head. A few tendrils (hurriedly wound around a curling iron in the privacy of her chamber, which artifice she would stoutly deny if asked so as not to be accused of the dreadful sin of vanity) trailed becomingly over her forehead and around her cheeks and nape. Looking into the tiny mirror as she twisted the last of these into place, Caroline had to admit that she was pleased with as much of her image as she could see.

A knock at her door made her thrust the iron guiltily back into the trunk from which she had unearthed it. Though such devices were used as a matter of course by English females, here in this Puritan land such artificial means of enhancing one's appearance were severely frowned on.

Caroline considered the stricture ridiculous and entirely in keeping with the stiff-rumped provincialism of the colony, but she had no intention of arguing the matter. Instead she would use her beauty aid with discretion and enjoy her own curls whereas others could, if they wished, feel righteous about their horsetail-straight hair.

"If you're ready, 'tis time we were off." Matt's deep voice on the other side of the door made her smile.

"I'm ready," she answered, and with another shamefully vain peek at her reflection she went out to join them.

Matt's admiring look was all she needed to justify what was, if indeed it was one at all, only a very small sin.

In honor of the occasion they were to take the buckboard that was generally used for trips to market. As distance went, it was farther to ride than walk—the footpath they commonly followed to the road was too narrow to permit passage of the cart, which necessitated a detour of some half a mile—but the time involved was about the same and they could be sure of arriving at their destination without the mishaps that normally accrued to small boys and their companions. Everyone was already piling into the conveyance as Caroline stepped from the house, the last one to do so, but she was touched to discover that the seat beside the driver—Matt— had been reserved for her, the lone female in the group. They were learning, after all. Wedged against Matt's hard arm, with Daniel planted solidly on her other side, Caroline barely felt the lurching as they headed over the pitted track toward town.

It was growing dark as they neared their destination. Even as Matt pulled up the horse and Daniel helped her down, excited chatter mixed with laughter reached her ears. Behind her, the remaining Mathiesons scrambled to the ground, already heading toward where light spilled through the open door of the Smiths' barn. Inside, awash in the golden glow cast by many lanterns suspended from thick oak beams, a large number of people were already assembled. Two huge piles of cut corn stood in the center of the gathering, and captains were busy choosing their teams. The object of the evening, as Matt had told her beforehand, was to see which team could shuck their pile of corn first. There were tables loaded with maple candy and spice cakes, apple and bayberry pies, and various kinds of meats and nuts. Cider was available in large vats, and a mug was thrust toward each of them, even the children, as their arrival was greeted with shouts on all sides. Friends clamored for their services, and Caroline found herself on one side with Thomas, Robert, and Davey.

Matt, Daniel, and John were on the other side—with Patience Smith and Hannah Forrester.

The sweet scent of hay mingled with the more pungent aroma of the cows and horses that had been removed from their customary lodgings for the night's festivities. Caroline shared a hay-bale seat with Mary, who along with James was also on her team. As she somewhat inexpertly pulled the green leaves and silken tassels from her share of the corn, she listened to the jokes and laughter going on around her with scarcely more than half an ear. Most of her attention was focused on Matt, who was sharing a bale and a chuckle with Hannah Forrester.

Though she was not conscious of it, Caroline's hands slowed and her fingers tearing away the tender silk became more vicious. Matt was smiling at something Hannah was saying to him, his blue eyes alight with amusement and his mouth quirked in a charming smile. The lantern light glinted blue off the black waves of his hair and cast a warm glow over features that were far too handsome even in the starkest daylight. He was in his shirt-sleeves as were most of the men in the face of so much thirsty-making work. The fine white Holland linen that she had fashioned, washed, and pressed with such care showed off the thick muscles of his shoulders and arms and the breadth of his chest to such advantage that Caroline feared Goody Forrester might actually drool from looking at them. His broken leg had healed; except for a slight scar where the bone had protruded, it was as good as new. But his other leg was thrust out straight before him as she had learned that it hurt him to keep the knee bent. In the black breeches and gray stockings that he wore, it was plain to see that he sported a very powerful leg indeed. Hannah Forrester had clearly made note of that.

"Why, Caroline, you've gotten the way of this very well!" Mary's soft voice jerked her attention back to where it should have been in the first place. The pile of shucked corn at her side had increased dramatically, she saw with some surprise and blushed as she realized the cause. But she managed to smile at Mary and rejoin with a light quip. Then she deliberately refrained from looking at Matt again, even when she heard Hannah Forrester's tinkling laugh.

Patience sat with Robert, her pretty face softened into near beauty by a sweet smile. Caroline was pleased to see that Robert was talking with her quite companionably, instead of responding to her with monosyllabic grunts as he would have done even three months ago. Like Matt, and all the other Mathiesons as well, for that matter, Robert wore a shirt and breeches that she, Caroline, had fashioned, and she took a proprietary pleasure in how fine they all looked. Thomas was quite the ladies' man as he divided his attention between Abigail Fulsom and Joy Hendrick, who perched on either side of him, while Daniel, who sat talking to James as they labored, was the object of longing looks from red-haired Lissie Peters. If the two of them were ever to wed, what a bunch of carrottops they were likely to produce, Caroline thought, amused. It was very possible that they would make a match of it, although Daniel seemed to have little idea of it yet. Lissie Peters had struck Caroline as a determined young miss, and Caroline's personal opinion was that Daniel would find himself wedded and bedded within the year. In fact, it was quite likely that the whole crew of them would disperse to their own homes within the next couple of years, and Caroline entertained the thought with some pleasure. She'd grown passingly fond of Robert and Thomas, and truly fond of Daniel, but caring for four grown men and two growing boys was exhausting work. She'd be relieved to pass on a large part of the burden to a gaggle of young wives.

But the logical corollary to that was that Matt would rewed as well. Hannah Forrester seemed quite as determined as Lissie Peters in her pursuit, but the idea of relinquishing her responsibilities for Matt and the boys to Hannah—or, indeed, to any other woman—made Caroline sit bolt upright on the bale, her hands stilling on the ear she held. Why, they were her family! She would not share them! Her eyes shot Matt such a look that had he seen it he would have been sure he had done something that mortally offended her. But he had joined in James's and Daniel's conversation, while Hannah had turned to talk to the woman to her left, and so he did not see the look. Of course, Matt had vowed never to remarry and had given Caroline no reason to doubt his resolution. There was no sense in borrowing trouble where none was likely to appear.

"Look at Hope, trying to climb up James's leg!" Mary said, laughing, and Caroline obediently looked. Hope was more than a year old now, toddling and babbling and as charming a baby as ever there was. Caroline watched, smiling, as James scooped up his black-haired little daughter and sat her on his arm while continuing his conversation with his brothers. Like Matt, James was an exemplary parent. Judging by their ease with their nephews and niece, Caroline thought it likely that Daniel, Robert, and Thomas would all become good fathers as well.

"Lookee there!" A great shout went up. Caroline looked for its cause to find that Daniel, red stealing up his cheeks, was staring down at a half-shucked ear that he held in his hands with an air of befuddlement. The kernels were deep orange rather than the customary pale yellow, and the sight provoked his brothers in particular to great gusts of laughter.

"What's happening?" Caroline whispered to Mary, all at sea.

" 'Tis a red ear! It means that Daniel gets to claim a forfeit from the girl of his choice."

"A forfeit?"

"A kiss, you ninny!" Mary said, laughing, and then they all watched as Daniel raised his eyes from the ear to look slowly around the loose circle of guests.

29

"*G*o on! Go on!" Daniel's face was almost as red as his hair as he got to his feet in response to the urgings of his fellow males. Caroline had to smile at how embarrassed he seemed, and watched with some interest as he stepped into the center of the circle. Whom would he choose? Her gaze moved to Lissie Peters, who had her eyes cast modestly down. Then, to her consternation, she realized that Daniel was coming straight toward *her*.

There was nothing for Caroline to do but sit where she was, blushing painfully, as with heightened color but a determined air as well, Daniel bent and pressed a quick kiss to her cheek. His lips just brushed her skin, warm and firm and not unpleasant, before they were withdrawn. Caroline felt no revulsion at his touch, but her mortification at being singled out in such a way overwhelmed her.

"Hurrah!" Laughter and applause rang out as the deed was done. Daniel, with a quick smile at Caroline, retreated again to the safety of the other side of the circle. For a moment Caroline felt herself the cynosure of all eyes, some laughing, some weighing, and some openly disapproving.

"Why, to think I never noticed! Daniel's sweet on you," Mary marveled at her side. Caroline turned to shush her, but Mary, brown eyes twinkling, would not let the subject pass so lightly.

" 'Tis as well I've grown so fond of you, because it seems as if we might be sisters soon," she teased. Eyes widening at the implication that Daniel might have serious intentions, Caroline frowned Mary into silence. Then, even as her hands reached for another ear and began to work, the better to hide her confusion, she could not forbear seeking Daniel out with her eyes. He was still red-faced as he weathered James's teasing. On Daniel's other side, Matt was not laughing along with the rest. Instead he was talking again to Hannah, seemingly quite composed.

Did the idea of his brother's kissing her really bother Matt so little? Across the floor, Lissie Peters was grim-faced as she yanked at the silken tassels, and the glance she sent Caroline's way was quite poisonous. Not that Caroline blamed her. She would feel poisonous too, if the object of her affection had openly been seen to prefer another.

If Matt had kissed Hannah Forrester, Caroline would be hard put to it not to murder them both!

Because Matt was the one she wanted. With a feeling of inevitability Caroline acknowledged the fact that she should have realized long ago. Her eyes sought him again. The black-hearted wretch was still conversing with Hannah Forrester. Daniel's kiss, which Mary had interpreted as almost as good as a declared intention, had clearly not disturbed him one bit!

Now that she thought about the matter, not during the whole course of the summer had he touched her in any way that was more than acceptably polite, and not by word or deed had he done anything that even the most optimistic female could interpret as an admission of interest. Had the physical attraction she had once clearly held for him died? Or had he, perhaps, decided that he was being led by his male passions down a path he had no real wish to travel, and deliberately pulled back? He'd said he had no intention of wedding again, and to make a mistress of her while she was living in his house and caring for the lot of them was obviously not a wise idea. Not that she would permit herself to become his paramour, of course. But his wife?

Caroline shied away from the question. With great deliberation she set herself to shucking her corn until, while she still had some half dozen ears to go, the other side was declared the winner. Then they ate and drank, and it was time to go home.

As before, she rode between Matt, who drove, and Daniel. The night had grown chilly, and wisps of clouds scuttled beneath a huge, orange-red moon. A harvest moon, someone at the husking bee had called it. The wind had picked up, causing the branches all around and above them to creak and sway. In the distance—Caroline hoped—a lone wolf howled.

The boys, tired into silence, were slumped against their uncles in the back. Robert and Thomas conversed in low voices. Beside her, Matt was still as a stone, his face unreadable as he drove, his arm hard and tense against hers. On her other side, Daniel was equally silent. The lighthearted air that had prevailed during the trip to the husking bee had vanished. Something heavy, though unexpressed, seemed to lie—if not over them all, then at least over the trio in the front seat. Caroline glanced from one to the other of the men beside her, thought of breaking the somber mood by lightly commenting on the evening just past, and then changed her mind. She was not feeling particularly jolly herself, and from the demeanor of her companions they were in no better spirits. Both appeared to have something weighty on their minds.

When they reached the house, Matt pulled up before the door to allow Caroline and the boys to alight. His brothers would accompany him to the barn to help put the buckboard and horse away and finish the chores that still needed doing. Caroline gave a fleeting thought to their working in all their finery, started to protest, and then, with a sigh, did not. She was in no mood to argue with anyone tonight.

The buckboard had barely started to move again before Caroline heard Thomas speak up from the back.

"Are you in *love*, Dan?" he asked in a twitting way.

"With *Car-o-line*?" Robert joined in. Caroline understood that they had merely waited until she was, as they thought, out of earshot before starting in on their brother. They would tease him mercilessly, of course, and she could only thank her lucky stars that she was to be spared.

"Shut up," she heard Daniel respond with more good humor than she herself would have exhibited under the circumstances, and then whatever else might have passed among the four of them was lost to her as the distance between them grew and she shepherded the boys into the house.

"Are you going to marry Uncle Dan?" Davey blurted as she shut the door behind them. He looked appalled.

Caroline turned to look at him, surprised that he had discerned so much when he had been busily engaged with his friends the whole evening. It was amazing how much children picked up when they seemed to be paying not the least attention to what was happening around them.

"No, of course not," she answered, more sharply than she had intended, and shooed them upstairs to bed. Halfway up John turned to glance at her.

" 'Twould be all right with me if you did," he said almost shyly. Looking at him, dressed in his best suit of clothes, which was a miniature of his father's, with his shock of black hair tumbled from the wind and his cheeks ruddily aglow, Caroline felt a surge of warmth. A smile began to curl her lips, only to be frozen in its tracks by Davey, who had already gained the upstairs hallway.

"Well, it wouldn't be all right with me!" he yelled, and then before anything else could be said he darted out of sight along the corridor. Seconds later a reverberating slam announced that he had run to his room.

John shrugged, his shoulders drooping as he continued on up the stairs. Accustomed by now to Davey's adamant opposition to what he felt was any attempt on her part to worm herself too firmly into the family, Caroline watched John go, then took herself off to her own chamber. As she went, she pondered the question: had Daniel's very public kiss been in the nature of a declaration of intent, or had it been no more than an affectionate gesture? Caroline found herself intently hoping that the latter was the case. If not, if Daniel meant to court her in earnest, then she could foresee that her hard-won peace would be subject to a degree of upheaval that she could look forward to with nothing short of dread.

But over the next few days Daniel neither said nor did anything to give credence to the suspicion that he had serious intentions toward Caroline. Indeed, he was out of sorts, as was the rest of the household. Davey and John fought constantly, and the other boys—she would not dignify them by calling them men, so childish was their behavior—bickered. Matt was for the most part silent, scowling at any and all who crossed his path, opening his mouth only to lambaste those unlucky enough to incur his particular disfavor. What ailed them all Caroline couldn't imagine, but whatever it was she heartily hoped that they would either soon die of it or recover forthwith.

" 'Tis not my fault that the blade rusted through, so you needn't behave as though it is!" Thomas growled one night at supper, responding to an implication by Robert that the hoe was ruined by having been negligently left outside.

"Oh, isn't it? Who was using it last, then? You're confounded careless with things, and if you were honest you'd admit it!"

"I don't know what *you're* grumbling about! 'Tisn't *you* who'll have to repair the thing, is it?" asked Daniel, sticking in his oar.

"*You* won't!" Robert retorted, switching his glare to Daniel.

"Why won't I? I always do! Were it not for me, we'd have no tools to work with at all! Both of you are always breaking things, or leaving them out to ruin!"

" 'Tis Thomas, not me, who's deuced careless!" Robert said in defense of himself.

"That's a jest! Ha, ha, I'm laughing!" Thomas scowled at his brother in marked contrast to his words.

" 'Twas Uncle Thom who left the rake out last week. I saw him," Davey piped up.

"Shut your mouth, bantling." Thomas transferred his scowl to Davey.

"I won't! I saw you! I . . ."

"What a slimey little talebearer you are," John said to his brother in disgust.

"I am not a talebearer! 'Tisn't bearing tales to say that! I saw him, and . . ."

"Oh, shut up!" John turned his shoulder in disgust.

"See there!" Robert was triumphant.

"Out of the mouths of babes . . ." Daniel muttered.

"I tell you I did not!" Thomas said defensively.

"For God's sake, hold your blasted tongues! I've heard enough and more from the lot of you!" Matt's roar from the head of the table made even Caroline jump. John and Davey looked scared and dropped their eyes to their plates. Thomas and Robert, their animosity apparently forgotten, exchanged speaking looks and likewise returned their attention to their food. Daniel chewed a mouthful slowly and swallowed. Then he looked at his older brother, his eyes narrowed, his jaw hard.

"Whatever the deuce is bothering you, I wish you'd stop taking it out on the rest of us! We're devilish tired of walking on eggshells around you for fear we'll put a foot wrong and get our heads snapped off for it!"

The silence that greeted that was fraught with tension. Caroline, fork suspended halfway to her mouth, looked wide-eyed from Daniel to Matt. Robert and Thomas seemed equally surprised. Davey goggled at his brave uncle, while John seemed to brace himself for an explosion.

"What did you say?" From the ominous quiet of Matt's words, John seemed in the right of it.

"You heard me." Daniel refused to back down. He met his brother's eyes without flinching. "You've been as tetchy as a bear with a cob up its backside for the last three days. You're making the rest of us suffer, and we're all miserable as a result. If you've got something on your mind, for God's sake spit it out. Or keep it to yourself, if you prefer, but don't take it out on us!"

"You"—Matt's eyes took on a ferocious gleam as they clashed with Daniel's—"can go straight to hell!"

He shoved his chair back from the table, got to his feet, and stalked from the room. The six of them who remained sat in stunned silence until the *thunk!* of the front door being slammed released them. They let out their breaths in a collective sigh.

"I ain't *never* heard Pa swear before!" Davey breathed, clearly awed. Caroline, sitting beside him, patted his knee reassuringly beneath the table. For her pains she received a scowling look, and the limb was moved out of her reach. But of course, what else had she expected?

"Do you think he's sick?" John sounded worried.

"We're men grown. He can't get away with snapping at us and ordering us about whenever it suits him." Thomas recklessly threw in his lot with Daniel.

"But it's not like Matt to be so blasted short-tempered. He never was, not even when"—Robert cast a quick glance at Caroline and the boys—"not even when things were real bad here."

Caroline understood him to be referring to when Elizabeth was alive. She dismissed her chagrin over Davey's continued dislike and frowned thoughtfully.

"Matt's been out of sorts, and that's why you've all been behaving like spoilt children," she deduced, marveling at her own insightfulness.

"Out of sorts!" Thomas snorted. "That's like saying the ocean's a mite wider that the creek!"

"But what do you suppose is bothering him?" Robert frowned.

"I don't know," Daniel answered tautly. "But if he gives me any more of his gaff, I'm going to punch him in his teeth!"

"You can't hit Pa!" Davey and John cried in unison.

"He's just talking," Robert assured them, although he looked at Daniel as if his brother had suddenly grown a second head. Indeed, such a threat was so out of character for Daniel that Caroline blinked at him.

"Someone needs to go talk to him, to find out what's wrong," she said. The adults all looked at each other. The unspoken question that hovered in the air was, who?

"You do it, Caroline," Robert said suddenly. "He doesn't bare his teeth at you."

"You make him sound like a mad dog. He's not *that* bad," Thomas said sotto voce.

"Isn't he?" Daniel returned grimly.

"Me?" Caroline ignored this last low-voiced exchange. The merest germ of a notion had begun to take route in her brain, and try as she would she could not dislodge it. "All right, I will."

Making up her mind suddenly, she got to her feet. She could feel all of them watching her as she left the room in pursuit of Matt.

30

*H*e was in the barn. As soon as she stepped outside, Caroline saw the faint light glowing through the open door. Gathering up her skirts, she headed in that direction, opening and closing the gate behind her and then stepping carefully through the barnyard to avoid any nasty surprises that might lie in her path. As she reached the open door, she caught just a glimpse of Matt seated on an overturned bucket with his lame leg outstretched, face grim as he massaged his scarred knee. Raleigh, who had been lying at Matt's side, spied her and jumped up with a mighty *woof!*

"Hush, Raleigh," Caroline said, annoyed at being announced when she would have watched unnoticed for a minute or two more. Was Matt's leg paining him, and was the pain causing his unusual irritability? At the notion, some of Caroline's confidence fled. He might not be upset over the idea of her and Daniel at all.

"What do you want?" Matt looked up, his expression in no way indicating that he was glad to see her. The moose came rollicking over to her, grabbing the hem of her dress and shaking it as an invitation to play.

"Stop that, you," she said sternly, and pointed the nuisance of an animal outside. When he went, head and tail drooping, she rolled the door shut behind him. At the moment she had no patience to waste on that buffoon of a dog.

When Caroline turned back from shutting the door, it was to find Matt scowling at her. He was still rubbing his knee, but the gesture was almost absentminded, as if his thoughts, focusing elsewhere, had little room for the pain or its easing.

"Shall I do that for you?" she asked, moving across the straw-over-packed-earth floor to his side.

"No." Matt's answer was rude in its brevity, but Caroline paid no attention to it, instead sinking to her knees and taking over from him quite naturally. It was a task she had performed before. When he had started using the crutches, and then the cane, as his leg healed, the extra weight on his lame leg had caused it to cramp with pain. But massaging eased it, and she seemed to have a particular knack. Even as he repulsed her with words, his hands grudgingly moved aside to let her take over the work.

For a moment, unspeaking, she kneaded the knee and the knotted thigh muscles above it much as she would have a loaf of bread. Even through the coarse homespun of his breeches, she could feel the heat of his skin. His thigh was hard and muscular and masculine, and she instinctively registered the feel of it as she worked to bring him ease.

"What do you want?" he asked again, no less hostile than before. As she glanced up from her careful attention to his knee, she saw that he was speaking through his teeth.

"Why, what should I want in the barn at this hour of the night? To talk to you, of course."

"Did they put you up to it?"

Caroline smiled a little, then turned her gaze back to his knee. "Of course. None of them dared face you. Except Daniel, and he was all for punching you in the teeth."

"Was he, by God! I'd like to see him try it!" Matt sounded so bloodthirsty that Caroline's hopes were increased. She looked up at him again, seeing if she could find anything in his face that might give her more encouragement.

"Brothers should not fight," she said, studying him. By the light of the single lantern that was set into a hook in a nearby support beam, he looked tired, tough, and so handsome that he nearly stole her breath.

"Cain and Abel did," Matt answered grimly.

"Yes, and look what came of it! Besides, you and Daniel are ordinarily the best of friends."

Matt grunted. Beneath her hands, Caroline could feel the easing of his thigh muscles, and she shifted her attention lower, to the knee itself and the stockinged calf below it.

"Davey was shocked to hear you send your brother to perdition," she told the knee. Her fingers found the hollows on either side of his kneecap, and she concentrated on massaging them while she waited for what he would say. "He has never heard you speak so before, he said."

"I should not have done that, especially before the children. I'm ashamed of myself, and I'll explain to Davey and apologize for it," he said heavily.

"But you were provoked."

"Aye, I was."

"By Daniel."

"Aye."

Caroline's hands stilled, and she looked up at him. She was kneeling now between his legs, half leaning against his sound thigh as her hands did their work on the other. She did not know it, but the lantern light turned her eyes beneath the silky black slashes of her brows to deepest yellow and emphasized the lovely planes and angles of her face, from her high cheekbones to her softly rounded chin. Her hair, black as midnight, was pulled simply back from a center part into a thick coil at her nape. The plain black and white of her dress might have been dreary on anyone else, but on Caroline it was superb. The fabric molded itself to her curves that were still slender but also round in a most womanly fashion, and the stark coloring echoed the tones of her hair and skin. She looked outrageously beautiful as she glanced up at Matt, and his mouth as well as all his muscles tightened in response.

"Why is that, I wonder?" She felt the stiffening of his thigh under her hands, and moved her fingers against the taut muscle. The wool of his breeches was rough to her touch. Beneath the cloth his leg was smooth and hard.

"What are you asking me, Caroline?" His eyes were hooded as they met hers.

" 'Tis no great mystery, is it? I am merely asking you why, after all these years of harmonious living, your brother should suddenly provoke you past all bearing?" If the words and tone were innocent, her intent was not. Her fingers smoothed the cloth, stroked up his thigh and then down again.

"Why? You want to know why?" His words were almost fierce. Without warning, his hands moved to cover and still hers, flattening them against his thigh. The size and strength of his hands as they rested over her own much smaller ones sent a flicker of heat racing along her spine. Arrested, she savored the sensation and the quickening in her loins that accompanied it. After months of cultivating a somnolent peace, it was surprising to find herself being jolted into quivering life again.

He started to say more, hesitated, and scowled at her.

"If 'tis your intention to wed Daniel, then you have no business being out here with me. I suggest you get up from there and hustle yourself back inside."

"I'm most fond of Daniel," Caroline replied with a pensive air. Her heart leaped at the sudden blue blaze that her admission caused to flare to life in his eyes.

"Are you indeed?" He bit off the words.

"And I believe he is fond of me as well. But he has not asked to wed me."

"He will."

"If he does, then I shall just have to—refuse." She smiled a little, and turned her hands so that her fingers sought and intertwined with his. " 'Tis not Daniel I have an eye to."

"Isn't it?"

"No." Emboldened by what she thought she saw in his gaze, she freed her hands and rose up on her knees so that her face was on a level with his. Her hands rested on his wide shoulders, while his, automatically, she thought, sought and found the slenderness of her waist. His eyes glittered into hers, restless and very blue.

" 'Tis you," she continued softly.

At that his eyes narrowed, while his hands tightened on her waist. Something that was far too intense to be termed a smile twisted his mouth, was gone.

"Are you making me a declaration, by any chance?" Underneath the deliberate lightness with which he tried to imbue the words, there was a wary note.

The heat that shimmered to life between them made speech increasingly difficult, but Caroline forced the words past her tight throat.

"And if I am?" she asked, her breath catching and holding as she waited, waited for his reply.

"I take leave to warn you that you are living dangerously." He was still striving for lightness, but his eyes, deep blue and hungry, said far more than his words.

"Indeed?" Uttering more than the single word was beyond her. Her hands shifted of their own accord along his shoulders, savoring the feel of the thick muscles through the shirt she had made. "And just what does that mean, pray?"

Matt looked at her for a long moment without answering, his face dark and his eyes restless. Then he laughed, a short, harsh sound that had nothing of amusement in it. "What does that mean, my poppet? Are you sure you want to know? But I'm going to tell you, since you've asked, whether you want to hear it or not. It means that you've been a raging fever in my blood for months. I can't think, I can't work, I lie awake nights going mad with wanting you. Is that enough to send you flying back to the house, or do you want to hear more?"

Caroline said nothing, but she made not the slightest move that might indicate incipient flight. Her eyes locked with his, and her breathing stopped.

"I burn for you." His voice was low and rough. "My flesh aches and throbs in a constant torment that must surely rival the tortures of hell. I can conceive of no surcease but that of easing myself in your flesh—yet I would not hurt you, or frighten you. So run away now, while you've still the chance. Or I warn you, you may sorely regret the outcome of this night's work."

"I am not afraid of you, Matt." It was the merest whisper, and not quite true. While she was not afraid of the man, she was afraid of the voracious passion that he held on so fragile a leash. She was afraid of what might happen when the quivering taut string that held him like that which strung a bow snapped.

"Are you not?" His eyes, dark with need yet blazing too, moved to her lips. "Then kiss me, Caroline."

It was a ragged taunt. Caroline's breath caught in her throat, and for a moment she hesitated. But he was hers for the asking now, she knew. She needed only to lean close and meet his challenge. Her eyes never left his face as she swayed toward him, sliding her arms around his neck. Her gaze was as intense as though she would commit his image to memory for now and forever. Only as their mouths touched did her lids flicker shut.

His lips were warm and surprisingly soft beneath hers. For just a moment he remained motionless, letting her feel the heat that arose from the simple meeting of their mouths. Then his hands shifted, sliding around her waist, and he pulled her close.

"Oh, Matt!"

She breathed his name even as she was crushed against his chest and he opened his lips over hers. His hand was on the back of her head, tilting it and positioning her mouth for his taking. Her lips had parted instinctively; his tongue slid inside, filling the warm wet cavity, claiming and taming it. The last time he had kissed her thus, he had gotten so far and no further before she had panicked. But this time, because he was Matt and she loved him, she forced from her mind the images of the past that rushed forth and concentrated instead on him: on Matt.

"You taste so sweet."

He was still holding himself back, withdrawing from the deep melding of their mouths as he pressed rousing little kisses to her lips, murmuring to her, gentling her so that she would not take fright. Caroline felt him reining himself in, and the knowledge that he cared enough for her to do so melted the last of the barriers that she had erected between them. In a sudden glorious burst of loving generosity she tightened her arms around his neck, pressed her body to his, and slid her tongue between his teeth. She would give herself to him, anything he wanted without restraint, because she loved him. He was more to her than the whole world.

"Caroline." He pulled back, sounding as if he were drowning. His breathing was uneven, his face flushed. She could feel the struggle he was having to hang on to his control. "If you kiss me like that again, I'm likely to lose my head."

"I want you to lose your head," she whispered against his mouth and, tilting her chin, fitted her lips to his again. This time, when her tongue touched his, he gasped. Then he gave her no quarter but crushed her closer, his mouth slanting over hers, his heart slamming against her breasts.

Even as he kissed her with hungry need he half rolled, half fell off the bucket, taking her down with him to the floor where he wrapped his arms around her and slid his legs over hers and let her feel the whole long hard length of him against her body. She tightened her arms around him and shut her eyes and held him close, not protesting when his trembling fingers found and fondled her breasts even though the ghastly memories were once again fighting to surface. But she held them at bay by repeating to herself, over and over, "This is Matt." Even when his hands slid down her legs to jerk at her skirt, she did not try to stop him, but clung to him as he yanked her dress and petticoat up around her waist and fumbled at his own breeches until his buttons popped with his urgency.

When he parted her stocking-clad legs with his knee she gritted her teeth. When he found the part of her that had been hurt before and that he would hurt again she sank her nails in his shoulders in grim acquiescence. When he pushed himself inside her, stretching her and filling her until she thought she must burst, she trembled with the horror that broke over her in waves as she could no longer hold it at bay. Yet still she held him, eyes shut, teeth clenched, and uttered not so much as a single sound of protest as, with hoarse sounds of ecstasy, he thrust himself inside her again and again.

Against her bare backside she felt the prickle of straw and cold earth. Over her and in her was the hard strength of groaning, heaving man. Her hands clutched his back, bunching his shirt in her fists, and her toes curled in her shoes as she resisted with every scrap of willpower she possessed the urge to fight what he was doing to her. He was Matt, her Matt, and she loved him. By this act he made her his. Clinging to that thought, she endured.

When he finished, with a great cry and a thrust so deep that she whimpered before she could stop herself at the ferocity of it, she held him as he collapsed shuddering atop her. She held him and stroked his hair and tried not to think of his body still wedged inside hers, or her soreness, or his seminakedness, or hers. Such thoughts would bring on shudders of disgust, she knew. Instead, as her hands smoothed over his shoulders and caressed his back, she concentrated on the certainty that she had pleased him enormously with her gift. As she had thought it would, that notion made the violation of her body far easier to bear.

Until, at last, he raised himself on his elbows so that he could stare down into her face. Looking up at him with a loving smile, she was stunned by the harshness she saw there.

"Damn you!" He gritted the words out even as his body tensed atop hers. "Why the hell didn't you stop me?"

31

"Why—why should I have stopped you?" Her eyes were huge with confusion and shock as they met his. He was clearly angry, his bright blue gaze narrowed and hard, his mouth set in an uncompromising line. Before tonight she had never heard him use such deliberate profanity, but he was suddenly making up with a vengeance for his normal temperateness. Even his body with its rigid muscles emanated hostility. Though why, when she had practically sundered herself in two to give him the dearest gift she had to give, he should be angry with her was beyond her ken.

"Because for all your sweet little seduction, you weren't a bit more ready for a man's loving than a twelve-year-old virgin!"

"But—that's because—you know." She was stuttering in her surprise.

"Yes, I know." Bitterly mimicking her tone, he surged to his feet. His face was red with temper as he adjusted his breeches without the slightest bit of modesty. Glaring at her all the while, he continued, "I've wanted to lift your skirts ever since I first laid eyes on you, sitting on your delicious little rump in the dirt with your gown half torn off and your hair tumbling over your shoulders, looking so mad you could spit. When you lay in my bed and I kissed you, do you know how hard it was for me to let you go? No, of course you don't. You don't have any idea. But let you go I did. And why? Because I had a fondness for you, Caroline, and you clearly needed to be cherished and kept safe. Trust was there between us, and trust is something I value far too highly to allow it to be tarnished by my lust. Before I took you to bed—if ever I did—I wanted to give you time, and a chance to heal. And by God, I did my part. I've kept my hands off you, haven't I? I've earned my spot in heaven with all the effort it took! But now—how the devil do you suppose we're going to be able to go back to what we had? We can't, because I'm going to go mad with wanting you, and yet knowing that if I take you you'll be sick with revulsion all the while I'm slobbering and panting away! Do you think I'm such a swine as to take a woman who doesn't want me? Especially a woman I have a care for?"

"But—but . . ." Words failed her. Never in her wildest imagining had she suspected that her selflessness would lead to such a denouement. His reasoning was beyond her at the moment, though she had clearly heard him say he had a care for her. That alone would have been enough to make her happy if he hadn't looked so fiercely angry.

Decent now, he was thrusting the ends of his shirt back inside his breeches. She bethought herself of how she must look, naked from her waist to the middle of her thighs where her white cotton stockings began, her legs wantonly sprawled, her skirt twisted about her middle. The sable triangle of her womanhood stood out starkly against her pale skin, and even the small indention of her navel was clearly visible to his view. Face crimsoning, Caroline thrust her skirt down and scrambled to her feet.

"I did want you to—do what you did. It's just that—I—I can't help it if I don't like it when it happens! Oh, Matt, can't you just accept the fact that I made you a gift, and be happy about it?"

"Be happy about it!" For a moment she thought he would punch the nearest wall. His face mottled with passion, and he clenched his teeth. "I neither need nor want any human sacrifices, thank you very much!"

"It wasn't like that!" she protested, almost wailing, but he was already stalking toward the door, running his fingers viciously through his disordered hair as he went. Clearly he did not mean to stay and discuss the matter further.

"Matt!"

Ignoring her, he yanked the door to one side, his temper and strength combining to make it slide as though its runners were greased. Then he stopped dead as he came face to face with Daniel outside.

Daniel stopped too, and for a pregnant moment the two merely stared at each other. Matt's back was to Caroline, but even so she could see the menacing stiffening of his body. Daniel, facing her, was still largely enveloped by shadows despite the pool of light that spilled out through the barn door, but she could sense the tension in him too.

"What do you want?" Matt growled, his big body planted so as to block both Daniel's access to and view of the interior of the barn. Daniel made as if to step around him, but Matt held him off with an answering move of his own.

"Where's Caroline?"

Matt laughed, the sound ugly. "Caroline is no concern of yours."

"She's as much my concern as yours! Where is she? She . . ." Daniel's voice trailed off as, over Matt's shoulder, he found Caroline with his eyes. She had hurried in pursuit of Matt, only to stop some paces behind him as he confronted Daniel. Now she moved so that Daniel could see her, and urgently shook her head at him. But Daniel, his eyes widening, was not pacified. Though Caroline didn't realize it, with her hair fallen from its knot to tumble over her shoulders, her lips rosy and swollen from Matt's mouth, and the pale skin of her cheeks reddened from his sandpaper jaw, she was the very picture of a woman who had just been, at the very least, thoroughly kissed.

"You—bastard!" Daniel said to his brother on an incredulous note. And then, without any warning at all that Caroline could see, he punched Matt in the face.

The blow resounded throughout the barn. Jacob, who had his own spacious stall at the rear, snorted in alarm, his gigantic body thumping against the wood. A cow penned nearer the door mooed loudly as Matt stumbled backward and then measured his length on the floor with a loud thud.

"Matt!" Caroline shrieked, running to Matt's aid as he sat up, a hand to his eye. She clutched his arm, crouching at his side and glaring up at Daniel with the ferocity of a lioness defending her cub. "You've hurt him! What were you thinking about? He's your brother!"

"You stay out of this," Matt growled at her, pushing her away and seeming to shake himself. Then he was coming up off the floor in a fast lunge, tackling his brother and staggering with him out into the barnyard. They fought furiously, trading blows and kicks and curses, both big, strong men and lethally furious. Matt was an inch or so the taller and the more muscular by a discernible degree, but he was hampered slightly by his lame leg and so the contest was more or less even. Darting behind them as they circled, grappling, the shadowy, shifting darkness obstructing much of her view, Caroline was reminded of nothing so much as a pair of dancing bears.

"Stop it! Matt! Daniel! Do you hear me? Stop it!"

Caroline grabbed at Matt's arm, only to be shoved back out of the way. At the same time, Matt, distracted, took another blow to the face. The splat of Daniel's fist connecting with Matt's jaw made Caroline cringe. Matt grunted, jerking his head back. Daniel followed with a blow to Matt's midsection, which, fortunately, Matt managed to avoid by twisting to one side. With a roar Matt planted a toe in Daniel's middle. Then, as his brother doubled up with a gasp, Matt followed with a bone-crunching punch to the face. This time it was Daniel who measured his length on the ground.

"Please stop! Please!"

But she might as well have kept silent, for all the good her cries did. Daniel flung himself at Matt again. Caroline, jumping from one foot to the other as she watched helplessly, remembered the bucket in the barn and ran to fetch it just as Daniel managed to lock his arm around Matt's neck. On the way back, she detoured just long enough to fill it with icy water from the trough. Then she stood beside them—'twas Matt who had Daniel in a headlock now—and sloshed the contents of the bucket impartially over them both.

"What the devil . . . !" They parted, gasping and spluttering at the freezing deluge. Both men rewarded her interference with identical glares. In the shifting moonlight, despite the differences in their coloring and height, they looked enough alike at that moment to be twins. Once the source of the intervention was identified, their eyes swiveled from Caroline to fasten on each other. Then, with identical snarls, they were at it again.

This time Caroline didn't even hesitate. She threw the bucket down on the ground, clenched her fists, and stormed toward the house. If the blasted fools wanted to kill each other, then she could only hope that they would succeed!

Once inside, she stalked into the kitchen, glared at the quartet who occupied themselves in various fashions around the room, and started gathering the trenchers from the table with a good deal more clatter that the task deserved.

Four pairs of eyes looked up at her with interest as she entered, and as they took in her disheveled state, heightened color, and obvious temper, at least two pairs of them widened with curiosity.

"Well?" Thomas finally said when Caroline, clanging utensils, seemed determined not to speak.

"Two fools are beating each other to death in the barnyard," she threw at him over her shoulder, speaking through gritted teeth. "And I, for one, don't care to watch!"

"What!"

After an appalled instant the four of them were on their feet rushing for the door. But what happened after that, Caroline didn't know, because she, tired of every single man who ever walked the earth, took herself off to bed.

Where she tossed and turned and fumed, and slept not so much as a single wink the whole night through.

32

*T*he atmosphere around the breakfast table the next morning was heavy as a thundercloud. Davey and John, apparently never having seen their father fight with one of their uncles before, were awed into unaccustomed noiselessness. They shoveled their corn mush and molasses down without so much as a peep and scooted off to school with only quick, scared glances for the adults they left behind. Robert and Thomas, after exchanging pregnant looks and attempting one or two conversational gambits that went unanswered, gave it up and concentrated on downing their food. Matt and Daniel ate with matching black frowns while Caroline slapped food into trenchers and trenchers onto the table in stony silence.

Matt sported a grotesquely swollen black eye, from, she thought, Daniel's first punch, and one corner of his mouth was cut and presumably sore. This she discerned by the way he winced as he ate and probed at the hurt area with his tongue. Daniel's nose was red and enlarged, and there was a massive dark bruise on the left side of his jaw. At first glance he appeared to have gotten the better of the battle. But he grimaced with every movement, and even sitting seemed to cause discomfort, so Caroline couldn't say for sure. In any case, she didn't feel the least sorry for either one of them. In her august opinion, it was a pity they had not beaten each other senseless!

Actually, she was quite glad to find herself so angry at the pair of them. It kept at bay the shame she would otherwise have been feeling over her disastrous attempt at lovemaking. It was Matt for whom she reserved her choicest fury, for taking an act that had been one of unselfish giving and twisting it out of all recognition, and then fighting with his brother over her, which was perfectly ridiculous. But she was angry at Daniel too, for hitting Matt and for acting as if she had betrayed him, Daniel, in some way. As if they had an understanding or something, which they most emphatically did not!

And she was angry at Robert and Thomas because they were Mathiesons, and men, and quite astute enough to have figured out the cause of their brothers' quarrel for themselves. Those two had been shooting the three principals speculative looks ever since they had all four thumped downstairs to discover Caroline banging pots in the kitchen, but so far neither of them had had the nerve to come right out and ask the cause of so much familial ill will.

Matt finally shoved his chair back from the table, his food only half eaten. For the first time in Caroline's memory, something had actually interfered with a Mathieson's appetite, but whether it was bruised emotions or a sore lip she wouldn't venture a guess. Robert and Thomas followed suit, but Daniel stayed where he was.

"You coming, Dan?" Robert paused on the way out the door to ask.

Daniel shook his head. "I'll be along in a minute. First I have something to say to Caroline."

This was accompanied by a challenging look at Matt, who had started around the table toward Caroline before being halted by his brother's words. Robert and Thomas both stopped what they were doing to stare at Daniel, while Matt turned to meet Daniel's gaze with an expression that did not fall far short of menacing.

" 'Tis I who have something to say to Caroline. And as I require privacy in which to say it, you can take yourself off." Matt's tone was deceptively quiet, but his glittering eyes belied it. As far as Caroline knew, it was the first word that either brother had addressed to the other since their fight. Though she wondered what Matt might have to say to her, she told herself stoutly that she was in no mood to hear it. Both he and Daniel had behaved like buffoons the night before, and if either of them had aught to say to her, they could just wait until she felt like listening! And when the words came, they had best be an abject apology!

"The devil I will," Daniel answered, abruptly standing up. His chair skittered back on two legs and was saved from crashing to the floor only by the fact that it smacked into the wall first.

"Oh, you will." Matt was coldly positive.

"Not on your say-so!" Daniel sounded as if he was spoiling for a fight.

They bristled with mutual animosity while Robert and Thomas, sensing another incipient battle, moved to grasp Daniel and Matt, each by an arm. Daniel suffered Robert's hold, merely ignoring him, but Matt shook Thomas off, though the younger brother still hovered watchfully close.

"Caroline has nothing to say to you." Matt spoke through his teeth.

"That's for her to say, not you. She's not your property."

Matt smiled then, a mere baring of his teeth. "Isn't she, little brother?"

"Wait just a minute!" Caroline, who'd listened to this exchange with growing outrage, slapped an empty trencher down on the sideboard. All four men started, as if they had forgotten she was there, and immediately switched their attention to her. She glowered from Matt to Daniel almost impartially, although there might have been just a dollop of extra venom in the look she gave Matt, who, in her opinion, was the more deserving of it.

"I don't care if you quarrel. I don't care if you fight. I don't care if you pound each other into matching bloody pulps, but you will not do it in my kitchen! Get out!" Her voice rose as she spoke, and by the time she finished she was shouting at them. When they continued to stand there gaping at her with as much surprise as though the wall had spoken, she snatched up her broom and waved it at them threateningly.

"Caroline . . ." Daniel began heavily. Matt shot him a murderous look, and opened his mouth to reply.

"Out! Out!" Caroline forestalled him, coming around the table with the broom. Thomas and Robert, eyes widening, beat a hasty retreat out the door. When Daniel, who was nearer to the line of fire than Matt, ignored her in favor of bristling at Matt, she brought the broom down across his shoulders with a *whack!* Daniel yelped, jumping sideways, which coincidentally brought him nearer the door.

"Hey!"

"Out!"

"But . . . !"

"Out!"

She swung at him again, just missing as he ducked, though the breeze caused by the motion ruffled his hair. Arms raised, spluttering protests, Daniel hastily backed away, stumbling over the threshold in his haste to get out the door. Caroline turned her attention to Matt, who stood his ground, eyeing her narrowly, while Daniel was routed.

"Get out of this house!" She hefted the broom.

"It's my confounded house and . . ."

Whack!

"Oww!"

Matt grabbed at the broom and missed as Caroline jerked it back. She knew that if he got hold of it, he could easily wrest it from her, and the contest would be ended in a moment. The idea of matching her strength with his was laughable. But she would not give him the satisfaction of seeing her back down, not when she was still so furious at him that she would gladly have carved him up for fish bait. Instead, raising the broom as a bludgeon, she raced at him with a cry that for sheer volume Jacob could not have bettered.

"I said, get out!"

As she ran toward him, screeching, she pounded the broom down on table and walls and chairs, in fact on nearly everything in her path, giving a wonderful imitation of a woman driven berserk by a man's idiocy. Matt fell back before her, hands lifted to ward her off, the surprise on his face almost comical, had she been in a mood to laugh, which she was not. She managed to plant one more lusty clout on the side of his arm that drove him, yelping, out the door. That done, she slammed the door and secured the latch before he could recoup himself enough to charge back inside.

Folding her arms over her chest, she glared at the door, satisfied. She stepped a couple of paces to the left, and with a martial air stood regarding her vanquished foes through the window.

Thomas and Robert flanked Daniel a little distance away. Daniel was saying something, and they were frowning as they listened. Raleigh frisked about their heels, delighted at this new game. Matt was closer, rubbing his arm where she had hit him and scowling at the closed door. For a moment she thought that he would forget his dignity enough to pound on it, demanding to be let in, and she almost relished the idea of daring him to break it down, because unlock it she would not! But he apparently thought the better of engaging her in battle before an audience of his brothers, with a day's work waiting to be done. After a moment in which the issue hung in the balance, he turned and strode away without a word to anyone. The other three, with Thomas and Robert exchanging looks and Daniel moving grudgingly, slowly followed.

With a grim smile Caroline left the window to get on with her own day. Though a small, woefully undisciplined part of her mind wondered what it was Matt had wanted to say to her—some tender sentiment, perhaps, or an apology for his sheer wrongheaded boorishness?—the rest of her was still too angry to care. The more she thought about the way he had behaved, both in his utterly uncalled-for anger over a gesture that had required considerable courage on her part, and his bristling-dog attitude toward Daniel, the madder she became. Fuming, she made a meal of the men's leavings—she was getting very tired of dining on leftovers!—poured Millicent her usual saucer of milk, and tidied the kitchen. She was just hanging the broom on its peg when she happened to glance again at the window.

A face was pressed to the glass, nose flattened so that the features appeared grotesque. The apparition was there for only an instant before it disappeared, more quickly even than Caroline could scream. But the skin had been the color of clay, smeared with stripes of yellow and red, and the hair had been black and lank. The savage! His appearance drove both Matt and her anger from her mind. With a shudder, Caroline backed away, thankful that she had latched the rear door, which was usually left open. But the front . . .

Whirling, she snatched the musket that stood in a corner of the kitchen by day while she was home alone and hurried toward the front room. The thing was kept loaded and primed. Matt had shown her how to put it to her shoulder, ease back the hammer, and pull the trigger to make it fire. But even in the direst emergency she had envisioned using it only to summon the men home, and she was not sure that she could shoot it at another human being, not even a savage. Although perhaps she could, if her back was to the wall.

A man was in the front room. With the corner of her eye Caroline caught a glimpse of him lurking in a shadow, and, gasping, spun to face him fully. To her chagrin, before she could even think to shoot fright caused the musket to drop with a clatter from her suddenly nerveless fingers. As the man leaped nimbly out of range of the probable blast, she screamed loudly enough to wake the dead.

"By Gideon, Caroline, 'tis only me!" It was Daniel. Her shriek made him jump again, his eyes flying to her face from where they had been fixed on the fallen musket, which fortunately had not discharged. Heart pounding, Caroline lowered her hands from her mouth and glared at him, as much because he had given her such a fright as because she was still angry with him, though she most certainly was.

"What are you doing here?" she demanded wrathfully, still collecting her wits, as he had well nigh scared her out of them. "But never mind that for the present! A savage was peeping in the kitchen window!"

"A savage!" Daniel looked astounded. "You must be mistaken!"

"I am not," Caroline said, "mistaken! Pray go and see for yourself!"

Daniel started toward the kitchen. Caroline picked up the musket and hurried after him.

"There's no one here," Daniel said, standing in the center of the kitchen floor and peering at the window and all around.

"He was outside looking in," she said through gritted teeth, thrusting the musket into his hand and shoving him toward the door. With a grimace that told her without words that he thought she had windmills in her head, Daniel crossed to the door, unlatched it, and stepped outside. Millicent, meowing, twined herself about his ankles.

"Move, cat. If there was a savage here, he's gone now." Daniel spoke with more unconcern than Caroline felt the matter warranted, and stepped back inside the door.

"There was a savage," Caroline insisted. Daniel lifted a hand pacifically.

"I'm sure there was. But he's gone, and Matt was right when he said they're generally harmless—and I have something of a very particular nature to say to you."

Her attention thus diverted, Caroline pushed the savage to the back of her mind and frowned at Daniel.

"I, on the other hand, have nothing to say to you." She turned her back on him and marched into the front room, determined to keep moving forever if that was what it took to escape the inquisition she feared was coming.

"Caroline, stop!" Lengthening his stride, Daniel caught up with her, grabbed her arm, and pulled her about. Angrily she slapped at his hand. He released her but planted himself squarely in front of her with the air of one determined to block her escape.

"I told you . . . !"

"Confound it, woman, I'm trying to make you an offer!" That exasperated roar sounded so like Matt that Caroline was momentarily shocked into silence.

"An offer?" she repeated when she could speak again, not sure that she had heard correctly. After last night, she had not expected this.

"You heard me." Daniel lowered his voice, but his expression was no less grim. "I want you to marry me."

He reached out, caught her hands, and held them. Caroline was too surprised to resist.

"Daniel . . ."

"Don't say no," he said rapidly. "I know—I'd have to be a blind fool not to—that there's something between you and my brother. 'Twas obvious last night. Before you get too deeply involved with him I want to offer you a choice. You'd do well to wed me, Caroline. I will treat you with all respect and . . ."

"Daniel." She tried to stop him, but he rushed on, regardless.

"You need not think that we must needs live here, once we are wed. I have a respectable sum put by, and we could buy our own place. 'Twas always understood that each of us would, when we wed."

"Daniel!"

This time she got through. He broke off to look at her inquiringly. Caroline shook her head at him.

"You do me too much honor," she said softly, looking up into his grave face, which bore definite signs of his recent war with Matt. Caroline felt a welling of affection for him, her first friend among the disreputable tribe, and it quite overcame her aggravation at him. "But I cannot be your wife, although I am very fond of you. We should not suit."

"You love him." The words grated, accused.

Caroline lifted her chin. "Whether I do or not is my own concern. I will not talk of this more."

Daniel stared down at her, his expression bleak. "I would still wed you. He will not, you know."

"You don't love me, Daniel. And, though I care for you as a—oh, as a brother—I do not love you. Not as I would need to, to be your wife." She finally succeeded in freeing her hands. Unobtrusively she flexed the fingers, which felt bruised from the strength of his grip.

"As you do Matt." Bitterness tinged the statement.

"That," Caroline said with a frosty glint rising to her eye, "is between him and me."

"I told him, this morning, that I meant to ask you to wed me."

"And what did he say?" The question was commendably steady, though Daniel had taken her by surprise.

"He told me to go ahead. Not what I would have said, were I he and had I wished to wed you myself."

"I told you, what is between Matt and me is between Matt and me. But you may believe me when I tell you that it has no bearing on my decision. Even if Matt did not exist anywhere in this world, my answer to you would still be the same."

Her words were perhaps sharper than she had intended, but the idea of Matt's giving Daniel permission to propose cut deep. He might at least have rushed to get his own offer in ahead of his brother's—but he had not. Though Matt had admitting to having a care for her—such a tepid term, it nigh turned her stomach!—he had said nothing of marriage, and it was by no means a sure thing that he ever would.

"You are firm in your refusal, then. Very well, I will not press you." Scowling, Daniel turned abruptly away. But instead of leaving, as Caroline expected, he moved toward the stairs, which he took two at a time.

"Where are you going?" she called after him, nonplussed.

"To pack a bag. Feeling as I do about you—and Matt—'twill be best if I move into town for the nonce. I can stay with James. Mary won't mind having me, I think."

"But . . ." Caroline's voice trailed off as Daniel disappeared from view.

Moments later he was back, carrying a valise with hastily shoved-in garments sticking out at all angles. He picked up the conversation where they had left off as he came down the stairs.

" 'Tis best, I tell you. Otherwise, Matt and I will be forever coming to blows. Because I—love you, Caroline, despite what you say. And I'll not find it easy to watch you making a fool of yourself over my brother."

And with that parting shot Daniel took himself out the door.

33

Somehow the men must have learned of Daniel's defection, and told John and Davey as well, because not a word was said that night at supper about the empty place at table. Now that her temper was cooling, Caroline's heart gave a little twinge every time she glanced at Matt, hoping—hoping —what? That he would apologize? Not likely! Whatever he had meant to say to her earlier he had apparently thought better of, because he was almost totally silent. His black scowls cast enough of a damper over the family so that, immediately after supper was over and their schoolwork done, the boys went to bed and Robert and Thomas retired to smoke out of doors.

Left alone with Matt, who ignored her as he scratched at some figures in a place he had cleared with his arm at the table, Caroline decided to abandon both him and the bucketful of dirty trenchers. She turned her back on Matt—who, if appearances were any indication, didn't even notice —picked up Millicent, went into her chamber, and shut the door very definitely behind her.

But it was earlier than her usual time to retire, and she was not about to let Matt Mathieson force her into lying sleepless in her bed when she had no wish to do so! Instead she decided to turn out her trunks, which were still lined up against the wall opposite the bed where they had been ever since she moved into the keeping room. From the time of her arrival she had been so busy caring for the men that she'd had little time to give to her own needs. Now she would pass a pleasant hour going through the relics of her past, and if the trenchers congealed in the meantime, then that was just too bad! If Matt wanted clean eating utensils, then he could just wash them himself.

As Millicent curled up, purring, in the center of the bed, Caroline settled herself on the wide plank floor, her movements cautious because of the slight soreness that lingered between her thighs. Although she had scrubbed away every lingering trace of him, even washing the gown she had worn the night before and pegging it out to dry, she could not erase the tenderness that reminded her of what had occurred every time she made an unwary move. While no longer technically virgin, her body was as unused to such experiences as a new bride's. His taking had left its mark on her body as surely as his anger afterward had marked her heart. Would she ever understand men? Caroline wondered with a fresh burst of fury. Then, deliberately, she banished the entire incomprehensible sex, and most particularly Matt, from her mind.

One trunk held what was left of her English dresses, the ones in the vivid shades that she had no use for here and had stored away when she turned herself into a Puritan. Which she had done purely to please Matt, as she knew she would admit if she were being honest with herself and permitting herself to think of him, neither of which she was, at the moment. A notion occurred to her and she gave the trunk a thoughtful eye— perhaps she could revert to her previous style of dressing just to irk him. There he was again, devil take him! Couldn't she keep him out of her mind? But she reminded herself that such behavior would be childish and undignified and would provoke comment among all those who saw her. Her quarrel was with Matt, drat him, alone, and she would keep it as private as she could. Already too many—if one counted four brothers, for she was sure Daniel would soon, if he had not already, confide in James, who would then certainly tell his wife—knew too much about a matter that concerned no one but the two most nearly involved!

Deliberately she shifted her attention to the second trunk, which contained what was left of her medicines, several books, and her personal papers. Nothing much of interest there, and she turned away from it in short order. She was left with the third trunk. It held her father's possessions and a few of his old clothes.

Caroline knelt beside this last for a long time before she found the courage to open the lid. The scent that assailed her as soon as she did so brought back her father as vividly as if he stood before her, his lean frame immaculately dressed as always, his black head cocked to one side, his tawny eyes alight with amusement as they had been during almost every phase of his life. Even as he lay dying he'd been able to laugh. It was she, caring for him, who had lost her capacity for joy. As the memories, some sweet, some bitter, flooded back, Caroline flinched as if from a blow and closed her eyes. It was a long time before she opened them again and with a tentative finger touched the lapel of the uppermost coat.

It was of rich bottle-green satin—no sober crow's plumage for Marcellus Wetherby—and her father had worn it often when he sat down to an evening of gaming. He had liked for Caroline to wear her peacock-blue silk when she accompanied him while he had on the coat—she possessed the gown yet—and had been smug about how well they looked together, dressed in this fashion. He'd wager what money they had—if they had any —or his lucky brooch if they had none (fortunately, as Elizabeth had told Matt, he almost always won) and they would stay at an inn of the highest caliber when he was flush, or of lower grade when he was not, but always there had been grand schemes and visions of a more prosperous tomorrow.

Her father had been a great one for generating grand schemes and visions. Caroline smiled sadly, remembering the number of times he promised to give her the world on a plate. The promises were empty, of course, but he believed them when he made them, and before she came to know him just that little bit too well, Caroline believed them too.

He was vastly unlike Matt. Her father had been mercurial, gay, determined to live for the moment. The only truly good thing she knew of him was that after her mother's death, he had come for her and kept her with him, never leaving her behind as, what with his nature, it had surely occurred to him to do. Of course, her looks had made her an asset to a man in his profession, but he had loved her in his fashion. In the years before his death they'd grown close. The ache of missing him came on her sharply now, as she had never let it do before.

Matt, on the other hand, was as solid and dependable as New England granite. For all his faults—and she would be the first to enumerate them, and call them many—he was the rock to which his family, and she herself, clung. In times of sorrow or trouble he would be a bulwark. For all his testiness, the man was as gentle as he was strong.

How could she love, so greatly, two such very disparate men?

Near the bottom of the trunk, tucked deep into a corner, a gleam of ruby red caught the candlelight and her eye. Her father's lucky brooch. Caroline drew it out and held it in her hand. It was a pretty thing, even to one who knew it for a fake, the vivid colors bright and twinkling and ready to fool the unwary. It had been her father's talisman—and the instrument that had brought her to Matt.

Her hand closed over it with convulsive tightness. As it did so, she almost seemed to see her father shimmering elusively just beyond the pool of candlelight; she almost thought she heard his voice bidding her to be happy. The illusion vanished even as she stared at it, of course, but the sweet hurt of it lingered and she shut her lids against the pain. Hot tears welled into her eyes, overflowing at the corners. But with the tears also came a sense of release.

All these months after his death, she was finally allowing herself to grieve for her father and let him go. Perhaps, soon, she could let go of the rest of her past, too, and put behind her the bitter memories that lay like a dark cloud over her new life.

At that moment the door to her room opened with no warning at all. Caroline's lids flew up, and she stared in affront at Matt, who stood on the threshold, one hand on the jamb and the other on the open door. So he had told Daniel to go ahead and make her an offer, had he? On top of everything else he had done, that was the proverbial straw that threatened to break the camel's back. Hoping that the small circle of candlelight was not enough to reveal the tears that his intrusion froze on her cheeks, she glared at him ferociously. He was scarcely more than a large, dark shadow himself, as the only illumination behind him appeared to be the minimal glow of the banked kitchen fire. His eyes glittered at her, bright blue even in the gloom, and his very stance told her that his purpose in entering was not to apologize.

"I told you when I first arrived that I expected to be treated with respect, did I not? Barging into my room without so much as the courtesy of knocking is scarcely my idea of respect." She spoke first, her tone icy.

"As this is my house, I scarcely consider myself to have barged in. In fact, I'll enter any room I like, anytime I like."

"You'll not enter my chamber without permission."

"Will I not? And how will you keep me from it, pray?"

"I will leave this house, if necessary." This was pure bravado, uttered on the spur of the moment. Of course she had not the slightest intention of leaving, and if he had been thinking rationally he must have known it. But apparently at the moment his thought processes were no clearer than hers.

"And just how will you do that? You are penniless, if I recall." His eyes lighted on the brooch she still held in her hand. "If you have any idea of using that piece of junk to trick some poor fool into helping you run away from here, I'd advise you to put it from your mind. Until your debt to me is paid in full, I'll seek you out wherever you go."

This growling speech banished Caroline's tears and brought her surging to her feet. She had dressed for bed as soon as she'd entered her chamber, and she wore not even her wrapper, only her white lawn nightdress, with her hair hanging over one shoulder in a thick braid tied at the end with a blue ribbon. Her feet were bare, and her breasts moved freely beneath the fabric that was thin enough to reveal just the barest hint of the dark circles surrounding her nipples and the triangular shadow at the apex of her thighs. Matt's eyes moved over her, narrowing even as the gleam in them grew almost savage. His mouth set into a hard, straight line.

"Get out of my room!" Her voice was low but raging. Her hand closed so tightly over the brooch that it cut into her fingers.

"Did you hear what I said? 'Twill avail you nothing to try to run away."

"Get out of my room or I'll scream!"

"Will you now?" But the threat of rousing his sons and brothers was a telling one, Caroline knew. Matt would be loath to make them—especially the children—privy to their private war. The only difficulty, she realized, was that she was equally reluctant to reveal so much and would be hard put to it to scream, knowing they were all so close.

"I will."

Her gaze met his with a hard brightness to match his own. Her chin was up, her stance belligerent. Matt might bully everyone else in the household, but he was not going to bully her!

"You were not so eager to be rid of me last night." There was a mocking undertone to his words that brought hot color rushing to her cheeks. How dare he remind her of that! She was suddenly fiercely glad that Daniel had blackened Matt's eye for him. Had he not, she would have been tempted to try to do so herself!

"Last night I had no notion what a complete jackass you are!"

His jaw tightened, and his nostrils flared, but if she succeeded in angering him, that was the only sign of it he gave.

"Your gentility is slipping, I believe," he said in a drawling tone that affected her temper like flame to a fuse. Her teeth clamped together, her spine stiffened, and her eyes shot golden bullets of fire at him.

"Get out of here," she hissed at him. When still he stood there unmoving, the very curl of his lips taunting her to be rid of him if she could, she drew back her arm and hurled the object around which her fingers curled —the brooch—at him as hard as she could. It should have hit him in the face, but at the last second he sprang aside, one hand shooting up to catch it in midair. He was inside her room now, making it seem ridiculously tiny as it was already crowded with her small bed and belongings, the washstand, and the kitchen supplies that were kept in there for lack of another place to put them. Caroline was reminded of how very big he was. He turned the brooch over in his hand, holding it between his thumb and forefinger and examining it with an expression of cold distaste. As the candlelight filtered through the faux gems, the spread tail of the peacock glowed with jewel colors: bright ruby red and sapphire blue and emerald green.

"What trash," Matt said between his teeth. Before Caroline had the slightest inkling of what he meant to do, he dropped it on the floor and ground it beneath his heel. The crunching sound that ensued reverberated through the air with the power of a gunshot.

"No! Don't!" Caroline rushed toward him, shoving him aside, but the damage had already been done. The dainty thing had proved itself no more than glass, and it lay crushed in colored shards with only a portion of the peacock's head still intact. Caroline stared down at it, feeling a hideous lump rise in her throat. Dropping to her knees, she gathered up what was left, cupping the jagged bits and pieces in her hands.

"I'll never forgive you for this," she said on a deep, throbbing note. Lifting her head, she fixed him with a look of glittering hate. His eyes were unreadable as they met hers, but a tiny muscle jumped once at the corner of his mouth.

"I'm sorry," he said, and she laughed, the sound bitter.

He opened his mouth as if to say more, and then, abruptly, he shut it again. Lips compressed, fists clenched at his sides, he turned on his heel and left her alone.

34

*T*he next day was market day. Caroline arose, prepared breakfast—though had it not been for Davey and John, she could have been boiled in oil before she cooked a thing—and got five Mathiesons out of the house without uttering more than a very few necessary words. And these she addressed to the boys. To Robert and Thomas she said nothing, because they were Matt's brothers, and to Matt she absolutely refused to speak. Like her, he was ominously silent. The animosity that lay between the pair of them was so blatant as to be almost tangible, and it was with an air of pardoned souls escaping purgatory that the innocent parties fled the house. Following his brothers out the door, Matt paused on the threshold and turned his head as if he wanted to say something to her. But apparently one look at her face was enough to dissuade him. Wisely, he went off to do his work without putting the degree of her rage to the test.

'Twas Indian summer now, and it was hot. All through the morning, as she did the chores that had to be done before she could go to town, Caroline was conscious of the heat. By the time she dropped the men's luncheon off in the west field—she literally dropped it, after a halloo to let Robert and Thomas know that she was there—she was of two minds whether or not to forgo the weekly trip to market. But the prospect of a visit with Mary was pleasant—although doubtless the other woman would be agog to know the details of what was going on between her and Daniel and Matt—and anyway she was restless. So Caroline put her basket over her arm, picked up the musket that she always carried with her outside the house since seeing the savage at the window, and set forth to Saybrook.

Squealing pigs were being herded along the road toward her as Caroline walked along. She surmised that they had been purchased by their herders —two youths and an older man who could have been their father—at market. Smiling a greeting at them, she carefully skirted the jostling animals, who stirred up so much dust that she coughed and choked, waving her hand in a vain attempt to dissipate it. A few minutes later the postrider galloped past, a thin youth on a sturdy spotted pony. He left a trail of dust in his wake too. Caroline found herself engulfed by a swirling golden cloud and resigned herself to it. There would be no surcease from dust on such a hot, dry day.

Grit seemed to have been shaken over her like powdered sugar over a cake by the time she reached town, and Caroline brushed her hands over her hair and shook her heavy skirts vigorously before she stopped at James's house. Mary greeted her with a cup of tea and a knowing smile, and before Caroline knew it she found herself seated at the kitchen table opposite her friend answering questions.

"Daniel actually proposed marriage? And you turned him down? And he came to us over that?" Mary sounded incredulous as she sipped her tea. In the corner Hope played with a cloth poppet that Mary had made for her, and both women sent her fond glances from time to time.

"Is that not what he told you?" Caroline parried, though without much hope. Mary was as inquisitive as a sparrow, and Caroline had little doubt that her friend would get the whole—no, not the whole, but something close to it—story out of her before she was permitted to leave her house.

"Daniel hasn't told me anything, though he may have said something to James. He no sooner showed up on my doorstep than James was asked by the selectmen to fetch a physician back from New London—you did know that the constable's wife and three others are down with a terrible sickness? No? Well, they are, and it is widely believed that Mr. Williams's very commendable skills are not sufficient in this case—and Daniel offered to go with him. I had not even time to question James, though I was dying to ask him how Daniel came by the bruises on his face." Mary paused, eyeing Caroline expectantly. When Caroline looked down at her teacup, and over at Hope, and then everywhere but at her friend, Mary snorted. The indelicate sound, coming from proper Mary, made Caroline look swiftly up. From the triumph on Mary's face, she deduced that that was precisely what the sound had been intended to do.

"Oh, all right." Sighing, Caroline gave in. "Daniel had a—disagreement —with Matt."

"A disagreement?" Mary's eyes widened. "Do you mean a fight? Over you?"

Glumly Caroline nodded.

"But how wonderful!" Mary exclaimed, grinning.

"How can you say that?"

"It does sound dreadful, does it not?" Mary chuckled. "But my dearest wish has been to see Matt happily married. He's had such a bad time, and he is such a dear man. James loves him, and so do I. He deserves some happiness after all he's been through. And you—you're perfect for him! I wonder that I did not see it before! But I kept thinking of you for Daniel, and that quite blinded me to other possibilities."

"Matt has said nothing of marriage."

"My dear, if he has come to blows with his brother—they're very close, the five of them—then he can mean nothing less. If he is hesitating at the moment, it is probably because he is feeling confused. Men are not nearly as clear-sighted about these things as we women are."

That notion was comforting, and Caroline allowed herself to be cheered up. After Mary had pried every bit of information she could from her guest—though Caroline kept Matt's lovemaking to herself—she at last was willing to let Caroline leave for long enough to get her shopping done. Though only on the condition that Caroline stop back by for another comfortable chat on her way out of town. She had to anyway, to get the musket that she left in a corner of the kitchen as there was no need for such protection in town, so Caroline readily agreed, though by this time she had little time to spare.

"I just knew we would be sisters, even if I was picturing you with the wrong brother," Mary said in parting, and she bestowed a quick hug on Caroline. Smiling, Caroline hugged her back, and though she thought Mary was assuming rather a lot about Matt's intentions, she was still smiling as she waved good-bye and stepped into the street.

On market day the usually peaceful common was transformed. Enveloped in a shimmering haze of heat, merchants bargained with farmers over produce and livestock displayed in carts and makeshift pens, peddlers hawked scissors and steel-bladed knives and the like, enterprising townspeople stood behind stands they had set up offering cold meat pies and mugs of cider, and even a couple of buckskin-clad Indians wandered through, offering to trade a string of pelts for various goods. A group of boys in leather aprons—apprentices, Caroline thought—sat in the shade of a spreading elm and made jocular comments as she passed. She ignored them and ignored too the dominie and his deacons, who were very much in evidence as they moved about, trying by their sobering presence to bring order to the sweating multitudes. Mr. Miller gave her a hard look as she passed him, but when Caroline boldly looked back he pretended not to see. Blue-coated bond servants mingled with the townspeople, doing the marketing for their masters. It occurred to Caroline that she could have been one of their number had it not been for Matt, but the notion so disgruntled her that she refused to entertain it further.

At that time of day the market, which had emptied for the midday meal, was filling up again with shoppers who had waited to take advantage of late-day prices. Caroline waved to Hannah Forrester and Patience Smith as she saw them at a distance, and waved again to Lissie Peters's father Simon. The town exciseman, he was paunchy and balding with no more than a memory of Lissie's red hair. To her surprise, he turned his shoulder to her and went on about his business without responding by so much as a twitch to her wave.

Apparently word had not gotten around that Daniel had offered and been rejected. If it had, Mr. Peters, with Lissie's hopes in mind, would likely have fallen at her feet.

Caroline was smiling sourly as she bargained for fresh cod to join the brace of ducks that she planned to save for later in the week. She added the fish to her purchases and decided to leave the rest of her marketing for the following week. It was so unseasonably warm that heat was rising from the ground in waves. Fanning herself with her apron in a vain attempt to feel cooler, she left the common, retracing her path down High Street.

On her way back to James's she passed the schoolhouse, a squat white building with all its windows open to combat the heat. From inside came the chant of children at their lessons. Caroline smiled faintly as she recognized the patter that Davey had practiced at home a few nights previously.

"Young Obadias, David, Josias—all were pious."

"Zaccheus, he—did climb the tree—our Lord to see."

Such joyless lessons, she thought as she had when she had first heard them, but then, most things in this Puritan land were joyless. While there were a few residents who did not follow the Roundhead ways, most did, and the ones who did not were frowned upon. The mere mention of King Charles was enough to provoke a hiss or a cascade of spittle from the most upstanding citizens. Caroline found it hard to understand how such fervently God-fearing folks could so openly thumb their noses at the divine right of their king, but they could and did. She had come to realize that they considered themselves God's chosen people, and any who did not either fall into line with what they believed or get out of the way could expect to be trampled upon.

Shouts from behind her caused her to turn her head. Exuberant scholars bounded down the schoolhouse steps for, she guessed, an afternoon recess granted because of the heat. The schoolmaster followed and stood on the steps squinting in the direction of the town square. He was not only in his shirt-sleeves but had them pushed up almost to the elbow. Bony and stooped, he appeared both hot and harassed as his attention shifted to his charges. Small boys looked much alike at such a distance, but Caroline thought she could distinguish Davey's and John's ink-black heads among the mob galloping around the schoolyard. Had she been sure of her reception, she would have turned back to speak to them.

She had gone no more than six strides farther along the road when she was stopped in her tracks by a quavering scream.

"Mad dog! Mad dog!" The cry sounded even as she whirled about to find children and adults alike scattering like leaves in a high wind in the face of a threat she could not see.

"Mad dog!" The warning came again. Grown men and women with children snatched up under their arms bolted in the face of the threat. Schoolchildren tore down the road toward Caroline. John the fleet-footed was at the head of the pack, she saw, and near the rear pounded little Davey with his schoolmates. Stark terror was on the faces of the littlest ones, and copybooks and primers were being thrown to the winds.

"John! Davey!" Instinctively Caroline shrieked their names. Dropping her basket, she started to run toward them. But already John and his followers were veering sharply to the left, out of the path of what chased them. Only Davey, hearing her cry, came on, heading straight toward her, his legs and arms pumping, his face reddened, his eyes wide with terror.

"Aunt Caroline!" he screamed, and then Caroline saw what was behind him.

It was a dog, surely not as much as half Raleigh's size—although its condition made it seem as huge as Jacob—a stocky, sleek-haired black mongrel with wild eyes and slavering jaws. Foam flecked its muzzle and dribbled in strings from its open mouth. It was some five yards behind Davey, closing fast.

Caroline reacted from purest instinct. She raced toward Davey, whose small legs were no match for the creature behind him, caught him up against her, and with his arms tight around her neck and his legs wrapping her waist fled with him to the nearest place to offer safety, a small beech tree left to grow in the corner of a yard. Boosting the child high into the branches, Caroline realized that she had no time to climb up herself, even if the tree could have held her, and she could have climbed it in her cumbersome skirts. She could hear the beast's labored panting almost on her heels.

Whirling, she flattened herself against the slender base of the tree as there was no time to seek other shelter. Terror awoke and raced along her spine as she beheld, at a distance of no more than a yard, the wide-open jaws studded with savage-looking teeth and pouring death-bringing saliva.

Too frightened even to scream, Caroline held out both hands in a vain attempt to ward the dog off—and then, to her shocked relief, the animal raced right past her.

Her knees gave out, and she sank, boneless, to sit trembling beneath the tree.

"Aunt Caroline! Aunt Caroline!"

Davey scrambled down from the tree, John pounded up from the stoop where he had huddled, and both boys dropped to their knees beside her, their faces white as they ascertained that she was unhurt. As naturally as she breathed, Caroline wrapped her arms around them, held them close, one on each side. They suffered themselves to be hugged, and even—she thought—hugged her in return. For a long moment the three of them clung together as the aftermath of terror shook them. In the distance she heard the sound of a shot and a bellow that announced that the dog had been killed. Over the boys' black heads she looked up to meet the cold stare of the dominie as he hurried with a rush of others to view the carcass. He said nothing to her but walked swiftly on, his robe raising a trail of dust behind it as he passed.

"You saved Davey's life." John straightened first, his eyes awed as he looked at her.

"I was so scared!" Davey still nestled close, and Caroline, greatly daring, stroked his silky hair. He did not pull away, nor did John frown at her for the familiarity, and Caroline realized that the last barrier that had held them from her had finally been breeched.

"I had no notion I could run so fast," Caroline confessed, and suddenly the three of them were grinning at each other like boozy fools.

"You threw me up in the tree like I was a feather!" said Davey.

"And that dog came at you like he was going to tear you limb from limb!" said John.

"I thought you was done for, Aunt Caroline," said Davey again.

"I did too, I must admit," Caroline responded. She hugged Davey, patted John's shoulder, and permitted them to help her to her feet as if she were a doddering little old lady, which was exactly how she felt. They were tenderly solicitous of her as they escorted her back to where she had dropped her basket. The cod had spilled into the street and was ruined, from dust and trampling, but no harm had come to anything else. Then they were summoned by their schoolmaster. Caroline waved them off, assuring them that she would be fine, and tottered to Mary's house where she all but collapsed on the kitchen floor. It was some time, many exclamations, and two mugs of strong tea later before Caroline felt restored enough to set out again.

The sun was low in the western sky, a hazy, reddish ball that bathed the landscape in an orange glow. The merest suspicion of a breeze blew in from the bay, which was flecked with small whitecaps and the color of tarnished silver. Even the water looked hot. For the first time, Caroline turned down the footpath that led to the forest with something akin to pleasure. 'Twould be cool in the depths of the trees.

Still jumpy from her fright with the dog, Caroline held the musket close beneath her right arm. The basket, heavy with the weight of her purchases, hung from her other hand. Dust motes danced through the air in front of her as she moved. Overhead, the leafy canopy was transformed by deep stains of scarlet and gold. Underfoot, leaves already fallen rustled.

Strange markings carved into the trunk of a tree near the path caught Caroline's eye. She paused, stepped closer, and looked at the meaningless symbols that had obviously been fashioned with such care. They almost appeared to be writing—but if they were, she could not decipher so much as a letter.

Frowning, she stepped back onto the path—and almost immediately someone or something leaped on her back. She screeched, staggered, dropped musket and basket—and went down as more creatures joined the first. After that first scream, a horrible-tasting rag was thrust into her mouth, and she ascertained that her attackers were at least human. Her hands were pulled behind her back and bound, and then she was yanked to her feet.

To her horror, Caroline discovered that her captors were a band of savages. Naked and painted, with naught but breechcloths and moccasins covering bodies that, from the look and smell of them, had been liberally smeared with bear grease, they were six strong.

Even as Caroline recognized, or thought she recognized, the particular hawklike features of the savage who had appeared to her both times before, she was being hustled through the forest, leaving the path behind.

35

"*P*a! Pa! You should've seen what happened today in town!"

His boys greeted him with excited yells as they burst through the front door. Matt, who had been prowling the house and surrounding area looking for Caroline to apologize to as he had meant to do the previous morning before Daniel forestalled him, listened to their prattle with half an ear at first. 'Twas not until they had nearly finished that Matt took in the ramifications of their tale, and recognized that his direst fear might have been realized after all: Caroline might have left home. Last night, when he heard her going through her trunks through the thin walls, he feared that she was planning to leave. When he opened the door to find that thrice-damned brooch in her hand, and her in that tantalizing nightdress that drove him almost out of his mind, his fear had crystallized into something hard and hurting. 'Twould be a long time before he forgave himself for crushing an object so precious to her, although he had already set the wheels in motion to make what amends he could. It would be even longer still, he feared, before she forgave him.

As his sons told of their encounter with the rabid dog, and recounted with enthusiasm how Caroline saved Davey's life, one fact at least became abundantly clear: she had gone to town, and she had not come back.

He had been home himself for some quarter of an hour, stopping work earlier than usual because of a completely irresistible impulse to make amends with Caroline. He had behaved inexcusably over the brooch, and he knew it. He had also not handled the aftermath of their lovemaking as well as he might have. He had hurt her while feeling the most exquisite pleasure himself, and the knowledge had made him feel like the lowest worm alive.

Would he never be able to rise above the demon of lust that had plagued him all of his adult life? In his right mind, he would sooner cut off a hand than cause hurt to Caroline.

But his lust had been all the greater because he cared for her. Even as he had taken her, tenderness had combined with desire to ignite him to a pitch far hotter than he'd ever been.

Then Daniel had thrust his oar in to muddy the waters even more. He did not like to admit to feeling such raging jealousy for a brother he dearly loved.

The worst of it was, he knew full well that Caroline would be better off with Daniel. He would come to her unscarred in both body and spirit, able to accept her love and return it with no shadows of the past to fall over their life together.

While he—he was no more, and no less, than life had made him.

But he meant to have Caroline, if he had to crawl on his hands and knees over sharp rocks to get to her—or knock his brother down again.

The boys were hungry, and he hurriedly got out bread, cheese, jam, and milk for them before heading out the door. If she had left those two to fend for themselves, then she must be very angry with him indeed.

Perhaps she did not intend to come back. The thought brought with it gut-wrenching pain. To hell with that, he told himself savagely, and fair knocked Rob and Thom down as they came in the rear door.

"Where are you going?" Astonished, they fell back before him.

"To fetch Caroline home," he snarled. "Stay with the boys."

They gaped at him, but before they could question or comment, he was gone.

With quick, angry strides he headed for the path through the woods. She would be at James's house, of course.

It required some doing for him to rap at James's door and inquire of Mary whether Caroline was within, because it occurred to him that someone, either Caroline herself or Daniel or James, had almost certainly told Mary at least a part of what had happened, and he hated her knowing so intimate a thing of him. But if her smile held a trace of teasing, and her eyes a touch of humor as she assured him that no, indeed, Caroline wasn't within, the sense of her message quickly banished his embarrassment and her enjoyment of it.

Since Caroline was not with Mary, and was not at home, then where was she?

Mary, almost as worried now as he, assured him that Caroline had left for home—yes, Mary was sure that was where she was heading—some hours before. And no, she couldn't have run off with Daniel (Matt had hated to broach the possibility, but he hadn't been able to keep it from taking possession of his mind) because Daniel had gone with James to New London the day before.

As that last rage-provoking notion was removed, stark terror struck at Matt's soul. He knew, better than most, the dangers that lurked in the woods. His first thought was of witches, but the coven met only in the darkest hours of the night and at certain phases of the moon. Caroline had disappeared in daylight, it seemed, so she couldn't have fallen into the hands of those who had tried to claim her sister for their own.

Begging a lantern from Mary, Matt headed back to search the road from town and the path through the forest. As he went, holding the lantern high, forced to move with maddening slowness so that he wouldn't miss what might be the smallest sign, he bethought himself of all the other things that could have happened to her.

She could have fallen and be lying unconscious somewhere. Perhaps he had passed right by her in his rush to get to town. She could have encountered a trapper, and the half-civilized brute could have borne her away to the Lord knew where. A mountain lion could have stalked her, a wolf could have made her its prey. . . .

But in the end, when he discovered the abandoned basket and musket, left where they had fallen by the side of the path not far into the woods, unmistakable signs pointed to a fate that had not even occurred to him.

Caroline had been stolen away by a band of Indians! Cold fear settled like a stone in his heart, and Matt set off at a dead run for home, praying for her safety as he went.

36

*A*ll night and all the next day Caroline found herself pushed, prodded, and dragged as she was forced to keep pace with her captors' seemingly tireless trot. They paused only briefly to eat, and not at all to sleep, conversing from time to time in what, to Caroline, were unintelligible sounds. When she stumbled for what must have been the dozenth time and they apparently realized that it was her long skirts that were making her so clumsy, they slashed her gown off at the knee. Sheer terror gripped Caroline as the blade hacked through the gray cotton skirt and white petticoat beneath. Visions of rape and murder danced hideously through her brain. But the knife never touched her flesh, and, savages though they were, they seemed to have little interest in her as a woman. With her legs bared from the knee down save for her white cotton stockings, they pulled the gag from her mouth, shoved a peculiar-tasting bread in her face, and held it, impatiently, while she ate. Then they gave her water from an oily-looking deerskin pouch, regagged her, and prodded her off again, following the course of the Connecticut River as it rolled away from the sea.

The river was wide and beautiful, with high grassy banks and a swift blue current in the middle. The forest crowded to the very edge of the banks. Beneath the trees the heat was a mere memory. The air was not merely cool, but turning cold.

Flagging badly but afraid that if she collapsed, as her body threatened to do, they would slay her and leave her cooling corpse as food for the wolves, Caroline gritted her teeth, forced all thought from her mind, and set herself to matching as best she could their curiously silent gait. When at last the little band stopped, toward sunset of the day following her capture, Caroline sank to her knees with relief. Were she to have no sleep this night either, she would not be able to go on in the morn. And then what would happen to her? She shuddered to think.

Trilling birdcalls whistled back and forth through the trees. It took Caroline a few minutes to realize that the nearest of these emerged from the leader's leathery throat. An answer, from somewhere no very great distance away, caused one of the braves to pull her to her feet and push her, stumbling, in the direction of the sound.

Like an army regiment escorting a prisoner, her captors closed ranks around her, and in this fashion they emerged through the trees into an Indian camp.

It was situated in a lush, well-guarded valley, at the side of a small deep-blue lake, though the term pond would have fit as well. Perhaps two dozen huts, unkempt pyramids of sticks and straw as scraggly as hayricks, composed the main of the village. Numerous small campfires dotted the enclave, while in its center a larger fire blazed. Squaws in shapeless, ragged garments turned from their cooking, incuriously, to eye the approach of the small band. Children and dogs watched with a degree more interest, a few of the former ceasing their play to gather round and a few of the latter bracing themselves to bark a greeting.

Caroline was taken through the camp to the center fire. There a quartet of old men squatted, passing a feathered pipe back and forth among them. They looked up, their eyes as black as their coarse hair, as the newcomers stopped on the other side of the fire. The blade-faced leader walked forward, while one of the four men, the one who looked the oldest, rose, and the two exchanged greetings. Then the leader, who was tall, muscular, and, Caroline thought, fairly young, gestured, and another brave pulled her forward to shove her in front of the blanket-wrapped old man.

His skin was the color of red mahogany, his eyes, set in a nest of wrinkles, dark, liquid, and intelligent. For the rest, he perhaps just topped the warrior's shoulder, and he seemed paunchy beneath the blanket. His nose was broad, his mouth no more than a slash in a face that was square and pitted and fearsome. Caroline felt a spurt of renewed fright as she realized that this was the chief and that her fate most likely rested in his hands.

He gestured. The gag was removed, and her hands were unbound. Caroline rubbed her wrists, ran her tongue along her dry lips, and waited for what would happen next.

The old man looked her up and down.

"You wise woman?" he asked. His English was guttural in tone, but understandable.

Caroline blinked. Whatever she had expected, it was not to be addressed, perfectly rationally, in her own tongue. She opened her mouth to deny it, thought better of it, and nodded once. Almost holding her breath, she waited to discover if her answer to his question was the one he wanted.

"Good. It is as we have heard from our brothers who visit the white man's village to trade. They told us that you held the Great Spirit of Death back from your man with your medicine. We have sickness here. You come."

He turned, heading toward one of the huts. A shove in the small of her back left Caroline in no doubt that she was to follow.

As she ducked to enter, the odor of illness inside the hut almost made her recoil. A small fire burned in the center of the hut, its smoke rising to the sky through a tiny hole in the peaked roof, but also filling the interior with eye-stinging haze. Refuse cluttered the earth floor. A young woman crouching beside a pallet turned to stare at them as they approached. On the pallet another young woman lay inert, swathed in blankets to her chin. It was clear from first glance that the supine young woman was very ill.

"This fever has killed six so far in our tribe. Our medicine does not help. Finally we think, it is white man's illness. We need white man's medicine. You will help my daughter."

Suddenly the reason for Caroline's presence became clear. Relief made her light-headed for a second as she realized that they meant her no harm. As she looked down at the unconscious maiden, it occurred to her that she might not be able to do anything to help the chief's daughter. If that were the case, if the girl died, would she then be killed?

"I will try," Caroline replied cautiously, and knelt beside the girl. The other young woman moved aside to make room. The victim's skin, when Caroline touched it lightly, was burning and dry. She seemed to have no awareness of anything at all.

"How long has she been like this?" Caroline asked the old man over her shoulder.

"Two days since. The others have all died in three."

The kneeling girl said something to the old man, who translated for Caroline's benefit.

"She has vomited, and has passed much waste matter that looks like rice water. My other daughter, Ninaran, says that her sister Pinochet is gravely ill."

"I will do what I can," Caroline promised.

For the next few hours, with the help of Ninaran, she labored to force liquids into the stricken girl. The Indians had few medicines that she recognized, but she did the best she could, and she thought that there was some slight improvement. Finally, when the fever rose so high that Caroline feared that it alone might kill Pinochet, she, with the help of Ninaran and two other women of the tribe, wrapped the girl in soaking blankets, just as she had done with Matt. And finally, as dawn streaked the sky, there was no doubt that the girl was better. Caroline thought, and said, that she would with careful nursing recover. What she kept to herself was the suspicion that no intervention of hers had turned the tide. God had selected this one to live, or the girl's own body had refused to recognize its destined fate. Because, in the hours before the fever broke, all Caroline's healing skills had told her that Pinochet would die.

So tired that she could scarcely focus, Caroline was at last led away to a pallet and allowed to sleep. When she awoke, it was to find the day well advanced. There was a squaw in the hut with her, regarding her with bovine eyes, but the woman made no move to hinder her as Caroline unwound herself from the nest of blankets and walked to the door of the hut.

It was a gray day, amazingly cold considering the heat of the day before, and very still. With no one to stop her, Caroline left the hut to which she had been taken and made her way to the one she thought held Pinochet. She was right, she discovered as she entered, and after a few minutes' check of the patient and a sign-language conversation with Ninaran, she left that hut in search of food.

As before, the three blanket-wrapped old men squatted before the center fire, passing their single pipe between them. A thick-waisted squaw stirred a pot suspended from a tripod, from which emanated a delicious smell. Her fear of the Indians having largely disappeared, Caroline headed toward the quartet and that enticing aroma.

She had just reached them when a horse and rider rode into the camp.

The rider was muffled up to his ears in a beaver coat, and a large black hat sitting low on his brow did much to conceal his face. Still, Caroline had no difficulty at all in recognizing him.

"Matt!" she cried joyfully, quite forgetting their quarrel and everything else in her pleasure and relief at seeing him.

"Ah," the old chief remarked knowledgeably, getting to his feet even as warriors surrounded Matt's horse, "your man?"

Caroline nodded, and with the chief's escort hurried toward the place where the young men of the tribe gathered, blocking Matt's access to the camp. Matt appeared unarmed, and there were no drawn weapons among the braves that Caroline could see, but if anything went wrong the situation could turn ugly very swiftly.

The braves cleared a path for their chief, and Matt dismounted as they approached. His stance was stiff, his eyes wary, his mouth grim. His gaze ran swiftly over Caroline as she neared him, seemingly to assure himself that she was unharmed. Her welcoming smile must have reassured him because a degree of rigidity left his jaw. Nevertheless, his right hand snaked out to grip her arm hard and draw her close to his side.

"I am Habocum, sachem of the Corchaugs," the old chief said to Matt. "You have come for your woman."

It was a statement, not a question, but Matt nodded. "Yes."

"She has done much good here. My youngest daughter was dying when she came, and your woman has restored to her the breath of life. We would gift her with many presents, except that we have been impoverished by the white man until we have little to give. But we give you, and her, our thanks."

"You're very welcome," Caroline said, smiling at the old chief. She would have said more had not a very hard look from Matt warned her to silence.

"I will take her home with me now," he said to Habocum, who nodded.

"You will need food for your journey, and blankets. The sky promises snow."

In short order the promised supplies were handed over and tied to the horse's saddle, except for one varicolored blanket that Matt wrapped around Caroline. She gave last-minute instructions about the continuing treatment that Pinochet would need to Habocum, who nodded gravely, and then, almost before she had finished speaking, Matt was lifting her into the saddle and swinging up behind her. He replied with no more than a nod to Habocum's hand lifted in farewell as he turned the horse about and headed out of the camp. As they passed the last barking dog, squaws were stripping huts. Possessions were being bundled up and fires smothered. It was obvious that the little band was breaking camp and preparing to move on.

"You were rude," Caroline said accusingly when they were under the protection of the trees and safely out of eyeshot and earshot.

"Rude?" Matt sounded as if words threatened to fail him. "That was Habocum, my poppet. Not half a dozen years ago he led a war party that decimated a whole settlement not far from Wethersfield. He was subdued, and his tribe largely wiped out, but he was never captured and has been on the run ever since. He's known for being bloodthirsty, and he hates the white man. I consider us fortunate to have escaped with whole skins, and saw no reason to linger to give him time to reconsider the matter."

"You came alone?" Matt's bravery in doing so was just beginning to occur to her.

"I did not want to waste time trying to recruit volunteers from the town, and James and Dan were away. Rob and Thom, being somewhat hot-headed, are not always assets on an expedition of this nature, and in any case they were needed at home. And in my dealings with Indians I have found that they respond more positively to a single, reasonable man than to an armed band threatening bloodshed. Besides, if you were to be recovered at all, it needed to be done swiftly. I feared what I might find if I tarried overlong."

The notion that Matt had been afraid for her made Caroline smile a little, and she rested her head against the plush fur covering his chest. He was dressed for the cold in ankle-length coat and knee-high boots, wide-brimmed hat and leather gloves. There were lines of fatigue around his eyes, and his jaw was bristly with blue-black stubble as he had not shaved in a day and a half. Even so, he looked very handsome, and so masculine that Caroline felt a tingling of her nerve endings as she looked up at him. Though since she had known him he rarely rode horseback, he seemed at ease in the saddle, and the horse that spent most of its days cavorting in a back field was docile under his hands. Whatever Matt did, he did it well, it seemed. Although, as she thought about that, she made a mental exception of his singing, and smiled again.

Riding before him in the saddle, his arm around her waist to keep her in place, Caroline was tired but content. Even through the blanket that swaddled her, she could feel the muscular strength of that arm and the spread thighs that cradled her buttocks. Settling herself closer against him, she faced the fact squarely: she loved the maddening, impossible man. She meant to have him and no other, whatever it took.

"I was glad to see you," she confessed.

"I was glad to see you too, especially alive and in one piece," he answered dryly.

"I was never really in danger, I think."

"Would that I had known that. I've probably lost a good dozen years off my life in the last day and a half."

"What would you have done, had they not let me go?" Pictures of a bloody battle made her shiver. But magnificent though Matt was, he would surely have lost. He was a farmer, not a soldier, and one man alone. What kind of battle could he have waged against a whole tribe?

"I would have bartered for you." Out of the corner of her eye she saw his mouth ease into a faint grin. "Horse, coat, musket, whatever it took. I even brought some skins along. And a side of bacon, and two jugs of rum. I was fairly confident I could get them to agree to the trade, if you were still unharmed when I caught up with you." He paused, and a shade of tension entered his voice. "You are unharmed, aren't you? They didn't touch you?"

Caroline shook her head. "I'm tired, and nigh perishing of hunger, but that's all. Were you truly frightened when you discovered I was missing, Matt?"

"A little."

She poked him with her elbow in retaliation. He grunted, but she thought he must hardly have felt it through the thick coat.

"When I found you gone, and discovered the basket and gun fallen beside the path—'twas a moment the likes of which I hope never to live through again."

The gruff admission made Caroline's heart stop. There was so much she wanted to say—and more that she wanted to hear him say—but she was tired to her bones, and the motion of the horse was lulling her almost to sleep. The conversation she had in mind was best postponed until she was fully in possession of her senses.

"Can we stop to eat, do you think?" was all she said.

"Did they not feed you?" Without stopping the horse, he turned in the saddle, rummaging in the bag tied on behind, and came up with an apple, which he handed to her.

"I'd prefer to get as far as we can before the weather hits, if this will keep you from starvation until we stop."

With a wordless grumble and a pained look at the apple, Caroline accepted it and bit into the red skin. The fruit, tart and juicy, tasted like nectar. She munched it, polishing it off until naught but the skinniest piece of core remained, then tossed it overboard while she licked her sticky fingers. When she glanced back at Matt, expecting to find him watching her amused, she discovered a frown instead, as he looked at the sky through the bare patches in the canopy above them.

"Is something wrong?" Caroline asked, worried by his expression.

"If I'm not mistaken, we'll have snow before nightfall."

"But we won't be home by then!"

"No."

"What will we do?"

Matt shook his head. "If it's bad, take shelter until it's over. If not, ride through it. I've done it before."

"You have?"

"Many times when we first came here, before the settlement was well established and the house built. You'd be amazed to know what a wilderness this part of the country used to be."

As it seemed a wilderness to her still, Caroline found the notion that it had once been wilder yet appalling. But now that the sharpest pangs of her hunger had been appeased, sleepiness was taking its toll. Huddling more closely into the blanket, she allowed her head to drop back against him, smiling at him when he glanced down at her.

"You look stove-in, poppet," he said, the curve of his mouth almost tender. "Why don't you give up and go to sleep? You can trust me to get you home safe."

"I know. But I'm not all that tired."

"No?"

"No."

He said nothing more, just settled his arm more firmly about her waist as he guided the horse toward home, using the river as his map. Lulled by the gentle rocking, the warmth of his body behind her, and the security of knowing herself safe in his hands, Caroline allowed her eyes to close. Just for a minute, to rest her heavy lids.

Moments later she was asleep. And while she was asleep the threatened snow began to fall.

37

*T*he cessation of motion woke her, she thought. Blinking, eyes widening as she saw nothing for a moment but a swirl of white, Caroline felt momentarily disoriented. She was aware that she was on horseback, with Matt behind her shouting something in her ear, and that the blinding, shifting curtain before her eyes was wind-driven snow.

"What?" she asked, but the wind blew the question away unheard. She had no need to worry, however. Matt was already repeating himself, his arm tightening about her ribcage and his bristly jaw grazing her ear as he roared.

"We're not going to make it. We'll have to take shelter."

"Where?" But this, too, swirled away with the snow. He was already dismounting, and Caroline acutely felt the loss of his heat and strength behind her. The wind buffeted her, driving icy needles of snow into the skin of her face as, by his going, he dislodged the fold of blanket he must have pulled up to protect her as she slept. She shivered, clinging to the saddle horn, fighting to catch her breath in the fierce cold. How had such a temperature change come on so fast?

Matt, on the ground beside the horse, shouted something that she couldn't understand. But when he held up his arms to her, she slid into them, allowing him to lift her down and set her on her feet beside him. The thick carpet of leaves that lay over the forest floor was covered now with perhaps half an inch of glistening snow. More snow, falling from a sky the color of pewter, was pushed by the whistling wind into white crusts that held fast to tree trunks and rocks. Matt pointed to what looked like a solid cliff face, and though she still couldn't understand what he was saying, she allowed him to lead her toward it. The horse, its reins trailing, was left behind.

With the snow clouding her vision she did not see the hollow in the rock until he pulled her into it. Not a true cave, no more than ten feet deep and perhaps eight feet wide, it looked as if a giant had taken a bite out of the cliff and then set it back down. Matt stepped inside it and pulled her in after him. The sudden discontinuance of stinging snow hitting her face and wind whistling in her ears was a blessed relief.

"We'll have to stay here until it stops." Matt was no longer shouting as he tested the depth of the leaves on the ground. Caroline, shivering in her blanket, turned to look at him. Snow glistened on the brim of his hat and beaded the dark fur of his coat. His eyes were very blue in the shadowy darkness of the cave.

"We'll freeze," she protested, but he shook his head.

"You stay in here out of the wind, and I'll get what we need," he told her and then strode back out into the curtain of whirling white. Clearly he meant to gather what they needed to set up camp, and he could use her help. Not that he would appreciate it, of course, but at the moment she doubted that he would take the time necessary to hog-tie her, which was what he would have to do to prevent her from doing her share. Setting her jaw in anticipation of his reaction to her disobedience, she nevertheless pulled the blanket closer and followed him out into the storm.

Though the horse, with Matt beside it, was less than a dozen feet away, it was hard to make out more than a dark blur. Matt, she thought, was not even aware of her approach until she reached his side. The look he gave her was narrow-eyed, but he did not waste his breath with words that the wind would prevent her hearing. Instead he quickly filled her arms with bundles stripped from the horse and turned her back to deposit them in the cave. He came behind her, bearing jugs and bags and the horse's tack. The bulk of this he dropped in an untidy pile just inside the entrance, though the jugs received more careful treatment. He straightened, his frost-rimmed brows meeting over the bridge of his nose as he scowled at Caroline.

"I told you to stay in here out of the wind, and I meant it," he said sharply. "I'm dressed for the weather, where you're not, and I'll get what's needed done a lot quicker if I'm not worrying about you. If you want something to do, go through our supplies to see what we've got. In an hour or less, we'll be stuck here for the duration, so I've no time to argue."

With that he turned and went back out into the crystalline whirlwind. Caroline watched him go, then turned back to do as he'd told her. His words made sense. She was scantily dressed for such numbing weather, and despite its warmth the blanket was in danger of growing damp from melting snow. Sliding it from her shoulders, Caroline shook it out, then rewrapped herself. She began inventorying and arranging their supplies.

An hour later the opening to the hollow was blocked with branches of scrub pine, dragged there by Matt and set in place against the outcropping of rock that formed their roof. A goodly supply of fallen branches for firewood was piled just inside this makeshift wall. An opening perhaps two feet wide had been left on its right side for the fire that would provide them with necessary warmth.

Matt knelt there, carefully arranging limbs, scrub, and tinder. When he opened his musket to sprinkle gunpowder over the whole, then disassembled the snaphance to procure a makeshift but functional flint and steel, Caroline could bear it no longer. He was deathly afraid of fire, as she well knew, though of course he was happily ignorant of her knowledge. She had been watching him covertly for some time, noting the increasing grimness of the set of his jaw, the determination in his eyes. But she thought that his fingers as he got ready to click the cumbersome fire starter together were not quite steady, and she could not even for the sake of his male pride keep her tongue between her teeth.

"I'll do that, if you please," she said briskly, moving toward him. Her words emerged as white puffs of smoke in the frosty air. Even in their newly cozy shelter, the heat of the fire was sorely needed.

Matt looked up at her, his eyes narrowed. But she noted that he stopped what he was doing, grateful, she suspected, for the slightest excuse for delay.

"Do what?"

"Start the fire. You may go out and see to the poor horse, if you want something to do."

"I loosed it. He'll fare better than we would, and probably even find his way home. But why should you wish to start the fire?"

"Starting fires is something at which I have a particular skill. 'Tis not fair that you're the only one who gets to show competence." She held out her hands for the flint and steel as she spoke.

But instead of meekly passing them to her, as Caroline thought he might now that he had a graceful way out of an abhorrent task, he stood up, stretching to his full height, which with his hat on was just an inch or so short of the roof, and eyed her narrowly.

"So you know about that, do you?" he said, clearly finding the notion displeasing. "Mary has been talking out of turn again, I suppose. If ever a man was loose-tongued, it must be James Mathieson!"

From the tight-lipped way Matt lingered over his brother's name, Caroline suspected that, were the maligned James present, he'd be in for a good trimming, if nothing worse.

"Now there you're wrong," she said, and while he was distracted she removed the snaphance from his hands and dropped to her knees to start the fire. Clicking flint and steel together, she made only a few tries before sparks fell on the tinder. Then, helped by a quick infusion of air as she leaned close and puffed, the tinder and surrounding scrub burst into flame.

As the fire crackled with growing strength, Caroline set the snaphance carefully by the rock wall and got to her feet. Matt had retreated to a distance of perhaps a yard. His cheeks were flushed, though the color could as easily have been from the cold as from embarrassment, and his eyes were wary.

Least said, soonest mended, Caroline thought, as warmth began to creep into their little haven. She eyed the assembled foodstuffs with interest.

"Was it Daniel?" Matt asked. The hat cast a handy shadow over his face that kept her from reading too much in his expression.

"No." Knowing that he would hate it if he were to discover in what precise fashion she had come by her knowledge, Caroline was not more forthcoming. Instead she bent to pick up some strips of dried meat that had been among the foodstuffs the Corchaugs had pressed on them. Her mouth started to water as the smoked aroma reached her nostrils. Next on the order of necessities was supper, she decided.

"Is this rabbit, do you suppose, or venison?" she turned to ask Matt, holding up the meat strips.

He looked both thoughtful and grim, but his eyes flickered with a glint of what she thought might be amusement at her question.

"Probably dog."

"Dog!" Horrified, Caroline dropped the meat as if it had burned her. Although she would never be one of Raleigh's unqualified champions, the thought of eating him or his canine brethren was abhorrent to her.

"The Indians consider it a delicacy." Matt retrieved the meat strips and set them carefully back with the other provisions. "Don't be too quick to turn up your nose at it. We may be glad of it before we reach home again."

"And when do you think that will be?" Caroline turned back to scoop up a fat smoked sausage, which Matt had brought with him from home. With the Indians' bread and what was left of the apples, it would make a substantial meal.

"When the snow stops."

She started to move nearer the fire, meaning to settle into the circle of its warmth while she sliced bread and meat for eating. Matt reached out to curl a hand around her arm through her blanket.

Caroline looked up at him inquiringly. Her head did not reach his chin, though she was tall for a woman, and the hand that held her arm was large and strong enough to break her in half had he a mind to do it. But his grip was gentle enough. Only his eyes were hard and, she thought, defensive, as he stared at her from beneath the sheltering brim of his hat.

"Are you going to tell me how you discovered that I have an—aversion —to fire, or are you going to let me guess the night away?" There was irony in his voice as well as a grittiness that she thought might serve to cover shame.

Caroline looked up at him, hesitated, and sighed. "Let me do this— 'twill only take a minute, and I am too famished to wait much longer—and I'll tell you all about it. Though I warn you that you're probably not going to like what you hear."

"There's little doubt of that," Matt muttered. As she quickly cut up the food he kicked the leaves into a pile against the right wall of their shelter— not too near the fire, Caroline noted as she watched with half an eye—and spread the horse's blanket over it. Then he picked up one of the stone jugs and set it close to the fire.

"To warm," he said as he caught her eye upon him.

"Rum?" she asked, cocking her head at him. Her disapproving tone made him smile.

"Aye."

"I didn't think Puritans drank rum."

"Puritans have many vices, my poppet, that I pray you continue to remain unaware of."

Caroline passed him his food and stood up, and they both retired to the makeshift seat he had fashioned. With their backs settled against the wall, they ate for a bit, and then Matt leaned his shoulder into the rock and looked at her.

"So?" he asked.

Caroline finished the last of her bread and sausage and picked up an apple. Taking a healthy bite, she chewed and swallowed before she answered.

"While you were out of your head with fever after the tree fell on you, you had a—bad dream," she said reluctantly. "From it I gathered that you were afraid of fire."

She would have left it there, but he would not let it rest.

"A bad dream?" he prodded. "What did I do, spell out chapter and verse for you in my sleep?"

Caroline started to take another bite of her apple, but he reached over and removed the fruit from her hand. She looked at it with a degree of longing, but a glance at Matt's face drove the thought of further sustenance from her head. His eyes were shuttered, his face closed, as if he would seal himself off from her. Caroline was reminded of him as he had been when they had first met, all flinty and aloof, and she could not bear to have him retreat from her again.

"Daniel told me of how Elizabeth set fire to the barn, and how you were burned rescuing her," she said clearly, her eyes fixed on his face so that she saw him flinch as if from a blow. "He did so because I had caused the fire to be built up in your bedroom, and when you awoke and saw it you panicked and began to scream."

At that Matt's eyes flashed to her, their color so opaque a blue as to look like midnight velvet. His jaw tightened, and the dark color that rose to stain his cheekbones was, she was sure, caused by shame at her knowledge of what he saw as his weakness.

"And so you have pitied me, and thought to shield me tonight by offering to build the fire." There was a harshness to his voice that made Caroline want to cringe at the hurt it strove to hide. She turned more fully to face him, her legs curling beneath her under the all-concealing blanket, her eyes earnest as they met his.

"I have not pitied you, Matt," she said. "I have understood."

When she freed a hand from the blanket and lifted it, meaning from sheer instinct to touch the scar on his face, he pulled back from her, then got abruptly to his feet.

"I don't want your 'understanding,' " he said tightly, his lips so compressed that tiny circles of white stood out at the corners of his mouth.

"Matt . . ." she began, starting to rise herself, but he was already walking away from her. "Where are you going?" she called after him when it became clear that he would leave their shelter. Her tone was high-pitched with concern.

"To take a walk." He glanced at her over his shoulder, saw that she was getting to her feet. "Don't worry, Caroline, I'll be back."

With that he moved aside some branches and stepped out into the snow.

38

He was not gone long, although to Caroline, standing in the center of their shelter waiting alone, it seemed a great while indeed. When he returned, stamping snow from his feet and removing his hat to shake the feathery flakes from it, she felt a wave of relief. Of course she knew that Matt wasn't in the least self-destructive by nature, that he was a tough, mature man able to weather the vicissitudes of life with fortitude, but still she had worried because she knew better than most how painful were scars.

"How is it outside?" she asked as she helped him brush the melting crystals from his coat, because she did not want to say anything that was too emotionally charged.

"Bad. A blizzard, the first of the year," he answered, replacing the branches to block out the soft howling of the wind and the quiet rustle of heavily falling snow. From his tone, and his expression as he turned back to her, she knew she had done the right thing in keeping her remark impersonal. The shuttered look was back, and she sensed that he had closed himself off from her deliberately.

"You mean there will be more of this?" she asked, aghast. Somehow the snowstorm had seemed like a freak happening, falling as it did when calamity after calamity was heaping on her head.

" 'Tis a mite early for such a heavy fall, but snow is the customary condition in Connecticut Colony from October to February."

"So what do we do all winter?" Such extremes of weather were foreign to Caroline's experience, and the idea of them appalled her.

"Stay inside out of the snow when it can be done, and work through it when it can't," he answered with a shrug.

At the thought of enduring months of being housebound, penned in as surely as a beaver in a trap by days upon days of snow, Caroline's opinion of the New World, never exalted, sank to a new low.

"You're cold," he said as he saw that she shivered. Despite the fire, the air inside the hollow was chilly enough so that her nose had reddened with it.

"Not overmuch," she responded, but even as she denied it her teeth began to chatter. Clenching her jaw, she controlled the betraying sound, but it was too late. Cursing himself for a blind fool, Matt made her lie down on the horse blanket and removed his coat to place it over her.

"But you'll freeze," Caroline protested, starting to sit up.

"Lie down." He knelt beside her and pushed her back. "Had I thought, I would have given it to you earlier. Believe me, I'm well able to withstand this degree of cold."

He was wearing shirt, breeches, and wool jerkin beneath the coat. Caroline saw that he would not argue with her over the matter, so she subsided meekly enough. Indeed, the heavy fur did bring with it a welcome degree of warmth. But that, she thought, lingered from his body and did not come from the fur at all.

When he had finished settling her, she had a saddlebag for a pillow and the animal skins he had brought as barter for her safety spread out on top of the coat. He would have doffed his jerkin as well, to put over her. But at that Caroline sat up, dislodging all his careful coverings, and told him vehemently that if he did so she would refuse so much as the blanket the Indians gave her and would sit out in the cold until she froze solid.

So he left the jerkin on, and indeed he did not seem to feel the cold as he moved about the shelter. Caroline, lying on her side, watched him quietly, feeling curiously content. Despite the fact that they were far from home, stranded in a makeshift shelter in the midst of a raging blizzard, the hollow with its curtain of branches and the fire burning brightly at its entrance seemed a cocoon of safety.

She must have dozed, because presently her eyes opened again and she discovered Matt slumped against the wall not far from where she lay. His eyes were fixed broodingly on the opposite wall. One knee was drawn up almost to his chest while his lame leg stretched out stiffly before him. His arms rested on his bent knee. By his side was the jug, and as she watched he reached down, hefted it by its handle, and took a long swallow.

"Are you not coming to bed?"

Her question, voiced without warning out of the stillness of the firelit darkness, startled him into choking on his rum. Recovering, he wiped the back of his hand across his mouth and turned to look at her.

"No."

"You mean to sit there all night." Mild sarcasm laced the words. It had grown colder inside the shelter, though warm as she was beneath the heaped coverings, she had not at first realized it. But her words were punctuated by little puffs of frost, and she guessed that, rum or not, he had to be feeling the cold.

"Aye."

"And why, pray?" His monosyllabic responses irritated her into sitting up and glaring at him. His eyes swept her, noting no doubt her disheveled hair that had escaped its pins entirely and cascaded over her shoulders and the hodgepodge of coverings in a blue-black tumble of silk, the sleep-flushed state of her face, and the wide somnolence of her eyes.

"Why not?" he answered obliquely as he took another swig of rum.

"Are you jug-bitten or just foolish?" Caroline came out of the coverings entirely, ire warming her as she marched over to him and stood, arms akimbo, scowling down at him.

"I'm not drunk. Go back to bed—you'll freeze," he muttered, his eyes running up her body from her slender legs, bare to the knee save for her shoes and thin stockings, to the swell of her hips, her waist, the curve of her breasts, all encased in gray homespun, then to the pale beauty of her neck and face framed by the inky spill of her hair. His eyes flickered. He averted his gaze and took another swallow from the jug.

"You're the one who'll freeze, you foolish, feckless man! I'm telling you to come to bed, and I mean it!" She spoke to him in the same authoritative, scolding tone she would have used to John or Davey.

He put the jug down, rested his arms on his knees again, and eyed her. "And am I now expected to say, 'Yes, Aunt Caroline,' and meekly do your bidding?"

That he read her so accurately made her lips compress, but Caroline nodded. "Yes, you are."

He laughed dryly. " 'Tis a pity that I'm more than ten years old, isn't it?"

Caroline looked him over. He still wore his hat, and he had to tilt his head back to see her as they conversed. His booted feet were planted firmly on the ground, and he seemed solidly settled in for the night. He was far too large for her to shift by force, and reason appeared to roll off him like water off a greased pig, so she would have to use guile if she held out any hope of getting him out of the cold.

Accordingly she sat down beside him, her posture mimicking his exactly. He turned his head to stare at her.

"What in the name of heaven do you think you're doing?"

Caroline smiled sweetly. "Joining you."

"I have no wish for your company."

"Now that," she said, "is a shame."

She reached for the stone jug—she had to use both hands, because the thing was amazingly heavy—and raised it to her lips, tilted it, and swallowed. The warm, spicy fluid nearly burned her tongue with its strength; it slid down her throat with a fire so potent that her eyes watered when she lowered the jug again. So that was how he had been keeping warm! It was certainly effective, even if the searing heat the fluid provoked was more illusion than reality.

" 'Tis heady stuff," Matt observed, his eyes narrowed as he waited for her to choke or cough. By superhuman effort Caroline did neither. Indeed, she managed an appreciative smacking of her lips along with a small slanting smile for him.

"Now then," she said, "what shall we talk about?"

"Go to bed, Caroline." He refused to rise to her bait.

"I'll not leave you sitting out here alone to brood and freeze."

"I am neither brooding nor freezing, I assure you."

"Fine, then." Gritting her teeth at the sheer impossibility of the man, Caroline said nothing more. Instead she stared determinedly at the opposite wall as he sipped the rum and cast her sidelong, considering glances. After passing perhaps a quarter of an hour in this fashion, Caroline began to shiver.

"You're cold!" he declared accusingly.

"Yes, I am."

"Go to bed."

"I won't without you. To sit up all night in such circumstances is so foolish that it borders on being lunatic! We can sleep front to back like spoons, if that is what's bothering you. 'Twill be far warmer if we lie like that, with the covers piled atop us both, than if either of us sleeps alone."

"I can't abide stubborn, shrewish women."

"Don't abide me, then, and we'll sit here until icicles form under our noses." Caroline clicked her tongue in irritation as she settled in for what threatened to be a long, cold night.

Matt grunted, took another swig of rum, replaced the cork, and got to his feet. "Come, then," he said, reaching down a hand to her, a peculiar note of resolution hardening his voice.

Suppressing a victorious smile, Caroline allowed him to pull her to her feet, then lay down at his direction on the horse blanket while he once again piled coverings atop her. She almost held her breath, waiting, but after only the briefest hesitation he doffed his hat, moved behind her, lifted

the edge of the Indian blanket—the bottommost layer of their coverings—
and slid beneath it.

When he had settled himself, keeping as aloof from her as he could,
Caroline could feel the whole hard length of him burning through the
layers of her clothes to her skin. Like hers, his head was pillowed on a
saddlebag, and he lay on his side, his front to her back. He seemed determined to keep a small space between them, but the rock wall was at his
back and he had not much room to maneuver. Gradually Caroline allowed
her body to soften and shift until she was lying full against him, her
bottom curved into the hollow of his lap, her back snuggled against his
chest, her head tucked beneath his chin. One arm he disposed of by curling
it beneath his head. The other, with nowhere else to go, found its way
around her waist, where it rested, stiff as a board as he refused to allow
himself to relax against her.

Caroline snuggled closer yet. Unobtrusively he tried to inch away from
her, but with his back literally to the wall there was nowhere for him to go.
She sighed as if with oncoming sleep as she felt him slowly going rigid
from his booted calves to his thighs to his chest to his head. Against her
thighs she could feel ample evidence of the effect of her nearness on his
body. He was hardly breathing now as he strove to minimize their touching. Though Caroline, feigning near-sleep, kept her eyes closed and thus
could not be certain, she had the impression that he was gritting his teeth.

With a wordless murmur she nestled her buttocks square against his
swelling maleness and pulled his arm closer around her waist.

Matt sat bolt upright, dislodging their covers and taking deep swallows
of cold air as she looked around at him with feigned innocence.

"I knew this was a mistake," he muttered, glaring at her.

At that Caroline decided to abandon all pretense. For good or ill he was
the man she would have, and so she meant to show him. If her body
shrank from the prospect of physical intimacy, why, her heart sang at the
idea of having him for her own. And it was her heart that drove her.

"No mistake," she murmured and sat up too, rising to her knees and
turning to face him as she looped both arms around his neck.

His hands came up and closed over her wrists as if to pull her arms
down. But then their eyes met, and his hands stilled. As he was sitting and
she was on her knees before him, they were much of a height, and she
could see every little detail of the emotions that flickered through his eyes:
first wanting followed by resolve, then wanting followed by doubt, then
just wanting. His eyes flared at her, hungry, bright-blue eyes that could
have belonged to a predator, as his breathing quickened and grew uneven.

For a moment longer Caroline allowed herself the luxury of looking at him, drinking in the way the firelight struck blue sparks in the tousled black waves of his hair, painted cinnamon his handsome face with its restless eyes and jaw-roughening stubble of a beard, danced over the broad shoulders and wide chest.

Then she leaned closer, letting her breasts rest fully against his chest as she touched her lips to his.

He quivered, and his hands tightened for one last moment over her wrists as his lids drooped shut.

"May God forgive me," he muttered against her mouth, and then his arms were coming around her and he was pulling her down into his lap, twisting her so that her head was cradled on his shoulder as he took her mouth with his.

He kissed her as if he was starving for the taste of her mouth, kissed her as if he'd been hungry for eternity and, now, having been offered the sustenance he sought, was determined to have his fill. This was no gentle wooing, but a hard, needy taking, and Caroline could do nothing but cling to his shoulders and open her mouth to his and yield. His mouth was hot and wet and tasted of rum, and he was kissing her so fiercely that there was no room in her head for bad memories or indeed any memories or thoughts that were not of him. His hand sought her breast through the layers of her dress and shift. Its heat seared her flesh, making her nipple tighten deliciously. To her surprise, Caroline moaned against his mouth, and the moan was one of pleasure, not regret.

At the tiny sound Matt stiffened, then shook all over as if with the ague. But it was not ague that ailed him as he twisted her down onto their makeshift bed, yanking her skirts up and fumbling at his breeches and coming into her before she could do more than obligingly part her legs. His claiming was hard and swift, and brought her no great joy except that of giving him whom she loved what he craved, but it caused her no great distress either. She held onto him, and thought of what it would be like to have this man beside her all the days of her life, and even smiled faintly as, having driven inside her with a last strong thrust, he groaned and spilled his seed. Then, as he lay atop her, panting and spent, she found her own reward in that male-oriented act by stroking his hair back from his sweat-damp brow and running her hands with proprietary gentleness along the breadth of his still-clad shoulders and down his back.

Finally he lifted his head to regard her searchingly. Caroline responded with a tender smile. Matt muttered something under his breath that sounded blasphemous, though she could not quite make out the words. He shut his eyes and then opened them again. Rolling off her onto his back, he pulled her against his side and stared up at the rocky ceiling for a long, pregnant moment before shifting his gaze to her again.

39

"*I* didn't hurt you, did I?" Matt asked wearily. He had battled his particular demon as long and valiantly as he could, and had finally, irredeemably, lost. Reality had to be confronted head on. Unless he was never to see her again—and that possibility was one he couldn't face—he had to admit the fact that it was as close to impossible as anything he'd ever attempted to keep his hands off her. He would be making love to her again, and again, and again, and again, just as surely as the sun would rise in the east each morning. Given the inescapable nature of that, it behooved him to take the matter in hand.

"Nary a bit," Caroline answered, quite cheerful. Her head nestled against his chest while her hand stroked his jerkin in the general region of his heart. Even that muffled touch made his pulse—and more than his pulse—quicken. The coverings were twisted around and under them, blocking her view of his still unfastened breeches and what they normally contained. That was all that preserved his modesty as his unrepentant body stirred awake. Already he wanted her again, but the sharp, fierce urgency of his need had been blunted enough so that he could begin, by gentle degrees, to teach her that there was more to coupling than she had yet discovered.

"I'm glad." If there was a trace of irony in his words, he doubted that she would detect it. She lay against him as trusting as a child, unaware that there was anything amiss. He had to bear much responsibility for that, of course. Except for the bastard who had forced her—would that the filth roast forever in Hell!—he had been her sole tutor in the delicate art of mating.

With an inward grimace Matt acknowledged that his lessons, as an educational tool for Caroline, left a great deal to be desired.

He shifted up to one elbow, looking down at her pensively. With his movement, her head had fallen back to rest against a saddlebag. She was smiling at him, a faint, sleepy smile, and her great golden eyes were shadowed with fatigue. The delicate pale oval of her face was marked in places by his beard. Matt made a mental note, once he had her safe home again, to begin shaving in the evening as well as the morn so as not to mar her skin. At the thought of the twitting he would take from his brothers over that, a corner of his mouth twitched down. 'Twas the penalty one endured for having a large, irreverent family, and so long as they kept their teasing from Caroline's ears he would suffer their barbs with what stoicism he could muster.

"You're beautiful," he whispered, leaning down to touch his lips to hers. She returned his kiss sweetly, that luscious pink mouth with its faint taste of rum soft and yielding.

Before he could be tempted to linger awhile, and then bewitched into forgetting what he was about entirely, he got to his feet and did up his breeches enough so that he could move about without their falling down about his shanks. She watched with interest as he restored himself to minimal decency, nothing about her frank gaze speaking of distaste.

She was healing, it was clear, and he thanked God both for her sake and for his own. If he was gentle with her, and careful, maybe he could yet teach her what a glorious thing the joining of a man and a woman could be. At the thought his body swelled against the restored restraint of his breeches, and it was all he could do not to drop back down beside her and commence her lessons at once.

If it was cold outside their cozy nest, he didn't feel it.

"Matt?" It was a lazy question, uttered by one clearly anticipating sleep. Matt smiled rather grimly to himself even as he reached down to haul her to her feet.

"What . . . ?" Clutching his shoulders as he set her upright, she blinked at him.

"We'll be more comfortable if I straighten the bed," he told her soothingly, and proceeded to do just that. But instead of leaving the prickly saddle blanket on the bottom, he covered the thick cushion of leaves with his fur coat. Then he took the few steps needed to reach the woodpile and from a safe enough distance threw a few stout limbs on the fire. For just a moment he looked beyond the blaze into the storm-ridden night, and then as the flames shot up to claim the new wood, he had perforce to turn away. As an afterthought he picked up the jug of rum and rejoined Caroline.

She still stood beside the pallet, her head cocked a little to one side, watching him. He set the jug down within easy reach, smiled at her, reached for her, and pulled her close. Then he bent his head to taste her lips as his hands sought the hooks that fastened her poor maimed dress up the back.

"Matt?" It was more question than protest, he thought, uttered as she discovered what he was about.

"We'll be warmer if we take off our clothes and huddle together under the coverings to share body heat."

Women's fastenings were infernal things, and he was sadly out of practice, but he managed to undo enough of them so that he could, he thought, get her out of the dress.

"You mean lie together naked?" She sounded shocked, as if such decadence had never occurred to her. Matt had to grin a little at the innocence of that.

"That was what I had in mind," he confessed.

"Oh," she said on a thoughtful note, and as he started to slide the the dress off her shoulders, he saw that she was frowning.

"Matt?"

"Hmmm?" Unable to resist, he bent his head to press a kiss on the creamy shoulder he had just bared.

"Do—is being naked the usual way?" She blushed scarlet as she asked the question, and her eyes dropped to study intently the toes of his boots.

"Some people prefer it," he told her gravely, pushing the gown down her arms. To his pleasure she helped him by pulling her arms out of the long, tight sleeves, and then, when he eased the garment down past her hips, she obligingly stepped out of it.

Standing there, in her thin white shift and ragged-edged, foreshortened petticoat, she was so enticing that it was all he could do not to wrap his arms around her and kiss her senseless, before proceeding to other, more fulfilling matters. But chill bumps were dotting her soft skin, and he knew that, though he was not, she must be cold. Some day he would have an opportunity to remove her clothing piece by piece, kissing each part of her body as he exposed it, but tonight was obviously not the night. Keeping a firm hand on demon lust, he finished stripping her as quickly and efficiently as he could—though he was unable to resist planting a few stray kisses here and there as he did so. Finally he dropped down on one knee before her to remove her shoes, and then, gritting his teeth as he fought with himself to do no more than the necessary task, reached up to untie her garters and roll her stockings down her legs.

Not tossing her on her backside and pumping out his lust between her legs there and then was the hardest thing he had ever done in his life.

He touched the cool, pale slenderness of her thighs, and his heart raced.

He slid the stockings down past dimpled knees and shapely calves, and he couldn't breathe. It was all he could do to force himself back to his feet, to find her blushing and looking at his boots again while he allowed himself just a moment to indulge his eyes.

Naked, she was the most beautiful thing he had ever beheld in his life. Her breasts were full and firm and very white, with lovely small nipples the color of strawberries. They jutted away from her narrow ribcage at a provocative angle, flauntingly feminine above a tiny waist and luscious, curving hips. Her belly was just slightly rounded, her navel a shadowy circle in its center. Her legs were long and lissome, and the nest of curls at the apex of her thighs was as black and silky-looking as sable.

Matt fought the impulse and was defeated. Breathing as though he'd run for miles, he bent his head and drew a pert nipple into his mouth.

It didn't taste of strawberries—it was infinitely better.

She gave a little moan and twined her hands in his hair. His hands were on her waist, large and dark as they splayed over the satin skin. He could feel her fingers tighten against his scalp as he suckled her breast. The heat was building in his loins, scalding pressure that he knew would in a matter of an instant prove too strong to resist—and from somewhere he found the strength to drag his mouth away from her breast.

Wordless, she lifted her face to him as he straightened, her eyes very wide and more amber than gold, her lips parted breathlessly. Looking down into her flushed, confused, and yet wondering face, Matt tightened his hands around her waist. He could not lose control yet.

The chill bumps on her arms stopped him yet again. Gritting his teeth, he picked her up in his arms and lay her on the soft fur bed, kissing her ear and the side of her cheek when she kept her arms about his neck and would not let him go.

" 'Tis your turn to watch now, poppet," he whispered into her ear, removing her arms from about his neck and then, though it pained him to do so, covering her nakedness with the Indian blanket so that she would not entirely perish with the cold.

When she was snugly ensconced, he undid his own buttons, first the jerkin, then the shirt, then the boots—he had to hop from one foot to the other for that, which was scarcely dignified although he was too aroused to care much—then the stockings. Finally, bare-chested and barefoot, he unbuttoned his breeches, hoping that the unimpeded sight of a fully erect man wouldn't daunt her too badly.

So far she had watched him in silence, though her eyes, peeping at him over the edge of the blanket, had grown bigger with each garment that he stripped away. Now he felt vaguely self-conscious, but determined too to show her all there was of him to see, and so shucked his breeches down his legs, shoved them aside with his foot, and stood before her in all his naked glory.

Her eyes were fastened on his member, huge and stiff as it stuck straight out from its bed of wiry black hair. As he looked at her looking at him, for one of the few times in his entire adult life Matt felt himself start to blush.

She seemed very young and very virginal, all big-eyed and pale as she gaped at him, her masses of black hair tumbling loose on either side of her face making her appear scarcely more than a child. Did the sight of him horrify her? Disgust her? Frighten her?

If she was truly too distressed from seeing him so to proceed, would he be able to force himself to leave her alone?

Yes, Matt told himself firmly, he would. If it killed him, he would give her time to get used to this new knowledge of men before he took the lesson any further.

Though from the way he was feeling at present, kill him it just might.

He waited in trepidation as she swallowed and lifted huge shadowy eyes to his face.

"Is that all there is to it?" she asked as if marveling at a long-feared object's innocuousness.

For a moment Matt couldn't believe his ears. Then he gaped at her like a wantwit. Finally he let loose with a shout of laughter. He was still chuckling as he crawled beneath the blanket and gathered her into his arms.

40

" '*T* is not funny! What are you laughing at?"

Indignant that he should be so consumed with hilarity at such a time, Caroline punched him on the shoulder. He winced, caught her fist in his hand, and pressed his lips to her clenched knuckles. But his chest still heaved with laughter he could not quite suppress as he held her close against him.

"I take it you were expecting something different?" The question was polite. Too polite. Caroline knew that he was still vastly amused, though she could not quite figure out why.

"From the feel of the thing, I thought it was huge," she said, a shade resentful because of his laughter at her expense that she could not share and could not understand why that sent him into guffaws again. He laughed until he choked, his arms holding her tight all the while as if he were scared that she would take umbrage and leave—which she might well have done if she hadn't been as naked as a babe, and shy with it.

When at last he had done laughing, he lay spent against the plush fur beneath them, his head pillowed on a saddlebag, his eyes alight.

"I'm afraid there's no more than that." His tone was apologetic, but Caroline knew when she was being made sport of. Still, he looked so handsome, so happy and at ease with his eyes a sparkling bright blue and his mouth stretched into a wide grin that made him look dazzlingly young and carefree, that she could not work herself up to a true anger, though she still did not understand what had provoked him to such paroxysms of mirth.

"If you're going to laugh at me, then I'm going to sleep," she said, flouncing onto her side and presenting her back to him just to see what he would do. Immediately he leaned over her, his body close against hers beneath the coverings that were piled atop them both. She could feel the whole hard length of him from his wide chest with its thick wedge of hair, to the powerful muscles of his legs and thighs, to the throbbing heat of that part of him that had been the subject of their conversation as it pressed against the roundness of her buttocks.

"Oh, no, you're not. Not just yet."

His arm slid around her waist, his hand seeking and finding a naked breast. Caroline felt a quiver of pleasure, stunning in its very unexpectedness, shoot clear to her toes as his fingers rubbed across her nipple. His hand splayed over the soft mound, squeezing and caressing, causing her breast to swell into his molding palm. She had not guessed that any part of the physical act between a man and a woman could feel good, but this felt unbelievably so. Then his hand strayed to her other breast, treated it as he had the first, and the resulting bedazzlement disrupted her breathing. Arching her neck so that he could more thoroughly address himself to the side of it, Caroline felt languid heat begin to coil in her belly, and she trembled.

"I love to touch your skin. I wondered for a long time if it could possibly feel as soft as it looks. It does."

The thickened quality of his voice was wildly seductive. Caroline quaked under the combined assault of words, kisses, and roving hands as, brushing the heavy curtain of her hair aside, Matt pressed quick burning kisses on her sensitive nape, then trailed his warm mouth along her shoulder and back again to rest, nibbling, in the delicate hollow below her ear. His beard, so masculine in its harsh abrasion that it made her bones melt, scraped across her tender skin. With one hand he continued to stroke and fondle her breasts while his other hand, sliding around her waist from beneath her, moved over her belly to explore her navel with a questing finger. Then his hand flattened and slid lower, covering that part of her to which she had never affixed a name. Instinctively she wriggled a protest, trying to shift his hold to some less intimate place, but he would not be dislodged.

"Trust me, poppet," he whispered in her ear. Caroline was briefly reminded of Eve and the serpent, who must once have murmured something very similar. But then his long fingers were moving lower yet, sliding down between her legs to touch her there so gently that the fire that ignited inside her as a result was almost shameful, and she no longer entertained any rational thoughts at all. Because surely that undemanding pressure should not in itself be enough to create such an inner burning! It was like liquid fire, a most pleasurable liquid fire that made her breathing quicken until she was almost panting and her body writhe against the hand that caressed her and the hard male body pressed close against her back.

Her eyes were closed, but she was aware of him with every pore. His breathing grew increasingly hoarse as he slid his mouth and unshaven jaw along the sensitive chord on the side of her neck. His arms enfolded her, the fronts of his hair-roughened thighs pressed against the backs of her silky ones, his broad shoulders dwarfed her own. He held her close against him so that she could feel the enormity of his maleness jutting against the nakedness of her rounded buttocks—funny how the thing felt so much more menacing than it looked! He caressed her breasts and explored the secret place between her thighs until she was shaken with involuntary tremors, in thrall to a burning sweetness that had her moaning and twisting in his hold.

Then he slid his fingers inside her, truly inside in the wet secret passage where she had never dreamed that they would go, and began to move them in and out in gentler approximation of the way he took her with his body.

Caroline's eyes fluttered open as she found herself on the brink of being consumed by an aching, swirling need the likes of which she had never dreamed she could feel. She gasped, tried weakly to hold it back, to squirm away, but found herself caught between his hand in front and his body behind. With a sound that was a cross between a moan and a sob she felt again the inexorable motion of those shocking fingers—and finally surrendered with closing lids and a shameful little cry to the wonderful quivering rapture that he had built within her like a carefully stoked fire.

When it was over, when she had returned to herself again, Caroline dared not open her eyes for the embarrassment of it. Matt still lay against her, holding her close, his hands possessive as they splayed over her breasts and the dark triangle at the apex of her thighs. His fingers were no longer inside her, for which small mercy she was thankful, but they still rested between her legs, and now that she was of sound mind again she found the extreme intimacy of his touch mortifying.

But not distasteful, or disgusting. Realizing that gave Caroline the impetus to open her eyes.

"Well, now, and what did you think of that?" He sounded both self-satisfied and curiously tense as he muttered the question into her ear, but it was the note of complacency underlying the question that brought her squirming around so that she could glare at him.

"I think you're conceited, and base, and . . ." she began wrathfully when she lay flat on her back on the soft fur looking up into his smirking, black-stubbled face. But despite the half grin at, she thought, her expense, what she saw in his eyes left her bereft of words. There was tenderness for her in the cobalt depths, and perhaps the faintest suspicion of triumph, but overshadowing all was hunger, feverish bright. He gazed at her as a starving man might look at meat, and Caroline let the smirk pass and the question die unanswered as she realized that he needed to be fed.

"I love you, Ephraim Mathieson," she whispered, the words drawn out of her of their own volition. Her hand lifted to caress his sandpaper cheek.

He trapped her fingers, pressed them close so that the heat of his skin seared her palm, his gaze never leaving hers. His eyes were suddenly vulnerable, defenseless as a child's, and his vincibility touched her as nothing in her life ever had. Shaken to the core by the force of what she felt, she raised herself on one elbow to press a kiss to the scar that was his badge of honor.

"God in heaven!" he muttered as her lips brushed the whitened ridge and were withdrawn. The grin disappeared entirely in favor of a grimace as his eyes flared and turned dark. Then he was pushing her back down and lowering himself atop her, kissing her as if he would steal her very soul, his hands everywhere, caressing and arousing and possessing, lifting her legs to encircle his waist even as his body staked the most primitive claim of all.

This time, as he made her his, Caroline was able to appreciate just how men could come to crave this physical act so, because the burst of response he'd engendered in her just moments before was nothing compared to the explosion of ecstasy that overtook her as he thrust for a final time deep inside her, crying out her name as he spilled his seed.

In the aftermath, they lay entwined, Matt on his back with Caroline sprawled across his chest, listening contently to the gradually slowing beat of his heart.

"Tell me something," she said idly after a long silence, tracing circles with a fingertip in the fascinating wedge of his chest hair. His nipples were flat and dark brown, like hers and yet most emphatically unlike, and she had rubbed and flicked them until, with a groan, he had caught her hands and requested her to desist. So she curled his chest hair around her fingers instead, various random thoughts occupying her mind. This one, for which she had wished an explanation for some time, had intruded out of the blue, faintly nettling her. "Just what did you mean when you told me that Hannah Forrester and I are very different kettles of fish?"

Matt lifted his head to look at her even as she tilted her chin so that she could meet his eyes.

"So that bothered you, did it?" Now that his passion was slaked, humor surfaced again. Too lazy to take umbrage at being laughed at—besides, as she thought about it, she decided that she was pleased that she could make him laugh—she merely put out her tongue at him.

"About as much as Daniel's kissing me at the husking bee bothered you," she responded sweetly, and tweaked a crisp chest curl.

"That much, huh?" Some of the amusement faded from his face and was replaced by a darkling gleam. He stilled her fingers, pressing them against him to keep them from doing him further hurt, and slid an arm, elbow bent, beneath his head to act as a pillow.

"Well?" She wanted an answer.

His mouth quirked into a half smile. "Why, that you, my poppet, are the most tempting sight I could ever hope to feast my eyes on this side of heaven—and she is not."

"And it had best stay that way." Pleased at his answer, she nevertheless fixed him with a severe stare. "Because you have given yourself to me, sir, and I warn you that I do not share!"

"Are you making me a declaration, Caroline?" The smile in his eyes as he repeated the question he had asked her once before was belied by the husky undertone to his voice.

"And if I am?" Her response was husky too.

"Then I would tell you that it's my turn."

"Your turn?"

"To make you one. But consider well before you answer. 'Tis a crew you'll be taking on, and a permanent one. If you would have me, you must also take Davey and John, and James and Dan and Rob and Thom and even the deuced dog. There'll be more babies, because I won't be able to keep my hands off you for more than a few hours at a time and babies are the necessary result of that, and all the work that they bring on top of everything else. Even a bond servant is freed when the term of indenture ends. You, on the other hand, would be giving yourself to me forever."

Caroline's eyes widened, and she pushed herself up on her elbows from her supine position on his chest to blink at him.

"Are you by any chance attempting to make me a proposal of marriage?"

"I suppose I must be."

" 'Tis a most negative one. May I be permitted to ask what prompted it?"

His brows shot up. His hands moved explicitly down the naked length of her back to linger on the curve of her buttocks. Caroline ignored the delicate tremors that shot along her nerve endings in the wake of his hands and frowned at him.

"You want me in your bed." If there was an ominous note to that, she couldn't help it.

"Aye, I do." His fingers tightened, pressing her against him so that she could feel his renewed arousal.

"That is the most insulting thing I've ever heard!" Barely managing to control the urge to hit him, she started to scramble to her feet, only to be forestalled by his arms wrapping around her.

"Whoa, now, Madam Spitfire, control that hasty temper of yours! Would you have me deny the obvious? I've wanted you in my bed since I first laid eyes on you, hightailing it across my field with that red cloak flapping behind you and Jacob on your heels. A woman who can run like that, I said to myself, is a woman far and away above the ordinary herd of females."

He was teasing her, she knew he was, but her feelings, so newly tender and sensitive to hurt, rendered her in no mood for it.

"Let me up, you randy oaf!"

She shoved against his shoulders. Matt must have seen the true pain in her eyes, floating just beneath the surface of her temper, because the smile in his died. Without warning he turned with her, holding her captive until she was pinned beneath him, not struggling but glaring at him with fierce hurt.

"Nay, I didn't mean it," he said quietly. "Or, rather, I did, but there is more to it than that, as you should know. I would wed you because I love you, Caroline, more than I have ever loved anyone or anything before in my life. I love you so much that the thought of losing you fills me with dread. I love you so much that, if you refuse me, I'm liable to spend the rest of my life howling at the moon like a wolf who's gone weak in the head."

The smile accompanying this was a mere flicker that did not reach his eyes and was quickly gone. Looking searchingly up into his face, Caroline realized that he meant what he said: he loved her. But like herself, he had been wounded by life, and so he sought to protect himself from his tenderest emotions with humor or whatever other means he could seize.

At that realization her pique died, and she lifted her arms to link them behind his head.

"I'll be proud and honored to be your wife," she said, and she smiled at him with all the love she'd kept inside for so long shining from her eyes and her voice.

Matt stared down at her for just a moment, his own eyes darkening. "No, my poppet, 'tis I who am honored," he muttered, and bent his head to lay his lips against hers in a long but achingly gentle kiss.

41

On that night the snow falling outside the shelter could have turned into a medley of cherubim singing in celestial chorus, and neither Caroline nor Matt would have noticed. They loved, and whispered, and laughed, and loved some more, and if the bliss they found together spoke more of earth than of heaven, it was still paradise enough for them.

Though the night was largely sleepless for both of them, when the dawn came Caroline awoke at the first creeping tendril of light. The interior of the shelter was amazingly bright because of the reflective properties of the snow outside. The fire was still burning steadily—Matt had fed it regularly, and though he had tossed limbs on the blaze from a careful distance, she had been pleased that he could bring himself to do so—but it barely took the chill off the air. Snugly wrapped in their cocoon of fur and covers, however, Caroline was toasty warm.

It helped, of course, to have a very large, muscular, hairy man sharing body heat with her.

His arm was around her waist with a hand resting just beneath her breast, and his leg was flung possessively over her thighs. She was curled, back to his front, as close to him as an apple to its skin, and it required some effort on her part to turn over enough so that she could see him properly.

Asleep, he had the look of a dark angel fallen to earth, his black hair tumbling in a riot of curls over his brow and around his ears, his thick, stubby lashes lying like sable crescents against bronzed cheeks, his features as finely delineated as if they'd been chiseled by a master sculptor.

On the mortal side, that unshaven stubble threatened to develop into a full beard, and her love slept with his mouth open.

In fact, not to put too fine a point on it, he snored.

Not loudly, but the rasping sounds issuing from between those classically carved lips were definitely not heavenly in origin.

Her eyes lighting with tender amusement as a particularly loud snore disturbed the pristine peace of the morning, Caroline thanked God, or Providence, or whoever was responsible, that Matt, for all his masculine beauty and staid Puritan ways, was no angel.

Because she loved him just as he was, snores, scars, beard, and all.

As she remembered the things he had done to her during that daft, wild night just past, she felt her cheeks pinken. Recalling the things he had taught her to do, the pink turned to rose. The recollection of their last coupling of what must have been at the very least half a dozen or more deepened the rose to burning red.

He'd caught her hips and pulled her down on him, and she'd ridden him with an abandon that would haunt her every time she caught his eye, for many and many a day to come.

At the thought of catching his eye, she panicked. What did one say to a man after such a wanton night? They had no more secrets from each other in truth now, and Caroline shut her lids at the thought of seeing his new knowledge of her reflected in his face.

Under his tutelage, she had discovered a capacity for strumpetry that she had never suspected lay dormant inside her. At the end, she'd no longer even needed his whispered encouragements to touch and caress, hold and fondle.

She'd done plenty of that on her own.

What she and Matt had done together bore no relationship to the horror that had, in her previous life, been forced upon her. The one was making love; the other was an abomination. After last night, the shade of Simon Denker would no longer cast a shadow of darkness over her life. She could put him and what he had done to her behind her, and get on with the business of living. Matt had set her free.

Was she really going to be his wife?

At the thought she almost fell to giggling like a silly schoolgirl. Only the knowledge that she must surely wake him if she gave way stopped her.

Suddenly she could not bear to face him as she was, naked and tousled with the marks of his lovemaking still everywhere upon her. She would get up from their bed and bathe and dress before he awoke. Besides, nature called, and the matter was growing increasingly urgent.

Getting up was not easy; even his limbs were heavy, and she had to shift them without disturbing him. But he seemed deeply asleep, and she managed to lift his arm and slide herself out from under his leg without even causing a disturbance in the rhythm of his soft snores.

Standing naked beside the rumpled pallet, Caroline discovered that it was, indeed, bitterly cold. Catching up Matt's shirt, she quickly put it on, amused to discover that the sleeves hung a good foot past the tips of her fingers and the tails reached down past her knees. She must look ridiculous, but there was no one to see, and she meant to have a quick wash if she froze to death making the attempt. Accordingly, she stepped into Matt's boots. She could almost have slept in one of them, so huge were they. Picking up the jug that was still half full of rum, she moved aside a few branches and headed out into the snow.

She went no farther than a step or so outside, wincing at the frigid temperature that made it hurt to breathe and stung her skin with icy fingers. The sun was rising, a hazy pale ball just visible as she looked toward the river, and the wind had eased. Though snow still fell heavily, it was no longer whipped into pellets that bit at the flesh. The sparkly blanket on the ground came up to her knees—she was thankful for the enormousness of Matt's boots—but the blizzard had passed. If not that day, then surely the next, they would be able to start for home.

What would Davey and John and the rest of them think of their news? She and the boys had crossed a crucial bridge on that afternoon in the village, but would their newfound affection extend to welcoming her as their father's wife?

Having taken care of the most urgent part of her business, Caroline emptied the remainder of the rum on a drift—everywhere it touched, strongly aromatic steam rose, and she was reminded of just how potent the drink had been—and quickly swirled the interior clean before filling it with snow. Then, shivering, teeth chattering, she stepped back inside the shelter with her prize.

"What the devil do you think you're doing?"

To her dismay, Matt was very much awake now. He stood, gloriously naked and apparently not a whit abashed, just beside their pallet, which he had clearly just left. His fists were planted on narrow hips as he scowled at her. She was so chilled that she could hardly speak, but she could look, and look she did.

With his archangel's face atop that magnificent body, he was a sight to stop any living, breathing female's heart. Caroline drank in the sheer glory of him, barely noticing how his eyes swept her in their turn.

"You little idiot, what possessed you to go outside like that?" Sounding far more irritated than a lover properly should, he reached down, dragged his fur coat from beneath the piled coverings, and stalked across the small space that separated them to wrap it around her.

Caroline, having set the jug close to the fire so that the snow could melt, was just straightening as he reached her, and she was grateful for the sudden warmth. Her teeth still chattered, and her skin tingled as it thawed, but she had not been outside for long enough to do herself any damage, she knew.

"We n-needed water for w-washing."

"You went outside practically naked for that?" The volume of his voice escalated to a near roar on the last word.

Caroline scowled right back at him. "Don't you dare roar at me, Ephraim Mathieson!"

"I'll roar if I want—and don't call me Ephraim."

"I will if I want to. Actually, I rather like the name."

"Oh, do you?"

"Yes, I do."

"You're feeling mighty cocky this morning, I see. Don't think I can't deal with impertinent chits."

"Pooh—you don't scare me! For all your big talk, I've never seen you so much as put a hand to the backside of one of your boys!"

"They're good boys and don't need that kind of correction. But don't think I won't put my hand to your backside, if you ever again do something so foolish as to go outside next door to naked in freezing weather to fetch water so you can wash!"

Put like that, it did sound rather witless.

"There were—other reasons too," she said lamely.

Her very hesitancy told him what she meant. As realization hit, his lips compressed and his frown lightened. "Next time get dressed first. Have you never heard of frostbite?"

"You're a fine one to be telling me to get dressed! Look at you, as naked as a babe!"

"You happen to be wearing my clothes!"

"Not all of them."

"Enough."

"You've breeches remaining, and stockings, and . . . ."

"Caroline, do you really want to spend the entire morning arguing with me?"

Put that way, the answer was clear. "No."

"Good. Because I can think of numerous things I would rather do." He smiled then, a slow wicked smile that set her insides to doing flipflops, then walked over to her and slid his hand under her chin to tilt up her face for his kiss. As his mouth touched hers she wrapped her arms around his neck and rose on tiptoe and clung, kissing him back.

"That's better." He lifted his head to flick her nose with his finger. "If you'll give me my boots, I, too, have business outside."

"Oh."

"Yes, oh."

Occupying such close quarters was going to have its embarrassing aspects, Caroline could see. She went pink to her ears as she passed over boots and coat, pulling on his stockings—they were of heavy wool, and far warmer than her own cotton ones—and wrapping herself in the Indian blanket instead.

Still naked beneath the coat and boots, Matt stepped outside for no more than a few minutes before he was back. Caroline had had time to remove the now-melted and warmed snow from the fire, but certainly not enough to wash. Crouching by the pallet, in the act of wetting a piece of linen she had ripped from her mutilated petticoat, she jumped as if caught out in some nefarious deed as he slid back inside and replaced the branches that she had dislodged.

"Surely you're not feeling shy of me?" he asked, seeing her jump and flush.

"I want to wash."

"So wash."

He was not perfect, this man she loved. In fact, he was far from perfect. Insensitivity to certain finer points of gentlemanly behavior was one of his failings. But if he could school her in the art of loving, then she could tutor him in manners. It seemed a fair enough trade.

"I require a certain amount of privacy," she said gently, and was not surprised when he looked at her with impatience.

"Is there something more of your person that I have yet to see?"

That was just the kind of response she had expected.

"Would you please just make yourself scarce for a bit?" Exasperation won out over gentle guidance, but then exasperation worked. Matt snorted as if at the folly of women, but—taking back his shirt, for which he exacted a forfeit from each of her breasts—he pulled on his clothes in a minimum amount of time, picked up his musket, and headed outside.

Keeping a wary eye on the wall of boughs, Caroline washed herself as thoroughly as she could, given the freezing conditions and inadequate facilities. From somewhere outside she heard Matt's voice roaring a hymn, and for a moment she stopped what she was doing to listen, a tender smile curving her mouth. Then, as the sound stopped, she recovered her wits, found her clothes, and began to dress. She was sliding on her last shoe when the *boom!* of the musket being fired made her stiffen.

She hurried to look outside and found him striding toward the shelter, the still-smoking musket in one hand and a freshly killed rabbit in the other. As he saw her, he grinned and raised the animal by its hind legs.

"Breakfast!" he said, and came inside for his knife. When he returned, in an amazingly short time, the carcass was skinned and cleaned and ready to be cooked.

"We'll have a feast." Caroline smiled at him as she relieved him of the meat, skewered it with a sharp stick, and propped it over the fire to roast. Matt shed his coat, washed his hands, and sluiced his face with the last of the water. He came up behind her to slide his arms around her waist. Standing, looking down with a frown at the juices that already dripped down to sizzle in the fire—would she do better to move the meat to a cooler part of the fire?—she was caught by surprise when his hands moved up to cover her breasts.

Instinctively she stiffened, and then, as he pressed his lips to the hollow beneath her ear, she relaxed. After a moment she turned in his arms, wrapping her arms around his neck and rewarding him with a lazy kiss.

Still, when she felt his hands start to unfasten the hooks at her back, she pulled a little away to frown at him.

"What are you doing?"

"Taking off your clothes."

"But I just got dressed!"

"And very fetching you look too. But I prefer you naked."

Exactly how he meant to occupy the rest of the morning burst over her like sunshine over the horizon. By this time her dress was unfastened to the waist, and he was tugging it off her shoulders.

"But it's full day!"

The sincere dismay of her protest drew a grin from him even as he bared her breasts.

" 'Twill make it all the better," he told her, and, stripping both her and himself, tumbled her down again into their nest. Rolling her onto her back, he kissed her protests from her, then with hands and mouth and body demonstrated to her that the day was a very good time for what he had in mind after all.

It was much later when Caroline, awakening from a doze, smelled burning meat and bethought herself of the rabbit.

With a shriek she catapulted out of his arms.

"What the devil . . . ?" Instantly alert to meet whatever threatened them, Matt jackknifed into a sitting position, the coverings falling away from his naked chest.

" 'Tis burned!" Caroline moaned, rescuing the rabbit from its funeral pyre with a stick.

"So we'll scrape away the burned part and eat what's left."

Unconscious of her nakedness in her distress, Caroline knelt and set the charred meat on a flat stone that jutted up from the floor just inside the entrance. To her annoyance, Matt began to grin, and then to laugh.

Then he was out of the covers and coming to fetch her.

"You are a constant source of joy to me, my poppet. Come back to bed."

"But the rabbit . . ."

"Never mind the confounded rabbit. You're naked, and it's cold, and we've nothing else to do but spend the day pleasing ourselves. 'Twill be awhile before we get another such chance."

"Yes, but . . ."

Even as she mourned the rabbit, Matt picked her up in his arms and carried her back to their pallet. It was quite some time later before she had another chance to think of food.

But finally, as outside the shelter the shadows of the trees lengthened toward the river, she did get to eat. With Caroline wrapped in the fur coat and naught else—Matt had taken the lesser warmth of the Indian blanket over her protests—they sat together on the pallet and devoured the remnants of the bread and sausage and apples, washed down with more water melted in the empty rum bottle. Matt took a swig from the other bottle— just a swallow, no more—and then they stretched out side by side, her head on his shoulder, replete.

"What will people think, do you suppose?" The question had been nibbling like a troublesome mouse at the edges of her happiness for some time.

"Think of what?" He ran a lazy finger from one sated strawberry-tipped breast to the other.

"Of us. Being wed."

"What should they think? 'Tis no concern of anyone save ourselves."

"But you—I—I'm not universally liked in the town, you know."

"You're not marrying the town."

"True. But . . ."

"Ahoy the cave! Matt, is that you in there?" The hail from outside the shelter startled them both. Caroline gasped, scrambling to make herself as decent as she could with the coverings pulled to her nose, while Matt stiffened and sat up.

" 'Tis Daniel, curse his black soul," he said to her tightly, then raised his voice to bellow back an affirmative.

42

"**G**et dressed." Matt was already on his feet stepping into his breeches as Caroline, not needing his admonition, searched for her shift. Spying it before she did, Matt tossed it to her, and her petticoat and dress as well. Caroline yanked her shift over her head while Matt threw on his shirt.

"Matt! *Cooee!*" A muffled imprecation followed this renewed shout. It sounded as if Daniel was encountering difficulty in getting to them, but giving it a good try.

"May the devil take you, little brother," Matt muttered, trying to stomp his feet into his boots and button his shirt at the same time.

Caroline frantically tied the tapes of her petticoat about her waist and reached for her dress while Matt, minimally decent now, headed for the bough barrier to hold Daniel off.

" 'Tis me, right enough," she heard him say in a rather more sour tone than Daniel's efforts on their behalf warranted.

"Praise the Lord! I feared that either Indians or the blizzard might have done for you, though I should have known better: you're too blamed ugly to kill."

If Matt responded to Daniel's attempt at humor, Caroline, who was in no position to see his face, couldn't tell.

"Is Caroline with you?" Robert asked. She started, fastening her dress as best she could and pulling on her stockings, wondering all the while just how large the rescue party might be.

At the thought of emerging from their love nest to confront a gossipy throng, Caroline shrank inside. Though no one could know for a certainty exactly how she and Matt had passed the night, they would no doubt speculate uncomfortably close to the mark. Tying her garters and hastily dropping her skirts, Caroline felt like the veriest Jezebel.

"Aye." There was something decidedly off-putting about Matt's terse answer. "You made good time tracking us."

"We did but follow the river, and then saw your smoke. Stand aside, brother. 'Tis confounded cold out here, and we could use a bit of the warmth from your fire."

With a quick glance over his shoulder to assure himself that Caroline was presentable, Matt stepped back inside the shelter. Daniel followed almost immediately, and Robert came after him. Both men were dressed in long fur coats and wide-brimmed hats and boots, and they stomped the snow from their feet as they entered.

Caroline had just finished wrapping herself in the blanket, and knew that she was as well covered as she had ever been. Still she could not prevent the bright red flags that flew in her cheeks as Daniel and Robert, who had cast quick, comprehensive looks around the small shelter, nodded at her. Daniel did not quite meet her eyes, while Robert's held an amused glint.

" 'Tis clear we worried and hurried for naught," Robert said, spying the second jug of rum that Matt had set to warm. Going down on one knee beside the fire to uncork the jug and then hefting it high, Robert availed himself of a long swallow.

"I see you've all the comforts of home," Daniel remarked, his eyes on the rumpled pallet even as Robert, with a nudge, passed him the jug.

Caroline could not have felt more ashamed if they had sewn the badge of an adulteress onto her breast.

"Caroline and I are to be wed," Matt announced abruptly, his eyes moving from Caroline's scarlet face to his brothers' knowing ones.

"Wed!" Daniel sounded poleaxed, his gaze shooting from Matt to Caroline and fixing there.

"Wed! Well, by all that's wonderful!" Robert's reaction was more exuberant. He crossed to Matt and clapped his shoulder, then grinned at Caroline. "Are you sure you want to marry big brother here? He's not my idea of a cozy armful!"

"Watch your mouth, Rob," Matt growled as Daniel came forward at last to offer his brother his hand.

"I wish you happy, Matt," Daniel said, his voice steady but his face pale. Caroline, watching as the two shook hands, felt a queer little pang in the region of her heart. There was so much love between them, among all the Mathiesons, in fact, that she wondered if she would ever get over the notion that despite Matt's declaration, she was an outsider looking in.

"Thanks, Dan." Matt's face eased into a smile as he cast a sideways glance at Caroline. " 'Tis better to marry than to burn, you know, and I've been burning for better than half a year now."

At that she stiffened indignantly, while the men exchanged hearty and very masculine guffaws.

"Did you fetch the doctor back from New London?" Matt was gathering their belongings together as he asked the question of Daniel. Watching him and then moving to help, Caroline realized with a quiver of sorrow that their sojourn away from the world was over.

Matt must have been thinking something along the same lines, because as he gathered up the makings of the pallet his eyes met hers. There was a gleam in them for her, and the sense of shared secrets heartened her. Whatever happened, she would have Matt.

"We brought him, and a learned man he is too. Which is fortunate, because we got home to discover half a dozen more stricken—and Mary ill."

"Mary!" Caroline's hand rose to her throat. Matt straightened and frowned. Daniel nodded grimly.

"Aye. She was not so sick as some, but I promised James I'd bring Caroline to her as soon as may be. He has already procured the services of the physician, but he is taking no chances with his wife."

"We'd best be away then. You brought horses?" Matt pulled on his jerkin, settled his hat on his head, reached for his coat, and then, to Caroline's surprise, settled the coat around her shoulders.

"You keep it. I'll be perfectly fine with the blanket," she protested, trying to shrug the garment off.

"Woman, if you are going to be forever arguing, I foresee a stormy wedded life ahead." Matt pushed her arms into the sleeves and came around in front of her to do up the fastenings. "I'll have you know that I mean to be master in my own house. I will be obeyed, or you will face dire consequences."

"Hoo!" Caroline said irreverently, but let herself be wrapped in fur to the chin.

"Lead him a dance, Caroline. 'Twill do him good to be brought down a peg or two," said Robert, his eyes alight with amusement.

"I daresay she won't make a particularly conformable wife," Daniel put in more slowly, a frown corrugating his brow. The thought appeared to afford him some comfort, and as they kicked snow over the fire he seemed a degree more cheerful.

There were horses waiting, four of them knee-deep in the snow. Three of them were borrowed, Caroline thought, and the other was one of the two kept for riding purposes on the farm. The animals stomped their feet impatiently, rattling bridles and stirrups, as their breath crystallized in the air.

The snow came well up over the tops of Caroline's shoes, which didn't occur to her until she was ready to step into it. The men all had boots, and she was girding herself not to mind the icy slush when Matt, seeing her dilemma, came from behind her to scoop her up in his arms.

"I can . . ." she began even as he plodded into the snow with her.

"There you go again." The words were grim, but his eyes teased her. Behind him, Robert burst into laughter, while even Daniel, at Matt's side, broke into a reluctant smile.

"I love you," she mouthed at Matt where no one could see. His eyes sparked down at her in silent but satisfying answer, and his arms tightened around her, pulling her more firmly against his chest. Caroline clung to his shoulders, wishing she could kiss the stubbled jaw so close to her mouth. But, conscious of her audience, she was too shy.

At the last minute, Matt set his hat upon her head and tossed her up in the saddle before she could protest. Then he wrapped the blanket around himself, and the three men distributed their gear from the shelter among the horses. Caroline, watching them work together with a minimum of words but the kind of efficiency that comes from long and easy knowledge, smiled into the fur that tickled her lower lip and settled Matt's ridiculously large hat lower on her brow.

The going was slow as the horses plodded through the snow, and the air grew increasingly chilly. Day turned into night, but the slender crescent moon reflecting off the thick blanket of snow lighted their way surprisingly well. The wind picked up, and from somewhere not too far away came the howling of wolves. Not one, but a pack, Caroline thought, shivering. The horses picked their way through the forest single file, with Daniel in front of her and Matt behind her. She was freezing, even with Matt's hat and coat, and she knew that Matt must be in worse case. But there was no help for it but to persevere. If the cold was unbearable when they were moving, it was worse when they stopped, as they had to do occasionally to eat and rest.

It was near noon of the following day when Robert at last sighted smoke rising lazily toward the sky over the tops of the trees.

"We've made it," he cried, and Caroline felt her weary spirits pick up at the knowledge that they were almost there. Had it been possible, she would have urged her mount on at all speed, but the careful gait they had maintained since leaving the shelter was the only one possible in the snow.

As they sighted the house through the trees, she swayed in the saddle. She was so tired, so deadly tired and so cold and so hungry and . . .

"Pa!" Davey and John erupted from the front door with Thomas behind them as the riders emerged into the clearing. "Pa!"

The children were jumping through the snow, uncaring in the way of small boys that they were not wearing their outdoor things and were wetting themselves to the waist. Raleigh bounded behind them, hopping through the snow like an enormous piebald rabbit as he barked his fool head off. The sheer exuberance of the greeting made Caroline smile even as she shook her head at the thought of the soaking the boys—and the dog— were getting.

"Pa!"

Matt reined in his horse, and blanket and all swung down to catch them up one in each arm as they reached him, giving them both a fierce hug that was just as fiercely returned.

"Why aren't you in school?" he demanded gruffly, putting them away from him as Raleigh, his barks deafening, bounced around the three of them.

"There's no school on account of the fever!" John said.

"Ain't that grand?" Davey echoed, and Caroline had to laugh at his cheerful self-centeredness. The whole world was well lost as long as he got out of school, it seemed.

"It's grand. Now go on inside the house while we put the horses up. Caroline, you go with them."

Matt put the boys into his saddle and led the horse the short distance to the house with the rest of them following. Once there, he lifted his sons down, then moved to hold up his hands to Caroline. With a wordless murmur she slid into his arms, feeling very cared for as she gave herself over to Matt's strength. Matt didn't set her down in the snow, but carried her, high against his chest, to the stoop, where he at last put her on her feet. Elevated as she was, their eyes were on a level. The sudden gleam in the blue eyes boring into hers was the only warning she got before he leaned forward to press a quick, hard kiss to her lips.

Then he turned and remounted without a word, leaving her pink-cheeked and flustered to face two wide-eyed little boys and their gaping uncle.

43

"*P*a kissed you!" Davey's words were almost accusing.

"Does he love you, Aunt Caroline?" John's eyes were every bit as wide as Davey's.

Thomas, while not saying anything, seemed to wait with as much interest as either of the two boys for her reply.

With an exasperated glance at her beloved, who was disappearing toward the barn with his brothers, the dog, and all four horses, Caroline shooed them before her into the house and shut the door.

For a moment she leaned back against it, so tired she could hardly stand. The warmth of the house was almost painful, and she grimaced as tingling life came back to her frozen fingers and toes. Food and rest were what she and her partners in adventure needed, and she knew a craven desire to plead hunger and fatigue and let her betrothed answer to his children and brother for himself. But the expressions on Davey's and John's faces stopped her. They were incredulous, their eyes enormous with questions.

"You're wearing Pa's hat!" Davey said as she took it off.

"And his coat!" John sounded scandalized.

"It was cold outside, and I had none of my own." Caroline must have looked hunted as she addressed herself to the least sensitive matter first, because Thomas, who'd been staring at her with much the same expression as his nephews, began to grin.

"But why did he kiss you?" Davey persisted. "He only kisses me, or John, and only when we're hurt or real sick. He don't kiss nobody else. Does he, John?"

John shook his head. Caroline sighed, opened her mouth—and found that she lacked the courage to tell them after all.

"Give me a minute to catch my breath, and then we'll talk about it," she temporized, moving away from the door toward the kitchen.

The hem of Matt's coat trailed the floor, and as she grew warmer she took it off. Millicent rose from her cozy bed by the hearth, stretched, and meowed a greeting. Something was bubbling over the fire in the kitchen— corn mush from the smell of it—and a sudden hunger pain cramped her stomach. The others would be hungry too, and she needed to think about making a meal. Then there was Mary, and after the meal she must hurry to her friend's side. All these fragments of thought ran through her mind in the time it took her to hang the coat on a peg.

She turned back to find three males regarding her foreshortened skirts with interest.

Caroline rolled her eyes, and headed for her bedchamber.

"But, Aunt Caroline . . . !" Davey protested as she shut the door in his face.

"I'll be right back," Caroline promised. "But I really must change my gown."

It took some fifteen minutes to wash and change her dress and brush her hair. Just as she stepped from her chamber, the men came in from the barn, stamping snow from their feet and brushing it from their clothes.

"Thom, you cooked!" Robert exclaimed on a note of appreciative surprise.

Thomas shot his brother a darkling look and continued to stir the mush.

"The boys and I had to eat, didn't we? 'Tis fortunate for the lot of you that I misjudged the quantities and made such a vast amount." He sounded almost defensive, and Caroline guessed that he feared being teased. Since she had lived with them, they had gotten in the way of considering such necessary tasks as cooking beneath their masculine dignity.

"Pa, why did you kiss Aunt Caroline?" Davey went right to the heart of the matter that was troubling him as Matt unwrapped himself from the blanket and sat down to pull his boots off.

"Come here, John, and help me," Matt directed. John, having clearly done this before, approached his father and straddled his foot, his back to Matt. Matt placed his other boot on John's bottom and pushed. The boot slid off.

"Pa! You're not paying attention!" Davey wailed.

John was repeating the exercise on Matt's other boot while Robert and Daniel performed much the same task for each other. Caroline shooed Thomas away from the pot and took over the cooking, just as the mush, too long neglected, was threatening to become lumpy.

"Yes, I am, Davey." Matt was in his stocking feet now, starting to unbutton his jerkin.

"Then why did you kiss her?"

"Because I'm going to marry her, half-pint." Matt said it almost teasingly, but the effect on the boys was dramatic. John stopped what he was doing to regard his father openmouthed, while Davey's lower lip quivered as if he would cry.

"Does that mean she'll be our mother?" John sounded horrified.

"I don't want no mother!" Davey began, very noisily, to sob.

So much for crossing bridges. This was worse than Caroline had expected. Hurt assailed her at the boys' unequivocal rejection, but she fought it off, striving to view the matter from their point of view. After all, their experience of having a mother had been disastrous—and they must be feeling very proprietary toward Matt as well. The notion that he might take another wife had probably never occurred to them.

"I can never be your mother," she interjected calmly, turning back to stir the mush although her attention was on the little scene behind her. "When I marry your father, I'll still be your Aunt Caroline."

"No!" Davey ran sobbing from the room. John, being older, had more control, so he merely pursed his lips and looked strained. "I'd better go after him," he said. With great control, he left the room. Then his stoicism apparently deserted him. Caroline winced, listening to his footsteps pounding up the stairs and across the floor overhead as, like his younger brother, he bolted for his room.

"You handled that well," Daniel said, scowling at Matt.

"You should have broken it to them gently," Robert seconded.

"Poor little tykes," Thomas muttered.

Matt, eyes narrowing, glared impartially at his brothers. "They'll come around," he said, and, getting to his feet, headed after his sons.

"Don't force them to accept me, please," Caroline said to his retreating back, but if he heard her, he appeared to pay her no heed.

Not more than ten minutes later, just as the mush was ready to be served, the three of them reappeared, with Matt, grim-eyed, herding his sons before him.

"We're glad you're marrying Pa, Aunt Caroline," John said glumly, his expression surprisingly adult for one of his tender years as he looked at her with barely masked anger.

"Thank you, John," Caroline answered as gently as she could, feeling a lump rise in her throat at the boy's stiff pride. How she longed to put her arms around them and assure them that everything would be all right! But instinct told her to hold back, to give them time to get used to the news. Their opposition was more the result of shock, she thought, than personal dislike, but she felt as though all the ground she had gained had been lost again.

Matt nudged Davey in the back. "Me too," Davey echoed his brother, obviously compelled by the weight of paternal authority. His expression was rebellious, and his lip still had a tendency to tremble.

Caroline smiled at him.

"Food's ready," she said, feeling it best to change the subject. "Sit and eat."

The boys, clearly glad to be released from onerous duty, immediately decamped for the table. Robert, Thomas, and Daniel joined them, while Matt lingered to smile rather grimly at Caroline.

"They'll get used to the idea, don't worry," he promised her under his breath. Caroline shook her head at him.

"You can't just order them to like the idea of our getting married," she warned, but he merely smiled at her, chucked her under the chin, and took himself off to the table.

When the meal was finished, Caroline wanted to head for Mary's home at once, but Matt insisted that she first needed to rest. She was gray-faced with fatigue, he told her, and he would not have her make herself sick. His concern touched her heart, and she found herself more willing to bow to his wishes than, she promised herself, would be the case once the newness of their betrothal wore off.

"Another hour or so can make no difference, and you're out on your feet. Besides, James will have had a true physician to her long before now" was the clincher, and Caroline had to concede that his words made sense. She was so tired that she could barely hold her eyes open. As soon as she climbed into her bed she was asleep, and then Matt refused to allow her to be awakened. Thus it was nearly nightfall before they set out for James's house.

Matt drove her in the sledge, wrapping her in thick fur robes and providing a hot brick for her feet. Clean-shaven now, he was pale from lack of sleep. Caroline snuggled close against his side as they whisked toward town, and would almost have enjoyed herself were it not for the seriousness of the matter that drew them there.

But likely Mary would be well on the road to recovery by now, and she was worrying needlessly.

The settlement seemed almost deserted, in thrall to a strange hush that Caroline attributed to the snow. The setting sun cast an orange glow over everything, painting even the bay the color of fire. Lights glowed in the windows of numerous houses, but only a lone figure, a man clad all in black, hurried along the street where James and Mary lived.

Even as Matt pulled the horse to a halt before their house, the door opened and James stood silhouetted in the aperture with the light from within spilling out around him. Matt raised a hand in greeting, came around the sledge, and lifted Caroline down. All the while James never moved, but merely stared at them as if he'd been frozen in place.

It was not until she stepped up on the stoop that Caroline got her first good look at James's face. White and haggard, his eyes red with weeping, he looked so distraught that Caroline felt a fist close around her heart.

He ignored her, looking past her almost blindly at Matt.

"She died. Mary died," James said brokenly, and as he said it he broke into wrenching sobs.

Caroline cried out as Matt pushed past her to take his brother in his arms.

44

*T*wo days later, at Mary's funeral, the drip, drip of melting snow was what burned itself most forcibly into Caroline's brain. Ankle deep in gray slush, she stood beside Matt, who was as sober as she'd ever seen him, clad all in black with his hat in his hands as he bent his head in response to the dominie's exhortation to the small gathering to pray.

"Our Father, who art in heaven . . ."

The familiar words of the well-loved prayer fell from Caroline's lips as she joined in with the others in ragged chant. On Matt's other side, James stood as if in a daze, his voice faltering a dozen times during the prayer he must know as well as he knew his own name. Matt glanced at him from time to time during the service, which was more hurried than usual as there were two more victims of the fever to be buried that day. His expression was nearly as drawn as his brother's. What one suffered they all did, it was clear. Daniel stood on James's other side, and Robert and Thomas were just slightly behind him, all white and still with misery that was as much for their widowed brother as for the woman he had lost. They appeared to form a guard around James, and Caroline knew that their hearts ached for him, as did hers.

Oh, and for little Hope! Tears slid down Caroline's cheeks as she glanced at the poor motherless child. Too young to know aught of her tragedy, Hope was clutched to James's chest, where she cooed contentedly and reached out from time to time to touch her father's nose or mouth. He permitted her explorations as if he was not even aware of them, but he would not give the child up for someone else to hold—Caroline had offered to take her, as had others of Mary's many friends. The little girl's bright blue eyes sparkled, and she was all smiles, because she liked to be in company and there was so much of it. Her unaware happiness was heartbreaking to see.

The hole at their feet already held Mary's pine casket. It remained only for James to throw in the first clod. Everyone waited expectantly—but James, staring blindly down into the grave, did not seem to realize that.

Mouth tightening, Matt bent and scooped up a fistful of earth, then pressed it into his brother's free hand. James looked down at his hand, then in anguish at Matt, as if his brother had done something to cause him terrible pain.

"Throw it in," Matt murmured.

James's face set into a bleak mask. Mouth working, he obeyed.

The clod hit the coffin with a dull thud, and Caroline shuddered along with James.

"God's will be done, world without end. Amen."

As the dominie's voice intoned the final words, Caroline chanced to meet his gaze. It was so filled with hatred for her that she was taken aback. His mouth curled at her in a sneer. Her eyes widened, and she took an instinctive step backward. But the service had ended, and Matt and Daniel, on either side of James, were already leading their brother away. Davey and John followed, both sad-eyed and solemn, though Caroline didn't think that Davey quite understood that they had put Mary into the ground forever, never to be seen on earth again. Which was as well, she supposed, as she fell in behind Robert and Thomas, who were discreetly shepherding the boys. Such a terrible reality mixed ill with the eternal optimism of youth.

The small crowd of Mary's friends and other relations parted for the Mathieson men, their eyes sympathetic, their murmured words consoling. But as Caroline passed through them, she was surprised to see eyes that had once regarded her benignly grow hard. Men dismissed her with contemptuous stares, while women whom she had never harmed pulled away their skirts.

Hannah Forrester stood weeping with her sister Patience, a handkerchief held becomingly to her eyes. Her gaze lifted to follow him as Matt passed—and then as he failed to notice her, her eyes found Caroline and turned hard. When Caroline nodded, Hannah deliberately turned her back, and Patience, whom Caroline supposed to be aping her sister, followed suit.

As she became aware she was being ostracized, a flush suffused Caroline's entire body. Had they somehow learned of what they would no doubt consider her sin with Matt?

"That's her—'tis the witch! Watch that she don't look at you—'tis those eyes of hers—see their color? If she looks at you, you'll come down with the fever too, and likely die of it, just as did poor Goodwife Mathieson, who befriended the creature," she heard one woman whisper to another. Surprised, she did turn to look at them, only to find that they cringed and raised a hand to ward her off.

Could they really believe she was a witch? Frightened, mortified, Caroline dragged her eyes from the speaker and her friend and almost ran after the men. Behind her, she heard the muttering grow louder and uglier in tone.

"She is evil, good people," hissed a voice that Caroline thought she recognized as the dominie's. "Ephraim Mathieson's paramour, skilled in alchemy, perhaps not even the sister of the first one who was his wife but the first one her own self, risen from the grave in new form to take vengeance on us for consigning her to hellfire. She's cursed our town, brought about the deaths of God-fearing folk with her spells! But we'll not be fooled! No, we shall not be fooled!"

There was a general murmur of agreement, and something soft hit Caroline squarely between the shoulder blades. A snowball! She whirled and found many among the small crowd of mourners laughing behind their hands while others turned away from her gaze. But there was none that she could identify as the culprit, and her shame at being thus publicly singled out was strong.

She did not cry out against the crowd, but whirled about again and hurried away in pursuit of the men, who were all oblivious to what had happened as they trudged toward James's house.

In the face of James's grief, she did not feel it right to mention the indignity she had suffered, and so she kept her tongue between her teeth as she cooked them all a meal, while James's brothers took turns sitting with him in the bedchamber he had, until two days ago, shared with his wife.

"He's in a bad way," Matt said to her later, when James had at last fallen asleep and they were preparing to leave. Daniel would stay the night with James, while Mary's mother, who had arrived from Wethersfield the day before, cared for Hope. As Mary had been her oldest, and she had young children at home, she could stay for only a few days. After that, 'twould be up to James to care for his little daughter as best he could, though Caroline decided she would willingly assume the charge if he would let her. She adored the sweet-faced baby, and parted from her with a squeeze and a tearful kiss.

On the way home, both boys were unnaturally silent. Caroline supposed that the lingering effects of the funeral had stilled their usually magpie tongues.

"Pa, will Uncle James find a new wife too?" Davey, who had been permitted to ride on the seat between his father and Caroline, piped up.

"Someday, perhaps. 'Tis a hard thing, to find another wife," Matt said after only a moment's pause, and ruffled his son's hair. Davey said nothing more, but he leaned against Matt and Caroline realized that he was comparing little Hope's situation to his and John's—and that he was coming, in some small fashion, at least, to accept the idea that she would be his father's wife.

Later that night, after everyone had gone to bed and the house was silent, Caroline sat for a time in front of the fire in the kitchen. She couldn't sleep, and thinking of poor Mary and Hope and James brought tears to her eyes. The world was a cruel, hard place, she was thinking, to sunder such as them.

A creak behind her made her jump and look around. In the doorway stood Matt, one arm resting against the jamb as he surveyed her. His face was somber, his eyes hollow with exhaustion as he had spent the intervening nights in helping James through his grief. Days had been spent on chores and burial details, and this was the first chance he had had for a decent sleep since coming to rescue her from the Indians.

"What are you doing up?" Her question was softly chiding.

"I heard someone down here and thought it might be you." He came away from the door to stand looking down at her. He was barefoot, clad only in black breeches. His bare chest and shoulders appeared very wide in the gloomy shadows of the kitchen. The breeches rode low on his hips, and above them the muscles of his belly were ridged and hard.

"You need to sleep." But she reached up to catch his hand and lift it to her lips.

"So do you." His eyes unreadable, he drew her up beside him and slid his arms around her waist. Caroline put her own arms around his neck, suddenly fiercely glad that he had come to her to share his grief, and rose on her tiptoes to place her mouth on his.

He pulled her close, kissed her well. Caroline allowed her eyes to close and her thoughts to give up their sorrow and focus on him. His hand slid up along her spine, pulling up the thin lawn nightdress with it as it went.

"Pa! Pa!" It was John, almost falling in his haste to get down the stairs. At the foot of the steps he saw them, still entwined in each other's arms although they had broken off their kiss as both turned to look at him, but his stride never faltered. "Pa! Aunt Caroline! 'Tis Davey! He's horribly sick!"

45

*F*or the next two days, as Davey's life hung in the balance, Matt hovered over the child's bed. So did John, clearly terrified that his brother might die, until Matt, afraid that he would catch the disease, forbade him to set foot inside the room. The others stayed out as well on Matt's orders, save for Caroline, who nursed Davey with a fierce devotion that could not have been more determined had he been her own child.

The physician, a learned man named Dr. Samuel Smith, came and went, shaking his head over the boy as he did what he could. The outcome in such cases, he told Matt and Caroline forthrightly, was largely up to God. Matt held Davey's hand and alternately prayed and turned the pages of the Bible as he searched for strength in this time of direst need. Caroline's heart broke as she considered what losing his son would do to him.

Part of Matt would die with Davey.

"Aunt Caroline, you won't let Davey die, will you? You saved Pa." Without school to occupy him, and banned from the sickroom, John had little to do but worry. Caroline's heart went out to him as she ladled more barley water into a jug for Davey, who was vomiting almost ceaselessly. John was halfheartedly playing draughts with Thomas, though such pastimes were in general frowned upon by the Puritans. But to keep their older nephew's mind off his little brother, John's uncles seemed willing to turn their hands to anything.

"I'll do my best," Caroline told him, quite unable to resist the temptation to ruffle his hair as she passed. To her surprise, in return John jumped up and gave her a hug.

"Davey and me—we love you, Aunt Caroline," he told her fiercely, his head buried in her soft breasts. "It really is all right if you marry Pa."

"Why, John, I love you and Davey too." Jug and all, Caroline wrapped her arms around him and dropped a quick kiss on his silky hair. "The four of us will be so happy together, you'll see."

Though she had grave doubts about Davey's survival, she would not tell

John that. Instead she strove to paint a cheerful picture for him for as long as she could.

"If Davey doesn't die," he said starkly, his head drooping again as he released her and returned dispiritedly to his chair.

"We must all pray that he won't," Caroline said with what steadiness she could muster, exchanging a pregnant look with Thomas over John's head. Thomas's eyebrows lifted, silently inquiring about Davey's condition. Caroline shook her head.

In the sickroom, Matt was already praying. Caroline, having tried every trick in her healing arsenal from the icy sheets to the medicines she still had, was helpless to do more for Davey than force liquids down him and bathe his burning body. His fate was truly in the hands of God—and he had already been sick for more than two days.

Nearly all the victims died in three.

As the clock crawled toward midnight, Davey was so still that several times Caroline feared that he had died already. Matt sat by the bed, holding his son's hand, and she exchanged only a few words with him as she sat on the other side of the bed.

She was sore afraid that they would lose Davey with the dawn.

"The Lord is my shepherd, I shall not want. . . ."

Clutching Davey's small hand with infinite tenderness in his big one, Matt closed his eyes and repeated the words of the ancient prayer. On Davey's other side, Caroline too clasped Davey's hand and joined in.

"Yea, though I walk through the valley of the shadow of death, I will fear no evil. . . ."

The words comforted her, as she hoped they did Matt. Davey, she feared, had passed beyond hearing.

Then, to her amazement, the child's eyes blinked open, and he looked, first at her, then at Matt.

"Pa," he said, as if relieved to find Matt there. "I'm mortal hungry, Pa."

With that his eyes flickered shut, and the hands they held went limp.

"Davey, oh, no, oh, please, God, no . . ."

Tears welled in Matt's eyes as he bent over his son. Caroline bent over the child too, her hand flying to his forehead, her eyes wide.

"No, Matt, he's not dead!" she cried joyfully, when her check confirmed her first wild hope. "He's not going to die! The fever has broken—and he's hungry! Once they're hungry, they never die!"

It took a moment for that to sink in. Then Matt slumped back in his chair, his eyes closing.

"Praise be to God!" he muttered. Caroline's heart broke as she saw a single tear emerge from beneath stubby black lashes to roll down a hard, bronzed cheek.

"Matt! Matt, my darling, didn't you hear me? Davey's not going to die!" Shaken to the core by the sight of Matt weeping, Caroline moved around the bed and slid her arms around his shoulders and held him close.

"I heard you." His arms came around her then, and he held her tight, burying his head in her breasts much as John had done earlier in the kitchen, and with as much innocence.

Caroline stroked the thick black hair, dropped kisses on it, murmured the soothing wordless things that she supposed women always murmured in times of emotional catharsis to the ones they love.

"Oh, God, I love you," he said in a queer, shaken voice. Now that the crisis had passed, his strength gave out. Caroline could feel exhaustion overtake him, feel his body growing limp and heavy against her. In a moment he would be asleep, right there in the chair, and she could either stay as she was all night or let him fall to the floor. He would be better, far better, in his own bed. Accordingly, Caroline half lifted, half urged him to his feet. Though he had insisted that she take a few hours' rest, he had been without sleep almost since the onset of Davey's illness.

"Davey's going to be all right, and you need sleep," she told him firmly when he protested being led to his room.

"I don't want him left alone." Matt was tired, but stubborn.

"He won't be. I'll go back to him when I've got you settled."

"I'm neither ill nor a babe."

"I know. But 'twould please me to tuck you in bed. And I'll ask Daniel to stay with Davey until I return."

As they passed Daniel's door she knocked, and when Daniel answered she repeated her request to him. His gaze flickered over the pair of them, leaning close together, Matt's arm around Caroline's shoulders and hers around his waist. A resigned expression came into his eyes as if he had suddenly discovered that they belonged together and would not dispute it more.

"Of course I'll sit with Davey," he agreed quietly.

He was already heading back along the corridor as Caroline guided Matt to his room. Once there, she lighted the candle from the one she carried, shut the door, and proceeded to help him out of his clothes as if he were a child. She unbuttoned his shirt, undid his breeches, pulled his stockings down his legs. When he was naked, she bundled him into bed, and was pulling the covers up around him when he reached for her.

"Tarry awhile," he muttered, his eyes and then his hands moving to her breasts. Then she understood that, despite his exhaustion, he had need of her, need of their life-giving act as an antidote to the angel of death. Without a word she slid out of her clothes and crawled into his bed.

"I need you so," he murmured as he found her mouth with his, and then he was showing her too, with his hands and mouth, until heat blazed between them bright enough to banish the darkness that had come so near.

*I*t was just past dusk on the following day when they came for her. Caroline was in the sickroom when a loud knocking shook the front door. She thought it odd that any visitor would bang so ferociously on a host's portal, but still as she went to answer it she had no real inkling of disaster. Supper bubbled in the kitchen, and the men, who had felt able to leave the vicinity of the house for the first time in many a day, were still in the south field, chopping into firewood the tree that had broken Matt's leg. Dragged to the side of the field, it had been allowed to season over the summer and now, with a hard winter facing them, it would be as useful in death as it had been in life.

But she expected them to return at any moment, and then they would all sit down to supper together. Despite their continued grief for Mary, with the threat to Davey lifted the meal would be in the nature of a celebration. She had cooked her men's favorites, and even combined corn-meal, eggs, wild honey, and milk together to fashion a small cake.

So all unsuspecting, Caroline opened the door to find herself confronting a crowd of perhaps two dozen men, and some fewer women, bearing flaming pine torches and muttering among themselves.

"Why, good evening to you all. How may I help you?" Though Caroline was surprised, she was polite. She had no clue as to their mission until, seeing her, the crowd grew suddenly silent. Millicent, drawn by the lure of the open door, came from her spot by the hearth to twine about Caroline's legs.

"That's her! That's the witch!" screeched a voice from the rear of the crowd. Peering into the darkness, her vision impeded by the flickering light of the torches, Caroline found it impossible to make out individual faces with any certainty. Though skulking in the background she thought she saw the flap of the dominie's robe, and nearer the center of the crowd a pate bald in the fashion of Mr. Williams's shone in the light of the torch the man held.

"Witch?" she repeated, confused.

"Look, she's got her familiar with her! 'Ware the cat!"

"Take her! My baby's dying, and it's all her doing!" There was hysteria in the woman's voice.

"Take the witch!"

Suddenly frightened, Caroline took a step backward and got a hand on the door to slam it. She stumbled over Millicent, who yowled and shot out into the darkness. Some in the crowd screamed, and others scattered. But as though her retreat made them bold, the bulk of them surged forward, grabbing Caroline by her arms and hauling her outside.

Caroline screamed.

"Aunt Caroline!" John, doing sums in the kitchen, ran to see what was happening. His eyes widened, his face paled, and then his fists clenched. Caroline saw that small though he was, he meant to fly to her aid against the multitudes.

"John, no!" she cried. "Run! Get help!"

She was silenced then by a hand clapping over her mouth.

"Get the boy! Get the boy!"

A shot rang out, and Caroline's blood froze.

"Deuce take you, Will, you knocked my aim off!"

" 'Twas apurpose, fool! We don't wish to harm the lad! 'Tis not he who's done wrong!"

"But he'll fetch his blasted pa, and the rest of 'em too, and we'll have a bloody war on our hands!"

"By the time he can get them here, we'll be done with what we've come to do. Hurry, now, and let's get on."

They were dragging her with them as they argued, her hands bound behind her, a blindfold over her eyes. She kicked and found herself lifted clear off her feet. Then, with hands beneath her armpits and others circling her ankles, she was carried into the forest. She could tell that that was where they were by the rustling of the leaves, the sound of clothing brushing against rough tree trunks, and the cries of night animals coming out to hunt and be hunted.

It was horribly clear that the mob that held her intended evil.

"Oh, please," she begged, terror hoarsening her voice. "Please, I'm no witch! Please don't hurt me!"

For she had recognized, or thought she recognized, the voice of one of the men carrying her. 'Twas Mr. Peters, Lissie's father, and she thought he was a fair man.

"Mr. Peters, please . . ."

" 'Tis no one of that name about. Hush, girl! Here, someone stuff something in her mouth."

Someone did, a woolen scarf that almost suffocated her and made her gag.

"We'd best hurry . . . !"

"Aye."

"Lift your torch over here. Is this the tree?"

"Aye, this is it, the one she carved her devil's words in! Look out that you don't touch the writing!"

"Pooh, writing can't hurt you!"

"How do you know that? 'Twould seem likely that it could. Anyway, why chance it?"

"Set her there, then."

Caroline was put upon her feet again, and felt the rough trunk of a tree at her back. She tried to kick at her captors and run, but in only a few moments they had her fast, bound to the tree.

They were piling things around her feet.

"Hurry up!"

"Quick, now!"

" 'Tis fitting that she should meet her end tied to the very tree that she marked with her evil. She can take her spells with her to the Devil!"

"Do you think we should take the gag from her mouth, so that she might pray?"

"Witches don't pray!"

"Maybe the fire will cleanse her soul before the Devil can claim it! Should that happen, I would not deny her the chance to pray!"

Fire! Caroline's blood ran cold as she realized what they meant to do: burn her at the stake!

"Do you wish to pray, girl?"

Caroline nodded weakly. The gag was removed, and she ran her tongue around her dry mouth.

"Why do you do this to me?" she asked piteously. The rope that bound her was tight, cutting into her arms and breasts and thighs. She struggled against it, but the knots were firm, and she knew that it would not be loosed by any efforts of hers. Tears filled her eyes, ran down past the blindfold, and wet her cheeks. Was it possible that she would meet her end like this? It could not happen so, not when supper was still cooking in her kitchen and her men would be coming in at any moment to eat and . . .

"I told you she wouldn't pray!"

"Do not think to sway us with tears!"

" 'Tis a devil's trick, to make us doubt! The evidence against her is ironclad!"

"Stop talking and light the faggots! We'll be here all night at this rate!"

"I am no witch! I pray you, you must believe me!" Caroline was sobbing with fear.

"Pay no heed to her entreaties! We all know that she practices alchemy, and the writing of her spells is carved into the very tree above her!"

"When a mad dog ran through the village, she turned it away with her eyes!"

"She looked at my Faith, and the next day the child contracted the sickness!"

"At night she sends her spirit into the soul of that cat, and roams the woods doing evil!"

"Light the faggots!"

"The cat is her familiar spirit! It looks like her!"

"Light the faggots!"

"She is a witch, and the sister of a witch!"

"Light the faggots!"

"No, please, you must listen . . . !"

"Ahhh!" It was a sound of satisfaction from the multitude, as if a large predator had just drawn first blood.

"Please . . . !"

Caroline was near hysteria. The crackle of fire reached her ears. The smell of burning pine tar rose to her nostrils. A sensation of heat attacked her feet, and she knew that the faggots had been lighted.

How long would it be before the flames spread to her skirt? When that happened she would be done for. . . .

Caroline screamed, long and shrill and loud, her head falling back against the tree. Watching, the crowd began to chant, first one voice, then another and then many.

"Burn, witch, burn!"

"Our Father, who art in heaven . . ." Caroline writhed against her bonds, against the heat that was increasing with every second, against the agony that she knew would soon be hers, against the impossibility of terrible, impending death.

"Burn, witch, burn!"

"Hallowed be thy name. . . ."

Her head scraped the tree, and her blindfold was dislodged. She could see the flames now, dancing ever closer, crackling with glee as they came to claim her, their prey. . . .

The crowd was almost gleeful now, swaying as they chanted, eyes gleaming at her like feral beasts' in the dark. They watched her panic with panting avidity.

They would enjoy watching her burn. . . .

The flames reached her feet, licked at the edge of her skirt, caught. The dark-blue homespun went up like a torch. Smoke seared her lungs, as the flames shot past her face, and Caroline opened her mouth for one last, terrified scream.

Shots sounded in the darkness. Men yelled, women screamed, people scattered. With the flames eating her, Caroline was aware of no more than this until a huge dark body attached to a hand holding a knife burst through the conflagration, sliced the ropes that held her, jerked her free. Stumbling forward, her dress still aflame, she was tumbled to the wet ground, rolled over and over as her burning dress was ripped away.

Through all that she never ceased to scream.

"Caroline!" It was Matt's voice that finally got through to her, Matt's face that impinged itself on the red fog of terror that filled her eyes, Matt's arms that held her.

"Matt!" She recognized him with a whimper, turned into the arms that held her against his chest, shivering and quaking and sobbing and gasping his name.

" 'Tis all right, poppet, I have you safe." He was crooning to her as he carried her, striding along the path that led through the forest to the house, with Daniel and Robert and Thomas and John, the first three bearing muskets and the last unarmed, for grim-faced guards. The crowd had vanished, melting like wraiths into the trees, and Caroline realized that she would never know the identity of most who had wished her dead.

It came to her then what Matt had done to save her.

"The fire," she whispered brokenly, her voice hoarse from the smoke, "you came through the fire."

He had braved the thing he feared most for her.

Epilogue

A month later, Matt and Caroline were married by an itinerant preacher in the front room of James's house. She wore one of her English dresses, the fine blue silk that Matt liked best, while he was in sober Puritan black. A delicate Mechlin veil that had once belonged to her mother covered her hair, and a prayer book that had been Mary's was in her hands.

James had given it to her, saying that Mary would have wanted her to have it. Caroline felt her friend's spirit very close that day.

James and Daniel, Robert and Thomas, John and Davey stood with them as they took their vows. When Matt slid the ring on her finger and Caroline turned her face up for his kiss applause broke out.

" 'Tis done, then," Matt said as if relieved, when his brothers clapped him on the shoulder and the minister, having been paid by Daniel, bowed his way out.

Caroline, who had more than ample reason to believe in the depth of his love, gave him a tender smile.

"Are you our ma now, Aunt Caroline?" asked Davey, looking worried.

"Only if you wish me to be," Caroline answered firmly.

"We do," John said and hugged her. Dropping down on both knees with no thought of what it did to her dress, Caroline hugged him back, then included Davey as he threw his arms around her too.

"I love you both," she whispered to them, and while they were too much the young men to confess to that, they submitted to a kiss each before squirming away.

The boys scampered off to play with Hope, the men turned to twitting their newlywed brother, and the bride was left to her own devices with nothing to do but observe her new family. Eyeing the five tall, handsome men—though her own husband was the tallest and the handsomest—Caroline felt a little bud of happiness burst into blooming life inside her.

She was loved, and she knew it. That night when Matt had dared the thing he feared most in the world for her sake, he had proved it without doubt. In the aftermath of saving her, he had watched over her tenderly while the doctor was fetched and her burns pronounced superficial and easily healed. In fact, she had healed, and her skin was as smooth and fine as ever it had been.

But the flames had seared a distaste for Saybrook forever into her heart.

Matt had told her of the witches who practiced their rites in the woods, and of how they had tried to recruit poor mad Elizabeth. He had examined the writing on the tree to which she had been tied, the writing she had noticed just before the Indians stole her away, and pronounced it to be composed of an alphabet of Celtic origin, called runes. The witches' alphabet.

And so, she had learned, the mob that came for her was been as crazed as she had supposed, because there really were witches in Saybrook. Only the identity of their target was wrong.

But still, they could not rest easy in their minds knowing that the same could happen again. So they were leaving, all of them, not only Matt and herself and John and Davey but Daniel and Robert and Thomas too, and James and Hope. The farm had been sold ironically enough to Mr. Peters, for so much money that Caroline blinked whenever she thought about it. The livestock were sold, too, along with most of the furniture. Three wagons loaded with everything they now possessed in the world waited outside. Raleigh—the menfolk had refused categorically to leave him—was tied to the last wagon, while Millicent waited in her basket on the front seat of the one in which Caroline would ride.

They would go south, maybe to Maryland, maybe beyond. Someplace where they could live, all of them, untroubled by the past.

"Well, if we're going, let's get to it," said James, outwardly recovered from Mary's death but inwardly, Caroline feared, badly crippled. But healing, as she well knew, could not be hurried. Perhaps it would come to him in time.

With a whoop the boys hurried outside, excited at the adventure awaiting them. The men followed more sedately, but Caroline got the sense that they were excited too. Only Matt held back, holding her back too with a hand on her arm.

"I've a wedding gift for you," he said gruffly, producing from his coat pocket a box that he handed her. For a moment Caroline stared at him rather than at it, her pleased surprise showing in her smile, her love shining from her eyes.

"Well, open it."

She did. When she saw what was inside her eyes widened. It was a brooch, almost an exact replica of her father's lucky peacock. Only the gems in this one were not paste.

"It's real," he said, confirming her guess as she looked at it, speechless. "Aren't you going to say anything?"

Lifting the exquisite thing from its box, she held it up to the light. The colors glowed bright, ruby red and sapphire blue and emerald green.

"Wherever did you get it, and how did you pay for it?" she gasped, for it was impossible to imagine such a thing being made in Saybrook, and the jewels alone must have cost a fortune.

"I commissioned Tobias to buy it for me in Boston," he answered. "And as to how I paid for it—Jacob. Tobias was more than happy to take him off my hands in exchange for your brooch."

At the thought of the huge bull being traded for the dainty piece of jewelry, Caroline started to giggle. Matt looked at her as if she'd grown a second head for a moment, and then he too began to grin.

"How fitting," Caroline gasped, collapsing into his arms.

"Fitting indeed," Matt murmured, and stopped her laughter with his mouth.